THE
KEEPERS
OF THE
LIBRARY

Also by Glenn Cooper

LIBRARY OF THE DEAD
BOOK OF SOULS
THE TENTH CHAMBER
THE DEVIL WILL COME

GLENN COOPER

THE KEEPERS OF THE LIBRARY

HarperCollins PublishersLtd

My thanks to Peter Denenberg,
who was my guide to the Yorkshire Dales and Mallerstang.
However, any errors I may have made are mine alone.

Isle of Wight, 1775

Hold the lantern steady," the old man told the girl.

The wind was howling and the pale moonlit clouds seemed to be moving across the sky at the speed of a three-master in a gale. Close by, the sea was loud and churning.

They were watching two rum-fueled laborers digging a hole through the frosty and hard January ground.

"Are you certain this is the right place?"

The girl said it was, but the old man could tell from her face that she didn't know for sure.

He clutched his cloak to his throat, and said, "If it is not, I will have you back at the baron's house tomorrow, and you will hear from me no more."

Her teeth began to chatter.

One of the workmen tried to be helpful though his words were slurred from the drink the old man had given him. "There's legends 'bout this place, Squire. Since I wuz a boy. Wouldn't be surprised if there's something to wot the lass says."

The old man answered, "If that is the case, why have you or your fellow islanders not investigated?"

"Scared," the other laborer said. "Used to be a monastery here. There's tales of ghosts of hooded monks prowling about at midnight, which it most likely is now. Have to be daft to come here."

"Then why did you agree to come with us tonight?"

"No one's offered to pay before, have they?" the first man said. "But if there's something down there, you're bloody well on your own."

The old man eyed the tall ladder the men had carried to the site. He doubted he could manage with his gouty foot, but he also doubted they would discover anything at all. In that case, a cozy bed awaited him at the inn in Fishbourne.

The spadefuls of dirt grew into a pile.

"You're not from these parts, are ye?" the second man said.

"No, I'm from across the sea, in Philadelphia."

"Oh yeah?" the man asked. "When war comes, which side are you on then?"

The old man sighed. "I do not want a war. I hope there is no bloodshed, but if I must choose a side, then I will."

The man persisted. "If you're not for the king, then I'll dig no more for you."

The clink of iron against stone brought them all to attention and allowed the old man to evade a response.

"Is it a big 'un?" the other digger asked.

The scrape of a spade revealed that it was large.

"Expose it," the old man said. "See if there's an edge."

In a while, the verdict was that they had found a good-sized flat stone abutting another one.

"Get your spade under it, man!" the old man exhorted. "See if you can shift it."

The girl drew nearer and dangled her lantern, casting light and shadows on the bluestone. The old man saw her shutting her eyes tightly.

Was she praying?

The stone was levered a few inches into the air, and the girl was instructed to bring the light closer. The edge of the stone appeared to have been resting upon a stout beam. Underneath was pure blackness.

"Christ Almighty!" one of the workers said. "This was made by the hand of man."

"Keep raising it!" the old man ordered. "But don't let it fall in. Slide it to the side."

They did that and left behind a hole large enough for a man to enter.

"Abigail," the old man said. "Get on your belly and put the lantern into the hole. Tell me if you see anything."

Without hesitation, she did as he asked, but the diggers began to back away. The old man swore at them, but he couldn't see where they were going as he was obliged to hold her ankles for safety.

"Can you see anything, child?"

"There's books!" she cried. "Lots of 'em. There's a library down there, just as I said there'd be!"

She stood up. By the light of the lamp, the old man could see her face streaked with tears of relief.

"I suppose we'll have to go down there, won't we?" he said. "You men, fetch the ladder."

But the laborers were already yards away, retreating at pace.

"Where are you going?" the old man cried into the wind.

"Like I said, you're on your own, Squire," was

the reply. "We weren't here tonight, and we won't be coming back. This place is cursed. We should've turned you down flat."

"What about the money?"

The voice was far away now. "Keep it."

"Well, it's just us, young lady." The old man sighed. "Let's investigate this library of yours, shall we?"

If the ladder had been only slightly shorter, their plans would have been thwarted. The man sent the girl down first as he thought she'd be agile enough to climb and hold both lanterns.

When her head disappeared, the old man grasped the end of the ladder.

The salty wind gusted fiercely and lashed his face.

Was some higher power furious at their intrusion?

The old man sucked up his apprehensions, turned his back to the hole, and found the top rung of the ladder with his gouty foot.

And with that, Benjamin Franklin took his first step down into the Library of Vectis.

Panama City, Florida, 2026

The snoring, low and vibratory, was the first thing Will Piper heard on waking. For a moment, he thought someone had started the motors, for the guttural sound coming from the guest stateroom uncannily resembled the harsh rumble of the cruiser's twin 454 Crusaders at idle. Those antique engines were irritable relics requiring constant fussing and coaxing to make them do what they were supposed to do.

Just like me, Will always said.

He stared at the teak ceiling in the master stateroom before parting the curtains and popping the window. The flat bright haze was typical for January. It would burn off soon enough. If the forecast was right it was going to hit seventy. Not bad considering Washington was supposed to get another four inches of slop. He thought about his morning mission, a simple enough challenge, persuading Phillip to come along on a tuna run into the Gulf.

His pillow was warm. Nancy's was cool and unused. He pulled it under his neck and closed his eyes. Phillip's snoring wasn't letting up, but even if it had, he knew he wasn't going to get any more shut-eye. At sixty-four he'd lost the black, dreamless sleep of youth, and though he missed it terribly, he was grateful that at least he'd firmly held on to his hair and his potency.

Young Phillip, on the other hand, was a finely tuned sleeping machine, a mattress Ferrari. It took almost nothing to tilt him into unconsciousness and Herculean maneuvers to rouse him out of it: thrust-open curtains, shoulder shaking, cajoling, the smell of bacon. And if the past week had taught Will anything, they'd be arguing before his son's big feet hit the deck.

The boat gently bobbed and tugged at its lines in the shifting tide. The freshening wind pacified him as it always did. But suddenly the twin motors of the yacht in the next slip noisily started up. His mood turned sour, and he peevishly peeled back the duvet. Peace and quiet were off the menu.

Then he remembered that his neighbor was out of town. Who the hell was monkeying with Ben's boat? He bounded topside to investigate.

His wardrobe varied little from day to day—swim trunks with or without a T-shirt, today without. On deck, he scratched his hairy chest like the big primate he was and squinted, adjusting his eyes to the daylight. His skin was bronzed and sunbaked, with an amusing swath of whiteness from waist to thighs. He still looked fit, with a flat enough stomach and large, bulky shoulders. Though he hadn't jogged or worked out in years, he ran up and down keeping the old boat afloat, and that probably did the trick, but if genes had anything to do with it, he wouldn't know. His old man had kicked off well before reaching his sixties.

Ben Patterson's new Regal cruiser was purring in neutral, but no one was at the wheel, and the lines were still tied.

Will went portside, leaned over his railings, and called out, "Hello!"

Two blond heads and plenty of bare flesh emerged from the Regal's salon. He quickly smoothed his sandy gray hair with a finger comb.

"Hi there!" one of the blondes called out. They were in their thirties, he reckoned, a good decade. They quickly introduced themselves. One was Ben's sister, Margie from Cape Cod and the other one, Meagan, was her best friend. Meagan was a looker.

"What's your name?" Meagan asked.

"I'm Will. You girls heading out?"

"You bet," Margie said. "We couldn't take the winter anymore. Ben's a sweetheart to let us come down and use the boat for the week. Got to enjoy life while it lasts, that's what everyone says. Want to come along?"

"Love to, but I can't. My son's asleep."

"How old is he?"

"Fifteen and change."

"Great age."

"Think so?" Will asked. "I'd say the two of you are a great age."

Meagan wagged her finger at him, the universal bad-boy sign. "Hey, you look familiar. I'm sure I've seen your picture somewhere."

He shrugged. He didn't want to go there but before he could change the subject she had her mobile in her hand. She pointed it in his direction and it lit up with matching images.

"Oh my God, Margie! He's Will Piper. *The* Will Piper. The Library guy."

"Guilty as charged," he confessed.

"What's going to happen next February?" Meagan asked as if he'd never heard the question before.

"Beats the hell out of me. Want help casting off?"

Phillip sat in the galley zombielike, staring at his mobile. Will couldn't help seeing the faces of his inane friends emerging from the screen in 3-D, bantering to one another in an unintelligible Net patois. The English language had officially gone to hell. Then he recognized the snarky hatchet face of Phillip's best friend, Andy, and made out the word "homework."

Seizing the opening, Will interrupted, "You've got homework?"

Phillip hit the mute button and took a bite of toast. "An essay."

"What kind of essay?"

"Just an essay."

"When are you going to do it?"

"It's almost done. Don't sweat."

Will grunted his approval. "It's going to be a good day. I'd like you to come out with me."

"Fishing?"

"Uh-huh."

"No thanks."

"Why not?"

"I'm not into killing harmless creatures."

"We'll do catch and release."

"I'm not into harming harmless creatures." He hooked his lip with his index finger and affected an expression of torment.

"Jesus, Phil."

"I'm meeting some friends."

"What friends?"

"Just some girls."

"I didn't know you knew kids down here."

"Now you do."

With that, Phillip took the mobile off mute and tuned his father out.

Girls, Will thought. Like father, like son.

Later that morning, when Phillip shoved off, Will made sure to amble up to the marina office to spy on him. From the windows, he saw a yellow convertible pull up, and three pretty girls collected his only offspring. The kid was a tad gangly but he was a good-looking boy with his father's big bones, tall for fifteen, with unruly sandy hair. Fortunately, he'd taken after his father on height. Nancy was pint-sized—until she got mad. Then she seemed to dwarf Will. Lately, he'd had enough long-distance blasts from her to be feeling reasonably small.

Will grabbed a pen from the front desk and with the instincts of a current father and a former FBI agent, he jotted down the convertible's plate number. You never knew, you just never knew.

He reboarded *Will Power,* looked at his neighbor's empty slip and sighed. He should have gone out with the ladies. The day stretched in front of him. Since fishing was off the table, what then? He'd been putting off an overhaul of his refrigeration system. Reluctantly, he decided that today was the day to get greasy.

Hours later he heard the Regal coming back in. He happily abandoned his tools, wiped his hands on a rag and emerged into the warmth of a fine afternoon. He figured the ladies were going to have problems docking the cruiser in reverse, and he wasn't wrong. After two aborted attempts where Margie missed the pivot point around the piling, he volunteered to board and land it for them. He nailed it perfectly and tossed the lines to a pair of outstretched arms reddened from a day of exposure.

"Our knight in shining armor," Meagan said. "Want a drink?"

"Let me grab a shirt."

Aboard *Will Power* he pulled a polo shirt out of his dresser and started talking to himself, unaware of the irony of his little speech given the name of the boat. "Have some goddamned self-control, for Christ sakes, Will. Try not to be a complete idiot, okay? Can you go do that? Do you think?"

When his head popped through the collar he found himself staring at a picture of Nancy at the FBI swearing-in ceremony in Washington, which elevated her to Executive Assistant Director for the Criminal and Cyber Branch. She looked good that day, very happy. He'd almost ruined the affair by acting so miserably, mooning about having to live in Washington. They'd worked through that, made an accommodation. Now, if he wasn't careful, he'd screw things up.

Will relaxed in a deck chair on the Regal and guzzled a beer. He was careful about his drinking and it was early in the day, but he felt entitled to a slice of good time. Except for her fleeting visit to Panama City lasting all of three days at Christmas, he hadn't seen Nancy for the better part of two months. And Phillip's forced school vacation with Dad hadn't exactly been as much fun as a barrel of monkeys.

The sunburned ladies had a full cooler, lots of snacks, and an unlimited supply of chirpy conversation. They fussed over him, and Meagan especially, kept feeding him beers and stoking his ego: his boat was cool. He had a great tan. He was in really good shape (for a man of his age). He was the first celebrity she'd ever met up close.

"So when did you get your boat?" Margie asked.

"About fifteen years ago. I traded a bus for it."

"A bus?"

"It's a long story," Will answered.

She accepted that and moved on. "You down here for the duration?"

"However long that is."

"Hopefully more than thirteen months," Meagan said.

"Hopefully."

An hour passed, and Margie nodded off from sun and beer. Meagan asked if he'd join them for dinner. Will texted his son and quickly got an answer. Phillip was otherwise occupied.

"I'm in."

"I'll let her sleep," Meagan said. "I'm going to make some pasta. Do you know how to use Ben's stove?"

Belowdecks, the boat rocked pleasantly in the afternoon wind. Will turned the propane valve and fired up the burner then lounged on the settee while Meagan chopped and cooked. He stared hypnotically at the clingy bikini fabric covering her firm bottom. Searching for spices, she happened upon a bottle of scotch in one of the cupboards. "I love this stuff," she purred. "Mental note to self. Replace bottle before we leave. Want some?"

He knew Ben's brand. It was Johnnie Walker Black, his best friend and his worst enemy. He sighed. "I'm on the wagon."

"You've had three beers!"

"The whiskey wagon."

"Alcohol is alcohol."

"Oh no it's not."

"What's the worst that can happen? We won't let you fall into the water. Besides, I'm a nurse. I can handle anything."

"My wife could call."

"That's what voice mail is for, honey."

The first generous sip conveyed the familiarity of a homecoming. It was dark and tonal, awakening his palate and tingling his throat. Seconds later, he felt it in his head, a rush of numbing pleasure. Hello, Johnnie, he thought, where've you been, pal?

While she sautéed, he finished one glass and started another.

When the sauce was simmering she joined him on the settee, poured a second for herself, and turned serious.

"I know I treat it like a joke most of the time, but I'm scared. No one seems to have any answers. What's really going to happen on February 9, 2027?"

"I don't have any special insights," he answered. "It's not like I'm sitting on inside information."

"Yeah, but you're the reason we know about all this! I'm sorry to press you, but I can't believe I'm actually sitting here with Will Piper! I'd kick myself later if I didn't take advantage of it."

"I've been out of the loop for over fifteen years. I'm more than out of the loop, I'm persona non grata with the government." He had another mouthful. "If I didn't have a trump card, I'm sure they would have bumped me off years ago."

"The database."

He nodded.

"You're BTH, right?"

Beyond the Horizon. "Yeah, I'm BTH."

"I guess at this point, I am, too," she said. "Still, could you look me up?"

"Believe me, I don't have access to the database."

"I guess I really wouldn't have ever wanted to know."

"I hear you."

"But it's awful to think that everything's going to

end in something like four hundred days, whatever the number is—you know people have countdown clocks on their screens! The world's totally obsessing and stressing."

"I don't think about it very much," Will said. "I just live."

"Yeah, but you've got a son."

He held out his glass for a refill. "That, young lady, is the hardest part. Plus a daughter probably older than you from a previous marriage."

"Any grandkids?"

"One. Laura's got a son, Nick. A very good kid."

"So you *do* think the world's going to end."

"Yes, no, maybe, maybe not, probably, probably not. Depends on the day you ask."

"Today?"

He wet his finger and held it up to the air. "Today? Yeah, we're toast."

"Then why are you on the scotch wagon?"

He waved his glass. "I think we've established I've fallen off."

"I mean in general. Most people I know are heavily into eat, drink, and be merry."

"If it were just me, I'd probably be a world-class hedonist. Nancy—that's my wife—wouldn't stand for it. There're certain things worse than death. You don't want to see her when she's pissed off."

Meagan clucked at that. "Where is she?"

"In DC. She's got a big job with the feds. My son lives up there with her."

"Separated?"

"Nope. She hates seeing me mope around our place in Virginia. It's the way we've worked things out. I'm from down here, always liked it. In a year or so, when we get close to the Horizon, we'll see where we park ourselves."

She put her glass down and ran a finger down his shirt from neck to navel, her fingernail against cotton making a rough, unzipping sound.

He knew what was happening, but he asked innocently, "What's this all about?"

"My sauce tastes best when it's simmered a long time."

"I like a good red sauce."

"Then come along to my bunk or berth or whatever you call a bed on a boat."

"Margie's right there."

"She's a really heavy napper." She placed one of his big hands on her left breast. "I think we should have some fun, don't you? I liked you right away."

He struggled with a response. His thinking wasn't crisp anymore, and her breast felt lovely and soft. "You're some kind of bikini-clad devil, aren't you?"

She inched closer and kissed him on the lips.

After half a minute he pulled back, and said, "You know, I think I'm going to have to decline your awfully kind invitation."

"Your wife?"

He nodded. "I've made promises. To her. To myself."

"Yeah, but don't you find me attractive?" She slid a hand over his crotch.

His head was swimming. "I certainly do."

"The world's going to end. Shouldn't we just enjoy ourselves?"

He admired her legs. "That's a commonly held point of view. But . . ." He took a deep breath and when he exhaled, something happened.

He felt like the air wasn't expelling, like it was building up, pressurizing his chest. He tried to stand up, but he couldn't.

"Are you okay?" she asked.

"I . . ."

The pressure overwhelmed him, and he struggled for air. There was a sound in his ears like a train passing very close. He'd been in some tight jams in his life, he'd been in firefights with men intent on killing him, but he'd never felt the kind of panic washing over him now.

He was dimly aware of Meagan's fingers on his carotid, and a faraway voice saying, "My God, I think you're having a heart attack."

Through the salon window the sky was still blue but darkening. He didn't want to stop looking at it but he lost sight when he slumped onto the carpet.

I'm BTH, he thought. I'm not supposed to die today.

What February 9, 2027 Means To Me
An Essay by Phillip Piper

As of today there are 394 days left until the "Big Day," the "Horizon," the "Last Day of School" as a lot of kids are calling it. Everyone is wondering what will happen, and people are going different shades of mental. Are we going to be blasted out of existence by an asteroid the size of Rhode Island? Swallowed up by a black hole? Fried by gamma rays from the sun? Or is February 10 going to be just another day?

I'm no different from everyone else who's been thinking about mankind's fate except for one thing. My father is Will Piper, the man who told the world about February 9, 2027.

This essay is a little hard for me to finish because my dad is really sick. He had a heart attack, and he's in the hospital. I know he's BTH, but that doesn't mean he's going to be all right. No one knows if he's going to walk or talk again or be able to respond to us. He's on a breathing machine in intensive care. They're giving him a new medicine, and we'll see if it helps. But I know if he was conscious, he'd be all over me to turn this essay in by the deadline, so that is what I'm going to do.

I wasn't even born when all this went down in 2009 and 2010. I found out about it and the part my dad played when I was twelve, I think. He wrote a book which I admit I never read. I saw the movie, Library of the Dead, *instead. It was a pretty cool movie, but it was weird watching actors play your father and your mother. My mother always said she wished she was as pretty as the actress who played her, but my father was never interested in speaking about it. He said the movie was silly and filled with inaccuracies and that he wished he'd never let it be made. The truth is, he's never been someone who wanted to be in the public eye.*

In 2009, my dad was an FBI agent in New York. He got involved in a case involving someone called the Doomsday Killer. A man in Nevada was sending postcards to people in New York City announcing the date they were going to die, and all nine of them wound up dying on the exact date. No one could figure out what was happening since there was nothing to link the victims, and all of the "murders" were completely different. My dad was the lead agent on the case and my mother—she wasn't my mother at that point—was a junior agent. They were a team, and I guess you could say they still are.

Nothing was making any sense and they kept hitting dead ends. But my mom and dad were really smart and figured out that the postcards were coming from a computer geek named Mark Shackleton who worked at a top secret government lab at Area 51 in Nevada. Not only that but my dad actually knew the guy from when they were freshmen roommates in college. Back in 2009, everyone thought that Area 51 was some kind of secret weapons facility or maybe a place where UFOs were studied. It turns out the real truth was even more amazing.

Area 51, as everyone knows now, is the storage vault for the famous Library of Vectis. In the year 777, on the seventh day of the seventh month a baby who was the seventh son of a seventh son was born in England in a place called Vectis (it's now called the Isle of Wight). The boy grew up to be some kind of a savant who had a preoccupation of writing down lists of birth dates and death dates for people from all over the world, people he never met. Some monks in an abbey took him in and realized that what he was able to do was miraculous. They created a secret order to take care of him and recruited women to give birth to his children and his children's children. Over the centuries, thousands of these savants produced a giant underground library of books, over seven hundred thousand of them, with the birth and death dates of everyone who was going to live through February 9, 2027.

No one knows how they did it. Some people say they must have had some kind of psychic connection to the universe or to God. I guess we'll never know. But in the thirteenth century, something happened. All of a sudden, when they were working on their parchment pages for February 9, 2027, they stopped writing names. Instead, they wrote Finis Dierum which is Latin for End of Days. Then all of them killed themselves.

After that, the Library was sealed up by the monks, and no one knew it existed until British archaeologists found it 1947. Winston Churchill gave the Library to the Americans who realized it could be very valuable. The US government set up Area 51 to hold the Library and spent a lot of time and money figuring out how to mine the data for political and military purposes. For example, if you knew that fifty thousand people with Pakistani names were going to die on one particular day you could do some serious planning on an American response to the crisis. For fifty years, no one outside the government knew about the Library until my dad found out.

Mark Shackleton had his own ideas what to do with the data. He wanted to make money off it and invented the Doomsday Killer as part of his scheme. My dad discovered the truth about the existence of the Library and shut Shackleton down. He got a hold of a copy of the database for all the births and deaths of everyone in the United States through 2027. If your death wasn't recorded in the database, you were considered BTH, Beyond the Horizon. He checked out himself, my mom and me, and some of our *relatives. We were all BTH. He hid the database in Los Angeles as an insurance policy.*

For a while, my dad kept the secret of Area 51 because of an agreement he made with the government. I don't think he was too happy about that, but he wanted to protect me and the rest of the family—I was born in 2010—and besides, he always believed that if people knew the dates of their deaths, that could seriously mess with their minds and create a bad situation. He and I never talked about it, but in the movie his character really agonizes over the decision to keep quiet. I think that part was accurate. But when I was only an infant, he was contacted by some men who had retired from Area 51. They were part of a group called the 2027 Club, who were trying to figure out what was going to happen in 2027.

One of the books from the Library of Vectis dated 1527 wound up at an auction house in London. They wanted my dad to help them get ahold of the book. It was the only book missing from the Area 51 Library, and they thought it might hold some answers about 2027. They were right. There was a sonnet hidden inside written by a very young William Shakespeare. My dad went to England, and in an old house called Cantwell Hall, he followed clues in the sonnet and found out about the End of Days stuff and the savants committing suicide. He also found out that knowledge of the Library of Vectis had an influence on some famous historical figures like John Calvin and Nostradamus, not to mention William Shakespeare.

There were security people at Area 51, government agents who were called the watchers, who were sent to stop my dad, and they got close. They tried to poison our whole family with carbon monoxide. I almost died, but they killed both my grandparents, whom I never got to know. My mom and I went into hiding, and my dad went to Los Angeles to recover the hidden database. He got shot by the watchers and escaped to the home of the head of the 2027 Club in Las Vegas. He was captured there, but my mom saved him, which was pretty cool.

My dad gave the database to my half sister's husband, Greg, who was a journalist with The Washington Post *because after thinking about it for a long time, he decided that people had a right to know what the government knew. Greg published a sensational story about the existence of the Library, and my dad became a reluctant celebrity. My mom kept working at the FBI. She's still there.*

The database never got published. The government sued the newspaper and the case went all the way to the Supreme Court. So people never got to know about their personal dates but everyone knows about February 9, 2027.

It's funny, but I never spent much time thinking about February 9, I mean really thinking about it, until my dad got sick. No one close to me since I've been old enough to understand has ever died or even gotten seriously sick. It took my dad's heart attack to change that. Now I realize how fragile life is and how, just like that, it can be taken away. Now I'm scared about what will happen to him, and I'll admit it, I'm scared about what will happen to me, my mom, my friends, and everyone on the planet.

I don't have any answers. I may be Will Piper's son but I'm as clueless as the next guy on what's going to happen to us. But here's what I think. I think that we should try to make each of these 394 days count. We should try to be extra nice to each another, try not to be jerks, try to smile a lot, and try not to complain and moan about everything or be superdepressed. We ought to live each day to its fullest and enjoy ourselves.

The way I figure it, we can either have 394 awful days ahead or 394 terrific ones. I'm going to go for terrific ones.

I think that's what Will Piper would choose too.

Through the impenetrable fog of illness he'd heard voices, some comforting and recognizable, others not. The foreign voices spoke hard, strange words: troponin, CK, left anterior descending, MCEs, cine MRIs, wedge pressures, dopamine, O_2 sats, vent settings, cardiomyoplasty.

Time was unfathomable. Later, he would liken his perceptions to Dali's melting clocks. A second. A day. A month—they were all the same. He was mostly aware of the discomfort of a breathing tube in his nose, and it became his nemesis.

When he was a young FBI agent, a star player in the twisted world of serial killers, he would pursue his target with an all-consuming passion and aggression, invariably to the detriment of whoever shared his bed and his life at the time. Now the tube was his enemy. He wasn't sure why it was crammed down his throat. Rational thoughts about it drifted away because of the sedatives given to prevent him from yanking it out. And just in case he lightened up between doses, his wrists were nightmarishly bound to the railings of his bed.

One day the fog lifted and he became gradually

aware of his surroundings. He was propped in a half-sitting position. His throat burned but he could no longer feel the stiff plastic in his nostril. He reached up, expecting the tug of restraints, but his hand moved unrestricted to his face, where he felt for the absent tube.

He looked to one side then the other. He was in a glass-walled room with muted lights. There were softly beeping machines. There was an intravenous line in his hand. He reached down to address an irritation in his crotch. There was a catheter. He gave it a tug and wished he hadn't. When he yelped, his body snapped forward, and his pillow slipped away.

A pretty nurse came in. "Hi, Mr. Piper. I'm Jean. Welcome to the land of the living."

She leaned over and repositioned his pillow. Her breasts came close to his face. The land of the living is good, he thought. But he demanded a little more specificity. "Where am I?"

"Miami. This is the Miami Heart Institute."

"I hate Miami."

She laughed.

"My throat's killing me," he croaked.

"I'll get you some lozenges. We only pulled the breathing tube at 2 A.M. It's 6 A.M. now."

He pointed down. "Can you pull this thing out?"

"It's coming out real soon."

A larger question came to his mind. "What happened to me?"

"You had a heart attack. A big one."

"How long have I been here?"

"Five weeks. You were a week in Panama City before they transferred you here."

"Jesus."

A phlebotomist came in to draw blood. She smiled at him then poked his sore, black-and-blue arm.

The nurse hung a bag of medicine, then said, "Your wife's been notified you're off the ventilator. She should be here soon. Dr. Rosenberg will be here for rounds in an hour. She'll fill you in on everything that's happened."

"She?"

"Yes, she."

"I'm surrounded by women." It didn't come out as a complaint.

Dr. Rosenberg had fiercely pulled-back hair. She was all business, not the kind of woman Will instinctively took to, but in this case he had a lot of time for her.

He'd had a whopper, she explained. A ruptured plaque high up in his left anterior descending artery which, because of poor collateral flow in other vessels had left a fair bit of his left ventricle, the main pump muscle, weak and useless. His heart failure was severe.

In the old days his options would have been limited to a mechanical pump, a piece of machinery that would have made him ambulatory though permanently tethered to a battery pack, or a heart transplant, with all the attendant risks.

"Screw the old days," Will rasped, painfully sucking apple juice through a straw. "What did I get?"

"Fortunately, there's been a revolution in the therapy of post MI pump failure," the doctor said. "We gave you MyoStem, a new FDA-approved preparation of cardiac-muscle stem cells. I injected them directly into the damaged areas through a catheter. They've taken beautifully. I liken it to reseeding a barren lawn. You still have a few bare patches, but it should fill in completely."

"Will I get back to normal?"

"Are you a marathon runner?"

"Not in this life."

"Then you should get back to normal."

"Sex?"

"Patients usually ask," she said amused, "but not in the first minute. Sexual activity shouldn't be a problem."

If I can fish, and I can screw, then I'll be okay, he thought.

At least until February 9.

When Nancy arrived he was sitting upright with his hair combed and teeth brushed. He instinctively grinned with the same sheepish smile he always sported every time he'd messed up with her.

She just stood there at the foot of his bed, crying.

"Hey, kiddo," he said.

She looked so small and thin. She's lost weight, he thought. Poor kid. The things I put her through.

When she was younger, stress had made her put on weight. The opposite was true now. In the early years of their marriage, he'd dropped little remarks which had sent her into mental tailspins, then a diet. But when she reached her midthirties and seriously started climbing the FBI org chart something shifted. Maybe it was the pressure of management jobs or the burden of being married to the likes of him or her excessive early-morning gym routines, but her body had turned lean and firm. He wasn't complaining.

Almost two decades separated them. She was still a fairly young woman; he was entering his self-admitted crotchety years. He considered himself all too predictable, but to his mind, she was as changeable as the prevailing winds. Some days she came off as tougher than nails, demanding, and hugely self-assured; other days she seemed diminutive, needy, and doubt-ridden. Some days, she complained to him bitterly about being up in Washington essentially leading the life of a single parent and making him feel like a selfish rat for not joining her. Other days, she said she'd had it with the bureaucracy in DC and just wanted to pack it in and move to Florida.

Now this.

"I didn't . . ." She couldn't finish the sentence.

"Come here," he said.

The bed rail was down. She leaned over and kissed him, wetting his cheek with her tears. He took his free arm, the one that didn't have an IV stuck in it, and enveloped her. He tried to squeeze but he was as weak as a kitten.

"I'm sorry," he said.

She straightened herself. "Sorry for what?"

"For being a pain in the ass."

"Since when did you start apologizing for that?"

"I guess it's a new thing."

"It won't last. Jesus, Will, we thought we were losing you."

"I'm BTH, remember?"

"You know what I mean. Like Mark Shackleton."

Mark Shackleton, he of postcard fame, who'd operated with a sense of impunity because he'd known he was BTH. Shot in the head by Area 51 agents fifteen years ago, he was still alive, a vegetable in a coma.

"I put you through a lot. I'm glad I didn't pull a Shackleton. I saw Doctor Stick-up-her-ass this morning. She said I got some new treatment."

"Dr. Rosenberg. Unless a woman's a bimbo, you think she's officious."

He smiled. "See, we're arguing again. Just like old times."

"I missed you."

He nodded and asked in rapid fire, "How've

you been holding up? Where've you been staying? Where's Phillip?"

"I've been trying to hold things together as best I could, especially for Phillip. He's back at school, staying at Andy's house. Andy's parents have been great. I've been in a hotel near the hospital."

"On leave."

"That was the plan, but it got derailed. We got busy. I've been coordinating things from down here, using the Miami office. I called Phillip this morning to tell him the news. He's arriving this afternoon, with Laura and Greg."

"Is Laura okay?"

"She's been down here a couple of times. She's been worried sick."

"And Nick?"

"He's fine too. He's away at school." Nancy set her jaw, a look he knew all too well.

"What?" he asked.

"I don't want to bring up any unpleasantness at a time like this, but before Phillip arrives I wanted you to know he's had a confusing time of it."

Will waited for more.

"It's the circumstances of your heart attack. The paramedics found you with a couple of young women inside Ben Patterson's boat."

He frantically searched his memory, came up blank and assumed the worst. "Christ. I'm . . ."

"Please don't apologize to me, Will. I'm not looking for that. I just want you to be sensitive to Phillip's feelings. He's been struggling with a lot of emotions."

Will teared up and summoned her for another hug. "I swear to you, Nancy, for as long as we have on this earth, I'm going to be a better man."

* * *

They bought him a small cake with a single battery-operated candle—real ones were verboten in the oxygen-rich intensive care unit.

The nurses dolled Will up in his own, now loosely fitting clothes, and wheeled him in a lounge chair so he could receive visitors more comfortably. He remained attached to intravenous lines and monitors and required oxygen prongs in his nostrils but to the surprise of everyone who had borne witness to his coma, he looked very much himself.

Though his voice was hoarse, his lips were cracked and coated in Vaseline and his complexion was sallow, his eyes retained their old sparkle, and the corners of his mouth sported his trademark self-deprecatory crinkle.

The powers that be limited the visit to twenty minutes. Nancy, Greg, and Laura hovered over him in an awkward homecoming while Phillip lurked at the doorway.

Laura had never outgrown her free-spirited youth. She was still a postmillennial flower child who dressed in long cotton frocks, her flowing hair streaked with gray. She was a novelist with a steady following of like-minded women who took to her stories of quirky love, abandonment, and randomness. It hadn't hurt her career that she was Will Piper's daughter; some of her fans combed through her books as if they were sacred texts looking for hidden truths about 2027, a subject she had long embraced.

Her son Nick was an only child, a few months older than Phillip. It had always been a source of family tension that Will's son and grandson were the same age. Laura had made no secret of her opinion that Nick had drawn the short straw and had been deprived of the unfettered attention of his grandfather. Nevertheless, Will genuinely liked the kid, always had, and on Nick's infrequent visits to Florida, found him a better fishing buddy than his son. But ever since he went off to boarding school in New Hampshire, they rarely saw each other.

His son-in-law, Greg Davis, was his usual saturnine self and during the visit, the two men exchanged a single obligatory bear hug and few words. The animus was largely one-sided—Will didn't particularly love the guy but he certainly never disliked him. If Greg was good enough for his daughter, he was good enough for him.

The difficulties lay with Greg's chronic disappointment and his belief that his career might have blossomed if Will had only been more helpful.

Will had always rejected the notion out of hand. When Greg was a junior staff reporter at *The Washington Post* back in 2011, hadn't he handed the kid the scoop of the century? Hadn't Greg become instantly famous as the journalist who first reported the existence of the Library of Vectis and Area 51? Hadn't he landed a Pulitzer Prize? Was it Will's fault that Greg's plans to write the book of books about the Library got shot down by a Supreme Court ruling that compelled the *Post* to cease and desist and return Will's pirated copy of the US database to the government? Was it his fault that Greg was forced to adhere to the government's nondisclosure agreement? Was it Will's fault that publishers fell all over themselves to get their mitts on *his* book about the Doomsday case?

Greg had left the *Post* after the Supreme Court verdict and ridden his journalistic notoriety for a while with jobs at the *New York Times*, then a succession of magazines and entrepreneurial publishing ventures, none of which had amounted to much. His latest project was a portfolio of NetZines aimed at immigrant communities living in America, and he and Laura lived in Brooklyn now, supported dispro-portionally by her novels.

Will found the cake too challenging to swallow and just ate the icing. "Best thing I ever tasted," he said.

"When you get home, I'll give you cake every day," Nancy said.

"Did they tell you how long they were keeping you in, Dad?" Laura asked.

"No, but the doctor said that when the MyoStem takes as well as it has for me, the recovery is fast. I'd leave today if it were up to me."

"It's not up to you," Nancy said sternly.

He changed the subject. "Been able to write?" he asked his daughter.

"I've been a little distracted."

"How about you, Greg. How's your business get-ting on?"

Greg had carried his angular body and sharp-featured face into middle age, but his curly mass of hair had wilted away. The dome of his head was now bony and geographic. The question seemed to ani-mate him. "We've been busy, crazy busy, because of Nancy's thing. Extra editions, you name it."

Nancy looked at Greg sharply.

"What thing?" Will asked.

"Nothing," she said, shooting Greg a dirty look. "I'll tell you later. It's nothing we need to talk about right now."

Ordinarily, Will wouldn't let a comment like that go—he'd dog it until he had an answer, but he was too weak and foggy to pursue it. He let the bone drop from his teeth.

He called his son over. The boy took a few paces into the room. "I hear you're staying with Andy."

Phillip nodded.

"How's that working out? Getting any work done, or are the two of you just farting around?"

"It's okay," the boy answered sullenly.

Will sniffed back some tears. "I'm sorry I put you through all of this."

"It's okay. Can I go downstairs so I can use my NetPen?"

"Don't you want to tell your father about your award?" Nancy asked.

"No," the kid said, slipping away. "You tell him."

"Phillip?" Will called after him, but he was gone. "What award?"

"His school had all the kids write about what February 9, 2027 means to them. All the essays were entered in a national contest. Phillip won first prize."

"You're kidding!"

"It's online, Dad. It's everywhere," Laura said.

"I even reprinted it in my NetZine," Greg added.

Nancy had a copy in her purse. "I'll leave it on the bedside table," she said. "Read it when we leave. You're in it."

"Am I?" Will said, unable to prevent a soft, shuddering run of sobs.

Nancy was gushing. "You look so much better!"

Will was on a regular hospital floor, disconnected from all but a small IV port in his hand.

"I'm feeling better," he said.

She'd found him walking the halls in sweatpants and polo shirt, doing a circuit of the ward. Every so often he would stop, check his pulse, grunt, and carry on.

"Breathing okay?" she asked.

He was. He was also pain-free except for his bruised, needle-punctured arms.

They made their way to his room, where he claimed the chair, she, the bed.

"They're doing an exercise test tomorrow," he said. "If it's good, they're sending me home."

She nodded enthusiastically, then repeated the word with emphasis. "Home."

He knew what she meant.

"I hate it in Virginia. You know how I feel."

"I can't leave you on your own."

"I don't *want* to be alone."

"Will, don't you think that your . . ." She looked

like she couldn't bear saying heart attack. ". . . your problem changes things?"

"I agree," he said. "I do think it changes things. I think you should retire. This was our tipping point. I want you and Phillip with me. Down here. Phillip can go to school in Panama City. Or not go to school at all as far as I'm concerned."

She closed her eyes in a show of anger and frustration. He expected her to come out fighting, but when she reopened them, it was apparent she'd reined herself in. She spoke evenly with supreme control. "We agreed not to let the Horizon change the way we live. Whatever happens, we'll be together as a family next February 9, and we'll be laughing or crying together, maybe a little of both. Until then, Phillip needs to stay in school, I need to keep working, and you need to keep fishing."

It wasn't what he wanted to hear but it wasn't surprising. Nancy was tough. That's what he liked about her even when it worked against him. "Then at least spend a month in Florida until I'm all better. Then we can go back to Plan A."

"I can't."

He lost his cool. "Why the hell not? Is it the 'thing' that Greg said you were busy with? Tell me how this 'thing' is more important than me."

She sighed. "It's not more important than you. It's a new case. A big one. I'm up to my keister in it."

"Christ, Nance, you're so high on the totem pole, all you need to do is take names and bust asses these days."

"You'd think. I almost feel like a field agent on this one."

He saw the anxiety in her face. It was paradoxically calming. "You want to tell me what it is?"

"Postcards," she said. "We've got more postcards."

What little pink there was in his cheeks blanched out. "You're not serious!"

"I'm completely serious."

"Where? How many? Who's got the capability or the motive? Why the hell now?"

She motioned for him to slow down and emphatically told him she'd only talk about it if he promised he wouldn't work himself into a state. He reached for a water bottle and agreed.

"To be honest, I thought you'd have seen it on TV or the Net the last couple of days or heard about it from someone in the hospital. I'm glad it's coming from me."

"You know I hate the news, and why would anyone have told me?"

"Because you're Will Piper?"

He saw her point.

"It started two weeks ago. Five postcards, all postmarked on the same day. It's the same pattern as seventeen years ago, a printed name and address on the front with no return address. On the back there's a hand-drawn picture of a coffin and a date. And like before, each recipient dies on the date."

"Only five?"

"It's fifteen now."

"Nevada postmarks?"

"New York City."

"Let me guess. Different causes of death, different MOs, maybe not even homicides at all," Will said automatically.

"Right."

"And no linkers or patterns."

"It's a little different from 2009. All the recipients are Chinese."

"What?" he said in amazement.

"The first ten lived mostly in Chinatown in New York. The five newest ones are in San Francisco."

"Who's working it?"

"New York, San Francisco. We've got good people assigned. Problem is, it's got my name all over it because of past history. The Director called me in on the first day and told he was cutting through six layers and putting me directly in charge. I'm briefing him personally morning and night. He wanted me in New York, but because of your illness he let me work it from Miami."

"Other than the curiosity factor which, believe me, I'm not discounting, why the hysteria? It's obvious it's a Shackleton-type situation. Some jackass from Area 51 is leaking names again."

"It's because of the China angle. The Chinese government and their Ministry of State Security is all over it. Even though the postcard victims are mostly American citizens the Chinese government is highly agitated. They also think it's coming from Area 51. They think it's an act of provocation. China's the second largest economy in the world. We're declining, they're closing fast. They're convinced we're screwing with them, playing psych-out games. They've let it be known through diplomatic channels that unless we find the leaker they're not going to roll over our debt payments. They call a few hundred billion in notes, and bad things are going to happen here."

Will signaled he wanted to switch places, to lie down. He sprawled out and said, "It's so damned juvenile. The world may end in a year, and we're playing these stupid games right to the last day."

She nodded wearily. "What can I say? It's official US policy to maintain the status quo."

"While NASA and every astronomer in the world

keeps looking for the big one with our name on it," he said. His eyes drooped.

She sat beside him and stroked his hair. "You look tired, honey."

"I'll do it," he said.

"Do what?"

"I'll go back to Virginia with you. Until I'm better. Okay?"

"I love you," she said.

His lip quivered ever so slightly. "Right back at you."

"And I forgive you."

He had a mental shot of Meagan in her little bikini and wished he could remember how much forgiveness he needed.

Roger Kenney rode Elevator One six floors up to ground level and left the chilled air of the Truman Building for the sandy heat of the Nevada desert. It was only a short walk to Rear Admiral Duncan Sage's office in the Admin Building but he sweated out the armpits of his fatigues by the time he was back in air-conditioning.

Admiral Sage kept him waiting, which was nothing new. Kenney always suspected the waiting game was a display of theater and power on Sage's part, a brittle show of dominance. It wasn't as if the base commander at Area 51 was the busiest officer in the US military these past several years. He wasn't the only landlocked admiral in the US Navy, but he was certainly the only one stuck on an ancient dry lake bed in the desolate Nevada desert. It was only an accident of history that put the base under naval jurisdiction back when it was established in 1947, and Sage was the last in the line of ducks out of water.

Kenney thoroughly and unreservedly hated Sage's guts. He considered him to be a pompous and insecure son of a bitch whom he wouldn't trust to shine his shoes in civilian life. To his confidants in the ranks of the watchers, the roster of majors who reported directly to him, Kenney seditiously referred to Sage as the banana slug after the creature so territorial and guarded that it bites off its own penis inside the female to prevent others from depositing sperm. He couldn't recall how he knew about the mating habits of banana slugs, but it was the typical kind of factoid he was always picking up and tossing around to the amusement of the men he commanded.

Sage's new PA, a civilian who, rumor had it, had been a showgirl on the Strip, moved papers around her desk in a transparent attempt to appear busy. All service branches of the military had been operating under a mandate to be essentially paperless by 2025, but out-of-the-way bases like Area 51 weren't visited by auditors and it wasn't clear that Sage could operate all his productivity devices.

Kenney sat stiffly, watching the PA. She was reasonably ripe and attractive and wasn't totally out of his age range. He stared intently at her sweater with radium eyes and concluded he wanted to make a move on her. Unless the old banana slug had already bitten off his penis inside her.

"Anyone in with him?" Kenney finally asked her.

"He's on a conference call, Colonel," she said. It sounded like a lie, but there was nothing he could do about it. He settled into a game. He was self-assured about his own attributes: dark, cocky features, lean, strong, and fast. He stared hard at her and tried to use mind control to make her look up. When she did, he'd hit her with a devilish little smile. Fifteen fidgety minutes passed. He needed to get back to the

Truman Building. For the first time in his five years as head of watchers Kenney actually had some serious work to do.

Groom Lake Building 34, the Truman Building, had become a shadow of its former self. At its high-water mark, over 700 government employees made the daily commute by charter plane from Las Vegas to the remote desert base. Now there were 134, 16 of them watchers.

After the existence of the Library became a matter of public knowledge gawkers and the press gathered at the security fences at McCarran Airport focusing binoculars and long lenses on commuters. Some Area 51 employees were followed from the parking lots back to their homes in Las Vegas and surrounding suburbs, prompting the security force at Area 51, known not so affectionately as the watchers, to go into overdrive, monitoring employees to make sure they could not and did not leak highly classified information on birth and death dates from the Library database.

The watchers had been knocked on their heels by the Shackleton affair and its aftermath. Their chief, Malcolm Frazier, had been killed by Will Piper's wife in an FBI shoot-out at the home of a dissident Area 51 retiree. Will Piper had gone to the press and blown the lid off of sixty-four years of maniacal secrecy. They had been disgraced, plain and simple. With an acting chief on board, an outsider dropped in by a Pentagon in crisis mode, they had been relegated to calling the Las Vegas police to deal with paparazzi chasing their analysts around Sin City.

But perhaps no one at Area 51 had been as affected as Roger Kenney. When the shit hit the fan, Kenney had only been a watcher for five years, but he'd already caught the eye of Malcolm Frazier in a big way.

Frazier had latched onto the gung ho kid and put him on a promotion fast track. He'd given him plum assignments and habitually singled him out to the rest of the watchers for his accomplishments. Whenever Frazier had pulled a graveyard shift, he'd made sure that Kenney was there too and the two of them would drink coffee and trade dirty jokes all night long.

And Kenney had loved the attention he'd gotten from the big boss. Frazier had been a stickler for regs and a general hard-ass, but he was a man's man who had the reputation of supporting his subordinates to the max and being a mentor to a chosen few. When Frazier died Kenney had cried like a baby, and he was still crying days later when he was one of the pallbearers at the funeral.

In the aftermath of his death, Kenney fell into a black hole. The medical officer at the base ordered him to see the Groom Lake psychiatrist. Kenney, being a man who'd rather puke than practice introspection, had been a reluctant participant in the exercise. The day he abruptly ended his therapy sessions was the day the shrink was wondering out loud whether Malcolm Frazier hadn't perhaps become something of a father figure to the young man.

"Tell me about *your* father, Roger," the shrink had asked.

"Never knew the man, Doc. The guy was nothing more than a sperm donor if you know what I mean. My mother raised me solo."

"I see. Do you think there might be a link between your grief over Colonel Frazier's death and your fatherless childhood?"

Kenney had shifted uncomfortably as if ants had invaded his shorts, and he suddenly rose. "This is voluntary, right? These sessions of ours," he asked.

"Beyond the initial consult, yes. Completely voluntary. I've already certified your fitness for duty."

"Then I am so out of here."

In time, Kenney returned to his sunny ways, the hysteria waned at the base and life at Area 51 returned to a semblance of normality. While politicians and the courts decided on the fate of Will Piper's leaked database, analysts got back to their routine. There were still sixteen years to the Horizon, still work to be done, and the watchers were as vital to the effort as they ever were.

The buzzwords at Area 51 and the Pentagon had always been research, planning, and resource allocation. The CIA and the military had used the Library as a tool since the early fifties, when, after its discovery beneath the ruins of medieval Vectis Abbey, a deal was struck between Winston Churchill and Harry Truman for the Americans to take control of the asset.

The Library, all seven hundred thousand volumes, was flown by the US Air Force from England to Washington. A nuclear-proof vault was built under the Nevada desert. It took twenty years to digitize all the forward-looking material. Before digitization, the books were precious. Afterward, the Library became largely ceremonial, a symbol of the awesome power of Area 51.

One of the early tasks for the staff at Area 51, a motley group of eggheads, braniacs, and military overlords, was figuring out how to exploit the data. After all, the ancient hide-bound books only contained names, written in their native alphabets, and dates of birth and death. Without correlates, the data was useless. Thus began a multidecade quest for virtually every digital and analog database in the world,

birth records, phone records, bank, marital, utili-
ties, employment records, land deeds, taxes, insurance data. North America was filled in first. Within
twenty years Area 51 analysts had some form of address identifier for nearly 100 percent of the population. Europe followed suit. Asia, Africa, and South
America took longer but the blank spaces on the
globe got filled in eventually. Now, with 8 billion
people in a world where virtually all personal data
was digital, the picture was complete.

In the fifties and sixties, as soon as Area 51 analysts
worked out the methodology for correlating names
with addresses and geographic coordinates, attention
turned to exploiting the data. Clearly, there were singular dates of national importance. A stunned Vice
President Lyndon Johnson was notified on November 19 that John Fitzgerald Kennedy would die on
November 22, 1963. He had four days to work out
a succession plan smooth enough to steady a shaken
world.

But there were bigger geopolitical treasures to mine.
Outcomes could not be altered but large events that
included fatalities could be predicted. If you could
predict large events you could plan around them,
budget for them, set policy, perhaps soften their blow
or exploit their outcome. Ever-more-powerful computers processed data around the clock, searching
for worldwide patterns. Area 51 analysts predicted
the Korean War, the Chinese purges under Mao, the
Vietnam War, Pol Pot in Cambodia, the Gulf Wars,
September 11, famines in Africa, natural disasters
like floods and tsunamis. When Pakistan and India
each launched a single nuclear missile against each
other on March 25, 2023 resulting in over half a million casualties, the US government was as prepared
for the disaster as humanly possible.

And from the moment the Library was discovered, the secrecy and integrity of the database was paramount. Because of that, the watchers were supreme. Their prime job was assuring that the existence of the database was never leaked and that the United States never lost its first-mover advantage. Furthermore, they were charged with keeping a tight lid on individual pieces of data. There were enormous concerns about what might occur if the public had access to any of it. Would society become altered or even paralyzed if people knew the day they were going to die— or their wife, or their parents or children or friends? Would whole segments of the population succumb to a predeterminist funk and drop out of their productive routines thinking, what's the point, everything's already been decided? Would criminals commit more crimes if they knew they weren't going to be killed on the day. All manner of unpleasant scenarios were on the table.

Over the years, the watchers kept the drum sealed. Yes, there were isolated incidents of an analyst here, a research assistant there, violating confidentiality and looking up the name of a family member or an enemy—and these incidents were dealt with in the most draconian ways, including, it was rumored, assassination, but there had never been anything like the Shackleton affair.

Post-Shackleton, there had been a shake-up—more of a purge, really—among the ranks of the watchers. Even more layers of security were added. Shackleton had been a high-level programmer, an expert in database security, a fox very much inside the chicken coop. The hole he exploited to purloin the database was plugged. But the US database was already out of their control, in the hands of *The Washington Post*'s lawyers. For that reason the government conducted the largest cyberinvestigation in its history to ascertain that the *Post*'s copy from Will Piper was the only one in existence. When the copy was returned following the Supreme Court ruling in the government's favor, Area 51 was confident the situation had been contained. And in the years that followed, Kenney lived up to the potential that Malcolm Frazier had recognized in him and steadily rose through the ranks of the watchers until he got the promotion that put him behind Frazier's old desk.

Sage's secretary answered her phone. "The admiral will see you now," she told Kenney.

Admiral Sage had a full beard. He was a portly throwback to the naval officers of a bygone era and seemed better suited to a nineteenth-century world of sailing the bounding main in brass buttons and gold braid than being a technocrat in the modern military.

He told Kenney to sit and grumbled at him, "You don't want my job, Kenney. Believe me, you don't want it."

"No, sir, I don't."

"I mean, I come here with the expectation it's going to be a plum assignment: I preside over the last few years of database functionality, I mothball the base, send the Library packing to the Smithsonian, pick up my second star, and if the goddamned world doesn't blow up next February, I retire to Rancho Mirage and play golf till I keel over. But that hasn't happened, has it?"

"No, sir."

"Instead, we get Doomsday II, and I'm in the middle of an international incident. The Pentagon is up my butt. The White House is up my butt. I'm late to supper every night, so my wife is up my butt. So who's butt am I going to get up?"

"Mine, sir."

"You're damn right. Give me your report."

My report, Kenney thought. You mean my Kabuki dance, where I pretend to bring new facts to the table and you pretend to listen.

As the investigation dragged on there were no new substantive facts, so Kenney had come to repeat himself, laboring to find a few incremental tidbits to extend the briefing long enough to save each party from the embarrassment of vacuous silence.

In the days after the appearance of the first tranche of postcards, the investigation had proceeded along two fronts. The FBI took the lead on reopening Doomsday I and the watchers spearheaded the search for a new Area 51 leak.

On the FBI side, the chain of custody of the *Post*'s copy of the database was reexamined and all living personnel who had been involved were reinterviewed. That list included Will Piper, Will's son-in-law, Greg, and Nancy Piper. Nancy Piper who was now running the investigation made doubly sure that no punches were pulled with her or her family lest she be accused of a conflict of interest. The FBI ran the traps and concluded that their original 2011 investigation had been complete and proper, that no hard copy of the database had ever been printed out and that the *Post*'s only copy of Shackleton's digital file had been returned to the government.

That threw the spotlight onto Area 51.

On the first day the case broke Kenney had assembled his cadre of watchers and addressed them in his easy Oklahoma drawl, "Okay, boys and girl," he began—he had a single female on his staff, an ex–military policewoman. "I'd rather lick a cat's ass than have to do this to you, but until further notice, you're all mine, twenty-four/seven. Forget about weekends and vacations, forget about your precious kid's softball game and your wife's birthday. You are restricted to base. We are in emergency ops mode. You are going to work your tails off until we find the leaker or prove this is coming from outside our shop. Is that clear?"

Redmond, the lone woman had said, "I'm going to need to work out more babysitting."

"Well, work it out then," Kenney had snapped.

"Can I claim for it?"

"Are you dumb as a sack of hammers, Redmond? You know you can't claim for that kind of shit."

Lopez, a muscular former Ranger who lived in the same Las Vegas subdivision, had said, "Keisha can stay with us."

"Aren't we just one big happy family?" Kenney had muttered before continuing his briefing.

They started by running all 134 employees through lie-detector tests, including, by protocol, the watchers and the base commander. A half dozen tests came back equivocal and those lucky few got put through the ringer.

Then the forensic audits began. The database-security group, the algorithm jockeys, as Kenney referred to them, began scouring the servers for any sign of data intrusion they might have previously missed. Shackleton had been an algorithm jockey in his day so Kenney got permission to get a super-nerd to check up on the nerds. In the old days, that would have been impossible since it took a year or more to grind through the Pentagon's security clearance system before someone could be brought inside the Area 51 tent. Now that every ten-year-old in the world knew what went on at Groom Lake, it wasn't a problem. On the recommendation of CIA database and encryption analysts, a professor of computational sciences from Stanford was airlifted in and given unfettered access to the system. He'd been at it since the first week but he still couldn't find a damn thing.

Kenney believed in a multipronged approach. He didn't understand database-security algorithms on a technical level but he believed he had a pretty good understanding of people. He started delving into personnel files looking for personal data and psychological nuggets that might add up to motive. That's how he became focused on Frank Lim, one of Area 51's China analysts.

Lim had his Area 51 twenty-five-year pin. He was a slight, unassuming man who did his job thoroughly, kept largely to himself and didn't share much of his aboveground life with colleagues. As operations in the Truman Building wound down and head counts were progressively cut, the department that suffered the fewest hits was the China desk. With the collapse in the Russian economy and the hobbling of India in the wake of its nuclear disaster, China was the only country that really mattered to the US. Every geopolitical equation had the China factor on one side and the US factor on the other. So even though there was only one more year of functionality in the Library, the China database was still being milked every day.

The more Kenney dug into Frank Lim, the more he distrusted him. He was the only Chinese-American analyst. His parents had both been born in Taiwan. A branch of the Lim family was still there. He had a history of wiring money to cousins, ostensibly to help with their children's education. One of his cousins was a prominent KMT nationalist politician who was a sharp advocate for full Taiwanese independence. Was it a huge stretch to think that Lim was behind some kind of act of political theater designed to intimidate the People's Republic of China? Were the Doomsday postcards a veiled threat to the government, as in, "Your days are numbered too"? Besides, Lim was one of the Area 51 personnel with a less-than-pristine lie-detector-test result.

A week into the crisis, Kenney and Sage, with the backing of the CIA and the Pentagon, agreed to roll up Lim and place him on administrative leave. Subject to the draconian terms of his employment agreement with Groom Lake, the watchers did not need judicial clearance to search his personal computers and phone records. When you entered the murky world of Area 51 you voluntarily gave up due process. The search came up empty but he remained under suspicion, and his house in Henderson was under twenty-four-hour surveillance.

When Kenney described the mundane details of Lim's visit of the day before to the supermarket and Home Depot, Sage seemed to perk up.

"How did he look?" the admiral asked.

"Look? I don't know. I wasn't personally on the surveillance," Kenney replied testily.

"You get photos, don't you?"

"Yes, sir."

"Well, let's see them."

Kenney pulled out his NetPen and unfurled its retractable screen. A couple of swipes later he had the images from the most-recent reconnaissance. He handed the device to Sage.

"Look at his face," Sage said, peering at a close-up. "He looks like he's hiding something."

"That may well be," Kenney said.

"Question him again. Do it personally."

"Yes, sir."

Sage closed his file folder, his way of showing a meeting was over. "On your way out, tell my PA I want to see her."

I'll bet you do, Kenney thought, you damned banana slug.

Inside the Truman Building Kenney strode into Elevator One and was about to push the −6 button for his office when he was seized by an urge he hadn't had for years.

He stepped out before the doors closed and headed for the V Elevator. He summoned it with a special access key and entered the brushed-aluminum interior. There were only two buttons, G and V. He hit V and inserted his security card in the slot below the button. The doors closed, and he began the smooth sixty-foot descent.

Kenney had personal knowledge that no one except for the environmental monitoring team had visited the Vault for a year or more. In years past, visits had been more frequent. There was a tradition at Area 51. On their first day, new employees would be escorted by the Executive Director of the Research Lab for a personal tour, but there hadn't been a newbie in a good while.

Stony-faced watchers with sidearms would flank the steel doors. Codes would be punched, and the bomb-proof doors would swing open. Then the newcomer would be led into the enormous, softly lit chamber with the rarefied atmosphere of a deserted cathedral and stand in awe at the sight before them.

The Library.

But now the existence of the physical Library had become something of an afterthought, fading into the dim recesses of collective memory. But in the midst of his first major crisis as the head of security, Kenney suddenly felt a need to connect with the past.

He emerged, the only soul on the Vault level. Outside the massive doors he entered the appropriate codes and stooped slightly for the retinal scan which triggered the hydraulics.

He stepped into the chilled dehumidified atmosphere and began walking, first a few feet, then a few dozen, finally a few hundred. He periodically looked up at the domed, stadium-like ceiling. As he walked among the bookcases he randomly touched some of the bindings, something that would lead to a reprimand if it were detected and reported up the chain. He assumed one of his own men was watching on CCTV from the sixth floor but no one would be filing a report on him.

The leather was smooth and cool, the color of mottled buckskin. Tooled onto the spine were years, escalating as he moved toward the rear: 1347—replete, no doubt, with victims of the Black Death in Europe, 1865—Abraham Lincoln's name was buried inside one of these volumes, 1914—filled with World War I victims. At the rear were the last volumes, thousands for the present year, 2026, but many fewer for 2027. The last recorded date was February 8.

He made his way to one side of the Vault, where a narrow stairway took him to a high catwalk. There, he leaned into a railing and took in the totality of the Library.

There were thousands of steel bookcases stretching into the distance, over 700,000 thick leather books, over 240 billion inscribed names. He took it in, absorbing the enormity of it all.

Area 51 was seventy-nine years old. There had been a total of sixteen security heads since inception. He would be the last. Each man had sworn an oath to protect the security and integrity of the Library. Each, he was quite sure, had stood on this exact spot and contemplated that oath and the spiritual implications of the Library's very existence.

Only one of his predecessors, Malcolm Frazier himself, had faced a breach of security as massive as the present one, and he had paid for it with his life.

Was that the fate that awaited him too?

Kenney played things by the book, but then and there he decided to look himself up in the database.

It was chilly, and it irritated Will that he needed a coat to take his walks. Down in Florida it was sunny and warm, but Reston, Virginia, was still in the grip of winter.

He'd always hated everything about their neighborhood—the cookie-cutter houses, the small, square backyards, each with a deck and a barbecue grill, the ubiquitous cul-de-sacs, which looked like lollipops on aerial views. Every morning at 7 A.M. a mass exodus occurred as one or both members of each household clutched their briefcases, got in their cars, and headed to nearby Washington. The March of the Lemmings, he called it.

Theirs was a modest three-bedroom house, comfortable, not luxurious. They'd never made much money, not that he particularly cared. Nancy's salary was fine at her level, he had a pension from the FBI and he had his social security, though receiving the monthly payments made him feel geriatric. He'd made a few dollars from his book years earlier but the money had gone mostly into boat refittings, a coveted car and a college fund for Phillip (in case there was a Beyond after the Horizon).

He took his prescribed exercise regimen seriously. At least two times a day he made a circuit around his neighborhood, and, just as his doctor had predicted, his walking had steadily improved as his heart grew stronger. Along the way, he weakly bonded with some dog walkers and stay-at-home moms, who lavished attention on the new brawny man in their midst and tried to draw him into their book clubs and afternoon coffees.

He'd gotten to the point where he could jog a few hundred yards, walk, then jog again. Nancy had bought him a wristband heart-rate monitor and he checked it assiduously, staying within his strict limits. Taking orders and obediently following rules rankled him as much as it always had but he never wanted to lie in a hospital bed again.

During the daytime he was alone. Nancy was one of the Washington lemmings and Phillip attended South Lakes High School. When Will wasn't doing something aerobic or working with barbells to restore his depleted muscle mass he read and very occasionally turned on the TV. The TV news and talk shows dispirited him with their countdown clocks to February 8 midnight and their so-called experts who reported on the motion of every piece of rock within the solar system.

He blamed the media for whipping folks into an agitated frenzy and it didn't surprise him that things were going from bad to worse. Productivity indices were down as people started drifting from their jobs. The "what the hell" and "eat, drink, and be merry" ethos was taking hold everywhere, and government sloganeering couldn't break the momentum. Markets were down and alcohol sales were up. Marriages were straining and cracking. Suicides were on the rise. The Chinese Doomsday case wasn't helping as it seemed to be reminding a dispirited, creaky world that the end was nigh.

So he avoided current events, took no calls from numbers he didn't recognize and slammed the door on those reporters who sought him out to tap his "unique perspective."

It was more comforting retreating into the realm of books but even that made him cranky because bookstores had become a pathetic rarity—there weren't any left in Reston. He'd never made a comfortable migration from cardboard and paper to plastic and bits but he could either pay a hefty premium for a real book to be delivered by a UFedEx van or take the path of least resistance and use one of several tablets that Nancy and Phillip possessed. So he grumbled every time he swiped a screen to turn a page but he enjoyed his Shakespeare and Dante, Steinbeck and Faulkner, all wells he wished he'd plumbed more deeply when he was young.

It was sleeting, and the sidewalks were getting slick. He altered his jogging style to come down flatter on his soles so he wouldn't slip on his ass and cause one of the housewives to bound from her front door like a St. Bernard with a brandy keg. The street looked less slippery so he hopped off the curb only to be honked at by an approaching car.

The car stopped abruptly, and the window slid down. It was Phillip.

"Goddamn it, Phillip!" Will exclaimed. "I hate electric cars. You can't hear them coming."

Phillip shook his head. "You want to get in?"

"I'm exercising. Why aren't you in school?"

"I'm done for the day."

"It's not even two o'clock. Don't you have to stay through the last period?"

"Honor students get open-campus privileges."

"What about wrestling?"

"I quit."

Will gritted his teeth. "Why?"

"What's the point?" Phillip said, driving away.

When Will got home, he went straight for the master bathroom to turn on the shower and while the water was heating he made for Phillip's room. Inside, the music was blaring and he had to bang loudly.

The music stopped and Will heard a dull, "What?"

"Can I come in?"

The door unlocked. Phillip was back on his bed before Will entered.

"I can't believe you dropped wrestling."

"Believe it, it's true."

"Don't cop an attitude with me. Why'd you quit?"

"I didn't like it anymore. I'd rather wrestle with girls."

"You were good at it."

Phillip shot him an attitudinal glance. "How do you know?"

He was right. Will knew because Nancy peppered him with e-mails of articles from the local e-paper. He'd never seen him wrestle.

"If you'd have gone to school down in Florida I wouldn't have missed any of your matches."

"So it's my fault you're practically split-up with Mom."

"I didn't say it was your fault."

"Whatever."

"And we're not split up. It's a compromise. You know the score. You were always free to choose Florida."

"And live on your boat? No thanks."

"I would have gotten a condo. I'm still willing to do that when your mom decides to retire."

"What's the point? Feb 9 is in less than a year. Just leave me alone to ride it out on the suckmobile, okay?"

"What about the things you wrote about in your essay, about having a positive attitude, making each day count, living life to the fullest?"

The boy gave him a patronizing grin. "It was just an essay."

"You didn't believe the things you wrote?"

Phillip didn't answer.

"You didn't believe the things you wrote about me?"

The kid pointed at the ceiling. "I think you left the water on."

Phillip's NetPen chimed. He yawned, turned his music down with a hand gesture and clicked the pen onto speech mode.

"What?" he said to it.

"Friend request," it said in a sweet robot voice.

"Who?"

"Hawkbit."

"Accept. Gimme pic."

"No photo available."

He was about to raise the music volume when the pen chimed again. "Message from Hawkbit."

"Yeah."

"I need to speak with you," the pen said.

He switched the pen from the female voice to an androgynous one. He didn't like to use his real voice with people he didn't know. Net Safety 101. He replied, "Chat mode: And you are?"

"Hawkbit," the pen said in a masked voice.

"Well, duh? Do I know you?"

"Not yet."

"But that's about to change, right?"

"I hope so."

"You XX or XY?"

"Sorry?"

"Male or female?"

"Female."

"Okay, you've got my attention."

"Do you know how to tunnel?"

"Sure. Don't you?"

"No."

"Not into tech?"

"Sorry."

"Why do you want to tunnel?"

"I've got to talk to you. In private."

"This is private."

"No, superprivate."

"Why?"

"I need your help."

He furrowed his brow and was about to ask if Hawkbit was a scam artist. The Net was full of them. "Do you even know who I am?"

"You're Phillip Piper, the son of Will Piper. I read your essay. You're the only person in the world I can trust."

FBI Director Parish didn't look good on one of his good days and he looked particularly gaunt and sallow today. Nancy approached his desk the way one might approach fresh roadkill, guarding against the shock of a sudden leg twitch.

"Talk to me," he said. "For Christ's sake, give me some good news."

She sat, crossed her legs and opened her briefing book. She noticed his furtive eye motion directed to her thighs and shrugged it off. She was used to it but if she ever mentioned it to Will she knew he'd knock the guy's block off. Will was old-school. What was good for the gander wasn't good for the goose.

"Another eight postcards were found yesterday, bringing the total number to thirty-six."

He rubbed his eyes and gazed out onto Pennsylvania Avenue. "I said good news."

"Well, I suppose the good news is that they're intercepting about a quarter of them at post-office sorting stations so some of the targets aren't getting them anymore. The volume of physical mail is way down these days."

"Hooray for that," he said sarcastically.

"The new batch of postcards is fitting into the same overall pattern. These were postmarked three days ago and passed through the Village Post Office on Varick Street in New York. That means they could have been dropped off in any of twenty-one street boxes. It's the seventh different post-office branch that the sender's used. So he's moving around. We're going over CCTV footage, of course, but as you can imagine, the image volume is overwhelming so I place a low probability of tagging an identifiable suspect making a drop into one or more boxes."

"What about the addresses?"

"Also the same pattern. About a third of the addresses are stale. The recipient's moved in the last ten or more years."

"Suggesting?"

"As you know, we've secured the cooperation of Area 51 on this. They think whoever is responsible is working off an old database, about twenty years old."

"How long has Frank Lim worked there?"

"Twenty-six years."

"So he could have stolen the database years ago and waited for his moment."

"I suppose so."

Parish folded his hands behind his neck. "You don't sound convinced."

"I think it's a stretch. I mean the guy has legitimate access to current data. If he wanted, he could have been committing a few names and addresses to memory every day and writing them down when he got home. Why rely on an old database? Besides, the postcards were sent from New York. We know Lim hasn't been out of Nevada."

"The theory goes that he may have a confederate in New York."

"I know that. I also know I haven't seen a shred of evidence along those lines."

"Have we drilled him on that angle?"

"Area 51 Security is in control of him. The watchers haven't given us access."

"Who's watching the watchers, that's what I want to know," Parish complained.

Nancy, more than anyone, had no love for them. "Exactly."

"I'll work through the White House to get us into position to interview Lim. Meanwhile, I may want you to go to Beijing. I want you to use your charms to pacify the brass at the Ministry of State Security. This thing is about to boil over into a major international crisis and we've got to do everything we can to defuse it. The White House thinks that VidCons aren't cutting it. Only way to show proper respect is to kiss their butts in person."

She said nothing.

He clearly didn't like her nonresponse. "What?" he said testily. "Your husband's okay, isn't he? You can travel now, right?"

It was the last thing she wanted to do but she kept a game face. "Yes, sir. Not a problem."

* * *

It was a Saturday morning and Will was determined to arrange some sort of family group activity
but beyond that kernel of a thought he had nothing.
If they were in Florida he'd have suggested—what
else—fishing, but what was it that people did in Virginia? Search for virgins? Nancy poured him a coffee
at the breakfast bar, sounding a skeptical note. Phillip wasn't the family-outing type, she warned. And
besides, she'd be amazed if he woke up much before
midafternoon.

"We could take a drive," Will said hopefully.

"Where?" she asked.

"Panama City?"

She padded her slippered feet behind him and
kissed his ear. "We'll ship you back pretty soon."

"I'm ready, you know."

"You're doing great but don't rush things."

"If I pass my exercise test at Georgetown, I'm heading south, okay?"

She sighed. She hadn't told him yet. "Whatever you
say, but I'd like you to wait till I'm back."

"What do you mean, back? Where are you going?"

"Beijing." She held her breath.

"Jesus, Nancy."

"Parish wants me to brief the Chinese government
personally. I can't duck it, Will. This thing is becoming a major international thing."

"That's nuts. If someone with database access
wanted to provoke China they'd send postcards to
Chinese cities, not American ones!"

"I don't disagree. All I can tell you is that isn't the
way the Chinese are seeing it. Anyway, Parish is in-
sisting."

He put his cup down hard. "I'm going out."

"Will!" she called after him. "Can't we talk about it? Don't go running out on me like you always do!"

He didn't want to talk. He didn't know why he *had* to talk. Living on his own was easier. He hated the art of give-and-take and compromise. He liked things his way—always had, always would.

He sat on the front stairs lacing his sneakers tight. Truth be told, the thing that bothered him the most about Nancy's going to China was that he'd be left alone with Phillip. Maybe on an intellectual level he knew that the kid probably loved him but the resentment on the surface was palpable. Not so different than the resentment he'd harbored against his own dad. But his old man had been a violent brute, a nasty drunk, a certifiable bastard.

He wasn't that guy.

Phillip had it easy. He didn't know what a lousy father was.

He rose to start his circuit. Physically, he was feeling strong. Maybe he'd start jogging straight off instead of walking.

Something caught his eye; rather, something didn't catch his eye. When he was an FBI agent, his ability to scan a crime scene and notice the smallest detail had been legendary. That was a long time ago but some things stayed with you.

As he approached the garage he peered into the small windows in the garage doors.

Where was Phillip's sideview mirror?

He cupped his eyes and looked through the glass. Nancy's car was there but Phillip's wasn't.

He ran inside the house.

"Nancy, Phillip's car is gone!"

She came out of the bedroom. "It can't be!"

"Why not?"

"I was up early. I didn't see him leave."

Will was already heading to Phillip's bedroom. He didn't bother to knock.

"Christ . . ." he muttered. The bed hadn't been slept in. He felt his knees go weak. Nancy was behind him and instinctively reached out to steady him. When Will spoke his voice was frosted with fear. "He's gone."

Yi Biao was notorious for keeping an uncluttered desk. As an ardent supporter of technology, he had all but banned paper from his office and he demanded that e-mails and reports be kept to a minimum of verbiage. Though he had a voracious appetite for information he liked to receive it crisply and concisely with no more than three action items per issue. And he banned the use of PowerPoint presentations from members of his staff. "Stand up and tell me what you have to say," he would demand. "I want to see your face and your heart, not a list of bullet points."

So his large desk was sparsely populated with objects—only a small collection of framed photos, a platinum- and diamond-encrusted Montblanc pen for signing state documents, a leather blotter and a pop-up computer screen. The photos told his story. His parents, both hardworking party members at his boyhood house in the countryside. His wife, a former actress who used to be more famous than he, his son, a graduate of Yale and Oxford who was now a rising star in the Ministry of Foreign Affairs, a stiffly posed shot with General Secretary Wen Yun and his favorite, his induction ceremony as Vice Chairman of the Central Military Commission.

That was the penultimate stepping-stone in a long and calculated career stretching from his first job as a minor provincial official in Gansu to the highest seat in the land. He was the heir apparent to Wen, and it was only a matter of time before his turn would come as the next General Secretary and President of the People's Republic of China.

The transition would probably have occurred already if it weren't for the Horizon. Although it was the official policy of the government to disavow the significance of February 9, 2027, there were enough Politburo members who were concerned about a coming cataclysm that Secretary Wen had decided to postpone his retirement until later in 2027, assuming that the Horizon skeptics were correct and China and the rest of the world still existed!

For Yi, the Horizon was a burr under his saddle, a constant annoyance. He counted himself in the skeptics' corner, not that he didn't acknowledge that the Groom Lake database was unfailingly accurate. He simply asserted that it was a bridge too far to believe that the last book in the Library equated to the earth's last day. It was his strongly held position that the most populous and complex nation in the world should orient its planning functions for a long and glorious future far beyond the Horizon, which was precisely why he was incensed that Wen Yun had delayed his ascension.

He looked out his office windows over the skyscrapers of smog-blanketed Beijing. He was high up, on the top floor of the August 1 Building, the vast headquarters of the Central Military Commission. It was early and the sun was just rising. He waved his hand at his screen and asked for his secretary. She immediately entered from the anteroom.

Yi noticed a cat hair on his suit jacket and irritably plucked it off. He didn't like his wife's cats but he had to live with them. "When General Bo arrives, send him in and make sure his visit isn't logged into my official diary."

General Bo Jinping arrived precisely on time, sat across from Yi and accepted a cup of tea. He had been Yi's handpicked choice to head the Ministry of State Security though it was a choice that hadn't been without controversy as the position traditionally went to a civilian. But Yi wanted a military man heading up the spy services. He'd always found PLA officers more straightforward than civilians, less Machiavellian, more apt to accept orders without pushback. And Bo was an appreciative acolyte.

"You're looking well, General."

"Thank you, Vice Chairman."

"I understand your son was promoted to captain."

"Yes, we are very proud of his accomplishments."

Yi put down his teacup, signaling that the small talk was over. "General, I would like an update on the postcard affair in the United States."

Bo was in command of the facts and didn't require notes. "As of yesterday, thirty-six postcards were received. The most recent six were in San Francisco."

"No other cities?"

"Not yet."

"And the American response?"

"There are extensive resources being allocated to the problem involving the FBI, CIA, Department of Defense, and the internal security service at Groom Lake."

"And what do they think they are dealing with?"

"There is dissension among the various departments. However, the Groom Lake security group has cast suspicion upon one of their analysts who is Chinese and has family in Taiwan."

Yi smiled broadly. "Excellent news. And tell me how they are reacting to our protestations."

"There is a high level of concern, Vice Chairman. In general, they believe we are overreacting and being opportunistic, but they cannot deny that it is a legitimate issue for us. They continue to insist that we should not see this as a provocation against Chinese people or the PRP, and they are further taking the position that there is no evidence of any US government involvement in these mailings. They wish to send over a delegation of FBI and CIA officials to reassure us of their innocence."

"Ha!" Yi exclaimed. "A waste of a meeting if ever there was one."

"Shall I accept their offer?"

"Go ahead. Why not? What I'm more interested in, General, is where this affair is heading. When do you think we will see the next wave of postcards?"

Bo smiled. "I think it could be soon, Vice Chairman."

"Very well," Yi said. "Keep me informed so I can keep the General Secretary informed. You know my views on this. Wen Yun is a little old and a little stubborn." Yi leaned forward and raised his voice to match his rising emotions. "He fails to appreciate that the time has come to declare ourselves as the one great superpower in the world. He fails to recognize that the Horizon is a distraction and that the time is right to settle Taiwan once and for all and assert ourselves across the globe. We must convince the General Secretary that this postcard affair is indeed an intolerable provocation. He must understand that it is a deeply offensive and symbolic threat to the Chinese people and that it flaunts the geopolitical advantage that the United States has long had by possessing the Vectis Library. Ever since I was a boy everyone was worried about challenging the United States too directly or too harshly and risking a world war. Let me tell you something, General," he said, thumping his palm repeatedly with his fist for emphasis. "I have no worries about a world war. If we push America to the brink, I believe they will back down. And if I am wrong, then we will defeat them. In either scenario, we will fulfill our rightful destiny."

Nancy spent the first frantic hour after their discovery calling all of Phillip's friends and their parents. No one knew anything or had seen him the night before.

Will called the Reston Police and the local hospital. They knew nothing about a Phillip Piper. A police sergeant recognized Will's name and helpfully offered to initiate a missing person's protocol if the boy hadn't surfaced by the afternoon but he reassured Will that 99 percent of kids who didn't come home one night were safely in their beds the next.

"I don't buy it," Nancy told Will. "A mother knows. *You* know. Phillip doesn't do this kind of thing."

"We had something of an argument yesterday," Will said quietly.

She jumped on him angrily. "Why didn't you tell me? About what?"

"About dropping wrestling. But things with Phillip are always about something else."

"What did you say to him? I swear, Will, if you said something to make him run away, I'll never forgive you."

Will sighed. He was always the bad guy, wasn't

he? But Nancy was traumatized, so he wouldn't take umbrage. "It wasn't much of an argument, Nance. I shouldn't even have called it that. I'd be shocked if it was the reason he pulled this stunt."

They were in Phillip's bedroom. She was rummaging through his desk and drawers.

"Is anything missing?" he asked.

"Plenty. His NetPen, some jeans, shirts, maybe some underwear, a backpack."

"Did he have any cash?"

"Maybe. I don't know. He uses his NetPen for charging things."

"How much was in his account?"

"A few thousand. He's saved all his money from jobs, birthday, and Christmas presents. For years."

"You're on his account, right? I mean he's still a minor."

She nodded vigorously, pulled out her own NetPen, unfurled the screen, and started issuing voice commands. As he watched her a lump formed in his throat, and the years dropped away. It was as if they were working a case together again, but this wasn't a case. This was their son.

"Oh crap," she said with a rasp. "He withdrew $2,800 last night at 6:05."

"From where?"

She looked like she was going to lose it. "From an ATM. At Dulles Airport. We can't do this alone, Will. I'm calling the Bureau."

Director Parish authorized an all-out push on Phillip's case on the theory that any suspicious disappearance of a family member of one of his top officials was a potential act of terrorism until proven otherwise. And as far as he was concerned, the timing with respect to the Chinese Doomsday case was a coincidence he couldn't ignore.

By midafternoon, their house was crawling with agents from the Washington field office. Special Agent in Charge Linda Ciprian was a woman Nancy had personally mentored for over a decade and the two of them talked in the living room, trying to strike the right blend of personal concern and professional conduct.

Will stood in his son's bedroom like a big statue, mutely watching a couple of young clean-cut agents picking through Phillip's belongings.

One of them found a hash pipe in a sock.

"Your son into drugs, Mr. Piper?"

He shrugged. "Couldn't tell you."

The agent sniffed it. "There's residue."

"Shocking," Will said.

"You never smelled it coming from his room?"

"I live in Florida. I'm not here much."

The agent looked down his nose. "I see."

The other agent asked what SocMedia sites the kid used. FB? Socco? Light Saber?

Will asked him which ones had 3-D images.

All of them, was the incredulous reply, as if he were a caveman for asking.

Through a Q&A process about Will's recollection of sites from the times he'd seen Phillip online, the agent decided he used Socco. He unfurled his own NetPen to find Phillip's public page. After Nancy confirmed she hadn't a clue about his logon ID, the agent obtained an e-summons from a federal duty judge and shot it to Socco security. The whole well-worn judicial process took less than an hour before the agent was on Phillip's private pages.

"Bingo!" he said with brass in his voice. "He was chatting with someone new to him named Hawkbit yesterday afternoon at 2:35. At 2:42, they were tunneling."

"What the hell is that?" Will asked.

The agent showed him little deference and less patience. "You haven't kept up with things, have you, Mr. Piper."

"I try not to, Special Agent—are you Finnerty or Johnson?"

"Johnson," he replied sharply.

"You need name tags. You look like twins."

"Tunneling is a hacker term for using a key-management-encryption system for ultraprivate NetChats. Using anything more than a 604-bit-key elliptic-curve algorithm is illegal since we can't break it."

"Oh," Will said blankly.

"Hello!" Agent Johnson said suddenly. "He used a 620-bit key. That's a potential crime, Mr. Piper. It's a big no-no, and I suspect your son knew it."

"Whatever you say, pal. Are you telling me you can't decipher it?"

"Not a chance."

"And any fifteen-year-old can get it off the Net?"

"The world we live in," the other agent said. "The terrorists are like pigs in shit with tunneling. We break the keys, the hackers keep coming up with longer ones."

"Show me the stuff you *can* read. From this Hawkbit."

Will read the chat transcription. Hawkbit was a girl. Huge surprise.

Nancy burst in with Linda Ciprian. "They found his car! It's at the long-term parking garage at the International Terminal at Dulles."

"Is anyone checking the airlines?" Will asked.

"We're all over it," Ciprian said.

"Nancy, he was online with someone he met yesterday who called herself Hawkbit," Will said. "She read his essay and told him he was the only one she could trust. Then they tunneled, which I just learned is . . ."

"I know what tunneling is," Nancy said.

"Looks like I'm the odd man out. My guess is this Hawkbit called, and our Phillip answered."

Nancy was surfing her Pen. "Find Hawkbit." She held up the thin screen and showed him a picture of a yellow, daisylike wildflower. "They grow in Europe, parts of Asia, Australia, and New Zealand."

Will sighed. "Well, twenty-eight hundred bucks will get him just about anywhere in the world, at least one way. He didn't even leave us a note! When I find him, I swear, I'm going to beat the stuffing out of him."

"Do you have the IP address of Hawkbit?" Nancy asked Johnson.

"We're working on it," he said. "It looks like it's offshore. We'll need an international warrant."

"Get a judge and get a signature," she barked.

In short order they learned that Phillip had boarded United Flight 57 from Dulles to Heathrow which had departed at 8:20 the previous night. He'd paid for a round-trip open-return ticket with cash. The flight had landed at 8:30 A.M. in London so he had a nine-hour head start on them. It didn't look like he'd taken a connecting flight so the presumption was that he was still in the UK though a dash to the Continent via the Chunnel or ferry couldn't be ruled out.

"How does a minor just buy a ticket and get on an international flight?" Will had asked incredulously.

Johnson (or was it Finnerty?) had the answer. Phillip had downloaded a parental authorization form from the United Net site and forged Nancy's signature.

Nancy and Will withdrew to their bedroom and closed the door.

"I just talked to him. Parish won't let me go," Nancy said, shaking with anger. "He said that he couldn't spare me."

"Screw him," Will spat.

"He also told me that the field assessment was that this wasn't a kidnapping or a terror snatch, just a runaway kid with social issues."

"Those two clown twins downstairs. I'm going to bust their heads together," Will said, heading for the door.

She stopped him. "Will, calm down. Parish did offer to ask for help from MI5 as a favor to us. They're going to put an agent on it to see if they can figure out where he is. Check CCTV feeds, track his NetPen, things like that."

"Damn it, Nancy," he seethed, "I'm not going to sit in the living room and wait for my phone to ring! This is Phillip we're talking about!"

"I know, I know," she said mournfully.

"I'm getting on the next flight to London."

"You can't, Will! You almost died two and a half months ago!"

"I'll be fine. I can do this Nancy," he said, opening the closet and pulling out a suitcase. "I'm going to find our son and I'm going to bring him home."

The economy cabin of the Boeing 807 was darkened for sleeping and most of the passengers were at least trying to get some shut-eye. Will was an exception, uncomfortably shifting his large frame in his middle seat, staring at the plane's flight path on the chair-back screen.

The last time he'd been to England was when Phillip was an infant. He'd taken Nancy and the baby to the Isle of Wight to have a look at the ruins of Vectis Abbey. They'd strolled on the grassy field among grazing sheep and looked out over the rolling waves and chop of the Solent. Beneath their feet was the ruined vault of the Library, destroyed by army demo men after the books had been cleared out in 1947 and turned over to the Americans. At the time he'd felt he had to go there, to see it for himself, but when it was done, he moved on and didn't dwell on it. He had a life to live. He'd resisted the pleas to lecture and do TV appearances, and decided to tell his story once, and once only in a book. And when the book finally faded from the best-seller lists, he faded too, onto his boat, into the blue-green waters of the Gulf of Mexico.

On the flight fifteen years earlier, Phillip had irritated Will by crying his way from Newfoundland to Ireland. Now the boy was irritating him again. He stewed fitfully: Why had he run off? What was he trying to accomplish? Was it rebellion? Was Phillip so angry at him for being a lousy father that this was the way he chose to express himself? Had he met a girl on the Net who snake-charmed him across the Atlantic? Or was something more ominous afoot?

When he had mulled over every conceivable scenario, he started to fret over his heart. Sure he'd told Nancy he was fit enough for the journey, but truth be told, he wasn't convinced. He had lied. He never called his cardiologist for clearance. You've got to do what you've got to do, he had told himself. Mind over matter.

At Heathrow's Terminal Six he cleared customs, picked up some currency and rolled his bag to the meeting point. A man in an overcoat held a paper sign with his name. He followed the driver outside and waited while he retrieved the car and brought it around. It was chilly and damp; the sky was dull and monochromatic, just like his mood.

A traffic-filled hour later he was in central London at Thames House on Millbank. On one hand it was the London he remembered, a bustling mix of old and new, but the sounds and smells were different. It was as if he were wearing earplugs. Gone was the rumble of diesel and petrol engines and their stinky chemical haze. All the buses and cars were electric or the newer fuel-cell models and street noises were reduced to the soft whine of drive trains and the whir of rubber on asphalt. Back home, especially in the smaller towns and cities like Panama City, there were still some holdouts spending twenty bucks a gallon for the privilege of being petroleum throwbacks, but these were dinosaurs like himself who couldn't give up their youths. His own toy was a 1969 Firebird, a beautifully restored machine he'd bought for himself in 2012 with some of the advance money from his book. It got six miles per gallon—a very expensive baby to run but worth every penny when he gunned it at a light change.

Will passed through the massive arched entry into Thames House where he presented himself to reception. He figured he wouldn't be getting priority treatment, and forty minutes later, his suspicions were confirmed when he was still waiting. Finally, a young woman came down to fetch him. He initially thought she was a PA—partly because of her youth and partly because her skirt seemed too tight to be an agent's. In his experience, albeit outdated, operatives usually didn't try to draw attention to their asses. But he was wrong.

"Is this Mr. Piper?" she asked him. "I'm Annie Locke, the case officer assigned to assist you."

She had short blond hair, intensely blue eyes and very white skin.

Another pretty thirtysomething with good legs, he thought, disdainfully. Just what I don't need right now.

"Call me Will," he said.

"Right, Will, hope you had a good flight over. Let's go back to my office, shall we?"

"You lead, I'll follow," he said, positioning himself to take in her swaying rear.

Her office on the fifth floor was tiny and it said everything he needed to know about her rank. Without Nancy's connections, he wouldn't be here at all, but this was clearly a lip-service assignment with no horsepower behind it.

"How long've you been with the Security Service?" he asked.

"Five years now," she said, sitting at her desk and offering him a chair.

"And before that?"

"University," she said.

Jesus, not even thirty, he thought. "I see."

"So," she said. "Your son. Any new developments since last night?"

He shook his head. "I called my wife from the car. There's nothing."

"And nothing other than timing to suggest that his sojourn to Britain has anything to do with the Chinese Doomsday case."

"No."

"I'm sure you understand, Will, that the upstairs boys agreed to devote resources to the case only based upon the slimmest of chances that there might be a connection."

"I understand that, Annie." He didn't ask for permission to use her first name. "I also understand that this is being done as an interagency courtesy."

"Quite so."

"Well, I appreciate it. And I'm grateful. I hope I'm not pulling you off something you consider more important."

She gave a voice command and Phillip's face appeared on her wall screen. "Let's just find your son, shall we?"

She was efficient, he'd give her that. She had all the relevant intel at her fingertips and on her screen. CCTV image captures at Heathrow, the underground, King's Cross station. And her presentation was crisp. In some ways she reminded him of a young Special Agent Nancy Lipinski back when she was thrust upon him on the Doomsday case. But Annie Locke was less earnest, less eager, and she possessed a dash of cynicism, a quality which had always been dear to him.

He watched the screen grabs of Phillip with a certain pride. The boy was clearly on his own. Someone might well have been tailing him, but no one was guiding him. He was out there, maneuvering a foreign city alone. The few shots that captured his face suggested to Will a trace of anxiety tempered with a determination to accomplish his mission—whatever that mission was.

"This is not the picture of a child who's been kidnapped or coerced," Annie said. "He's purposeful. No meandering or sightseeing. He uses his NetPen to buy notes after he clears customs, leaves Heathrow on the Piccadilly Line and goes directly to King's Cross station, presumably purchases a ticket with cash, and disappears."

"You don't know what train he caught?"

"Afraid not. We couldn't pick him up on CCTV."

"Where can someone go from King's Cross?"

"Points north. The Midlands, Cumbria, Yorkshire, Scotland."

"You couldn't track him on his mobile?"

"Seems he's turned it off."

"Son of a . . ."

"I expect he knows his parents have the wherewithal to locate him more easily than most parents."

"He's a smart kid."

"Will Piper's son. That's what you'd expect, right? We had a case study on you in our training program, you know."

The remark made him feel like a fossil. "I'm flattered," he lied, "but Phillip takes after his mother. She's the one with the brains. So that's it? He's missing somewhere in the north?"

"Not exactly. What do you know about this Hawk-bit girl?"

"Nothing. From their conversation, it looks like it was a fresh interaction."

"I agree. It's also a new moniker. I haven't completely exhausted the databases, but I haven't found a single other SocMedia or NetMail instance of a Hawkbit."

"Apparently it's a wildflower."

"So I understand. Not really into botany."

Will leaned into her desk. "So what do you have?"

"The message to your son on Socco was sent from a NetPoint in a public library. Don't look so shocked: we still have a few left! It's in a small town, Kirkby Stephen, in Cumbria, the westernmost part of the Yorkshire Dales. It's a point served by a rail line that originates at King's Cross, so it all fits well enough."

Will snapped himself to a standing position. "So let's go to Kirkby Stephen."

"I've already booked us train tickets," she said. "We've got enough time to stop at the commissary for a bit of breakfast and a coffee."

"Trains? We're not flying?" he asked.

"You surely haven't seen our budget. Don't worry, we'll get there in excellent time."

The northbound train sliced through the middle of Britain: Peterborough, Doncaster, Leeds, Bradford. With the population of the country swelling to nearly 70 million, the concentric sprawls around each metropolitan area meant fewer expanses of green farmland and countryside than Will had remembered from his last English train ride years earlier. He sat by the window welcoming the periodic splashes of sun that worked through cloud breaks and made the morning seem less dismal. But north of Peterborough, the clouds formed a dense blanket; then there was no respite to the gloom.

Annie sat opposite him nursing an orange soda, glued to her unfurled NetScreen, a pair of wireless earbuds firmly planted. He couldn't tell whether she was doing work, chatting with friends, or playing a damn game. And he didn't much care. This was a babysitting assignment for her—he understood that. If he got one or two useful things out of her a day, that would be good enough. Phillip was his son, and if you wanted to call this a case—it was his.

He got up a couple of times, ambled down the aisle to the lavatory to splash his face. The bar car was open. He was sorely tempted.

It was midafternoon, cool and misty when they pulled into Kirkby Stephen. There were few people on the platform and they had no competition at the taxi rank. The driver got out and unplugged the car from its power point. He climbed back in and dully asked with the look of a man who'd been napping, "Where to?"

"Do you want to check in first?" Annie asked.

"No," Will answered abruptly. "The public library."

"No libraries down south, marra?" the driver asked.

The library in Kirkby Stephen, though relatively new, was housed in the oldest building in town, the sixteenth-century Old Grammar School. It stood in Vicarage Lane across from an old rectory and boardinghouse. Like most of the ancient town structures, it was built of coarse red sandstone. The library windows were plastered with posters of town events and book readings.

When they entered Will was struck by the emptiness of the place. There were some stacks of books by the entrance but they seemed to be there mostly for show. Who read real books anymore? Only the old guard, the diehard, clinging to the feel and smell of paper with their last breaths. The few libraries that had survived state funding cuts had mostly reinvented themselves as social clubs for seniors and places to leave off children while busy mums shopped. Add to that Net access. Net devices were cheap, and most everyone had one, but this was a poor part of the country, and there were household gaps. The entire middle of the ground floor was given over to Net-Points with sound-resistant baffles so people could use voice commands to navigate the tilted wafer-thin screens without disturbing their neighbors.

Annie went to the central desk and got the attention of the librarian, a prim white-haired lady with a bright, hand-knit jumper.

"Hallo, is this Mrs. Mitchell?" she asked.

The woman smiled. "Yes, Gabrielle Mitchell. You must be the government lady."

"I am indeed." Annie showed her ID card, which seemed to impress Mrs. Mitchell no end. "I love books about spies," she cooed.

"Me too," Annie said.

"So I take it you haven't found the boy yet," the librarian whispered, as if there were people crowded around the desk who ought not hear the conversation.

"I'm afraid not. This is the boy's father, Mr. Piper."

The librarian's concern for Will's plight melted into something else as she took on the demeanor of a red-carpet gawker. "I'm very pleased to meet you, despite the circumstances, Mr. Piper. We don't get many celebrities up here." She wanted a handshake, and he obliged. "He's so handsome," she whispered to Annie as a gossipy schoolgirl might.

He put an end to the nonsense. "Could you show us the NetPoint used to message my son."

It was at the end of a row, no different from any of the rest, a padded chair, a desk, a blank polymer screen that came to life with the Cumbria County logo at the wave of a hand. Of the twenty workstations only half a dozen were occupied.

"Is there a user log?" Annie asked.

"No, we don't do that," the librarian said. "There'd only be a user identifier recorded if they logged in to borrow an e-book, and that apparently did not happen during the session in question."

"So anyone can use these terminals anonymously?" Will asked.

"Absolutely. We don't have a watchdog mentality. We wish to encourage the use of the Net for learning and recreation."

"Most public places make some sites off-limits," Annie offered.

"We use filters to restrict pornography and locations with objectionable content for minors. It's the standard Public Libraries Association filter. Which site was used to communicate with your son, Mr. Piper?"

"Socco."

"Popular, very popular," Mitchell observed. "Especially among the younger ones, as I understand. It's very technical, a little too colorful for our seniors."

"It was three days ago, around 8:40 A.M.," Annie said. "By the look of things, there aren't many people about on weekdays."

"Every day is different, dear."

"Get many people in before 9 A.M.?" Will asked.

"We open at 8 A.M. Some mornings, we have students stopping by on the way to school to meet up with friends. We have snack- and coffee-vending machines that are highly rated. You have to offer these kinds of services to be relevant, you see."

"Were you here that morning?" Annie asked.

"I was."

"There was a girl. Or a woman. She used the screen name Hawkbit," Will said.

"So I was told. Hawkbit rings no bells."

Will was trying to be polite. "There was a girl who spent over half an hour online with my son three days ago sitting on this chair, and you're telling me you can't remember who it was?"

"That's exactly what I'm telling you, Mr. Piper. If it were a book, perhaps I'd remember it. I'm not nearly as good with people."

Will pulled out a picture of Phillip. "This is my son. Have you seen him?"

She shook her head.

"Annie, give Mrs. Mitchell one of your cards. If you see him around here, please call her right away."

The librarian nodded like a bobblehead doll. "He's a handsome boy, isn't he?"

They walked the short distance to the Black Bull Hotel and checked into side-by-side rooms. A pre-arranged hire car, a Ford Maltese, was waiting for them at a charging stand in the car park. Annie suggested that Will have a bit of a rest but he brushed off the suggestion and told her to meet him in the lobby in fifteen minutes.

He sat down on the thin mattress. The patterned red carpet and the burgundy walls made him queasy. He could hear Annie, muffled through the thin wall, opening and closing her wardrobe.

He fished his phone from his pocket. He'd never gravitated to NetPens. His phone was basic; there was little commercial demand for the old models anymore. All it was good for was phone calls, texts, and basic Web browsing on a small, antiquated LCD display. No unfurling screens, no 3-D or gesture commands. He used the keyboard to type a short text to Nancy: he'd hooked up with MI5, he'd arrived in Kirkby Stephen, nothing to report yet.

They spent the rest of the afternoon canvassing. First stop was the local police station, an unmanned office administered from Kendal. A community patrol officer whom Annie had called earlier un-locked the door and offered to put on the kettle. Annie presented her credentials to the young man who seemed over the moon to be involved in a Home Office case. The officer helped them copy a stack of photos of Phillip emblazoned with the police phone number, then he joined them, walking the streets and squares of Kirkby Stephen, leaving the pictures off at pubs, cafes and local businesses and asking passersby if they'd seen the boy.

Officer Brent Wilson, tall and lean, chatted ami-ably and gave a running commentary of his patch. "It's a nice little town," he said. "Quiet-like. The occasional problem, of course, but it's usually the same bad actors over and over. You get a call-out t' a certain address, you know precisely what's going t' transpire. Mostly, it's th' economy that causes the problems. Hit us hard here. The 9 February busi-ness, but I expect you know more about that than I! Jobs've dried up. People are listless, depressed-like. More drink. More drugs. Worst off, we've had a bunch of youngsters, some as young as thirteen, hanging themselves. They leave the most pitiful messages behind. It's like an epidemic." He sighed, his voice trailing off, "Oh well."

Will knew the story. The same thing was playing out in towns and cities in America, and from what he'd read, the rest of the world. The Horizon was coming. It was weighing hard, and the vulnerable weren't coping. For his part, he was determined to ignore February 9. *Que sera, sera* was his public posture on the Horizon. *Fuck it,* was his private one.

At dusk Will and Annie made their last stop of the day at Kirkby Stephen Grammar School, a small secondary school at the edge of the town with fewer than four hundred students. The headmistress received them sympathetically and let them post the photos on the community bulletin board and in the library. Hawkbit? A local wildflower, wasn't it? And that was all she had to offer.

Will was dragging. Annie told him she'd be fine on her own and urged him to have some food in his room and a good rest but he was too old-school for that, and besides, he thought she was treating him geriatrically. He insisted on joining her for dinner in the Bull's restaurant.

The dining room was dimly lit. It smelled of beer. Only three tables were occupied, and the waitress went through the motions as if drugged. Will kept trying to check her pupils to confirm his suspicion. The meal was some kind of pasta affair pulled from the deep freezer. He ate it automatically, more interested in the bottle of French wine, which wasn't half-bad. He was medically cleared to drink in strict moderation but moderation for him was a squishy concept. Splitting a bottle of wine was moderate enough, he reckoned.

Annie wasn't keeping pace. It seemed to Will she

wasn't going to get off more than a single glass. He playfully asked about it.

"When we're in the field, we're considered on duty twenty-four/seven. One drink with dinner's generally allowed, but that's it, I'm afraid."

"Seems Puritanical," he said. "More of an American attitude."

She laughed at that. "I haven't been in the Service long enough to learn which rules can be bent. Better to follow the straight and narrow."

"I don't think I've ever come across a straight line," Will said, putting back the rest of his glass and reaching for the bottle. "So why'd you decide on this line of work?"

"It seemed rather exciting on the face of it. Important work and all that. It was this or the City—all my brothers went into finance—and I'm afraid I would have been bloody awful at making money."

"That makes two of us. Apparently you weren't one of your generation who used the Horizon as an excuse to slack off."

"No, but a lot of my school friends did. Many of them seem exceedingly pleased with themselves, I must say. Cracked the code and all that. The worker bees keep all the essential goods and services operating right till the end while they party like there's no tenth of February."

"If that's what the code says, it's pretty depressing, not that I'm intolerant of hedonism. I've been a practitioner most of my life."

"You never worked again after the Doomsday case?"

"I was close to my twenty years of government service. They pensioned me early to get me off the stage. Got pulled back into things a year or so later, went public with the Library as a survival mechanism, then settled into permanent retirement."

She tapped her fingertips together pensively. "Can I ask you something? I've always wondered—and we even had a module on this at school—whether your personal motivations extended beyond the personal safety of you and your family. I mean, did you have a philosophical or moral viewpoint about the public's right to know what an elite element of the government already knew?"

It was a question Will had publicly fielded over and again when he'd done his book tour years earlier. At the time, he'd articulated a high-minded position about the rights of an individual to know what their leaders knew, that people had the absolute right to the knowledge that their date of death was predetermined. He left it to wiser men than him to decide whether an individual ought to know his or her own death date. He said he was ultimately supportive of the decision of a presidential commission that stated that individuals and society as a whole would be best served if the dates remained closely held and subject to strict safeguards to protect individual rights.

Now he was a little drunk and as tired as he'd been in a long time. "You want to know why I blew the whistle on Area 51 and the watchers? You really want to know?"

She did.

"Because those fuckers really pissed me off."

Back in his room, he stripped and collapsed on the bed. He was woozy but had the presence of mind to do his nightly heart check. He placed the Heart-Check cup on his chest and waited for it to issue an audible report.

Heart rate 74. Normal Sinus Rhythm. No action required.

He grunted, put the cup away, and shut off the light.

Tomorrow they'd repeat the exercise of handing out Phillip's photo in the nearby towns of Appleby and Sedbergh. Then they'd hit up smaller villages. What else could they do?

Through the wall, he heard Annie getting ready for bed.

In the old days—

It was almost pitch-dark. The moon was out but it was shrouded in cloud, a diffuse ruddy disc high in the night sky. Without illumination all he could do was run and stumble, get up and run and stumble again.

Nothing in his life had prepared him for this. The fear was like curare, gradually paralyzing his legs; he had to struggle to keep the muscles pumping.

The terrain was uneven and treacherous. It had rained earlier, and the heavy grass was slick as ice, particularly on the slopes. He steered by gravity. Every time he found himself going uphill, he corrected course.

Level is good, he thought.

Uphill is bad.

The hills led to wilderness and isolation.

The flats were more likely to lead to a road.

He stopped to catch his breath and listen.

The wind whipped past his ears. Beside that, all he could hear was his own shivering. He wasn't dressed for a February in these parts and he'd gotten thoroughly drenched from the wet grass. Otherwise, it was quiet. Completely quiet. He felt for his NetPen. It was still in his pocket despite multiple tumbles. He had no idea if it had a charge, no idea if he'd get a signal.

It *had* to work.

He trotted again, wanting desperately to make further progress before daring to stop to use the mobile. How long had he been running? A half hour? Longer?

Blinding pain!

He'd run into something hard and unyielding and it put him down. His knees hurt, and he tasted blood in his mouth.

He felt the obstacle with his hand. It was a low stone wall, and he'd rammed it hard enough to make his teeth hurt.

He picked himself up and carefully climbed over the waist-high structure.

Then he heard something behind him. A voice in the distance. He was sure of it.

He crouched behind the wall and looked over it from the direction he'd come. There was a distant streak of bluish light.

Then he saw dark shapes moving slowly toward him.

He wanted to get up and run again, but his knees hurt, he was exhausted and he was too scared.

The shapes got closer.

He closed his eyes.

Baaaaa.

From the blackness, a sheep emerged.

He put his hand out, unafraid of the comforting touch of woolly warmth, but the animal stopped dead in its tracks before being joined by more beasts. The sheep halted their advance and stared at him. Then the flock, as one, slowly and cautiously retreated.

On the other side of the wall there was another voice. Two men calling out to each other. "Th't weh," he heard in the distance. "Aye, th't weh."

He pulled the NetPen from his pants pocket and held his breath while he pushed the ON button. It glowed red: only seconds to minutes of battery life.

Unfurling would drain power.

"Send emergency beacon," he whispered into the unfurled pen.

"Recipient?" the pen asked. He lowered the volume.

"Will Piper."

"Attach a message?"

"Yes."

"Dictate message," the pen instructed.

The chime was light and melodic and wouldn't have awakened Will if he'd been sleeping soundly. But the alien mattress, the stuffiness of the room, and his incipient jet lag contributed to fitful sleep.

He blinked awake and tried to pinpoint the source of the insistent tone.

His mobile phone.

It sounded like the tone from a text message but it didn't extinguish: it kept chiming.

He reached for the device on his nightstand, touched the screen, and read the message:

> Emergency Beacon Received from Phillip Piper.
> Play attached message? Yes/No.

He sat upright, breathing hard, and touched yes.

It was four in the afternoon at Groom Lake. Roger Kenney was at his workstation six floors below the parched desert floor, getting ready for the afternoon exodus, the ritual known as the Strip 'n Scan, where every employee had to undergo a high-tech strip search to make sure the database never left the premises. Of course, that hadn't stopped a genius like

Mark Shackleton from beating the system back in 2009 with a plastic thumb drive up his rear end, but the scanning technology was foolproof now.

With an alert, a window opened on his wall screen.

The screen announced: Priority Alert. Significant activity on Surveillance File 189007, Will Piper.

Kenney looked up, mildly interested. He'd put up a routine data-collection matrix on Piper when he learned the FBI had requested MI5 liaison assistance about the disappearance of his son. He did it on the off chance it had something to do with Chinese Doomsday. "I'm a thorough son of a bitch," he liked to tell his people. "You want to get ahead in this world: walk like I do, talk like I do, act like I do. I'm not arrogant, people, I'm just right." Besides, there were few people on the planet Kenney hated more than Will Piper. He hadn't pulled the trigger on Malcolm Frazier but he might as well have. Any legitimate excuse to spy on him was welcome. And you never knew. One thing might lead to another. The thought of a reckoning was more than appealing.

"Display file," Kenney commanded.

Audio file. Sent 60 seconds ago from NetPen registered to Phillip Piper. Emergency Locator Beacon. Latitude = 54.4142, Longitude = -2.3323, Pinn, Cumbria, United Kingdom.

A sat-map came up of undulating green terrain devoid of man-made features except for a web of stone walls. The middle of nowhere.

"Play audio file."

It was a boy's voice, a tight, frightened voice in a half whisper.

Dad. It's me. I'm in trouble! I escaped. The Librarians. They're after me. Help me! I . . .

Five minutes later, Kenney was in Admiral Sage's office, replaying the intercepted transmission.

"What does he mean by the Librarians?" the admiral asked.

"No idea, sir. The term isn't in our databases."

"I don't like it."

"No, sir."

"You did good by putting a screen on Piper. Good piece of lateral thinking. The history of Area 51 has taught us that with Will Piper, where there's smoke, there's fire."

"Thank you, sir."

"Your reward is to get your ass over to the UK immediately to personally monitor developments and intervene as appropriate. I'm giving you full operational control. Take a team. If this has anything to do with Chinese Doomsday, it's Groom Lake that's going to break the case, not some minor-league outfit like FBI or MI5. Now pack your bags and get your wheels up."

Isle of Wight, Britain, 1296

It was the twenty-eighth day of December, three days after the Christmas Day feast of thanksgiving. Clarissa had been anticipating Christmas fervently, counting down the forty days of St. Martin by placing forty pebbles on her washstand. She began on the eleventh day of November and removed one pebble each day. When the great day finally arrived her sixteen-year-old heart leapt with joy. The Abbey of Vectis was a hard and dreary place for a young girl who hadn't yet committed to a monastic life, and any day that offered sweetmeats, presents and a sense of community cheer appealed to her immensely.

But now that Christmas had come and gone she settled back into her monotonous routine. The bells for Lauds awakened her as they always did. It was dark in her small chamber and devilishly cold. Her single window rattled in the stiff, pulsing wind coming off the sea.

She instinctively reached under her cover to feel her belly. Against her palms it was smooth and tense.

Only two months to go. She was told there'd be no kicking and there wasn't.

But she knew her baby was alive and well. She was certain of it.

He was hers, the only thing in this world she possessed, and she loved him.

Having her own chamber was an unimaginable luxury. Growing up in the wild northern frontier of Cumberland as the sixth child of a Norman farmer, to the age of fourteen she'd shared a bed with four sisters and a single room with her entire family. She had come to Vectis Abbey a year earlier. Baldwin, the Abbott of Vectis, had stopped at the market town of Kirkby Stephen on his return from an arduous journey to Scotland seeking patronage for his order. Following the death of the abbey's principal patron, the Countess Isabella de Fortibus, Baldwin had been forced to leave his island enclave and travel throughout the Kingdom of Wessex and far beyond, courting earls, lords, bishops and cardinals to support Vectis Abbey, a jewel in the Benedictine crown which possessed the finest cathedral in the land. Baldwin's entourage had found itself in need of two fresh horses and in the market square the abbot met Clarissa's father, who had horses on offer.

A deal arranged, Baldwin had a question for the farmer. He was also in need of obedient young virgins to populate the ranks of novices at his abbey. Had the man any daughters to spare? For a price?

Indeed he had. But the question which farmer was which one? His oldest had caught the fancy of the son of the local blacksmith and he was expecting good things from the union. The youngest was too young and the next youngest was his wife's favorite; he didn't fancy the slings and arrows coming his way if he dealt her off. That left the middle two. Both were good enough workers but Mary better met the abbot's criterion for obedience. Clarissa, on the other hand, was strong-willed and feisty, questioning everything, a burr under his saddle. After he'd made up his mind, he'd showed his wife the coins and told the sobbing woman, "We'll leave it to the church to tame her."

Clarissa had left Yorkshire with a mixture of trepidation and wonder. She knew well the strife in store for her if she stayed on the farm. There was no allure to that life beyond the solace of her family's bosom. She'd work the fields and herd the sheep till her bones ached—right up to the day her father married her off to some village oaf who'd snatch her away from her dear sisters anyway. And the only consolation of the union with that husband who undoubtedly would have bad teeth and onion breath would be a baby. How she longed to have and hold a baby one day! She'd seen her mother with her newborn youngest sister, and when she cuddled her to her milky breast, that haggard woman appeared happy for the only time Clarissa could recall.

And it was that thought that weighed on her during her monthlong journey to Vectis. If she were to marry Christ and not a man, she would never have that baby. How sad, how sad. But she was treated with solicitude by the abbot's minions and was regaled with stories of the grandeur of the cathedral and the wonderful tranquillity and holiness of the abbey. So she thought about God and wondered if he materialized on earth what he would look like? A handsome young man with a beard as she had seen on crucifixes? An old man with a white beard in a long robe? And how would she feel as the bride of Christ?

She remembered well her first sight of the cathedral spire. She had pulled her new woolen cloak to her throat to counter the slicing wind. With her free hand, she gripped the ship's rail hard enough to turn her knuckles white. The sea behaved like it was trying to prevent her from completing her journey. She'd never seen the ocean before, and it seemed like a dark, evil thing, spraying salt in her nostrils and sickening her stomach. But a kindly old monk who had been her protector of sorts during the expedition grasped her shoulders and told her she had nothing to fear. The boatman, he said, had the situation well in hand.

"Just keep your eyes on the spire, child. We'll be there, soon enough."

The spire, appearing black against the gray sky, was God's outstretched hand pointing straight to heaven. Vectis would be her home, her sanctuary. She would devote herself to God, and if she were worthy, she would become a nun. The peacefulness that descended upon her at that moment was the loveliest feeling she'd ever experienced in her young life.

On arrival, she kissed the beach and walked the short distance to the abbey, trailing at the rear of Baldwin's entourage. Entering through the heavy portcullis of the walled abbey she was amazed at how bustling it was. With a population of six hundred it was the second largest city on the Isle of Wight, and it seemed that all six hundred of them came rushing out at once to greet the returning abbot. Baldwin dropped to his knees on a grassy verge before the grand cathedral and gave loud thanks for his safe return.

Clarissa had been left drifting in the hubbub until a severe-looking nun approached and, without so much as a greeting, instructed her to follow. Sister Sabeline, the Mother Superior of the sisters of Vectis, was a dried-out husk of a woman, so bony and shriveled, it seemed that the weight of her heavy black habit was all that prevented her from being tossed into the wind. Wordlessly, she led Clarissa through the extensive grounds. Beside the grand cathedral there were some thirty stone buildings at Vectis including the chapter house, abbot house, kitchens, refectory, cellery, infirmary, buttery, hospicium, warming rooms, brewery, stables and dormitories. To Clarissa, it was unimaginably complex.

Clarissa's destination was the sister's dormitory, a low structure toward the rear of the abbey near the perimeter wall. Sister Sabeline placed her into the care of a plump, elderly nun named Sister Josephine who took her to an open dormitory lined with straw-stuffed wood-framed beds. On each bed was a neatly folded coverlet, and beside it, a chamber pot. On a low nightstand was a candle and a ceramic basin.

"Have you started your menses, girl?"

"Me what?"

"Oh heavens! Your flowers!"

"Oh, aye"—she flushed—"but not at t' moment."

"Lift up your skirt, girl," the nun commanded.

Clarissa froze.

"You heard me!"

She slowly obeyed.

The nun had a good look at her nakedness and grunted her approval, but no explanation was forthcoming.

"All the girls are working," Sister Josephine told her. "You'll meet them after Vespers. This one will be your bed. Do you know how to pray, girl?"

"I know t' Lord's Prayer," Clarissa said.

"Well, it's a start, isn't it? And do you know how to peel and chop vegetables?"

Clarissa nodded.

"Good. Let's get you to the kitchen, so you can start earning your keep."

"I want to be a nun, Sister. How do I do it?"

Sister Josephine snorted. "You start by peeling potatoes."

Gradually, week by week and month by month, Clarissa realized her lot was different from most of the other girls in the dormitory. Although she attended prayer hours in the cathedral with the others she was never released from kitchen duty to participate in daily tuition of scriptures and hymns. One girl who seemed to be treated much like her was a big-boned lass with a turnip nose named Fay. But she had disappeared one day, never to be seen again.

The other girls called themselves novitiates, and when they had been at Vectis for a year, they were allowed to take simple vows. And those who had been at the abbey for four years had their heads shorn and took their solemn vows, receiving the ring of Christ. As sisters of Vectis they were given their own sleeping cells and time off chores for solitary prayer and meditation.

Adding to Clarissa's sense of befuddlement and isolation, other girls shunned her and whispered behind her back. No one would tell her why she was different. She just knew she was.

When she had been at Vectis for six months, a new girl, younger than Clarissa, came to the dormitory. She was a fair-haired lass named Mary, deposited at the abbey by her father to serve at the pleasure of the abbot. The bed she was given was next to Clarissa's and they shared a peeling and chopping station in the kitchen. Before long it was clear that Mary too was not being treated as a novitiate.

Mary was as shy as she was and the two girls hardly exchanged a word for the first few weeks. When they finally did, their accents and dialects were different enough to make communication difficult, but in time they came to understand one another.

"Are we not to become nuns like the others?" Mary had asked.

"When I ask for an answer from Sister Josephine, I hear nowt," Clarissa had said. "When I pray for an answer from God, I receive nowt. Can I ask you something? When you arrived, did Sister Josephine look at you naked like?"

Mary nodded. "She said my hips were good'uns."

The girls became fast friends, bonded by their seemingly shared fate. To them the abbey was their entire world, and it was a strange and unfathomable place. They struggled to understand the hierarchy of the abbey and the jobs of the inhabitants. They knew that there was a brewery, but which monk was the brewer? They knew there was an infirmary, but which brother was the surgeon? They played a game, trying to guess who did what, sneaking about in the few minutes here and there when they weren't under the scrutiny of Sister Josephine or the cook, following a likely suspect around the abbey grounds as he went about his labors.

During these adventures the girls discovered two buildings in the complex they found particularly curious.

In a far corner of the abbey, beyond the monks' cemetery, was a simple unadorned structure the size of a small chapel connected to a long building without windows. To this building they had once seen a wagon deliver provisions of meat, vegetables and grain.

"There must be a kitchen," Clarissa had said.

"They must have their own girls doing the duties," Mary replied. "Less work for us."

The other strange building that caught their eye was close to this chapel and kitchen. It resembled a small version of the sisters' dormitory made of limestone blocks with rows of identical square windows and chimney stacks on both the short ends. On one of their walks they spied something that filled Clarissa with a turbulent blend of fascination and fear. Fay, the girl with a turnip nose who had vanished months earlier, was waddling from the small dormitory to the outhouse behind it. There was no denying it: she was heavy, very heavy with child.

How does a lass come to be bearing in a monastery, Clarissa had wondered?

That night, Clarissa lay awake on her straw pallet, the memory of Sister Josephine scrutinizing her naked hips weighing on her.

What was her fate to be?

The answer to her question came soon enough.

On a sunny day in June, as pretty a day as Clarissa had ever seen, the air sweet with honeysuckle and humming with orange bees, Sister Josephine approached her during morning ablutions and told her to gather up her few belongings.

As she was being led away her eyes met Mary's. They said good-bye to each other silently with trembling lips. She had no idea if she would see her friend again.

It surprised her not the least when Sister Josephine took her straight to the small dormitory at the edge of the abbey grounds.

Inside, the air was stuffy. The windows and doors had been shut keeping the breeze at bay. There was a central hall and individual cells on both sides.

Down the hall, she thought she heard the cry of a

baby, but it lasted only a moment. Then a girl's low words. Wasn't it the voice of Fay, the big-boned girl who was heavy with child?

"What place is this, Sister?" she asked fearfully.

"That's no concern of yours, child," she was told.

"When the time comes, you'll be told what you need to be told. Until then, all you must do is obey and behave."

"Yes, Sister," she said as faintly as a squeaking mouse.

She was ushered into a small chamber with a bed, a nightstand and some earthenware necessities.

"There's but a single bed, Sister," she exclaimed.

"You do not have to share it, Clarissa. It's for you and you alone."

"Me own chamber?" she asked incredulously.

"You must thank the Lord for your bounty, girl."

"Will I be working in th' kitchen?"

"You will not."

"What work will I do then?"

"You will pray and meditate. That is your work now."

"Will I go to th' cathedral for th' hours?"

"You will not. You will make your own prayer here."

"Are there others with me?"

"Enough questions! Sister Hazel will come presently with food and drink. She will be your superior. Do everything she says without fail."

Sister Hazel was a sturdy nun with broad shoulders and hair sprouting from odd places on her face. Everything she did, she did quickly, and she made it plain that she expected Clarissa to do her bidding smartly and without complaint. She was in absolute charge of the dormitory and there'd be no nonsense. The rules were simple: there was to be no fraternization with the other girls. Meals were to be taken within her cell and every morsel had to be consumed. Morning ablutions were to be done thoroughly and swiftly. She must report the beginning of her menses without fail. Her only time outside would be visits to the outhouse. She must be diligent in her personal prayers. And finally, Sister Hazel would not tolerate idle questions.

Clarissa settled into a boring period of solitude. She did her best to pray but she could only remember a few hymns and prayers from beginning to end. She was a prisoner in her cell, but the food was plentiful and her bed was comfortable. She strained her ears to listen for voices from other cells, and when she visited the outhouse, she tried to spy into the dark windows of neighboring cells. The only thing she knew with certainty was that there was a baby down the hall. She heard it crying from time to time as plainly as can be.

When her menses came she dutifully reported it to Sister Hazel who seemed pleased at the news. Two weeks to the day later her life changed forever.

On the appointed morning, Sister Hazel arrived after her morning meal and stood over her.

"Today is the most important day in your life, child. The Lord is calling you for a higher purpose, and that purpose will be fulfilled presently. I am taking you to a part of the abbey that only a privileged few know about."

"Is it the small chapel, yonder," Clarissa said, pointing.

"You're a very curious and clever girl, aren't you? Yes, that is where we are going. The girls who go there are truly the chosen ones. You are to be one in a long line who have done their duty and been rewarded with the knowledge and certainty that they have served God in a special and singular way."

"What am I t' do?" she asked, trembling.

"Just follow Sister Sabeline's instructions when you are there. She will personally supervise the ritual."

"What's a ritual?"

"Always the questions with you! All I will tell you is that some girls, the weak ones, become frightened by what they see. But you are not weak, are you, Clarissa?"

"Nae, Sister."

"No indeed. You will be brave, you will not cry, and you will obey Sister Sabeline."

"Aye, Sister."

"Then come along."

It was another fine day and she turned her face to the warmth of the sun. Her heart was fluttering with fear but she was resolute. If God had chosen her for some high purpose, then she would bend to his will. Whatever the circumstances.

At the chapel door Sister Sabeline was waiting for them. Sister Hazel handed Clarissa off and quickly left. The old nun sternly bade the girl to follow her inside. Clarissa was surprised to see that the chapel was entirely empty with a bluestone floor, adorned only with a gilded wooden crucifix affixed to the wall above a dark oak door at the rear.

Sister Sabeline pushed the door open, took Clarissa's hand, and pulled her through.

Clarissa found herself on steep, spiraling stairs that bored into the earth. There were torches set at intervals but she still had to take care with her footfalls. The stairs wound so tightly that after a while she felt her head spinning. When they could descend no farther an enormous door blocked their progress.

Sister Sabeline unlocked the door with a heavy black iron key affixed to her leather belt. To open it, she had to lean into it with all her might.

They were in a dim cavern.

Clarissa squinted and tried to make sense of what she saw. Wide-eyed, she stared at Sabeline and was about to speak when the nun told her not to utter a single word.

The chamber had a domed ceiling that was plastered and whitewashed to increase the luminosity of the candles spaced out on rows of long tables.

Clarissa stopped breathing when she realized what she was looking at. Seated at the tables, shoulder to shoulder, were dozens of ginger-haired men and boys with ghostly white skin, each one grasping a quill, dipping and writing on sheets of parchment producing a collective din of scratching that filled her ears. Some of the writers were old men, some young boys, but despite their ages they all looked similar to one another. Every face was as blank and staring as the next, green eyes boring into sheets of white parchment.

My God, who are these creatures, she thought.

What are they?

"Remember. Say nothing!" Sabeline warned her.

None of the pale-skinned men seemed to take notice as Sabeline dragged her in front of them one by one, row by row.

Suddenly, one man raised his head and looked straight at her. He was ancient, perhaps the eldest. His skin was wrinkled and slack, and there were only a few patches of reddish gray hair on his scaly, pink scalp. Clarissa noticed that the bony fingers on his right hand were colored with ink and that the front of his robe was stained yellow with food. He started to breathe heavily, emitting high-pitched wheezes. Then a low groan emanated from his throat, a primitive animalistic sound that made Clarissa's knees go weak.

"I cannot believe it," Sister Sabeline mumbled. "I simply cannot believe it."

The nun took one of the candles and yanked at Clarissa's sleeve the way one pulls at a stubborn mule, but when she remained rooted, Sister Sabeline yanked again, setting Clarissa's legs in motion. At the end of the row, the nun pulled her toward a pitch-black archway.

Clarissa didn't want to pass through into that void but she was a rag doll in the old nun's grasp. As she passed through the arch, she turned her head and saw the old wheezing man rise from his table.

The moment she passed through the arch, a hideous stench filled her nostrils. Instinctively she recognized it as the smell of death. She felt her stomach turning inside out but she was able to hold on to her breakfast.

The first yellow skeleton she saw by the light of Sister Sabeline's candle made her gasp in fear. Its jaw was wide open, as if screaming. There were bits of adherent flesh and hair. Its eyes had desiccated into masses the size of peas. Progressing farther into the catacombs she saw others—many others—skeletons too numerous to count, stacked into loculi carved into limestone. She'd seen a dead body once in her life, her grandfather laid out before the hearth before he was wrapped and carried out to the burial ground. But that had in no way braced her for the immensity of all this death.

"What is this place?" she gasped.

"Hush!" the nun said. "You are not to speak!"

They stopped in a small chamber, lined floor to ceiling with loculi. Sister Sabeline held the candle in her outstretched arm.

Clarissa was shaking like a dog that had just been pulled from the waters of a frozen pond. She heard a shuffle.

Someone was coming.

"Look at me!" the nun commanded. "Do not turn away."

Someone was behind her.

She could not obey. She pivoted and saw the immobile face of the old man in the flickering light. He was staring at her with his liquid, green eyes.

"You have no idea how blessed you are, girl," Sister Sabeline hissed. "This is no ordinary scribe. He is Titus, the most venerable, the most prolific. In all my years, he has never chosen a girl. You may be his first! Do your duty well."

My duty, Clarissa thought! God help me!

The old man started to make low, grunting sounds and began pawing himself.

"Lift your gown," Sister Sabeline shouted. "And bend over. Do it now!"

Her small pathetic life flashed through her mind. If she ran, where would she go? She had no one to help her, nowhere to hide, no money, no friends. There was only one thing for her to do.

She grabbed the hem of her gown and lifted it to her waist.

"Good, now bend toward me."

She felt pressure against her privates then a sharp jolt of pain as her maidenhead was breached. Growing up on a farm, she'd seen animals in heat. She knew about these things. She felt like a ewe being mounted. She closed her eyes tightly, clamped her jaw, and thought only one thought over and over.

I will have a baby. I will have a baby.

It didn't last long. The old man's grunting reached a crescendo, and when he was done he immediately withdrew and shuffled away.

"Stand up now," Sister Sabeline ordered.

Blinking away her salty tears, Clarissa stood and let her robe fall to her ankles.

"There. You have done your duty and done it well. I'll take you back to your dormitory now. You will lie on your back with your knees up for three days. All your needs will be attended to by Sister Hazel."

"Will I have a baby?" she asked plaintively.

"You will!" Sister Sabeline said. "A very special one."

Adrenaline purged Will's fatigue. He sat tense and rigid beside Annie as she drove their hired car south toward Pinn. It was a moonless night. Theirs was the only vehicle on the narrow road. In the high beams all he could see were hedgerows, drystone walls, and the occasional lonely, dark, limestone cottage.

Annie stifled a yawn. It spoke volumes to him. She wasn't committed to the assignment. She didn't have the zeal he had when he was a young Turk. Or the fire in her eyes that Nancy had when she was on a case. Maybe it was just Annie. Maybe it was the younger generation. Maybe it was the pernicious effect of the Horizon. He didn't much care. His son was some-where out there in the inky wilderness, in peril. And Will required the complete commitment of everyone involved in finding him.

"How far are we?" he asked.

"Not very. I'm looking for Officer Wilson's car. He should be there already."

Will had called Nancy and forwarded Phillip's message. She was working late at the Bureau and immediately pinpointed the coordinates of Phillip's beacon on a satellite map. "It's farmland," she had said. "Not many buildings around. What the hell is he doing there, Will?"

"Wish I knew, Nance. Is there a terrorist group in your files called the Librarians?"

He had listened as she issued voice commands to her computer.

"Nothing," she had said.

"They could be new. The name worries the hell out of me."

"Me too," she had said. He'd heard the palpable fear in her voice. She was a mother first. "It could be something ad hoc involving the Horizon. Maybe Phillip's connection to you made him a symbolic target."

"His essay was all over the Net," Will had said.

"Yes, it was."

"Is there a chance in hell this has got something to do with your Chinese case?"

"I don't want to rule anything out. Parish relented. I was able to duck the China trip. Should I try to get permission to fly over to the UK?"

"No, stay put. We may need you to do things in Washington that can't be done here. I don't trust MI5. They've given me a girl not much older than Phil."

There had been a pause. He had known what Nancy was thinking, but he'd been sure that under the circumstances she wasn't about to ask: "Is she pretty?"

Instead, she had said, "Will, find him and bring him home. And listen, take care of that silly heart of yours."

Ahead, in the dark, Officer Wilson's car was at the side of the road with its interior lights on. Annie slowed and pulled in behind him. They met in the frigid night air.

Wilson pointed toward the darkness. "It's a chilly night for a lad t' be out in th' Dales, eh?"

"Then we'd better find him fast," Will said flatly. "Are there many houses around here?"

"Maybe seven or eight t' a square mile. Nae many fowk round here," the officer said. "This is sheep country."

Wilson had a police-configured NetPen. The screen was deployed and was displaying a terrain map with a pin marking the satellite position of Phillip's beacon.

"How far is that?" Annie asked.

"About three-quarters of a mile. It's gey dark. I've only got the one torch—sorry about that—so unless you've got your own, we'll need t' stay close."

They found a gap in a hedgerow and began walking into a meadow, dark as sable. Will had no sense of the terrain beyond what he could see in the yellow cone of the policeman's flashlight. The grass below his feet was winter-clumped and crusty with frost. He shuddered at the thought of Phillip's stumbling about in the alien landscape.

After a while, he was aware from the tightness in his quadriceps that they were climbing. It wasn't a steep grade, but it was a steady one. He pushed on his neck to check his pulse and prayed that his heart wouldn't act up. There was a stone wall ahead.

"We'll go over," Officer Wilson told them. "Try not t' dislodge any stones or I'll have complaints in th' morning. Farmers around here aren't too jolly. And mind the sheep mess."

Wilson climbed it with ease and offered a hand with Annie who, because of her skirt, went over more awkwardly. Ordinarily, Will would have assisted but because she was showing so much skin, he elected to keep his hands to himself. When he crossed over, he felt a chest palpitation that made him pause and frown in self-loathing pique.

"You okay?" Annie asked.

"I'm fine," he insisted, picking up the pace. He cupped his mouth with his hands and called out his son's name.

The policeman swung his beam toward Will, and said, "Mr. Piper, I understand your concern, but I'd ask you t' wait a bit till we're better away from th' farmhouses. It wouldn't be pretty for an irate land-owner t' come out here with his shotgun looking for a trespasser."

Will resisted the urge to tell the guy to go to hell. He needed his cooperation.

After twenty minutes of climbing they had traversed another five walls. Wilson looked at his NetPen and declared, "This is th' approximate spot where your son set off th' beacon."

"I'm going to call for him now," Will said. "You okay with that?"

"We're high enough we won't be disturbing anyone in the valley."

"Phillip!" Will shouted. He waited and called again. "Phillip! It's Dad! Where are you?"

Will wandered a few yards in each direction and tried again.

The whistling wind carried no response.

The officer swept the hillside with his light.

"What's that?" Annie asked, pointing at some dark masses.

"Sheep, I reckon," Wilson said, "but we'll take a look. Stay together. We don't need more missin' people."

They approached the shapes, which were indeed a cluster of sheep huddled near a small field hangar.

Wilson checked inside. It was empty but for some straw. He poked around with his shoe and declared it clear but Will insisted on repeating the exercise himself.

They spent half an hour wandering the sloping pasture surrounding the beacon coordinates as Will desperately called for his son over and over. Finally, Wilson insisted that they were done for the night. He'd return with more officers in the morning, request a helicopter from the Cumbrian Constabulary, but any more tramping about blindly was pointless. Will reacted furiously, got into Wilson's face, and had to be tugged away by Annie, who pleaded with him not to alienate the local authorities.

"We don't have our own resources up here, Will. We need their continued help. Think about your son, okay?"

Will felt the fatigue buckle his knees and bowed to her gentle logic. They hiked down off the fells.

At 9 A.M. local time, Roger Kenney and his team disembarked from a US Air Force Sikorsky transport helicopter at the 421st Air Base Group at RAF Menwith Hill in Harrogate, North Yorkshire. It was sharply cold and the sun was harshly bright. The three Americans slipped on mirrored sunglasses and climbed into a Humvee.

They had landed in England directly from Nevada earlier that morning, touching down at RAF Mildenhall in Suffolk, the home of the USAF 100th Air Refueling Wing. There they immediately boarded a chopper to take them onwards. In transit, arrangements had been made to support the Groom Lake team at Menwith Hill, the National Security Agency/

CIA satellite ground station and communications data intercept post.

As the chopper approached, Kenney had pointed out the array of giant white antennae housed in globular white radomes stretching out over the countryside. "Kind of look like big old amanitas, don't they?"

He had two of his best trackers with him, Lopez, an ex-Ranger, and Harper, ex-Delta—both as loyal as they came, both BTH. Lopez yawned, and Harper contagiously followed suit. "What's that, chief?" Lopez asked.

"Death cap mushrooms. Good eating until they kill you. Just ask Emperor Claudius."

"Whatever you say, chief," Lopez said.

Soon they were comfortably belowground, their natural habitat, in a hardened bunker capable of taking a direct nuclear hit. An American NSA liaison officer showed them around their suite which had a situation room, a dedicated VidLink to Groom Lake, some bedrooms and a self-catering kitchen.

"Thanks for your hospitality," Kenney told the NSA man. "Feel right at home."

"Just close your eyes and pretend there are cacti up there," their host said. "Give us a shout if you need wheels."

"How long'll it take to drive from here to Kirkby Stephen?"

"How heavy's your foot?"

"Made of pure lead, man."

"About two hours."

While his guys washed up, Kenney logged onto his Groom Lake server and established sync with his surveillance programs. Within a few minutes he was up and running. There was a queue of audio files of mobile calls between Piper and his wife and text files between Annie Locke and her superiors at MI5.

He quickly learned that little progress had been made during the night but they were set to resume the search for Phillip Piper that morning. Kenney dragged Will's and Annie's photos onto the wall screen and as he called up the locations of their mobile devices on a grid map of Cumbria he cheerfully spoke to each photo in turn. "Annie Locke, you are a fine-looking young thing. I hope we get to meet, preferably under some nice fresh sheets. And Will Piper, I hope we get to meet too, real soon. I owe you for Malcolm Frazier. I am going to seriously fuck you up you sanctimonious son of a bitch."

Will paced restlessly in the hotel lobby after consuming a piece of toast and some bad coffee. There was no sign of Annie, and her tardiness irritated him. He was tempted to ditch her but she had the car keys so he marched up the stairs and banged on her door.

Through the wood he heard, "Just a sec!"

She cracked the door and when she saw it was him, she opened it fully. She had a brush in her hand, and though she was dressed her blouse was partially undone.

"Come in if you like," she said. "Coffee? I had a carafe sent up. There's plenty left. I'll just be a minute. I'm not late, am I?"

"Yeah, you're late," he said, ambling in and sitting on her unmade bed. He figured the best way to hurry her up was by planting himself.

She was already back in the bathroom. "Terribly sorry about that. I promise to make it up by driving faster."

"Have you heard from the cop?" he asked.

"Officer Wilson? Yes indeed. He rang to tell me that he and four other officers were going to be searching Mallerstang this morning. I believe they're in transit."

"Mallerstang?"

"That's the valley we were tramping about last night."

"What about a chopper?"

"Yes, well, that's a bit more of a challenge, apparently. It's being serviced."

"Well, let's get another one!" Will shouted, rising from the bed. "Call your people in London! Get one from the RAF."

"I did place a call. Got quite a lot of blowback, I'm afraid. That's why I'm running behind schedule."

"Jesus," he growled. "I'll call Washington to light a fire under their asses."

She emerged from the bathroom, hair in order. "By the time that's yielded results, the Cumbrian police helicopter should be back in operation. I'm hoping for this afternoon. Ready?"

Her blouse was still undone. He pointed helpfully, but when she didn't catch his drift, he said, "Your buttons."

She did them up without blushing and looked him in the eye. "When we find your son, I'd like to help you celebrate."

He sighed. This was familiar territory. "I'm possibly old enough to be your grandfather."

"You look just fine to me." She grabbed her coat and her shoulder bag. "You know, I felt I knew you before we met. I think I developed a schoolgirl crush when I saw your waxworks at Madame Tussaud's during a class trip."

He grunted in embarrassment. "That can't be on display anymore."

"I think they might have taken it out of storage and dusted it off in honor of the one-year countdown to the Horizon. Perhaps you can take Phillip before the two of you return to America."

They drove south on the same route they had taken the previous night. The B6259 wound through the floor of Mallerstang, a long dale carved into the Pennines by the River Eden. What had been black and unfathomable in the dead of night was now clear and sun-drenched. They were in a U-shaped trough of wilderness. To the east and west were high undulating grassy fells with limestone outcrops and scattered woodlands. The fells rose to nearly two thousand feet on both sides of the road. Down in the narrow valley, Will had a visceral and claustrophobic reaction to the fells. He felt they were leaning in, pressing his chest, making him work for air, a blunted version of the way he'd felt during his heart attack.

Up and down the fells he saw the complicated latticework of drystone walls like those they'd encountered in the dark. Scattered on either side of the road were gray stone farmhouses and barns, some at the end of winding dirt lanes. Because the drystone walls and the buildings were of the same limestone as the crags they seemed to be part of the landscape, thrust out of the bedrock, not man-made.

They passed a small iron sign. Pinn.

"Not much of a town," Will said.

Annie agreed. "There isn't even a pub."

Ahead were two squad cars. Annie passed them and pulled off the road. They were empty. Will got out and strained his eyes, looking for the policemen in the hills, but he couldn't make them out.

"Okay," Will said. "Hopefully, the police are doing

what they're supposed to be doing. Let's do our job. Where's the first house?"

They'd stuck a digital pin in the map on Annie's NetPen display and drawn a circle with a radius of one mile. Within that circle, there were eight houses plotted on the 1:10000 scale Ordnance Survey map. They'd start there, then extend the radius by half-mile increments.

Will scanned the fells. Someone in Mallerstang, someone in this damn valley knew where his son was.

"We'll walk to the first two, then hop back for the car," Annie said. "That house up there's got a charming name: Scar Farm. Think it's a different meaning than scar face, but nonetheless, perfect place to start."

The house at Scar Farm was a limestone cottage lying partway up the fell, as were most of the farms in Mallerstang. The meadows down to the road were for hay and silage, and those up on the fells were for rough summer grazing. Annie knocked on the door, then knocked again when there was no response. Will took over and slammed his heavy fist into it a few times.

A dog started barking behind the house. Will headed around back to investigate and saw a man on a tractor in the field beyond the barn; he climbed onto a low stone wall, balanced himself, waved his arms, and shouted out a series of "hellos." The man noticed him, pointed the old petrol-fueled tractor, and motored down the hill in their direction. At the same time a woman emerged from the barn and cautiously approached.

The farmer pulled his tractor up to the wall and dismounted. The dog was on his side of the wall and with a sharp command, he stopped its barking. He was a grizzled-looking old fellow in a tattered padded jacket and Wellington boots. Will was still atop the wall. The man shouted at him, "Divn't dee that yer divvy!"

"What did he say?" Will asked Annie.

"Haven't a clue I'm afraid."

The woman drew closer. She was a similar vintage to the farmer and just as weather-beaten.

"He said, 'get off our wall, you idiot.' This here's private property," she said.

Will climbed down. "Sorry, ma'am. I wonder if you've got a minute to talk to us."

"You lost?" the woman asked.

"No, ma'am. I need your help. Could I have a minute of your time? I'm looking for my son."

The farmer was fuming and shouting something unintelligible.

"Shut yer moy, John," she said. "The man's boy's gone missin'. Get back t' it, I'll take care of 'em."

The old man swore, got back on his tractor, and puttered off.

Will took a picture of Phillip from his jacket. "Thank you. This is my son. We know he was close to here last night."

"Up on that fell," Annie said, pointing at a hillside.

"What's your laddo doing in Mallerstang?" the woman asked Will.

"I'm not sure. I think he met a girl online."

"No girls here. Haven't seen your boy. You two are th' first strangers in a while. We get ramblers in the good months but nowt in th' winter."

"Have any of your neighbors talked about a boy's being in the area?" Will asked.

"We don't have time t' sit around at scordy. Farms don't run themselves."

Annie pulled a card from her purse. "Well, if you see or hear anything, please ring me, will you?"

The woman took the card without looking at it. "You're not a horney then. What are you?"

"Horney?" Annie asked back with an amused look.

"Police."

"No, ma'am. I'm with the Security Services. From London."

She turned to walk back to the barn. "Don't know nowt 'bout that."

The rest of the morning brought more of the same. By lunchtime they had visited five houses with receptions ranging from suspicious to hostile. No one had seen Phillip. Two households had teenage girls at school in Kirkby Stephen. They left Phillip's pictures behind with a request to be called if the girls recognized him.

Walking back to the car, Annie's NetPen chimed. It was Officer Wilson on his way back to town. They'd scoured the pastures and fells for hours without finding a trace of physical evidence.

"Shall we find a pub for a spot of lunch?" Annie asked Will.

"I'd rather we kept going."

She sighed, rummaged through her bag, and waved a chocolate bar. "I've got an emergency Fruit and Nut. Want to share?"

They finished the chocolate bar at the entrance to Lightburn Farm, then drove up the dirt lane around a hillock that concealed the property from the road. The ancient farmhouse looked much like the others they had visited that day—gray stone, rectangular, center entrance with asymmetrical windows and a sharply pitched slate roof. An attached barn was at a right angle to the house on the fell side.

A middle-aged woman with fiery red hair was hanging laundry on a line by the side of the house. She stared hard at them as they exited the car.

"Hi there," Will called out. "I wonder if you could help us, ma'am?"

"With what?" was her curt reply. She was a handsome-looking woman in her forties who might have passed for a beauty with a bit of makeup and better clothes.

"My son is missing. He came here from America. We know he was near here last night. Could I show you his picture?"

"You his mother?" the woman asked Annie.

"No! Bit young for that. I'm with the Security Services."

"From London?"

Annie nodded.

"So we've got a Yank and a lady minder from London. What's th' boy doin' up here?"

"We think he met a girl from here online," Will said.

The woman set her unhung laundry in a basket. "I see."

"Do you have any daughters?" Will asked.

"I do."

"Can we speak to them?"

"Just the one. She's at school. Tell you what, come into th' house. I'll offer you something t' drink, and we'll look at your picture, but I can tell you straight off we haven't seen any American boys."

As they followed her to the front door, Annie whispered to Will, "First glimmer of hospitality we've had so far. And I can even understand what she's saying!"

They found themselves inside a large single room dominated by a mighty hearth with a waning fire. To their left was a kitchen, to the right, a cozy sitting area with some old furniture, a hooked rug, and an ancient TV set—pre–flat screen, big, and bulky. The woman immediately went to tend the fire, adding a few lumps of coal.

Will had a good look around, and asked, "How old is the house?"

A man's voice came from the stairs. "Fourteenth century, parts go back farther. Who's asking?"

The woman quickly answered. "Daniel, come down. We've got visitors. This man's laddo's gone missin'. He's come all th' weh from America."

The man had black hair, long black sideburns, and several days of stubble. His right arm was in a sling.

"I'm Daniel Lightburn," he said. "I'd shake your hand, but mine's busted."

Will and Annie introduced themselves.

The woman joined in. "I'm Daniel's wife, Cacia."

"What a lovely name," Annie said.

"Sit down," Daniel offered. "Don't often get visitors. Cacia, offer them a bevvie."

"Tea or whiskey?" Cacia said.

"Tea for me," Annie said eagerly.

"I wouldn't say no to a whiskey," Will said, wearily sinking low into the shot springs of the old sofa.

He hadn't touched scotch since his heart attack. His doctors didn't want him back on his nectar of choice; Nancy didn't want him back on it. But his resistance was worn low by jet lag and worry. The drink hit his pallet sharply but went down with an easy familiarity.

He smiled at his hosts. "I don't mind telling you, but we've seen a bunch of your neighbors this morning, and you're the only ones to invite us in."

Daniel had two fingers of whiskey himself. "Fowks here aren't keen on offcomers."

"Some of them have an impenetrable dialect," Will joked. "You don't."

"Varies, I suppose," Cacia said. "We don't mix much with others. So we don't pick up all their ways."

"We're what you'd call, self-sufficient," Daniel said. "We grow our veggies, milk our cows, butcher our sheep and chickens. We don't want for much that th' outside world has on offer."

"It's just you and your daughters?" Annie asked.

"We've got two grown sons up tending th' sheep. And me brother and his wife and their wee 'uns are in th' other cottage out back. We've got a gey clan."

"Let's see your picture then," Cacia said.

Will handed over a copy.

"Good-looking boy, isn't he, Daniel, but like I said, we haven't seen 'im."

"What make you think he's around here?" Daniel asked.

"He sent a signal from his NetPen." They were staring at him blankly. "It's a mobile communicator. It operates on GWS, the global wireless system."

Annie held hers up to show them.

Daniel shrugged. "We're not big on technology. Th' telly was th' ol' fella's, may he rest in peace."

"The signal he sent last night tells us he was less than a mile from this house."

"Mr. Piper says th' boy met a girl online," Cacia told Daniel.

"Must be quite the lass t' come this far." Daniel laughed. "Where in the States are you from?"

"Virginia."

"How'd he manage to get all th' way here?"

"He ran away, bought a plane ticket, took a train from London."

Daniel said, "A motivated lad."

"How old is your daughter?" Annie asked.

"She's fifteen," Cacia said.

"Does she go online a lot?" Will asked.

"Not from here, that's for sure," Daniel answered. "We've no computers. Maybe from school. Wouldn't know."

Annie continued, "Has your daughter mentioned using the social networking service called Socco?"

"Never heard of it," Cacia said.

"Could you show her this picture of Phillip when she gets back from school and ask her if she's ever sent a message to him?" Will asked.

Annie passed one of her cards to the nodding woman.

"And one more question," Will asked, rising. "Have you ever heard the term the Librarians?"

"Well, I know what a librarian is?" Daniel said. "Don't think I understand th' question."

"Yeah, it is a strange one. Outside of the conventional meaning, is there any local group up here that goes by that name?"

"No, sorry," Daniel said. "Can't help you."

Annie hurriedly finished her tea and stood up too.

"Thanks very much for your kindness," Will said. "If your girl knows anything, please call Miss Locke right away."

Will was surprised when Cacia Lightburn took his large hands in her small ones and squeezed. She looked at him with unblinking green eyes and said with a sincerity that almost evoked his tears, "I know you're going to find your boy, Mr. Piper. I know you will."

They returned to the car.

"Awfully nice people," Annie said.

"Yeah, I guess they were," he said, his voice drifting off. His hands tingled. It was almost as if he could feel the lingering touch of that woman's rough palms. "Let's keep moving. Two more houses to go."

Through the front-facing kitchen window, Cacia watched the car disappear.

"They're gone."

Daniel rubbed at his hurt hand and started upstairs.

"Send Haven t' me as soon as her bus arrives."

"Daniel," his wife said. "If they come back here, what are we t' do?"

"Do? We'll kill 'em, of course."

Nancy fast-walked from her office to Director Parish's suite. She'd been having a cup of coffee and commiserating with her assistant about Phillip when all hell broke loose. She'd been forced to banish her son from her thoughts.

Parish started in before she could even take a chair. "Jesus Christ, Nancy. Jesus fricking Christ."

His phone buzzed. His PA was on the intercom. "The White House is calling. Chief of Staff Gladwell."

"Tell him I'm being briefed on the matter. I'll call him back in two minutes," Parish said. He turned to Nancy, "Tell me what we know."

"Details are still coming in, but the Chinese embassy in Washington received six postcards this morning by regular mail," she said, checking her notes. "They were addressed to the Ambassador, the Deputy Chief of Mission, the Minister for Cultural Affairs, the Minister for Economic and Commercial Affairs, the Defense Attaché, and an Information Officer."

"What date's on the cards?"

"All tomorrow."

"Is it a copycat?"

"Hard to say. We've got a team over there negotiating with their security people to take possession of the postcards for forensics. I'm told they're postmarked from Manhattan, like the others, and that the hand-drawn coffin appears identical."

Parish threw his hands up. "What the hell good are forensics going to be? None of the postcards have common prints."

"We can test the ink. So far they've been from the same brand of pen."

"Anything else?"

"I've got to tell you, Bob, I don't think this fits. Maybe it's a copycat, like you said, or maybe our perp is intentionally winding up the Chinese government toward some end. Think about it. Everything so far had pointed to an outdated database. None of these diplomats have even been in the States for more than a few years. And they don't live at the embassy. The Area 51 databases, as I understand them, are keyed to residential addresses."

"Well, we'll just have to wait to see if any or all of these diplomats are pushing daisies by midnight tomorrow, won't we?" Parish said caustically.

His intercom buzzed. It was the White House again. He had the call put through, hit speaker mode, and regurgitated Nancy's briefing to Dan Gladwell.

Gladwell was in the middle of a sentence when he told Parish he had to put him on hold. When he came back on the line he said, "Bob, I just got word from State that the Chinese are packing up and leaving. They're evacuating the entire embassy. They've got a plane heading to Dulles to pick them up and bring them home. They've lodged a formal protest. I need you over here five minutes ago to brief the President."

*   *   *

Will and Annie widened their house-to-house search concentrically and by the end of the day had visited all residences within a two-mile radius of Phillip's beacon. The word had spread around Pinn; some of the farmers knew about their visit in advance. A few were cordial; many were downright nasty about the intrusion. None of them shed a glimmer of light on Phillip's whereabouts.

They began their drive back to Kirkby Stephen in the creeping sunset, Will's mood matching the dullness of the evening.

"Let me buy you dinner," Annie said, her eyes firmly on the windy road. "I spotted a pleasant-looking place across from the hotel."

"Yeah, sure," he said robotically.

She snuck a glance at him. "We'll find him, Will."

"Can we get the police to do another air search tomorrow?"

"Honestly, I doubt it. Officer Wilson sounded like they were done for now, but if there are further leads we're to ring him."

He felt the valley squeezing him again and wanted to escape its grip to an open space where he could breathe easier. The terrain smoothed out soon enough and there was some relief in that. But Phillip was going to be spending another night somewhere in that gloomy valley. Hiding? Held against his will? Scared?

He texted Nancy a barebones status report.

Her texted reply was, Oh my . . . and he could hear the sigh in it.

He waited for more, then asked her if she was okay.

Yeah. U?

Hanging in there.
Big problems with China.
I need to hear that Philly is safe.
I'll get it done. I promise.

"Your wife?" Annie asked.

He grunted an affirmative.

"She must be worried sick."

"She is. So am I."

Back in his room, Will splashed his face and changed his shirt. He tuned the TV to the news and quickly got the drift of Nancy's "China Problem." She was in the middle of it like the yolk in an egg, that was for sure.

His mobile started vibrating and chiming on his bed. He figured it was Nancy but when he was a couple of feet away, he pounced on it.

The caller ID was PHILLIP!

"Phillip!" he screamed into the phone. "Where are you?"

There was a sickening pause where he heard nothing at all.

"Phillip?"

"I'm his friend." It was a small voice. A girl's voice. He'd heard the Cumbrian accent all day long.

Will sensed a fragility. If he pushed hard, he'd lose her. At the FBI, he'd been legendary at interrogation.

"I'm his dad."

"I know."

"Is he okay?"

A soft "Yeah."

"Can I talk to him?"

"I'm not with 'im right now."

"Where is he?"

"He's safe."

"Where are you?"

"Th' library."

"In Kirkby Stephen?"

"Yeah."

"If I go there, can I talk to you?"

"Only if you promise t' come alone."

"I promise."

"Do you have a car?"

"No. Yes. Yes, I have a car."

"Good. We'll need a car if you want t' see 'im."

"How will I know who you are?"

"I'll know who you are. You're Will Piper."

Will hung up and began to think furiously. If he involved Annie he might spook the girl and the door she had opened might slam shut. He could hardly use a taxi. In his prime he might have hot-wired a car and helped himself but he had no idea if it was even possible to boost one of the electrics in the car park.

Suddenly he knew what he had to do. He grabbed his phone and wallet and took off.

He didn't go far.

Annie opened her door to his knock. She was in a robe. "I thought we said half an hour."

"I know."

He gently pushed his way in. She closed the door and dropped her arms to her side allowing the robe to part.

He'd pulled this kind of stunt so many times in his life he couldn't remember. Sometimes he was sober, often not. Sometimes he knew the woman's name, sometimes not. He was never a big talker in these circumstances and he wasn't this time either. He simply pulled her in, kissed her softly on her upturned lips, and moved his hands over her back.

After a while she disengaged, smiling.

"Gosh, wasn't expecting that. I'm sure the restaurant will be open a bit later."

"I'm sure it will."

"I didn't think you'd be in the mood for a dalliance."

"I figured an attractive lady would take my mind off things."

"It's the least His Majesty's Government can do for you. Just give me a sec, won't you?"

He nodded, and she disappeared into the bathroom.

He wasted no time. The Ford's keys were on the bureau. He pocketed them and walked out quietly, closing the door behind him.

In a few minutes he was tucking the car away on a street behind the public library.

It was one of the two days per week the library had extended hours. There were many more users than his previous visit. The main floor had an inviting fluorescence compared to the gloomy darkness of Market Street. Despite his long retirement he still had the knack. He scanned the room and processed it in one fell swoop, hoovering it for evidence, getting the broad picture and finer details simultaneously.

He pegged the teenage girl before she made eye contact. It was the way she fidgeted nervously with a strand of her long red hair. And her hippie retro look, which his own daughter had adopted for a time: no makeup, long, gauzy dress with a pea jacket over it, low-cut work boots. She looked like the kind of kid who'd use a wildflower as a screen name.

The confirmation came when she saw him and affected a small smile. She motioned for him to follow her to the stairwell.

In the basement, among the stacks, she finally spoke.

"Did ya come alone?"

"Yes."

"Phillip looks like you."

"Where is he?"

"Not far."

"Okay, let's go get him."

"It's not that simple."

He trod lightly. She looked afraid. "Should I call you Hawkbit?"

"Me name's Haven."

An airy-fairy name. "Okay, Haven. Why don't you tell me what the situation is?"

"Can we do it when we're driving? I slipped away. Hitched a ride t' town. They'll find me missin' if I'm not back soon."

"Are we going to Pinn?" he asked.

She didn't look surprised as she nodded. "I was told you were around today."

He searched his memory to match Haven's features to the families he'd visited. "Lightburn Farm?"

She nodded again.

"I met your parents."

She nodded.

"My car's parked out back."

Haven showed him a back way to get to the B6259 without passing through Market Street. Annie would be prowling the town, looking for him, angry on so many levels. At least he'd been able to swipe the keys before he'd had to sleep with her. There was that.

And as if on cue, his mobile phone rang with a call from a UK number. He didn't remember giving Annie his mobile number but she was MI5 after all. She probably had a dossier on him. He switched the phone off. The last thing he wanted was for Annie or the local police bumbling into a situation and mucking things up. He was going to extricate Phillip from whatever jam he was in. He didn't need their help anymore.

It was fully dark. Outside the town he clicked on the high beams.

She sat beside him, a silent waiflike presence.

"What can you tell me, Haven? Why did you want Phillip to come here?"

"I thought he could 'elp."

It wasn't going to flow out of her. "Help who?"

"Me. And others too."

"How could he help you?"

"By getting th' word out."

"About what?"

"About what we do up on th' farm."

He asked the question as gently as he could, fighting the urge to scream at her to spill the goddamned beans already. "What do you do on your farm?"

"I'll show ya, not tell ya."

Was that the line she'd used on Phillip? Was this a ruse orchestrated by her parents to lure him there? "Under the circumstances, Haven, how do I know this isn't some kind of trap?"

"It's dangerous, but it's nae a trap. Phillip got caught, and I feel bad 'bout that. Truly awful. I was the one who got his NetPen away from Uncle Kheelan. I helped 'im get off."

"But he got caught again, right?"

She sounded mournful. "On th' fells."

"He said he was being chased by the Librarians."

"Did he?"

"What did he mean by that?"

"You'll find out."

"Are you sure he's okay?"

"Me dad fell over and busted his hand, but Phillip's fine. They're cross wit' me. They're not letting me see 'im, but I know he's cared for."

He needed to formulate a plan. "Is he in the farm-house?"

"No."

"The barn?"

"No."

"The other cottage?"

"No."

"Where then?"

"Under them."

"A tunnel?"

"More than that. You'll see."

"How do I get to him?"

"There's a secret way in. I'm taking you there."

"Do your parents or your uncle have any guns?"

"Shotguns."

"Any handguns?"

"Don't think so. Don't know."

"How many men are at your farm?"

Her response puzzled him. "How do you mean men?"

"Adults. Brothers, cousins, you know."

"There's me father, me uncle, me two brothers, and me two cousins, but they're girls. And me aunt, but she's a girl too, I 'spose."

The sign for Pinn was in the headlights.

"In about a mile we're going to pull off th' road and hide th' car in a little thicket," she said. "We'll walk the rest of th' way through th' fields. I've brung a torch."

He was always good at reading people—very good—but he wasn't confident that his skills applied to teenage girls from Mallerstang. If this was a trap, no one would have a clue where he'd gone. Someone from the farm could come back for the car and drive it to another town or hide it in a barn. He'd be on his own. He didn't love any of his options. He'd have to figure something out when he got there. He wasn't an FBI agent any longer. He was a retiree with a mend-ing heart. But he'd always been able work through tough scrapes, and he wasn't about to stop believing in himself with his son's life on the line.

"Okay, Haven," he said. "Whatever you say."

Kenney awakened from his nap to the sound of his NetPen firing off an alert. He fumbled for the light in the officer's guest room and grabbed the device, commanding it to read the message.

> **Incoming voice communication from Phillip Piper to Will Piper. Received 18:22 GMT.**
> *Phillip! Where are you? Phillip?*
> I'm his friend.

Kenney listened to the rest of the conversation and laced up his boots. Soon he was flicking the light switches down the hall in the guest dormitory.

His men alerted fast, sparing him the dazed and confused routine.

"Lopez, Harper, get your asses in gear. We're blowing this taco stand. We're going to Kirkby Stephen."

"That a person or a place, chief?" Lopez asked, slipping on his civilian khakis.

"It's a town, jackass. Piper's on the move, and so are we."

Isle of Wight, 1297

Clarissa swung her feet off the bed and paused before standing lest she have a dizzy fit. She pressed her hands against her swollen belly and sang a little ditty to her unborn child, a rhyme her mother had fancied:

> *Diddle, diddle dumpling, my son John,*
> *Went to bed with his trousers on;*
> *One shoe off and one shoe on,*
> *Diddle diddle dumpling, my son, John.*

Sighing, she pushed herself upright, slid her feet into sandals, and shuffled to her water basin.

Her simple morning wash complete, she rapped her knuckles against her locked door and called for Sister Hazel.

The door opened but Sister Hazel wasn't there. Instead it was another nun she'd never seen before.

"Where is Sister Hazel?"

The woman had a thick Germanic accent. "She took ill last night with the flux and is being attended in the infirmary. My name is Sister Ingrid. How may I help you?"

"I would like t' go to the privy closet before I take my morning meal."

The elderly nun seemed flustered and unsure of herself.

"I sent another girl there, did I not? You're not supposed to see or speak to one another. Those are my instructions. Wait here till I come back for you."

Sister Ingrid clopped down the hall in a trot, neglecting to shut or lock the door. From the far end of the dormitory Clarissa heard the sound of a woman crying. Gingerly, she stepped into the corridor to see if anyone was there. When she saw it empty, she began to creep toward the sorry sound.

Some of the doors along the way were closed but others were wide open. Peeking through the open ones she saw rooms identical to hers though unoccupied and unused. The crying grew louder as she approached the last door on her right. She put her head against the wood. A desperate sobbing filled her ear.

It *was* Fay, the turnip-nosed girl she thought she'd heard months ago. She was sure of it.

"Fay? Is that you?"

The crying abruptly stopped. Clarissa heard a muffled, "Who's there?"

"It's me, Clarissa."

Fay said nothing.

"Can I come in?"

"The door's locked!"

She looked down. There was a black key lodged in the lock. She glanced down the hall, turned the key, and slipped in.

Fay was sitting on her bed, alone, her eyes red as beets, tears still flowing despite her newly found quietude. But then the girl saw Clarissa's pregnant belly and she started loudly bawling again.

"Fay," Clarissa said, "what's the matter?"

"They took him!"

"Who?"

"My baby!"

"Why?"

"He was finished suckling," she sobbed, "so they said he was ready."

"Ready for what?"

"To be with his own kind."

"What do you mean, his own kind?"

"You know. Deep in your heart, you know. What happened to me happened to you, didn't it? You saw them down there in that horrible place."

Clarissa had done her best to block that terrible day from her mind and concentrate on her gestating baby. But in her dreams—or nightmares—the smell of the catacombs, the rows of mute, pale, ginger-haired scribes, the shriveled old man who took her as if she were a farm beast—these things came to her in frightening sparks.

"They took your baby down there?" she asked.

Fay bit her lip and nodded.

"What will they do t' him?"

"When he's older and can grasp a quill, he will join the others. That's what I've been told."

"What do they do? What are they writing, anyhow?" Clarissa asked.

Fay went quiet again and wiped her face dry. "They'll tell you when they take your baby away from you. Sister Sabeline told me because she said I'd done good, and they were going to have me do it again. As soon as I'm ready, I'm to go back to the catacombs. But before that, I'll be able to see my son." She sobbed anew. "I miss him so much! He was a quiet one. He wasn't a smiley boy, but I know he loves his mummy."

Clarissa was insistent. "Fay, I want you t' tell me what it is they write."

"It's a secret. One that's been passed along since the early days. Our sons are special-like. They have a gift that comes from God they say. They know when a person will be born and when that person will die. They write that down on parchment, and the monks bind the sheets into great books which they keep under the ground in a library. Our sons are blessed ones. They're holy scribes."

Clarissa shuddered. "There were some of 'em that were really old." She thought of the one who violated her. "Do you mean t' tell me they spend their whole lives under th' ground?"

"I don't know," Fay said. "I think so."

"Well, they're not taking my baby away!" Clarissa declared. "They're not!"

With that, Fay buried her face in her hands and cried a storm.

Clarissa backed away, and once in the hall, she locked Fay's door again for both their sakes. Through an open door and through a window, she saw Sister Ingrid scurrying back to the dormitory.

In an instant, Clarissa made a decision. She removed the key from the latch of the open door and closed her fist around it. Then she ran back to her own room, shut the door behind her, and sat back upon her bed trying to compose herself.

Sister Hazel swung the door open, muttering, "Oh my! I left your door unlocked."

"I did not notice, Sister," Clarissa said. Just then she remembered the key in her fist.

"Well, it matters not. The privy closet is free now. Come with me, girl."

Clarissa rose and pretended to swoon. Dropping to her knees she buried the key into the straw of her mattress.

"Heavens, child! Let me help you!" the nun said, grabbing her by the shoulders.

"It's all right, Sister. The feeling has passed. I'm better already."

From that moment a single thought would come to consume Clarissa's every waking minute.

I will not give up me baby.

I will not give up me baby.

But who was she to stand up to the power of Sister Sabeline and perhaps the Abbot himself? She wasn't even a nun. She was a lowly nonentity. A girl who was useful as a vessel, no more, no less.

And how would she escape from this fortress of an abbey? On an island. In a strange land. Her home far, far away. She could just as easily find the way to see the Pope in Rome as her own village. And if, by chance, she could overcome all these obstacles, how would she survive her journey without benefit of coin?

It was this last consideration she chose to dwell upon. While her father had never deigned to give her a shred of advice, she'd heard him wistfully say time and again how a purse filled with silver could solve any problem if only one would drop into his lap.

Where, she thought, would silver be kept at the Abbey? She'd seen some shiny altar objects at the cathedral, but these were impossibly out of reach. Then it dawned on her: perhaps the Abbot had items of finery and value at his own house.

An audacious plan began to brew in her head, and her desperation drove her to test it one ice-cold January morning well before the dawn. She always slept through the cathedral bells which rang at half past four to call the slumbering inhabitants of Vectis to Lauds, but this morning she awoke.

She prepared herself by lighting a stubby, thick walking candle from her ever-lit room candle. Then she waited until the bells chimed again to mark the beginning of the cathedral service. At the last peal she put her ear to the door, said a quick prayer, and placed her stolen key in the latch hole. She commenced wiggling it and rotating it to dislodge the key she knew was in the other side of the lock. When she heard it drop to the floor with a too-loud clang she got down to the business at hand.

She pushed the purloined key all the way into the mechanism and slowly turned it. There was a clunk as the bolt disengaged. The key worked! She was free!

The vaulted hall was black and deserted and her candle cast wild shadows. She tiptoed through the corridor and left the dormitory, emerging into an icy swirl of snow flurries. She knew the way to the abbot house well enough for it was by the cathedral. A waning half-moon showed itself through gaps in the clouds. She kept to the shadows of buildings and trees cupping the candle with her hand to hide its light from any stray soul who wasn't in the cathedral and to prevent the wind from extinguishing it. She trod deliberately, wary of slipping on the sleety path. The thought of landing on her pregnant belly terrified her.

Her gown was not intended for inclement weather. She reached the abbot house shivering uncontrollably. Over the clattering of her teeth she heard the sweet chants emanating from the cathedral. Baldwin's beautifully carved door yielded easily to her push, and, despite her fear of discovery, she was immediately comforted by the warmth of the fire blazing in the great hearth of his reception chamber.

The fire burned so brightly she hardly needed her puny candle. The room was empty of people but not of objects. No, not of objects. It was replete with all manner of wondrous things: tapestries, colorful rugs, padded furniture, and achingly lovely paintings of Christ the Lord. And silver. Silver candlesticks and plates, and a great silver crucifix on one wall half the size of a man.

In a moment of madness she imagined staying, warming herself thoroughly, immersing herself for a while in the finery of the place. But she shook off the folly and left. She had accomplished her task. She found that the abbot did indeed have silver. Now she only needed to retrace her steps and return to her bedchamber undetected.

Clarissa bided her time, waiting for her courage to build and for the night sky to be moonless. She kept to her routine, doing her ablutions, eating as much as she could for the sake of the baby, and engaging in prayer and meditation. But the nature of her prayers changed. She was no longer reciting her memorized scriptures and psalms; she was praying for the precious life growing within her.

I will not give up me baby.

The month of January passed, and February was upon them. By night, Clarissa kept two blankets over her for warmth and by day wrapped herself in one of them as she paced her room. The purloined key was secreted in her mattress. She didn't think its absence had caused a problem. The day after she stole it another had taken its place. Sister Hazel, absentminded as she was, had probably thought that she herself had misplaced it.

At night, when she visited the privy closet, she took note of the state of the moon. She reckoned that in less than one week, on the twelfth day of February, the moon would be dark. That would be her night.

Leaving the outhouse one night she saw Sister Hazel escorting a new girl by the arm. But it was more than escorting; it was far rougher treatment. The girl was crying and struggling, looking like she might break and run. Clarissa made eye contact with the girl—strong contact. The two of them seemed to stop time and bond in wordless communication.

The girl—no more than sixteen—had small, delicate features, a perfect chin, high cheekbones, and pearl white skin. Her eyes were moist and acutely sad, seemingly calling to Clarissa to come to her aid.

Time unfroze and Clarissa passed by.

Back in the dormitory Clarissa recognized the new girl's room by its open door and unmade bed. She resolved to pay her a nocturnal visit.

That very night she used her stolen key to go to her. As quietly as she could, she unlocked the girl's door and entered.

The girl was awake, propped up high in her bed, illuminated well enough by the candle on her nightstand for Clarissa to see she looked like a frightened, motherless fawn.

Clarissa put her finger to her lips and hushed her. "Don't be scared. I'm just down the hall."

"How did you get out of your room?" the girl asked.

"Promise not t' tell?"

The girl nodded.

"I stole a key. I can come and go as I please,"

she declared proudly. "As long as I'm right careful. What's your name?"

"Elizabeth."

"I'm Clarissa."

"You're with child," Elizabeth said.

"Well along. Two months to go, maybe three."

"How did it happen?" Elizabeth asked.

Clarissa hesitated at that. The girl looked too petrified to tell her the truth. "The usual way these things happen."

"Did they take you down to the crypts?"

"How do you know of that!" Clarissa exclaimed, catching herself speaking too loudly.

"Other girls were talking. They'd heard of dark doings in such a place though none had ever gone there."

"I can attest that it exists, but more than that I won't say," Clarissa said.

Elizabeth responded to her admission by crying. Clarissa sat upon her bed and offered the comfort of a held hand.

Suddenly, Elizabeth staunched her tears, and asked, "This key of yours. Can you use it to give me the pleasure of stealing a few moments of company with another?"

"Who?" Clarissa asked.

"A young monk. His name is Luke."

Clarissa was stunned. "What will you do with this monk?"

"Do? Nothing but talk, though I think I may love him. We have seen each other time to time on the abbey grounds and have exchanged but a few words. But I can tell he is smitten by me, and I myself have an ache in my heart I can only believe is love. I will ask him to take me away from this place. I do not want to suffer your fate, Clarissa."

"My fate," Clarissa repeated softly, dropping Elizabeth's hand and rubbing her own pregnant belly. "I am not altogether a servant to my fate. They aim to take my baby away from me when he is born and suckled. I will not let that happen. I aim to leave this place too."

"And go where?"

"Home. In the north country. Cumberland."

Elizabeth grabbed her hand back. "Will you help me, dear Clarissa? Will you help me see my Luke?"

Clarissa said nothing while pondering the matter. Finally, she answered, "In five days time, when the moon is dark, I will be leaving here. I'll give you my key then, and you may do with it as you want."

Elizabeth grabbed Clarissa's hand again and squeezed it so hard it ached. "You're like an angel who's come to me in my hour of need."

"I'm no angel. I'm just a lass like you who wants t' go home."

On the twelfth of February, the night was dark, cold, and cloudy. Clarissa made her final preparations and waited for the cathedral bells to summon all worshippers to the cathedral.

For the past week she'd been requesting extra food and had hidden nonperishables like dried fruit and hard bread in a kerchief, which she stashed under her mattress. When the dormitory was quiet and locked, she bundled the foodstuffs into her spare blanket. Rolled with its ends tied together, it made a fine across-the-chest shoulder bag to hold provisions and booty for her journey.

When the bells rang she waited just long enough for worship to begin. Then, clutching her small candle, she used her key to free herself for the last time.

Quiet as a flea, she unlocked a door down the hall and entered Elizabeth's room. The pretty girl was waiting for her, fully dressed. "You came!"

"I told you I would. Now, take my key. I'll lock you in when I leave but use the key to let yourself out. I beg you t' wait for a good while before you exit. In case you're caught, say nothing about me and tell them you stole th' key. I must have time to get off th' isle. Will you promise?"

"I'll do as you ask, dear Clarissa."

"You'll meet your young monk then?"

"In the stables. I managed to speak to him this afternoon when I went outside to the privy closet. He was waiting nearby in case I emerged. Blessedly, Sister Hazel was attending to another girl with a fever."

Clarissa embraced her and kissed her cheek. "Then good luck to you, Elizabeth. Be careful. I wish you a long and happy life."

"And I wish you the same. I will pray you make it home safely."

Clarissa patted her tense belly. "I beg you to pray that both of us make it home safely."

Clarissa crept from the dormitory and followed the rehearsed route to the abbot house, where she found everything exactly as it had been during her scouting mission. She helped herself to a pair of silver candlesticks and a silver plate, its rim encrusted with jewel stones. She could not and dared not take more. Her blanket bag was now considerably heavier as she slipped from the abbot house and made her way to the main abbey gate.

She quenched her candle and let her eyes grow accustomed to the darkness. Through the predawn murk she could see the rudiments of the great iron portcullis that secured the entry arch. She prayed the gate was unattended, but if not, her plan was to heave a stone and hope a dim-witted gatekeeper went looking for the source of the noise.

As it happened, the gate was not attended but that created a different problem, one Clarissa had not anticipated. The iron portcullis grate was fully lowered. How would she ever pass? Certainly, she was in no condition to climb over!

Tucked against one of the archway pillars was an iron ratchet wheel. Her heart was beating out of her chest as she grabbed the cranking handle and turned it. With all her weight into it, the wheel moved and ratcheted a turn. The grate raised a mite.

It seemed she'd be able to manage the infernal machine but it wouldn't do to run off with the gate left open. Someone would notice, and she'd be caught!

An idea came to her which immediately she ascribed to God's helping hand. A dried branch lay nearby, blown from a tree overhanging the abbey wall. She took the branch and commenced ratcheting the wheel again until the gate was lifted just enough for her to be able to slither underneath on her back. With her shoulder pressing hard against the crank shaft she slid the branch between the ratchet and the nearest tooth of the wheel. When the branch was in place she eased her shoulder off the shaft and heard cracking as the weight of the ratchet crushed the tree limb. But it held the gate in position.

Quickly she got to the ground, lay on her back and with sandaled feet, pushed herself under the portcullis with the terrifying cracking and popping sound of a pinched branch in her ears. If it fell, her baby would be the first to be pierced, and both of them would die a sad, painful death.

Mercifully, she cleared the gap and rose triumphantly at the other side of the abbey wall. Then with all the strength in her body she pulled down on the grate with both hands and hung from it.

There was a snap and the branch gave way, followed by a ground-shaking thud as the portcullis slammed shut.

She turned her back on Vectis Abbey and looked for the path to the ferry.

Horses shuffled and whinnied when Luke, a brawny young monk, came into the stables. It was black and cold, and he was frightened by his own boldness for even being there. "Hello?" he called out in a half whisper. "Is anybody here?"

A small voice answered, "I'm here, Luke. At the end."

Luke used the slice of moonlight penetrating the open stable door to find her. Elizabeth was in the stall of a large bay mare, huddling beside its belly for warmth.

"Thank you for coming," she said. "I was afraid you wouldn't." She wasn't crying anymore. It was too cold for that.

"You are freezing," he said.

"Am I?" She held out her arm. When he felt her alabaster wrist, he encircled it with his hand and would not let go.

"Yes. You are."

"Will you kiss me, Luke?"

"I cannot!"

"Please."

The young monk looked distressed. "Why do you torture me? You know I cannot. I have taken my vows! Besides, I came to hear your plight. When last we met, you spoke of crypts." He let go and pulled away.

"Please do not be angry at me. I am to be taken to the crypts tomorrow."

"For what purpose?"

"They want me to lie with a man, something I have never done," she cried. "Other girls have suffered this fate. I have met them. They have birthed babies that are taken from them when they are suckled. Some girls are used as birth mothers again and again until they lose their minds. Please do not let this happen to me!"

"This cannot be true!" Luke exclaimed. "This is a place of God!"

"It is the truth. There are secrets at Vectis. Have you not heard the stories?"

"I have heard many things, but I have seen nothing with my own eyes. I believe what I see."

"But you believe in God," she said. "And you have not seen Him."

"That is different!" he protested. "I do not need to see Him. I feel His presence."

She was growing desperate. She composed herself and reached for his hand, which, in an unguarded moment, he allowed her to grasp. "Please, Luke, lie down with me, here in the straw."

She carried his hand to her bosom and pressed it there. He felt the firm flesh through her cloak, and his ears filled with rushing blood. He looked like he wanted to close his palm around the sweet globe, and for a moment, he almost did. Then he regained his senses and recoiled, banging into the side of the stall.

Her eyes were wild. "Please, Luke, don't go! If you lie with me, they will not take me to the crypts. I'll be of no use to them."

"And what would happen to me!" he hissed. "I would be cast out! I will not do this. I am a man of God! Please, I must leave you now!"

As he ran from the stables, Elizabeth's soft wails mixed discordantly with the neighing of disturbed horses.

Clarissa was sure she was on the right path because the sound of the sea grew ever louder in her ears. At the water's edge, the ferry boat was tied up against a wooden pier for the night. Bedside the pier was a small cottage, its windows black. The ferryman was asleep, she reckoned, but when he woke at dawn, she would be there to make him an offer.

In the morning, storm clouds lay low and heavy over the island. Luke had lain awake through the night, fitful and troubled. At Lauds, it was almost impossible to concentrate on his hymns and psalms and, in the brief interval before he was obliged to return to the cathedral for the Prime Office, he rushed through his chores.

Finally, he could bear it no more. He quietly approached his superior, Brother Martin, clutching his stomach and asking for permission to forgo Prime and attend the infirmary.

Permission granted, he put up his hood and chose a circuitous route to the forbidden buildings. He picked a large maple tree on a nearby knoll, close enough to watch but far enough to conceal himself. From that vantage point, he stood guard in the raw, gray mist.

He heard the bells ring for Prime.

No one came or left the chapel-sized building.

He heard the bells ring again to signify the end of the office.

All was quiet. He wondered how long he could pass unnoticed and what the consequence of his subterfuge would be. He would accept his punishment, but he was hopeful that God would treat him with a small measure of love and understanding for his pitiful frailties.

The bark was rough on his cheek. Consumed with fatigue, he dozed briefly but awoke with a start when his skin chafed on the jagged surface.

He saw her coming down the path, led by Sister Sabeline as if towed by a rope. Even from a distance, he could tell she was crying.

At least this part of her tale was true.

The two women disappeared through the front door of the chapel.

His pulse quickened. He clenched his fists and softly beat them against the tree trunk. He prayed for guidance.

Crouching behind a bush, Clarissa watched as the dawn sky seemed to touch the sea and bring it to life. The wind picked up, and the waves rolled higher and stronger. She feared the ferry might not embark into the peril of a storm.

The thin wisps of smoke from the ferryman's chimney turned heavy. He was stirring. The effluent of a chamber pot was flung from a window, and, before long, the ferryman emerged, his eyes on his ship and the heaving waters.

She stood and approached with a tacked-on expression of cheer to belie her fugitive status.

"Good sir. I would like passage this morning," she said.

"And who might you be?" the hoary seaman asked.

"Just a lass from Newport who must reunite with her husband."

"You been here all night?"

"Nay, sir, I've just arrived after spending a night with a relation in Fishbourne."

"You don't sound like you're from Newport," the man said.

She thought quickly. "I was born up north."

The ferryman tugged at his beard. "It's rough this morning, and I see no other passengers. It's hardly worth my while to risk my boat on one lass."

She looked at the brightening sky. Sister Hazel would soon be coming by with morning victuals, and she'd be found out. She lost the pretense of good humor. "I must go now! I cannot wait. I can pay. I can pay handsomely."

The seaman arched one brow skeptically and asked to see evidence of her claim.

She knelt and unrolled her blanket just enough to produce one of the candlesticks. "I can give you this," she said.

He took it and felt its heft in his hand then scratched at it with a thumbnail. "It's a fine piece of silver, it is. Did you steal it?"

"I did not! It was a gift from my relations."

His smirk was evidence enough of his nonbelief, but he pressed her no further. "Is there more treasure in that blanket of yours?"

"No more for you, sir. That is more than enough for a ferry ride I reckon. I have a long journey to the north country, and I will meet other men who will want to be paid for their services."

He shifted the candlestick from hand to hand while considering his decision, then said, "Right then. Prepare yourself for rough passage. If you've eaten, you'll lose it, that's for certain."

She nodded and silently thanked God.

Come my baby, we're going to sail away from this place.

"I'd like to keep more of that treasure of yours in *my* family," the ferryman said. "On the other side, I'll bring you to my brother, who has a horse and a cart. If I know him, for silver like this he'll take you where you want to go."

Sister Sabeline pulled a terrified Elizabeth through the chapel door and led her down a stairway that plunged into a netherworld.

Like a lamb to the slaughter, Elizabeth was shepherded through the Hall of the Writers, where one puny, spindly youth raised his ginger head and grunted, and from there she was led into the sickening void that was the catacombs.

Inside, candlelight flared against grotesque skulls, and the old nun had to use both arms to keep the fair-haired girl upright.

They were not alone. Someone was beside the girl. Elizabeth whirled around to see the dumb blank face and green eyes of the young writer blocking the passageway. Sister Sabeline withdrew. Her sleeve brushed the leg bones of a corpse, and they clattered musically. The nun held the candle high and watched from a short distance. Elizabeth was panting in fear. The ginger-haired man stood inches away, his arms limp by his sides. Seconds passed. Sister Sabeline called to him in frustration, "I have brought this girl for you!" Nothing happened. More time passed, and the nun demanded, "Touch her!"

Elizabeth closed her eyes, bracing for the touch of a living skeleton.

Suddenly, she felt a hand on her shoulder, but it was not cold and bony, it was warm and reassuring.

Elizabeth heard Sister Sabeline shrieking, "What are you doing here! What are you doing!"

She opened her eyes, and, magically, the face she saw was Luke's. The ginger-haired man was on the ground where Luke had roughly shoved him.

"Brother Luke, leave us!" Sabeline screamed. "You have violated a sacred place!"

"I will not leave without this girl," Luke said defiantly. "How can this be sacred? All I see is evil."

"You do not understand!" the nun screamed.

From the hall, they heard a sudden pandemonium.

Heavy thuds and crashes followed by flopping and thrashing sounds as if great fish had been hauled onto land.

Elizabeth's ginger-haired youth turned away and walked toward the noise.

"What is happening?" Luke asked.

Sister Sabeline did not answer. She took her candle and rushed toward the hall, leaving them alone in the dark.

"Are you safe?" Luke asked her tenderly. He was still touching her shoulder. He had never let go.

"You came for me," she whispered.

He helped her find her way from the darkness into the light, into the hall.

It was no longer the Hall of the Writers.

It was a place of gruesome death.

The only living soul was Sister Sabeline, whose shoes were soaked with blood. She aimlessly walked among a sea of bodies, draped on the tables and cots, crumpled in piles on the ground, a mass of lifelessness and quivering involuntary twitching.

She had a glassy expression, and could only mutter, "My God, my God, my God, my God," over and over, in the cadence of a chant.

The whole chamber was slowly filling with the blood that was spurting from the quill-pierced eyes of scores of ginger-haired men and boys.

All of them dead or dying, and at the center of the carnage was the ancient scribe Titus, with his quill buried so deeply it looked like a feather was growing from his eye.

Luke led Elizabeth by her hand through the carnage where he had the presence of mind to glance at the parchments that lay on the writing tables, some of them soaking up puddles of blood. How could he know that, many years hence, the small act of grabbing one of the parchments would come to save Elizabeth from ruin and destitution long after his own demise?

They ran up the winding stairs, through the chapel, and out into the mist and rain. They kept running until they were far from the abbey gate. Only then did they stop to catch their breaths and listen to the cathedral bells pealing out an alarm.

In the distance, the ferry boat was coming back to the isle from its first run of the day. People were milling by the pier waiting for passage. Luke felt in his robe for the few coins he had kept when first he had journeyed to Vectis as a young man seeking the cloth. He and Elizabeth would join the queue and leave the horror of the morning behind.

The hem of the Abbot Baldwin's white robe was soaked with blood. Each time he stooped to touch a cold forehead or make the sign of the cross over a supine body, his garment got bloodier.

Prior Felix, a burly Breton with a black, bristling beard, was at Baldwin's side, supporting him by the arm so the abbot wouldn't tumble on the blood-slicked stones. They made their rounds through the carnage, pausing over each ginger-haired writer to check for signs of life, but there were none. The only other beating heart in the Hall of the Writers belonged to old Brother Bartholomew, the keeper of the underground Library, who was making his own grim inspection at the opposite end of the chamber. Baldwin had sent Sister Sabeline away because her hysterical crying was unnerving and preventing him from collecting his thoughts.

"They are dead," Baldwin said. "All dead. Why in God's name has this happened?"

Bartholomew was systematically going from row to row, stepping carefully over and around bodies, trying to keep his footing. For an old man, he was moving briskly from one station to another, plucking manuscript pages off the table and making a stack of them in his hand.

He made his way to Baldwin, clutching a ream of parchments.

"Look," the old man said. "Look!" He laid the pages down.

Baldwin picked up one and read it.

Then the next, and the next. He fanned the pages out on the table to see more of them quickly.

Each page carried the date 9 February 2027, with the identical inscription.

"*Finis Dierum*," Baldwin said, "End of Days."

Felix trembled. "So this is when the end will come."

Bartholomew half smiled at the revelation. "Their work was done."

Baldwin gathered up the pages and held them to his breast. "Our work is not yet done, Brothers. They must be laid to rest in the crypt. Then I will say a mass in their honor. The Library must be sealed, and the chapel must be burned. The world is not ready to know what has happened here."

Felix and Bartholomew quickly nodded in agreement as the abbot turned to leave.

"The Year 2027 is far in the future," Baldwin said wearily. "At least, mankind has a very long time to prepare for the End of Days."

Prior Felix began his lamentable chores.

He oversaw the placement of the slain writers into their crypts and walked through the vastness of the Library amidst endless shelves of sacred books.

With a heavy heart, he climbed the stone stairs into the chapel for the last time, clutching the pages upon which were writ *Finis Dierum*. He would use these as holy tinder.

At his direction, bales of hay were carted to the chapel and placed around its perimeter.

When the job was done, he called for a torch and glumly lowered his head, awaiting its arrival.

He lifted his eyes at the sound of Sister Sabeline calling his name. She was coming from the special dormitory, with Sister Hazel in tow.

The two nuns were wide-eyed and puffing at their exertions.

"Tell him!" Sister Sabeline demanded. "Tell him what has happened."

Sister Hazel wheezed and sputtered until she was able to form the words. "One of the girls, Clarissa by name, heavy with child, she was. She's gone!"

"What do you mean, gone?" Felix asked with the weariness of a man who had just lived through a cataclysm.

"She must have stolen a key and run away after last night's supper," Sister Hazel said.

"That's not all she stole!" Sister Sabeline added.

"There's silver gone missing from Abbot Baldwin's house. This wicked girl's planned her escape well. I sent a brother to the ferry. The girl sailed at dawn though the ferryman wouldn't say how she paid."

"If this is so, she's not the only one who's left," Felix said, blinking at the revelation. "Her unborn child has also left, the child of Titus the Venerable. In the long history of the Library, a scribe has never left, born or unborn. And now it has happened!"

Felix looked at the bundle of parchments in his fist, and muttered, "Why did they take their lives as they did? Was it because they had in their travails recorded the last day of life on this earth and had no more to write? Or was it because they sensed a great rift caused by one of their number being snatched from their midst? Was it *their* End of Days?"

Sister Sabeline covered her face with her hands and sobbed.

"I think we shall never know," Felix said.

Felix lit the parchment pages with the torch and used them to set the hay alight. He watched as the timbers were consumed by fire and saw the building collapse upon itself.

But he did not, as Abbot Baldwin had instructed, throw a torch down into the vaults.

He told himself that he could not bear witness to the destruction of the Library. He told himself that this decision should rest solely in the hands of God Almighty.

He stayed on the spot for the rest of the day, gazing at the smoldering ground, uncertain whether the great Library had been destroyed by the conflagration. Only when the bells chimed for Vespers did he leave the patch of hot earth to quench his soul in prayer in the winter cold of the cathedral.

Walking through the shrouded fields, Will could only sense the foreboding presence of the undulating fells looming over them. Haven was quick and sure-footed so he had to use his long legs to keep up with the beam of her flashlight.

He hated being unarmed. His Glock retired when he did, stashed away, clean and oiled in a small safe he kept in the engine room of his boat. He didn't even have a penknife on him. The only things in his pockets were car keys.

In his younger days he'd been highly rated in hand-to-hand combat, not because he was the quickest guy on the mats but because he was so damned big. When he would get his fists and feet in motion he was a buzz saw. But now was under doctor's orders to keep his heart rate under 130. Like it or not, his best weapon was going to be his brain.

"Are we close?" he asked.

"Not far."

With that, Haven clicked off her flashlight and slowed so Will could follow in the blackness.

In the distance, there was a glowing window.

"Is that Lightburn Farm?" he asked.

"Yeah. Quiet now."

They'd been walking parallel to the road, but now the girl steered them away upland at roughly a forty-five-degree angle. The tall grass was heavy with frost and Will had to high-step to avoid tripping on a clump.

A shape materialized, a few shades darker than the night. Closing on it, Will saw that it was some kind of barn or storage building. The farmhouse was a good two hundred meters down the slope.

It was a small, open-sided barn, a hangar, with a sloping slate roof made of the same stone as everything else in the valley. Haven entered one of the bays, and Will cautiously followed.

There was little to be seen, just a few bales of hay and some long-poled farm implements. He scanned the interior for a weapon—a hammer, a scythe, an axe—but there was nothing suitable. Should he grab a rake? He thought not.

"What's the deal?" he asked the girl.

"Th' deal?"

"What is this place? Where's Phillip."

"Help me shift th' hay," was her answer.

They pushed the heavy bales to the side and Haven shined her beam onto the floor. An iron ring lay in a circular recess. She stooped and tugged at it, grunting, "It's heavy."

Will intervened and took hold of the ring. The hatch creaked on its hinges and yielded. He laid it down flat. Without light, there was only a dimensionless void; with the benefit of the flashlight, there were stairs. Rough wooden stairs, a long straight run of them pitched at a steep angle.

"Let's go," she said. "Mind your step."

"No electricity?" he asked.

"When we get down, there's light. Swing th' hatch back after yourself."

He counted stairs and tried to keep track of the depths to which they were descending. At the last step, he decided they were about ten meters below the surface.

They were in an anteroom of sorts, a limestone box hewn from the natural bedrock, the pickax swipes left rough. There was an old door. This one was locked. He watched Haven press on a section of wood above the keyhole until she found the right spot. A small panel swiveled open; there was a key in its hollow.

Very clever, he thought. Hidden in plain sight.

The lock yielded with a clunk, and she slowly swung the door open and switched on a light. They were in a much larger room, also low-ceilinged, but this one was a storage area lined with cheap metal bookcases stocked with all manner of goods. In the yellow glow of old-fashioned incandescent bulbs Will saw a trove of tinned and dried foods, jerry cans marked "water," and rolls of toilet paper. It looked for all the world like a survivalist's bomb shelter.

He was about to ask her if that's what it was when he noticed another set of shelves. These were packed with reams of printer paper and boxes of Papermate Black Biro pens.

"What the hell?" he said.

Haven hushed him. "We've got t' be quiet now. Really quiet. We're going through th' next door. You're going t' see another room, but we're not going t' turn on th' lights. I'll use th' torch again. It's quite a big room, but it should be empty."

"Should be?"

"Should be," she repeated. " 'Cept for Phillip."

Will felt prickly with anticipation. "Then let's go."

She switched off the lights in the storage room and opened the other door at its far end. She held her hand over the business end of the flashlight, torch restricting the beam to the space between her fingers.

This new room was warmer than the other though not by much and just as dark. As they walked down the middle of the room, Will made out what was lining the walls: beds. Low camp beds with pillows and blankets in heaps. All of them empty.

At the far end of the room, Will saw a rectangle of orange on the ceiling. Drawing closer, he realized there was a partition, a pen made of walls that didn't reach the full height of the room.

There was a humming sound. The orange glow was coming from a space heater, he thought. Someone was being kept warm.

Phillip.

He tried to prepare himself.

He'd have to postpone his normal impulses to greet him loudly and volubly, to give him a great hug, to transition at speed to a scorching scolding.

This was going to be a snatch and run. He'd save the father-son thing for later.

They'd leave the way they came in. Hopefully, Phillip was in good shape and could make it on his own steam. If not, Will was prepared to put his healing heart to the test and do a fireman's carry. Once outside, he'd take Haven's flashlight and send her on her way and get to the car as fast as they could.

He'd leave it to the police to figure out what the hell was going on underneath Lightburn Farm.

Drawing closer, he heard a low, guttural rasp. Snoring. Phillip asleep.

Will picked up the pace to cut in front of Haven and in a few long strides he was at the flimsy door to the partitioned space. He pulled it open. There were several camp beds inside, one occupied.

He dropped to a knee, felt for a shoulder under a

rough blanket, turned the sleeper from his side to his back and peeled the blanket back from his face.

He heard Haven say, "Oh God!"

In the orange light he saw a face, but not Phillip's.

It was the face of another young man, who awoke with springing eyelids revealing bright green eyes.

At that instant, Will felt a blinding pain on the crown of his head and he went down very hard and very fast.

When he awoke, he thought he was back in the hospital. There was the same disorientation as after his heart attack. He knew who he was but he didn't have the foggiest idea where he was or what had happened to him. Had he had another coronary? Or was he awakening from his first? Had everything he thought had transpired merely been a dream?

But the ache was in his head, not in his chest. He tried to touch the spot with his right hand but he couldn't get to it. Something was keeping his hand from reaching higher than his shoulder. In the low light he tried to figure out why and found himself staring curiously at an iron manacle around his wrist. It was then that he realized he was lying on his back, and recent memories began to flood back.

"Dad?"

He turned his head and there, sitting on a second bed inside the partition was Phillip.

"Phillip," Will said weakly.

"You okay?" the boy asked with a concerned look.

"I'm not sure. How the heck are you?"

"Reasonably shitty," the boy said. "This wasn't supposed to work out like this."

Will tugged at his manacle. "You think?"

"Kheelan saw you and Haven in the fields."

"Her uncle, right?"

"He's big, and he doesn't have a sense of humor."

"Is he the one who nailed me?"

"Uh-huh."

"You sure the girl wasn't in on this?"

"I'm sure," Phillip insisted. "She's not like that. She's in big trouble now. I hope they don't punish her too bad."

Will swung his feet over the low bunk and discovered that his left hand was free. He used it to rub at the painful area on his head and discovered a sticky patch of coagulating blood. "Are you chained up?"

Phillip showed him his manacle. "It sucks. They let you go to the bathroom, if you want to call it a bathroom, but that's pretty much it. It's really boring."

The boy didn't look bored. He looked scared.

"Did they hurt you?" Will asked.

"No."

"You sure?"

"I said no."

"I got your emergency beacon," Will said.

Phillip pursed his lips, and Will could see he was struggling to keep himself from losing it. "Thanks for finding me."

Will remembered the storage room chock-full of provisions and the blank-faced young man who had been lying on the bunk that Phillip occupied. He waved his hand at the rows of empty beds in the dimly lit chamber. "What goes on here?"

"You don't know?" Phillip asked.

"Phillip," he said testily, "I don't know a damned thing. I don't know why you ran away. I don't know why we're being held. I don't know what the hell is going on in this goddamned farm in the middle of goddamned nowhere. So if you'd care to enlighten me, I'd be much obliged."

Phillip shrugged. "I just thought you were further along."

"Well I'm not!"

"Okay, okay, I'll tell you what I know, but first tell me one thing. Does Mom know where we are? Is the SWAT team coming?"

Will softened his tone. There was palpable fear in the boy's voice, and it was time to stop being an irritable jerk and time to be a father. "She doesn't know. No one knows. There's no SWAT team, just you and me, kiddo. We've got to get ourselves out of this. I don't know about you, but I think we'll make a pretty good team. But first I've got to know what we're up against."

Phillip nodded and was about to speak when the door opened, and two men swept in.

Daniel Lightburn, his arm still in a sling, had a poisonous look on his face. The other man, Kheelan Lightburn, was taller by a head, with the same straight black hair as his brother. His clothes were dirty, and his boots were muddy. Will locked onto the frightening size of Kheelan's fists and the complete absence of animation in his face. At best, he's dull-normal, Will thought. At worst, he's a psychopath.

Will liked to seize the high ground even when the chips were against him, so before one of them could say anything, he said, "Hello, Daniel. Nice to see you again. And this handsome guy must be Kheelan."

"Shut it," Daniel said.

"So tell me, Kheelan, did you use a club on me or just one of those hams attached to your wrists?"

"Let me ask *you* something, Mr. Piper," Daniel said. "Do you want t' get kilt in front of th' lad?"

Will had the information he needed: their captors weren't screwing around. They meant business. He adjusted himself to the situation. "No, let me tell *you* something, Daniel. The police and MI5 are on the way here. Things will go a lot better for you if you let us go. And if that's too much for you, let the boy go."

"I very much doubt it," Daniel said. "Haven tells me you agreed t' come on your own. You wouldn't have risked a cocked-up police operation on account of Phillip here."

"The MI5 are pros."

"Are they now?" Daniel said with a harsh laugh. "Maybe down in London, but not up here. Just to be safe, I searched you good for bugs or whatever they're called. Bashed your mobile phone for good measure."

Will said, "Look, friend, you can think whatever you want about the authorities, but you tell me, what do you think your move is?"

Kheelan spat back in an accent even thicker than his brother's, "Our move, marra, is t' keep you lot in chains till we decide when t' finish ya."

"I told you he was a real comedian," Phillip said, shakily.

The threat didn't much unsettle Will, but he hated that his son was inside a pressure cooker. Will knew full well that he, Phillip, and Nancy were all BTH. He'd never told Phillip—it wasn't the kind of thing he ever wanted to talk about with his son—but if he thought the goon's threats were getting to the kid, he'd tell him the score when they were alone.

"This isn't the kind of thing you can get away with," Will said evenly. "You will be found. You will be caught. You'll go to jail, and whoever in your family is complicit will do time as well. You will lose this farm. Whatever operation you've got going on here will be shut down. Trust me. These are facts."

"Mebbe so," Daniel said. "But the Horizon's

coming, in'it? That's what you're famous for, Mr. Will Piper. If we do go t' jail, our sentences'll end next February, won't they?"

With that, Daniel and Kheelan started laughing so hard they appeared loose-limbed.

"What's so damned funny?" It was a woman's voice, and Cacia came through the door, carrying a tray of food. Trailing behind her, Haven carried another tray of drinks.

Daniel challenged her. "Why'd you let Haven out of her room?"

"She's been cryin' her eyes out," Cacia said. "She feels bad about what happened t' Mr. Piper. And she wanted to see th' lad."

"She should be feeling bad about what she done t' us!" Kheelan shouted. "She's brought in offcomers! She's ruined us! She's a wicked creature who needs t' pay!"

"How-ee then!" Daniel shouted back. "She's my daughter, and I'm th' one who'll decide what's t' be done."

Kheelan lowered his voice. "I'm just sayin' "

"Get out now, you two," Cacia said, shooing her husband and brother-in-law out. "Go and keep watch with Andrew and Douglas. And make sure his car's well hid. We'll tend t' this lot."

The men silently assented and left.

Will decided to stay quiet and observe mother and daughter for a few moments. He couldn't tell if Cacia wore the pants in the family, but she was a force to be reckoned with, that was certain. He could see the masseter muscles in her face rippling as she clenched and unclenched her jaw. Was it in anger or frustration? Was her ire aimed at them or her own?

But Will had no doubt about her feelings toward her daughter. She passed instructions to Haven with tenderness. The girl might have gone rogue, but it seemed as if no transgression would be enough for Cacia to withdraw a mother's love.

Will also caught the furtive glances going on between the girl and Phillip. As Haven laid out a meal for the boy her face radiated sunshine. And Phillip responded in kind. Will could understand why. The girl was very pretty and shy, not the kind of out-there, brash girl his son hung around with in Virginia and Florida.

"Are you all right, Mr. Piper," Cacia asked. "Were you hurt bad?"

"I'm a little sore, ma'am. But I've been cracked a few times. Makes the skull thicker."

"Does it now? Well, have some soup and bread while they're hot. What do you think about having your father here, Phillip?"

He replied through a mouthful of warm bread, "It's good, I guess."

"You've got to let us go, Mrs. Lightburn," Will said.

"I hate being called that. Would you call me Cacia?"

"I hate being called Mr. Piper."

"Okay, Will," she laughed. "I wish t' God we could set ya free. I wish t' God Haven had talked t' me before luring your son over 'ere. I wish none of this'd happened, but it did, and we've got t' deal wit' it."

"Are you going to tell me what you do here?" Will asked placidly.

"Aye, I will," she answered. "In the morning, I'll tell ya, and I'll show ya."

I've lost him," Annie told her superior.

"What do you mean, you've lost him?" the voice boomed over her NetPen's speaker.

"He lifted my car keys and took off. I don't know why, and I don't know where he's gone. We came up empty today. It's not like we identified any good leads."

"Maybe he saw something you didn't," the voice said caustically. "He may be retired, but in his day, he was one of the best. But you wouldn't know that, would you, as you weren't born then?"

Annie took a breath and maintained a professional tone. "What would you like me to do, sir?"

"I'd like you to mobilize the police and find the man. I'm sending a team up there led by Rob Melrose. When they arrive, brief him, then follow his orders. I should have sent him in the first place."

"Yes, sir," she replied through gritted teeth.

"And I will brief Piper's wife in Washington, who will, in all likelihood, remove some vital parts of my anatomy."

Kenney tried to straighten his legs out, but there wasn't enough room. "Is this seat back as far as it'll go?" he asked no one in particular.

Harper was driving, relying on GPS navigation, which delivered instructions via a curiously sexy British voice. "We're almost there, chief."

Lopez was crunched into the backseat, his knees bent up. All three men had short hair, and with their jeans, sweaters, and leather jackets, they looked as American as they come. "No point in trying to look like Brits," Kenney had told them. "Couldn't do it if we tried. We're tourists, if anyone asks."

"Yeah, that'll work," Harper had replied, rolling his eyes. "Tourists with a trunk load of weapons and ammo."

Lopez started to snore.

Kenney reached behind and backhanded the side of his big head. "Keep sharp, for Christ's sake."

Lopez awoke with a sharp inhalation. "Sorry, chief."

"Hey," Kenney scolded, "I'm beat too, we're all as tired as a one-legged man in an ass-kicking contest, but we're on a mission."

Lopez's communicator beeped. "Surveillance alert. Subject Anne Locke, MI5 comm protocol. Decoding now."

"See, what did I tell you?" Kenney said.

Lopez grunted and turned up the volume.

As the three men drove through the dark countryside, they listened to a recording of Annie's conversation with her station chief in London about a missing Will Piper.

"Piper's three steps ahead of those clowns," Kenney said. "He's probably found his son. The question is, what the hell did his son find."

Lightburn Farm, 1297

The contractions were coming every few minutes now. The nether reaches of her body were ablaze with searing pain and she prayed to God the baby would come soon, or if that was not God's will, that her life would mercifully end.

Clarissa was on her back beside the family hearth, knees up on a heap of woolen blankets. She could barely hear the exhortations of her mother or the encouragements of her sisters.

All she could do was try to let her mind drift onto other things.

The journey from the southern shores of Britain to the north country had taken six weeks. Adam, the brother of the ferryman, proved to be a kind and faithful companion. It had struck Clarissa that the payment she had arranged was inequitable. The ferryman received a silver candlestick for making a two-hour crossing in rough seas. The cart man received the matching candlestick for six weeks of slogging on rutted roads, often sleeping in the open while allowing Clarissa to shelter in his lean-to. But Adam suffered the labors cheerfully, dodging highwaymen, changing horseshoes himself, negotiating meager rations in village after village. He was a poor man, far worse off than his nautical brother, and the silver, he told her, would transform the lowly state of his family. Why doesn't he just kill me and take the candlestick, she had thought? The answer, she had learned, was that he was a good, honest man, pure of heart and now, in her agony, she took comfort in remembering his goodness. "I'll get you and your baby home," he'd say time and again. "You can count on me."

In the final days of her journey to Yorkshire, upon entering the wild terrain of the dales, her heart had been stirred by a landscape she had thought she would never see again.

A single lamentable road led into the heart of the dales, but it petered out well short of her farm. Only sheep tracks penetrated deeper into the hills, and sometimes even these faded away and were lost. Clarissa and Adam had persisted, and, with the help of shepherds, they finally found their way to Pinn and the very threshold of Clarissa's farm.

Her father had been the first to see her climbing from the back of the cart, ripe with child. He had called for his wife and daughters, and soon, Clarissa was surrounded by joyful, crying women.

Her flinty father had looked as disgusted as she had ever remembered. "Is this th' father?" he had asked, pointing disapprovingly at Adam.

"Heavens no!" Clarissa had cried.

"Who then?" he had demanded.

Clarissa had sobbed and delivered the half-true story she had rehearsed in her mind. "It was a monk who done it. He took me by force. I had t' run away."

Adam was supped and his horse fed and watered. He loaded his cart with hay for the return journey and hugged his charge. "You take care of yourself and that baby," Adam had told her. "He's had a rough start to life, but that don't mean he won't be a big, important man once he's growed."

No sooner had Adam departed than Clarissa's father began complaining. Now there was one more and in time, two new mouths to feed! And she wouldn't be able-bodied for a spell. Her return was a pox on the Lightburns!

When he got so red in the face she feared he might do something terrible, she unrolled her blanket and presented him with the abbot's silver plate, its rim set with clusters of fine gemstones.

Her father grasped it, his eyes widening in amazement, and his knees buckled under his own weight. Kneeling, he sobbed, "It's me purse o' silver! I don't know how ya came t' have this, and I won't never ask. All I know is that th' Lightburns are now among the richest families in Cumberland. I welcome ya home, dear daughter, you and your bairn."

With a rush of blood and straw-colored fluid, the baby's head, then its shoulders, cleared her birth canal.

Her mother held it up for inspection and milked the cord before tying it with a strip of sheep hide.

Clarissa's sisters whispered to one another. The baby was curiously placid and noncrying. It had a striking shock of ginger hair and green eyes.

"It's a boy, all right," her mother declared. "Here, take him."

Clarissa clutched the slimy infant to her sweaty breast and said, "I knew he was a boy. His name'll be Adam."

*   *   *

Adam grew like a weed and at the age of seven he was tall for his age though spindly. But while his body grew, his mind lagged behind. Two of Clarissa's sisters were married and producing children at a rapid clip. Adam's cousins were animated, talkative little brawlers who delighted in taunting the mute boy and shoving him to the ground in an attempt to provoke a response. None was ever forthcoming. No amount of goading could crack the boy's impenetrable facade. He was branded a dullard, but Clarissa bristled at any slights. "He's a special boy," she would say. "You'll see. He's my precious, special boy." But even under her lavish attentions, he remained mute as a stone, never smiling or reciprocating a hug. And while the boys his age began helping with chores around the farm, Adam seemed incapable of even gathering twigs for kindling.

One day, Clarissa was in the farmhouse roasting a lamb in the hearth, when her mother came to her. "There's a man t' see you!" she said breathlessly. "An old man on a mule. He wears th' monk's clothes."

The news made Clarissa light-headed with fear. Her first instinct was to grab Adam and run to the fells, but she calmed herself, and asked, "Just one monk you say? No others?"

"Only one tired and hungry old man. He calls himself Bartholomew."

Clarissa wiped her hands on her apron and told her mother to tend to the lamb spit. She checked on Adam, who was in his favorite and darkest corner of the room silently playing with his omnipresent stick, then went outdoors to see this monk.

Bartholomew was standing by his mule feeding it hay by hand. She didn't recognize him from her time at Vectis, and by the strained expression on his face, she could tell that he didn't recognize her either.

"Are you Clarissa?" he asked.

"Aye."

"I am Father Bartholomew," he said.

She asked the question, then steadied herself for the answer. "Have you come from Vectis?"

"I have, child."

"Why are ya here?" she asked in dismay and anger.

The monk fed the last of the straw to his mule and patted its head. "I am not here to harm you or judge you," he said wearily. "I only wish to speak to you. This has been a long journey for an old man. Three months it took me with Petal, my lovely little mule, as my only companion. There were black and rainy nights when I thought we would not survive, but with God's help, we are here."

"You've nowt come t' take me boy?" she asked.

Bartholomew closed his eyes and moved his lips in prayer. When he opened them, his old face had softened in relief. "He survived. God be praised. No, I do not want to take your son. What do you call him?"

"His name's Adam," she said, limp with thanks.

The monk smiled at that. "Ah. The name of the brother of the ferryman—the cart man who bore you here. He is the one who told me where you dwelled, but he did so only after I promised I would bring you no harm. But Adam is a good name for another reason." He wagged his finger as if imparting a lesson. "God's first-created man."

"Would ya like some food and drink?" Clarissa asked.

"God bless you, I would."

Bartholomew begged to wash off the filth of the road before entering the house. She watched him dip a cloth in the horse trough and scour his frail body, his joints appearing gnarly and swollen.

At the threshold of the farmhouse Bartholomew stopped and peered in. He seemed instinctively to turn his face toward the far corner, where Adam sat shrouded in darkness. Clarissa told her mother she could return to her chores outside, then set Bartholomew by the hearth and ladled day-old stew into a wooden bowl.

Though he appeared tempted by the smell of the food, the old monk put down the bowl and kept staring into the corner.

"May I see him?" he asked.

She nodded and called out for the boy to come. There was a sound of scraping from the corner but no movement.

"He's not a disobedient boy," she said. "It's just—he's different. Let me fetch 'im."

"No," the monk said. "I will go to him."

Bartholomew rose and shuffled slowly toward the corner.

The scratching noises stopped.

"Will you bring me a candle?" the monk asked.

Clarissa obliged and gave him one.

He held it out and bathed the boy in dancing yellow light. Clarissa heard the monk catch his breath and hold it for a while. His exhalation sounded like a long sigh.

"I see Titus in him," Bartholomew said softly. "The redness of his hair, the length of his chin, the small ears, the most beautifully long fingers. It is as if Titus were reborn."

"Th' old scribe," Clarissa said. "Th' one who took me."

"He chose you that day. For decades he stood for no woman, but on that day he chose you."

"Why?" she asked.

"It is not for me to say, but in a way, you were blessed."

"At that moment in th' crypt I didn't feel th' blessing of God. But I loved 'im from the first time I seen 'im, and I still do even though he's a strange child."

"Hello, boy," Bartholomew said, staring at him in wonder.

Adam seemed to take no notice of the visitor.

"What's that in his hand?" the monk asked.

"It's his stick. He only lets go of it when he sleeps. The other children on the farm play with wooden toys or smooth stones from the river, but this boy wants only his stick."

"And what does he do with it?"

"Nowt that I can tell."

"Is that so?" Bartholomew lowered himself to the dirt floor grimacing from the pain in his knees. He pushed the candle forward until it brightly lit the earth where two walls joined. "Look! Do you see?"

Clarissa bent forward. "See what?"

"There! There! In the dirt. Letters and numbers! Your son is writing!"

The old monk made his case over supper: he wanted nothing more than a barn roof over his head, clean hay for his bedding and food and drink for himself and his mule. In exchange for these necessities Bartholomew offered Clarissa and her family something they did not have and until then did not know they were lacking: the personal services of a priest. And beyond that, he hinted of more. Adam, he told them, that special boy, held a key to a holy realm where the Lightburns would be God's knights. They would become anointed ones on earth and worthy of a seat at Christ's table in Heaven. And he would teach them how to use that key to unlock the door to a hallowed and blessed kingdom.

Clarissa's father chewed the gristle at the end of a lamb rib and listened intently to the monk. Clarissa's silver plate had transformed the fortunes of the family. He had extracted the jewels and melted the silver into small fat discs. With this currency he had begun to improve himself. He purchased a great number of sheep and a team of fine workhorses and soon found himself livestock rich and land poor. He dearly coveted two butts of land adjoining his farm held in serfdom by his neighbor, Thomas Gobarn. Like Gobarn, he was an unfree serf, paying tenure for his farm to Robert de Boynton, the king's knight for the shire. A few choice jewels to his lord had secured an elevation in his standing, and Lightburn became a vassal, eligible to hold a deed to his land. Robert de Boynton did honor him by coming to his farm and seisined him of the fief by handing over a ceremonial sod of land. Furthermore, a purse of silver coins persuaded de Boynton to deed him Thomas Gobarn's land as well. With the seal of his lord in hand, Lightburn triumphantly pushed down the stone wall that separated the two holdings to allow his sheep to graze on new pastures, and he began charging rent to Gobarn to farm a measly parcel.

Now, Lightburn considered what the priest was offering. As a vassal, he had an obligation of frankalmoign, a duty to pray for his lord's soul. In truth, he paid lip service to this duty, but with a priest living in his barn, he could do real service! If Robert de Boynton could see Charles Lightburn honoring him by retaining his own priest to pray for the lord's eternal soul, then he might be further elevated, becoming a man of the lord.

And what of this business of Adam, the dullard grandson being more—much more—than met the eye? Well, he was prepared to listen to the old priest. And why not? All Bartholomew was asking was to live in his horse barn and be fed.

Intrigued at the prospect that his future could be even brighter, Charles Lightburn told the monk that he was welcome to live, pray, and teach at Lightburn Farm.

In the coming days, Clarissa washed Brother Bartholomew's habit, mended the rips, and patched it where it was threadbare. The monk ate heartily to regain his strength and saw to his unruly beard with his newly honed belt knife. While declaring himself able-bodied, to Clarissa he still looked like a walking corpse, so thin and dried-out, but at least his eyes had gone from cloudy to bright.

Bartholomew assembled the Lightburn clan around their supper table to tell them his tale. The men and women of the extended family sat attentively while the monk stood and gesticulated in front of the hearth. The children played on and around their beds, and Adam kept to himself, scratching away with his stick.

Bartholomew told them the oral history of Vectis, which had been passed for centuries from the mouths of monks to the ears of monks. He told them how in the year 777, on the seventh day of the seventh month, in the presence of a fiery comet, a boy was born on Vectis, the seventh son of a seventh son, and that this boy, Octavus, came to live in the abbey. He told them that the boy looked much like their Adam, mute and pale with ginger hair and green eyes. And he told them that the child Octavus was found to have a marvelous God-given ability to write though he had never been taught, but more than that, to write the names of all men with their dates of birth and their dates of death, demonstrating to the amazed monks of Vectis that verily, God did determine the fate of men.

And those ancient monks did establish the holy Order of the Names to allow Octavus to perform his labors without interruption. And they provided the boy with quill and parchment and bound the pages of his labors into holy books. And he told them that when Octavus was older he seized a young novice girl and did impregnate her with his seed and the issuance of that union was another pale, mute ginger-haired boy with the selfsame abilities.

The Lightburns listened with rapt attention to Brother Bartholomew as he described an uninterrupted chain of mute scribes stretching from the olden days until Clarissa's last day on Vectis. He told them they lived their entire lives in an underground cavern dug into the bedrock of the Isle of Vectis, where they diligently recorded names of those who would be born—*Natus*—and those who would die—*Mors*—for centuries into the future, names entered in English, Frankish, Moorish, Hebrew, Chinese, and all manner of foreign characters. The scribes worked as if they were of one mind and one hand. They never duplicated the work of another, but all their efforts proved to be a seamless stream, centuries of labor that had yielded a vast library of books encompassing the years 777 through the ninth day of February 2027. And Bartholomew told them that he himself had lived his own life in service, mostly underground, as the monk charged with the operation of the holy scriptorium.

He told them that Clarissa was also one in a long

line of special servants to the Order of the Names, healthy and pious girls who were selected to bear the next generation of scribes.

"But you were a unique girl, were you not?" Bartholomew said. His words carried no venom, and Clarissa was relieved she was not to be castigated. "Perhaps your fiery nature was the reason that Titus the Venerable rose to the occasion. You would become the only girl who ever fled before delivering your issuance. And your action, dear girl, alas proved to be the end of the Library."

He told them of the horrific events of that ninth of January in the year 1297, when all at once the scribes to a man and boy seized their quills and thrust them into their eyes, deeply into their brains, effecting a most-horrible death on the tables and floor of their scriptorium. And he told them how he had gone from desk to desk collecting the last pages each one had writ and upon each finding the same words: *Finis Dierum*, End of Days. They were all working on names for the ninth of February 2027, a day far, far in the future.

"Is that th' day th' world'll end, Father?" Charles Lightburn asked.

"That was the opinion of myself and my learned colleagues. Until we learned that Clarissa had fled with her baby. That cast doubt. Baldwin, our abbot, did not alter his belief that they had borne witness to the day of destruction, but our Prior Felix and I wondered otherwise. Perhaps they were not notating the End of Days of mankind but that the end of their days, as the chain of scribes born to Vectis had been broken by Clarissa's actions."

Clarissa began to sob in heartfelt lamentation. "No, my sweet girl, do not cry," Bartholomew urged her. "You could not know. And if we have learned only one thing in the Order of the Names, it is that everything happens because God wishes it so."

"What happened next?" Clarissa's father asked.

"Baldwin ordered Felix to destroy the Library by fire because he expressed the opinion that mankind was not prepared to know its secrets. But Felix was not of the same mind. He razed the chapel that stood above the underground chambers but took care not to set torch to the books themselves. My personal belief is that the Library has survived though I cannot be sure. In the months and years that followed the calamity, the spirit of Vectis Abbey weakened, and some monks and sisters left the isle for other monasteries. I, for one, harbored a notion that grew inside me like the baby that grew inside of you, Clarissa. I am old, very old, and have little enough time left, but I had to know. I had to know! Did you survive? Did your baby survive? Did the Library carry on? Before I was too weak to hope to mount a journey such as the one I have accomplished, I resolved to leave my island sanctuary, my dear Vectis Abbey, and follow your route to your home to see if you and your son were alive. And here I am. In the warm bosom of your family, knowing that God had guided me here with a purpose."

"What purpose?" Clarissa asked.

"To honor the will of God, good people," Bartholomew said with tears in his eyes. "To plead with you to help me to continue God's work. To perpetuate the Order of the Names. To let the Library continue!"

Bartholomew lived for two more years. During his days in Pinn, he taught the Lightburns many things.

He taught them how to make ink from lamp black

mixed with gum. He taught them how to fashion quills from goose feathers. He taught them the art of making parchment by liming and stretching sheepskin. He taught them how to bind a book. And he taught them how to quarry away at the limestone below their dwelling to make a secret chamber to house a scriptorium.

And before he died in Clarissa's arms, gasping and hot with pneumonia, Bartholomew witnessed the completion of Adam's first thick book, spanning the ninth of February 2027 to the tenth of February 2027, filled with strange-sounding and often indecipherable names of people who would not come to be born or die for over seven hundred years.

Haven and Cacia leaned against a limestone wall, watching Will and Phillip. The boy had just awoken and was hungry. He scarfed down his breakfast but Will had no appetite. It had been tough watching Phillip sleep through the night. He'd nodded off after their meal before Will could extract any info from him. But he let him rest. He figured he'd get the facts soon enough, and that time had come.

"Did you sleep?" Cacia asked.

"I heard a lot of snoring from the other room," Will said. "Who else is down here?"

Cacia ignored the question. "I can get ya more food, Phillip," she said.

"No, I'm fine."

"And you, Will? Are ya sure you'll have nothing?"

Will smiled at her. "In the unlikely event we're here for supper, I'll reconsider."

"Right then," she said. "I promised we'd tell you th' score, so let's get t' it. Haven, you can tell 'im why ya contacted Phillip."

The girl was far too shy to look Will in the face. Instead, she talked into the floor. "I thought . . ." Her voice trailed off. "No, I knew Phillip was th' only one who could help me. Not only me. Our teacher had us read his essay, th' one that won that award. There's been all sorts of stuff about th' Horizon. It's been horrible like around 'ere. There've been kids all depressed and such. A girl in Kirkby Stephen one class ahead a me hung herself, and two boys in Kendal did th' same. On Socco, ever'one's going barmy about it. They're all scared what's going t' happen next February. I couldn't just sit 'ere and do nowt about it."

The girl was crying now. Will was struck by the emphatic way the girl had said, "I knew." "How did you think Phillip could help?" he asked.

"He's Will Piper's son, in' he? You were th' one who found out everything about th' Library, weren't ya? You know what t' do in these situations."

"What kinds of situations are we talking about?" Will asked.

Cacia said, "It's time t' show ya something. If I undo your handcuffs, I need ya t' promise me you won't hurt us or try t' run."

"I can promise you I won't hurt you," Will answered.

"Look," Cacia said sharply. "I can get Kheelan down here t' mind you with his shotgun, but I'd rather not have 'im with us. It'll . . ." she paused, " . . . limit th' experience. Besides, the men are all outside and you'd be caught straight out."

Will nodded. "Okay, you've got my word. How about you, Phillip, you in?"

"I'd rather make love than war. Besides, I want to take the guided tour."

Will chuckled and held up his wrist for Cacia's key.

Despite his pledge, Will thought about grabbing Phillip and making a run for it. They'd head to the storeroom, dash up the stairs, exit the hangar, and hoof it as fast as they could through the field and to the road, where they'd try to flag down a car. But a lot could go wrong, and with the Lightburns prowling the farm, the odds weren't good. He'd have tried it if he were on his own but he couldn't risk Phillip's getting hurt. Besides, he was curious as hell, so he obediently followed Cacia through the nearest door.

There was another small room which didn't seem to have any particular function other than to provide access to three other doors. It was lit by a single hanging bulb.

Cacia pointed to one of the three closed doors. "Would either of you like t' use th' loo?"

Phillip went first, and when he was done, Will pushed the door open.

It was closet-sized, carved from the limestone, a smelly dead end. There was a water pipe coming from above, which plunged through a drilled hole and into an old, rust-stained porcelain sink. The toilet flushed, so he figured it emptied into a cistern. As a way out, it was going to be a nonstarter, but one thing was sure: whatever was going on here was a serious, long-term operation.

Back in the anteroom, Will pointed at one of the two other doors. "This one?" he said.

"No," Cacia said. "Later. This one first."

Will said to Phillip, "Been through there yet?"

The boy answered, "Nope. But Haven told me about it."

Cacia opened it and sent Haven into the pitch-blackness to switch on lights. Before he could see, Will smelled it. A muscular sweet aroma of leather and mold, a scent of antiquity. In the instant before the lights flashed on, he was certain what it was and then, in the sickly yellow incandescence, his eyes confirmed what he already knew.

It was a library.

He simply said, "Jesus," and took a few steps inside.

Phillip's reaction was more prosaic. "Holy shit!"

The limestone chamber was cavernous and cool, the temperature of a wine cellar. There was a central corridor that carried through, straight as an arrow, as far as he could see. On either side were wooden bookcases standing floor to ceiling, each some five meters tall. The width of the chamber was easier to fathom than the length, about fifty-sixty meters, precisely bifurcated by the corridor.

The bookcases nearest them were barren, and as father and son silently followed mother and daughter into the chamber, it was clear there were enough empty shelves for thousands upon thousands of books.

"Room to grow," Will said.

Haven didn't seem surprised that Will understood the situation. "When it's full, I'll be long gone," she said. "So will Cacia. It'll be someone else's burden."

Phillip sprang ahead like an eager puppy and Cacia caught up with him. He made his way to the first full bookcase. By the time Will arrived, the boy had wriggled one of the books from a shelf.

It was thick and heavy, bound in fresh leather with the strong smell of a new pair of shoes, not the fusty scent of the ambient air. The spine had a hand-tooled number: 2566.

"That's a date, isn't it?" Phillip asked.

Haven said, "Aye."

Phillip opened the book to a random middle page while Will looked over his shoulder.

On the page were two columns of names, about a hundred per row. Names handwritten in black ballpoint ink. Will picked out ones in English, Spanish, Chinese, Portuguese. Beside each was the date 24 August 2566 and the word *Natus* or *Mors*.

"Still using Latin," Will said.

"We don't know why," Cacia said. "There's lots we don't know."

"You're not using parchment," he said wryly.

"Hardly," she said. "Copy paper from Asda. But at least we go all out on th' bindings. Good Yorkshire sheep hide."

Will shook his head. "A second Library. A second goddamned Library. There's no Horizon, is there?"

"That's why I had t' contact Phillip," Haven said. "The world needed t' know! Before more people did themselves harm."

Cacia sighed. "The world didn't need t' know anything, Haven. It wasn't our duty t' let 'em know. Our only duty's t' th' Library."

"Where are the books for 2027?" Will asked.

Cacia waved her hand down the corridor. "All the way down that end."

"Does it start on February 9, 2027?" Phillip asked.

"It does."

Will shook his head in wonder. "Why here? Why Yorkshire?"

Phillip slid the book back into the case and started walking toward the rear of the chamber the others following along.

"There's nothing written, only what's been passed down by word of mouth within our family, and who knows what's true and what isn't. But it's said that a girl, a Lightburn she was, was on th' Isle of Wight, at Vectis Abbey, in th' late thirteenth century. She was made pregnant and she fled t' her home 'ere in th' Dales. It's said her name was Clarissa but in truth, there's no way t' know. It's said too that 'er baby's name was Adam. The Lightburns of old recognized their responsibility to serve th' Library. We recognize that responsibility today, don't we Haven?"

The girl muttered "aye" under her breath.

"So the notation at Vectis—End of Days—meant something else," Will said.

"End of the days at Vectis, I suppose. Back then, Clarissa must've been a willful girl who brought ruin t' th' abbey. I only hope my Haven hasn't through her willfulness done th' same t' us."

The girl began to weep, then something made her abruptly stop. Phillip had taken her hand and was holding it tightly.

Cacia ignored the boy's advance at first. "For over seven hundred years, we Lightburns have been librarians. This is what we do. It's why we're on this earth. There are many books here, maybe a million, maybe more. We never counted 'em. We don't read 'em. We keep 'em. These books come from God, and we are God-fearing people. We never knew exactly how we figured into th' bigger picture until you exposed th' business at Area 51. It was all we talked about back then. We appreciated knowin'."

"Glad I could help," Will said.

"Come on, you two," Cacia called after the boy and girl. "Haven, it's time t' show 'em what's behind th' other door."

Yi Biao was in a dark mood. He sat alone in his study at his official residence in Zhongnanhai, close to the Forbidden City. General Secretary Wen's house was a stone's throw away within the heavily guarded compound, but it wasn't as if they were in and out of each other's places for tea and cakes. Even *he* had trouble gaining access to the old man these days.

His study was lined with mostly Chinese books, the collection of a lifetime. Though he had personally led the effort to modernize and ban physical books in schools and universities in favor of e-books, he still enjoyed the pleasure of holding a hefty traditional book, though the new biography of Hu Jintao, the General Secretary whose term had ended some fifteen years earlier, lay unopened on his lap.

He took a long sip of Southern Comfort and waited for the sweet, numbing sensation to travel from tongue to brain. He'd acquired the taste when he was China's Ambassador to the United Nations, and now he had it imported by the case. He took another syrupy sip for good measure and let his shoulders go lax in the armchair. His wife was out at a dinner with friends so he had the house to himself.

He laughed at the thought. Himself meant him and a live-in staff of six. He called for his aide, an earnest young man, and asked him to instruct the maid to run a hot bath and to summon his masseuse. He aimed to drink, soak, and massage the tension from his body and mind.

His meeting earlier in the day with Wen had gone poorly. Yi thought he had laid out a compelling case for immediate action, but Wen proved to be an immovable object.

The old man had listened carefully while puffing on one Red Pagoda Hill cigarette after another. How he escaped lung cancer, Yi would never know. It had always irritated him no end that the CIA knew Wen's date of death or whether he was BTH, but that information was unknown to him. It was galling beyond belief.

"Look," Wen had said when Yi was done with his recommendations, "we've made some strong responses already. We've recalled our ambassador. We've initiated a series of war games near Taiwan. Don't you think we should wait and see how these actions mature?"

"General Secretary," Yi had said, "don't you believe that sending these warning postcards to our Ambassador and his staff in Washington was the last straw? An intolerable humiliation. It is not only me. Other members of the Politburo see it the same way."

"I don't like the concept of last straws," Wen had spat. "There is always one more straw to be found. And don't forget, the Americans are vigorously denying their role in the affair. What proof do we have?"

"Of course they are hiding behind denials," Yi had asserted. "General Bo has told me he is 99 percent certain the postcards originated from Groom Lake agents."

"Ah, 99 percent," Wen had said with a sneer, showing his yellowing teeth. I will not take our nation to war based on anything less than 100 percent."

"If we attack Taiwan aggressively with surgical strikes to limit civilian casualties, I do not believe that the United States will intervene," Yi had said evenly. "I believe the island will be reunified within hours, and the only thing America will do will be to shout and impotently stamp its feet at the United Nations."

"No!" Wen had shouted. "You must bring me 100-percent proof—documentation that I can see with my own eyes—that the US government intended to threaten us with these stupid letters! You bring me something like that before I will authorize any of the radical suggestions you have made this afternoon. This meeting is over, Vice Chairman. Tread carefully. I had not considered the future leader of China to be so rash."

Yi finished his drink. His masseuse had arrived, and he had to change into his robe. In the morning he'd see General Bo again. Hopefully, the crafty fellow had something else up his sleeve.

We are close to the tipping point, he thought, treading slightly unsteadily on his slippered feet. So close! I need one more provocation to persuade Wen to seize the moment and capture our rightful place in history! I don't care if it comes from luck or skill, I need one more thing!

Rob Melrose arrived at the Black Bull Hotel in Kirkby Stephen and immediately went to Annie's room. Brimming with public-schoolboy arrogance he barged in when she opened her door and began dressing her down.

"There's a lot of displeasure in London," he said with a toffy accent that made her clench in irritation. "A lot of displeasure. Will Piper is a bit of a hot potato politically speaking, and you let him give you the slip. Career-limiting move, Annie. Very disappointing. I've got two men waiting downstairs. Let's get a move on, shall we?"

She was fully dressed but hadn't yet put on her walking shoes. She purposely kept him waiting by sitting on her bed, slowly lacing and tightening. When she stood up, she said, "Look, Rob, my remit wasn't to keep Piper on a leash. It was to offer assistance in the location of his son. He chose to run off. I don't know why. But I am blameless."

"I'm quite sure you'll have an opportunity to assert your blamelessness when you file a report, but for now, *my* remit is to locate two missing persons: Piper and his son. You know who Piper's wife is, don't you?"

"Yes, Rob, I do," Annie said wearily.

"Then you can imagine the shitstorm coming our way via the FBI and the State Department. My job is to find them today, and your job is to assist me in any way I deem appropriate. I suggest we find a quiet spot in the lounge and have you debrief us on all your activities in Kirkby Stephen and the surrounding environs."

"Yes, why don't we," she said defiantly, grabbing her shoulder bag. He might not have noticed she was mocking him when she said, "I believe we should be especially mindful of the—surrounding environs."

Kenney and his men rolled into Kirkby Stephen and parked their car just past the Black Bull. Kenney's surveillance people back at Groom Lake had gotten a precise bead on Annie Locke's location from her NetPen signal, and they'd been monitoring all her e-mail and telephone traffic, slicing through the MI5 encryption algorithms like a hot knife through butter. As Kenney liked to say in these situations: "We own her." His watchers had never met a code they couldn't break. It was what they did for a living. He was proud as hell of his people and their mission, but the end was nigh, as they say. He didn't have the slightest idea what he'd do when Area 51 was decommissioned. Sometimes, when he was off duty with a skin of booze in his gut, he secretly hoped that when the Horizon came, he and the rest of humanity were cleanly wiped out. That way he wouldn't have to settle for an inferior job.

But now, as he stretched his legs and checked out the geography of Market Street, he was mindful only of the job at hand. He was going to find Will Piper, find out what he and his son were up to, and find out who the hell "the Librarians" were. And when he'd accomplished that, if there was any way he could legitimize his actions, he was going to seriously fuck up Mr. Piper. Sure, Piper was BTH, but he could still be hurt, and besides, putting the hammer down would take care of unfinished business. He owed it to Malcolm Frazier and the honor of the watchers. As he was delivering the beatdown, he'd be sure to let Piper know that each and every blow was coming from Malcolm, fists from the grave.

Annie sat at a snug table at the rear of the hotel lounge with Melrose and two other MI5 agents. She knew the men, good enough blokes, she reckoned, who must have shared her opinions of Melrose but were clams in the presence of their boss. The beer mats on the table oozed a nasty yeastiness. She stacked them and tossed them onto an empty table. Melrose had waved off the server, saying they were neither hungry nor thirsty, then remarked at the waiter's scowl, "I do hate these provincial towns."

Annie delivered a crisp rundown of the houses and farms at Pinn that she and Will had visited. She dwelled the longest on the Lightburn Farm because that was their most substantial encounter. Most of their other interviews had been brief and rather unfriendly.

"The people up here don't seem to like outsiders," she said.

"But that wasn't the case at Lightburn Farm," Melrose said nasally. He had a map on his NetPen screen with red pins at each of their interviews. "Pins on Pinn," he had said, then waited for his toadies to chuckle. "They weren't unfriendly there, were they? What does that tell us, Annie?"

"As I concluded in my draft report, Rob, it indicated they were either a friendly lot or they were hiding something," she said.

"Well, in either case, it seems we should pay them a visit this afternoon. Let's see how friendly they are when the heavy mob descends on them."

Just then, Kenney, Lopez, and Harper came into the lounge and asked to be seated for lunch. Kenney gave the MI5 table a good hard stare.

"Who the hell are that lot?" Melrose whispered.

"Never saw them before," Annie said. "Americans by the look and sound of them."

"Well, the tall one seems to recognize you. Did you see the way he looked at you?"

She shrugged.

"FBI?" Melrose whispered. "CIA? Other?"

"Want me to go ask?" she said sarcastically.

"Heavens no! Bad form. I'll make some discreet inquiries. But I wouldn't be surprised if this isn't the machination of Piper's wife to shadow our investigation."

Across the room, Kenney was whispering to his people too. "Anne Katherine Locke. She looks just like her photo. Pretty little gal. Barely legal, if you ask me."

"What's our move, chief?" Lopez asked.

"Well, our first move is to pray to the Almighty Lord that there's something on this menu that won't turn our stomachs inside out. After that, we'll do what we do best. We'll follow their asses till they lead us to Piper."

"I think they made us," Harper said.

Kenney opened the menu. "What are they going to do? Outrun us in their dinky electric car?"

* * *

Nancy wasn't used to an empty house. It wasn't so much the part of being alone. Will spent most of his time in Florida while she was in Washington, and Phillip didn't exactly hang out with her. He stuck to his room most of the time. It was the quiet that got to her.

Phillip had a noisy presence. There was the constant thumping from the subwoofer in his bedroom. And his NetPen was perpetually chiming some kind of alert from Socco and his myriad Net sites. And he never turned the kitchen or living-room TVs off, so there was always a background of voices to squelch.

Now the house was as silent as a tomb, and she hated that.

She was dressed for work and filling her commuter mug with coffee when she began to cry. Her son was missing. Her husband was missing. And her hard-ass boss was asking her to put job and country first. It was too much.

She did what she had been doing obsessively—she voice-dialed Phillip's phone, then Will's, and got the same casual greeting messages that seemed so monstrously incongruous under the circumstances.

Next she checked her e-mails and found and reread the same one she'd picked up while still in bed. Ronald Moore, Deputy Director General of MI5 was reassuring her that everything was being done to locate Will and Phillip. One of their "best men" had been deployed into the field with a team to assist the younger case officer, Miss Locke. She could expect to receive regular updates.

Nancy had looked up the particulars on Annie Locke and had snarled at the pretty face on her screen, "Leave him alone, honey. He's got a bad heart." She imagined that Miss Locke would have gotten Will's old juices flowing the way pretty women always did. That rising sap of his had almost killed him at Christmas. But why had he taken her car and ditched her? He must have gotten onto something and didn't want the baggage of a tyro tagging along. But why hadn't he called to let her know what he had? Just a ten-second call!

Damn you, Will, she thought. You're the most exasperating man I ever met. And by the way, I love you.

Director Parish found her the moment she arrived at the Hoover Building on Pennsylvania Avenue.

"Guess what, you were right," he said, pouring them both coffees from a carafe on his conference table.

"Right about what?" Nancy asked.

"All of the diplomats who turned tail and flew back to Beijing are alive and well this morning."

"I told you it didn't fit."

"And I already told you, you were right."

"Then let me catch the next plane to the UK. I need to get over there and find my guys."

"Ron Moore tells me they've got good people on it, Nancy. Here's the situation. The Chinese aren't cooling down. They don't care that the last batch of postcards was a hoax. They believe—or they're saying they believe—that they originated from the same organization that sent the real ones. They're asserting they all came from Groom Lake. They've lodged a formal complaint with the State Department stating that the threat to their diplomats has taken the crisis to the next level, and they're demanding to know why the administration is engaging in hostile provocation. As of this morning, they've started rattling sabers. They've deployed two Shi-Lang-class aircraft carriers and a group of Type 094 nuclear attack subs into the South China Sea heading toward the Taiwan Straits. It wouldn't surprise anyone at the Pentagon if they used this as a smoke screen for an invasion of Taiwan. The White House, needless to say, is tied up in knots. That's where we come in. The best way to defang these guys is to prove the postcards did not originate from inside this government. It's up to us to break this case, which means it's up to you."

Nancy sighed, the weight of the world on her narrow shoulders. She had packed a case for England but it would have to stay in her car trunk.

She took the elevator to the fifth floor, where she had carved out a suite of offices and conference rooms for the Chinese Doomsday task force. Throughout her career as a senior-level administrator she'd been a practitioner of centralizing complicated cases. That hadn't always made her popular at the field-office level where Special Agents in Charge and their staffs often felt usurped by the long arm of Headquarters. But this case was a perfect example of the need for coordination. Postcards had been sent to New York City, San Francisco, Los Angeles, and now Washington. She couldn't have each field office doing its own thing.

She had plucked a Special Agent from the New York office to come to Washington to lead the task force, aware that she saw a lot of herself in Andrea Markoff, a ten-year veteran of the FBI and a real pistol, always on a full burn and as smart as they came. Markoff was over the moon at being mentored by the highest-ranking woman in the Bureau and was ferociously loyal.

When Nancy stopped by the task-force conference room, Andrea scampered to her side.

"Any progress on the videos?" Nancy asked.

"Cracked it like an egg!" Andrea said. "The new software programs got finished last night, and it looks like they're working."

"Let's take a look."

Nancy's mantra had long been: shoe-leather work breaks cases. She'd learned that working with Will on her first big case, and the lesson had been validated over and over throughout the years. The only hard evidence to latch onto were the postcards. All of them were postmarked in Manhattan and all passed through one of seven post-office branches. That meant the sender or senders had in all likelihood physically deposited the cards in several of the 167 street or central boxes that fed these branches.

It was easy enough to narrow down the days in question based on the postmarks on batches of cards and given the near-total blanket of CCTV coverage of Manhattan streets, there was good video for almost every box. The problem was the sheer volume of data. For any day in question, there were twenty-four hours of footage to review for some twenty street boxes or 480 hours of images to scrutinize looking for a recognizable face attached to a letter drop. And multiply that by the eight relevant days over the past two months that corresponded to each batch of postcards. The search for a common face or faces was a classic needle-in-a-haystack scenario.

Andrea's idea was to get the geeks involved. With Nancy's blessing, she created a posse of analysts to write code that would compress the videos and include only images where a person's hand could be seen touching the handle of a postbox.

"It's running now," Andrea said. "It's not perfect, but it's weeding out 99 percent of the crap."

An entire side of the conference room was covered by video screens. Andrea called up the January 8 video feeds, and the wall lit with the best angles for the twenty-one postboxes that fed the Village Post Office on Varick Street. "Run images," she said.

A group of agents and techs in the conference room fell in behind Andrea and Nancy as the chopped-up time-stamped video feeds began playing back.

The algorithms seemed to be effective. The choppy videos were pretty much limited to images of people depositing letters into the boxes.

"This would have been even tougher ten years ago," Andrea said. "I mean, when was the last time you mailed a letter?"

Nancy remembered. When Will was away from her in Florida, she liked to send him real cards, not e-ones. The last was a birthday card in November, something with a sailboat and a sunset. She pushed it out of her mind—she didn't want to get teary in front of her people.

It must have been a bitterly cold day because many of the people on the videos were wearing scarves and hats. "I'd say there's only going to be a 50-percent hit rate for facial IDs," Nancy said.

"If we're lucky," Andrea said. "But at least we've got time-shrunk material to work with."

Nancy's NetPen vibrated. She popped an earpiece in and stepped to the back of the room to take the call.

It was Ron Moore from MI5. She braced herself when Moore's assistant announced he was coming onto the line. But the call turned out to be an empty piece of courtesy. He was merely informing her that his London team had arrived on the scene in York-shire and was going to be deploying into the field shortly. They had a number of leads which they were going to investigate methodically. "Is there anything else I can do for you, Nancy?" he asked by way of signing off.

From the corner of her eye she became aware of something. On one of the video screens.

Her heart went into a full gallop.

"No, Ron. Thank you. Please call if you get anything." She pulled out her earpiece and shouted across the room, "Middle row! Second screen from the left! Freeze it and go back fifteen seconds!"

Andrea halted that screen with a palm gesture and swiped it into reverse with another. "Play," she said.

Nancy was close to it now at Andrea's side. "There! Stop!"

The screen froze. A hatless man had one hand on the handle of a postbox and another hand in the slot.

"Jesus," Nancy said.

"What?" Andrea looked puzzled.

"That one. Do a facial capture and run it against all your other footage. And do it fast. I know him."

Will had an inkling of what he was going to find behind the door, but his suspicion was hardly enough to blunt the numbing reality of seeing it.

He had imagined what it might be like to be in the same room as them, a fly on the wall, but these kinds of musings had been akin to imagining having a time machine to go back and witness the goings-on at the court of King Henry VIII or wander the grottos of Lascaux while prehistoric man painted frescoes.

There were seven of them.

The oldest was perhaps in his seventies, the youngest, not much older than Will's own son. They sat at two simple tables at the front of the room; unoccupied tables stretched into the black reaches of the chamber.

All seven looked up when they entered. Will saw seven sets of emerald eyes briefly staring at him before they all quickly resumed their work.

"It's all right, they're friends," Cacia said to them soothingly, but it seemed to Will that her words mattered as much to them as reassurances given to household pets. It was her tone that mattered.

There was no fear betrayed in their comportment,

no curiosity, no sense of a violation of privacy. They were mute and blank-faced, their lips relaxed in their labors, their eyes nonblinking. Every one of them had longish ginger hair, straight and fine, the older men thinning at the top, showing scaly scalps.

Will was drawn to their hands. Long, delicate fingers grasped black ballpoint pens depositing flowing, cursive script onto white A4-sized sheets of paper. They sat in padded wooden chairs, their paper illuminated by high-intensity lamps. All had the pale complexion of basement dwellers and the spindly habitus of men whose bodies existed only to support the mind.

As he had walked through the Library, he had imagined them wearing the flowing robes of ancient monks, but their garb was commonplace and, as such, incongruous. They had uniforms of a sort but the clothes spoke more to household convenience than regimentation—khaki trousers, white socks and sandals and light blue cotton shirts.

"Dad," Phillip said.

"I know," Will replied. "I know."

They fell silent again watching, slack-jawed as the ginger-haired men did what their kind had been doing since the eighth century: writing down names and dates. And next to each name was the simple notation—*natus* or *mors*, born or died.

"Can we go closer?" Will asked.

Haven ushered them in until they were standing between the two occupied tables.

"They're working on th' thirteenth of April 2611," Cacia said softly. "They've been on it for almost a week."

"In that time, about one hundred thousand people'll be born and one hundred thousand'll die every day," Haven said, using the hushed voice one uses in a library. "I totaled it one day when I had nowt better t' do."

"They'll be in balance," her mother said. "I hope it's a natural one."

"It's my job t' count th' pages," the girl said. "When they get t' six hundred, Andrew, one of me brothers, binds 'em in a book."

The body odor of the men, a sweet, fermented smell, filled Will's nostrils. "What do you call them?" he asked.

"They each have names," Haven said. "But we call 'em the writers. For twelve centuries that's what they've been called."

Suddenly Will and Phillip startled when one of the writers in front of them pushed his chair back and rose.

"Don't worry," Cacia said. "Haven, take care of Matthew."

Matthew was young, perhaps twenty, with reddish stubble on his chin and above his lip. He walked toward the door and stood before it, his hands at his side, shifting his weight on his feet.

Haven opened it for him and both of them left.

"He had t' go t' th' loo," Cacia said. "They're like children, really. They need constant attending. We've got t' feed 'em, clean 'em, shave 'em—cause they don't like beards, put them t' bed at night and wake them up in th' morning. I'm not complaining—it's what we do—but it's a lot of work, I can tell ya. All the Lightburns are involved. The entire farm exists to support 'em. You met me husband and 'is brother. Haven's got two older brothers, Andrew and Douglas, and an aunt, Gail who's got two girls, both small. Like I said, it's our duty. All of us do our part, all our wakin' hours."

Will could see that Phillip had shifted his attention

from looking over one of the writer's shoulders to listening to Cacia. "But Haven goes to school," Phillip said.

"She does, and not of her own choice or our choice. Not by a long shot. She's always been a free spirit, that one, wandering off, picking 'er wildflowers and following butterflies onto th' fells. Years back, th' headmaster of th' school in Kirkby Stephen was up walking the fells above th' farm when he happened upon 'er and was curious why he didn't recognize 'er. She was young at the time and admitted she lived down on the farm. Well, th' local authorities visited us and wanted to know why th' girl wasn't going t' school. It was a lot of bother. We live off the map as much as we can, you see. We don't use th' doctors, don't take benefits, and here they are, snooping around. We're used t' th' DEFRA people coming 'round t' tag th' sheep and cows, but we never had trouble with offcomers muckin' about with our children. We had to hide th' young'uns down here with the writers every time some busybody showed up. But they got their hooks into Haven, and we either had t' send her off t' school or jump through all sorts of hoops for home schooling, which was even worse since they'd come and inspect ya all th' time. So aye, Phillip, Haven's been the only Lightburn who's gone t' school. It probably accounts for why she did th' stupid thing contactin' you."

Will jumped in with a question. "There are seven writers. They get old, they die, but they don't die out, do they?"

Cacia sighed. "Ah, you've spotted our biggest challenge."

Will had found a weak spot. He had to exploit it even if it was going to upset his son. "Tell me, Cacia, is Haven next?"

Cacia nodded solemnly. "We want her t' be a wee bit older, but aye."

Will was right about Phillip because the boy almost came out of his shoes. "Are you serious? With one of them?"

The writers stopped their work at the shouting but resumed in unison a few seconds later.

"It's our way, Phillip. It's always been our way," Cacia answered patiently.

"Leave her alone!" Phillip demanded gallantly. "If it's your way, why don't *you* do it?"

Cacia touched a young writer lightly on the shoulders. "This lad's mine. And Matthew too."

Will kept drilling. "How does Haven feel about this obligation of hers?"

"She's not thrilled, is she? She's seen the outside world in school. She fancies boys. I reckon she fancies you, Phillip. Maybe all that played into her deciding t' contact ya. But she'll do what th' Lightburn women are supposed t' do. It's for th' glory of God. It's bigger than us. As it is, our generation's been slackin'. They're only seven of 'em now. Look at all the empty tables behind 'em. In the past, there's been twenty, thirty a time."

"So it's up to Haven, then her younger cousins, to get the numbers up," Will said harshly.

"Dad, we can't let that happen!" Phillip said.

"I'd respectfully ask the two of you not t' be judgmental of us," Cacia said sadly. "There are greater forces in the universe than th' sensibilities of young girls."

Haven returned with Matthew. "Dad's coming," she said. "We'd better take 'em back t' th' dormitory."

Will had a flood of thoughts. Grab one of the ginger-haired men around the neck and use him as a hostage to get out. Do the same with Cacia or the girl. Do something! But he kept returning to Phillip's safety and decided to fight with words only.

"Cacia, you've got to let us go," he said. "Haven was right. The world needs to know there's no Horizon. Billions of people are suffering needlessly, scared to death over something that's not going to happen."

"I'm sorry, Will. It can't be done. The world mustn't find out about us. They won't let us survive in peace. It'll be th' end of the writers and th' end of their work. We won't abide that. Now hurry. We've got t' go."

Based on Annie's briefing, Melrose decided they would visit Scar Farm first, Lightburn Farm second, and Brook Farm third. If those didn't pan out, they would carry on until they'd covered the entire list of properties.

Annie warned them that the folks at Scar Farm employed a somewhat undecipherable dialect, but Melrose nevertheless complained irritably, "I can't understand a bloody word they're saying. Really, do we need an interpreter in our own bloody country?"

"Fuck off," the farmer said.

"Shall I interpret?" Annie asked, smiling.

"Tell them we have a right to enter their premises under the Security Act of 2019," Melrose said.

"I'm gittin' me gun," the farmer said, disappearing inside the farmhouse door.

Melrose told one of his lads to apprehend the farmer and put him in restraints and after a brief scuffle, the old farmer was in plastic cuffs and his wife was hyperventilating on the kitchen floor.

While the other agent stood watch in the garden, one hand upon his holstered weapon, Annie kept an eye on the elderly woman, offering her a glass of water and some settling words. Melrose and his colleague searched the house and the outbuildings.

Kenney and his men had staked out some high ground in a thicket on the other side of the road. Now, he was watching the MI5 team through binoculars as they ran their paces.

"What kind of weapons you think they have, chief?" Harper asked.

"Peashooters, more than likely," Kenney said. "And no telling whether they can hit a target."

Will broke down and ate the lunch Haven brought down for them. Father and son sat chained to their beds in the partitioned room inside the larger dormitory. The girl explained it was used as an isolation room when one of the writers came down with a cold or a fever to prevent its spreading.

"What are your mom and dad saying they want to do with us?" Will asked her as casually as he could.

"They're not sayin' in front of me," Haven said. "They don't trust me any more. But I can hear 'em arguing."

"Can you get us the keys to these?" Will said, holding up a manacled wrist.

"They've hidden everything from me," she said. "The keys, Phillip's NetPen."

"Can you call the police?" Phillip asked.

"Nae! They'll see me using th' phone in th' lounge."

"Can you sneak away and go to a neighbor?" Will asked.

"Not likely!" she said. "My uncle and brothers are keepin' watch. It's only because mum's told 'em she's short-handed, they're letting me bring th' meals."

The girl sat on Phillip's bed while he ate, close

enough for their shoulders to touch. She asked him if he was done and he responded by giving her a peck on her cheek, changing its color from pale to rouge.

She hastily gathered the trays and left, saying she'd be back when she could, then turned her head to give the boy a shy smile.

"Good maneuver," Will said. "She's already on our side, but every little bit helps."

"It wasn't a maneuver," Phillip replied in a bothered tone.

The kid's smitten, Will thought. "She's a nice girl," he said. "You got good taste."

"When we get out of here, you've got to promise me you'll make sure nothing happens to her, okay?" the boy demanded.

"I'll go to bat for her. You've got my promise."

"We are going to get out of here, aren't we?" Phillip asked, suddenly less confident.

"Yeah. Definitely."

"We've got to," the boy said, stretching out and yawning. "The world's got to know about this place."

As the boy snored the afternoon away, Will lay on his bunk, his arms folded defiantly over his chest, trying to work the angles. The kid already had Haven in a spell and he'd have to work the Piper charm on the girl's mother. They weren't getting out of this by resorting to violence. It was too risky. Like his son said, they'd have to make love not war.

He was starting to drift off himself when the door to their little room opened and Cacia came in with a couple of mugs of tea. She saw Phillip was asleep and whispered, "Why don't we have a chat?"

Will nodded and held up his wrist.

"Do I still have your promise?" she asked.

"I'll let you know when I retract it," he said.

She unchained him, left Phillip's tea by his bed, and escorted Will to the three-doored anteroom.

He sipped at the milky tea and gestured at the Library door. "Want to take a walk?"

Inside, she switched on the lights, and Will inhaled the ancient vapors.

"It's quite the place," he said.

"'Tis that. It's magical. That's why we've got t' protect it."

Will began his semirehearsed speech. "Let me give you my take on this, Cacia, okay? Your writers or savants or whatever you want to call them—I don't have a clue where they get their abilities. I've never been really religious, but I guess there's no getting around the fact that their talent speaks to some kind of higher authority. Maybe that's God. Maybe it's something else. But one thing I do know is that the names written down in these books represent real people. The names of most of the billions of people alive today are here. The names of billions more who haven't been born yet are here. It's about people, isn't it? It's not about books."

They began to move down the central corridor.

"What are you sayin', Will? That we should turn away from our obligations t' perpetuate the Library so people can know their fate? I don't know why this Library exists, but I know it's our obligation t' protect it from th' prying eyes of th' outside world."

"Look, I've thought about this every day of my life since I discovered the first Library. I don't think it's healthy or natural for people to know the day they're going to die. People ought to be focused on living, not dying. And I think it's despicable that my government used the data for decades for geopolitical purposes. But it makes me sick that the entire world is walking around with the mistaken belief—which in a way I'm responsible for—that they're under a death sentence. People are in anguish over the Horizon. I think it's time to let them know that next February 9 is just going to be another day."

"If it were possible t' accomplish that without compromising what we do 'ere, I wouldn't have a problem," she said.

He turned to face her. They were near a stack with books for the twenty-fourth century.

"But you do have a problem. A big one. Phillip and me. You can't just make us disappear. We're not just a father and son off the street, Cacia. Because of my wife, we're high-profile."

"Tell me about Mrs. Piper, then," she said with a toss of her red hair and a trace of a smile.

"She's a really great lady, a good mother, and for the purposes of this discussion, she's the number three person at the FBI. She'd be here now if she hadn't gotten trapped by a big case back home."

"So, she's a powerful woman then. Do ya like strong women, Will?"

Will had a good idea what was going to happen next so he wasn't bowled over when she rose to her toes and kissed him. He kissed her back, briefly enjoying her soft, yielding lips before pulling back.

"I guess I like women, period," he said. "But I get along fine with strong ones. How does Daniel do with strong women?"

"Ach, don't talk about me husband," she said, hands on hips. "You're the one on me mind at th' present."

"You two having an argument?" Will asked, smiling. "It wouldn't be about what to do with us, would it?"

She nodded.

"He and your brother-in-law want to kill us, don't they? There's a problem, they take care of it. I get the psychology. The problem is, we're BTH. So for whatever reason, it isn't going to happen before next February 9. That means the only way to keep us quiet is to hold us down here for over a year, which also isn't going to happen. Because of who my wife is, the British Security Services are already looking for us, and they'll have a good idea where to find us. This isn't going to end well for you, Cacia. You've got to save yourselves. Keep your own counsel, don't rely on Daniel and Kheelan."

She said something under her breath, a personal aside, a thought escaping on a sigh. It sounded like, "I know how this'll end."

"I'm sorry, what did you say?" Will asked.

"Nothing. Nothing at all. By the way, your wife's big case. I've a notion she'll solve it."

Will furrowed his brow at that but said nothing. Instead, he began slowly walking again.

"Are you interested in taking more exercise or do you want to peek into your future? You can browse 2027 if you like," she said.

He laughed. "I sincerely don't want to know what's going to happen to me and my guys. Years ago, I *had* to look. I guess I was relieved we were BTH, but it never sat well with me. I felt I'd crossed a line I wasn't meant to cross. How about you?"

"I've not searched for me own date, if that's what you're asking me. Nor the dates for my family. We leave the books alone. Besides, for all I know, our dates aren't in this Library at all. Maybe they're in th' other Library."

"I sincerely hope that's not the case."

She kissed him again, longer this time. As he held her, he dangled the tea mug from his finger trying not to spill what was left down the back of her dress. When she'd had her fill of kissing, he held her head against his chest with his free hand. She was murmuring again, but he didn't try to understand what she was saying.

I'm getting somewhere, he thought. This make-love-not-war thing has its merits.

Looking over her shoulder at the nearest stack of books, he noticed something peculiar. All the volumes in the library were a uniform five inches thick, but on one of the middle shelves, the second book from the end was slim, only half an inch wide and devoid of markings on its blue spine.

Driven by an intense curiosity, Will let the tea mug slip from his finger. It shattered on the stone floor.

He apologized profusely, but while Cacia dropped to her knees to gather the ceramic shards, he reached for the slim volume and stuffed it down the front of his trousers, making sure his shirttails covered the evidence.

"We'd better go back now," she said. "I'll get a dustpan. I don't want Daniel or Kheelan findin' a piece. They don't need t' know we've taken a stroll if ya know what I mean. Jesus though, I'll hate to have t' lock ya up again."

He smiled at her. "At least you've given me something nice to think about," he said.

He willingly went back to his bunk and allowed her to rechain his wrist. Phillip was still snoring. When she left, he immediately reached into his pants.

The book had a fancy binding of ample royal blue leather with red corners.

He opened it and stared at disbelief at the cover page. He scanned it once, then a second time to make sure he fathomed the floridly confident, hand-drawn script.

*Being the Personal Journal of My Visitations
to the Extraordinary Libraries of Vectis and Pinn
Benjamin Franklin
1775*

Then, with an unsteady hand, he slowly turned the page and began to read.

It is with considerable Trepidation that I sit to pen my Recollections of recent Events. The Things which I have seen may scarcely be believed, but as a Man of Science who has a certain Reputation for Powers of Observation, I would hope I might be more believed than Most. Yet I must admit to Myself that I have not decided if I shall ever divulge the Contents of this Journal. Yet my Memory, which is now quite excellent, may not be always so. I have seen Men in their Onage who can scarce remember where they have left their Slippers. Should in the future I choose to enlighten Others concerning my Discoveries and find Myself bereft of Recollection, then this Journal shall serve as my Aide Mémoire.

Indeed, as I sit here in semi Darkness with the oddest Assortment of Companions, I must wonder if I Myself will ever see the Light of Day. I am not a Captive here, but neither am I entirely a Free Man. My Fate, as I understand it, is being debated some-

what furiously by my Hosts. I am always in
favor of a good and robust Debate, but as I
am the Subject of such Discourse, I admit
to a certain Queasiness. Adding to my Dis-
comfiture, the early Twinges of the Gout, my
most unwelcomed Friend, arrived again last
Evening.

I think it best to begin this Tale in the
Summer of 1761, when first I met a most re-
markable Gentleman, Baron Le Despencer,
who in those Days was less grandly known
as Francis Dashwood.

"Benjamin, a gentleman is here to see you."

Benjamin Franklin opened the door to his bed-chamber and looked over the top of his glasses at his landlady and companion, Margaret Stevenson. She peered at his unfinished tray of victuals and clucked at him.

"I've been too busy to eat," he mumbled, showing her his ink-stained fingers. "Who is it?"

"His name is Francis Dashwood. Polly is in the sitting room keeping him company, but I don't want to leave her alone with him too long." She rolled her eyes. "He seems a lively one."

"Very well, you go and rescue the dear girl. I shall be down presently."

Franklin had lived as a lodger on Craven Street since his arrival in London in 1757. It was a four-story house owned by the widow Stevenson, situated near Whitehall between the Strand and the Thames. He had found the lodgings quite by accident shortly after his arrival on a packet boat from Philadelphia.

He had come to England in the official capacity as Agent of Pennsylvania, representing the colony's interests before the powers that be. While unrest and dissatisfaction existed up and down the American colonies, Pennsylvania had a particularly vexing set of problems, which Franklin was tasked to solve. Pennsylvania was owned and governed not by the crown but by the descendants of William Penn, who had been granted a proprietorship of the territory in 1681 by King Charles II. There were some Pennsylvanians, Franklin included, who believed they would do better answering to Parliament than the capricious Penn heirs. Franklin's remit was to lobby Parliament to release the colony from the Penn yoke.

Franklin had been the overwhelming choice of Pennsylvania's political class to represent them in England as he was far and away their most accomplished citizen. He had risen from a humble boyhood in Boston to become a colonial printer and the publisher of the most respected newspaper in America, *The Pennsylvania Gazette*. He had given himself over to public service and had a long-standing seat in the Pennsylvania Provincial Assembly. He more than dabbled in the natural sciences, becoming a world-renowned inventor, scientist, and philosopher. By the time of his appointment as Pennsylvania's agent, he had amassed a trove of political and academic honors.

He had also amassed the trappings of an unconventional lifestyle. His marriage to Deborah Read of Philadelphia had been of a common-law nature due to bigamy laws. Her first husband had absconded to Barbados with her dowry and was never heard from again. His eldest child, William, was all-but-openly acknowledged as the illegitimate product of Franklin's union with a lady of disrepute. But rather than banish his son to a life on the edges of society, Franklin embraced the boy and warmly tucked him into his household. Deborah, a plain and simple woman,

seemed to tolerate Franklin's skirt chasing and settled into a marriage where her husband was away for
years at a time. Their first son, Francis, died of the
pox at a young age, but their second child, Sarah,
was a healthy fourteen-year-old when her father departed for his assignment to London.

Franklin enjoyed domesticity every bit as much as
he did ribaldry, and in London he quickly settled into
a surrogate family life with his landlady and her teenage daughter Polly, tutoring, mentoring and flirting
with the pretty lass. He even brought his son, William, to England to expose him to politics and diplo-
macy and had tried his hardest to push him and Polly
together to no avail. But outside the Craven Street
household, Franklin prowled the bars, coffee shops,
and salons of London, sporting his fancy suits and
glittering reputation, his owlish eyes searching for all
the amusements a teeming city of 750,000 could offer.

When Franklin entered the sitting room, Polly Stevenson, a pretty twenty-two-year-old, looked as relieved as if the warder in the Tower of London had
come to release her from captivity. She smiled sweetly
at Franklin and scurried away.

"Sir Francis," Franklin said with a polite bow. "I
am honored to be in your esteemed presence."

"You know of me?" Dashwood asked, his fleshy,
moist lips curled in delight.

"Indeed I do," Franklin said, straightening the
jacket of his blue velvet ensemble. "Member of Parliament for New Romney, Treasurer of the Chamber,
tipped to be the next Chancellor of the Exchequer,
heir apparent as the Baron Le Despencer, the premier
barony of England."

Dashwood, though fifty-two years old, nearly the
same age as Franklin, was so delighted by this recitation of his particulars that he jumped up and down in

glee like a little boy, spilling some of the brandy Polly had given him. He had a round, full face with small, dark eyes and a corpulence commensurate with his affluence.

"I was told you were a clever one, and indeed you are! But how is it you know my *curriculum vitae*?"

"It is my business to know the inner workings of His Majesty's Government. The good people of Pennsylvania are paying me to know these things, for how else can I effectively represent their interests in England?"

"Well, it's all very logical," Dashwood said. "But beyond the dry bones of my political life, what else have you heard of me? Pray tell!"

Franklin gestured for Dashwood to sit and did so himself. "Well," he said, "I ask for forgiveness in advance if this story is untrue, but I was told that as a young man on your grand tour of Europe you once observed the worshippers in the Sistine Chapel pretending to whip themselves for their sins in a most perfunctory and ineffective way. Thereupon, the next day, you returned with a large horsewhip concealed under your cape and at the appropriate moment, produced the instrument and had at yourself with great drama and vengeance."

Dashwood roared. "Indeed it is true! And for my impudence, the Swiss Guards escorted me to the gates of the Eternal City and bade me not to return. I'm afraid my views on Catholicism have not much changed with advancing age though my powers of discretion have marginally improved. Marginally."

"I would enjoy having a conversation about religion with you, Sir Francis, preferably over a good bottle of claret. I myself am a Christian, to be sure, but I'm a picker and a chooser. I take what I want of it and discard the rest."

Dashwood giggled at this and told Franklin he was sorry he'd been remiss in not reaching out earlier. He was certain, he said, that the two of them shared a great many views on a great many subjects. "I wonder," Dashwood said, "if I might entice you to come to my country house in Buckinghamshire for an extended visit. In a fortnight's time, a number of gentlemen will be joining me there for social activities."

The loaded way he said "social activities" piqued Franklin's interest. "And who might these gentlemen be?" Franklin asked.

"Ah, the likes of Sandwich, Wilkes, Bute, Whitehead, Selwyn, Lloyd. That lot."

That lot included some of the most influential men in England, fellows whom Franklin had been courting and lobbying for years with varying degrees of success.

"You have my complete attention," Franklin said.

"Yes, I thought as much. We need to include an American gentleman in our circle. That's what's been said, and who better than the esteemed Dr. Franklin?"

"I would be honored," Franklin said, removing an errant strand of flowing gray hair from his face. "Might I know more of the social activities you mentioned?"

"I do not wish to spoil the fun. Suffice it to say that we call ourselves the Friars of St. Francis of Wycombe. But you need not bring your Bible. Our worship is directed toward wholly more earthly realms."

"I see," Franklin said, his eyes twinkling.

Dashwood finished his brandy. "And wait till you see our nuns!"

* * *

Franklin had a notion he was going to enjoy his sojourn at West Wycombe the moment he arrived at
Sir Dashwood's country estate. The footman was
dressed in some sort of flowing Arabic robe, and the
butler looked something like a sultan. All manner of
libations were laid out on a tray in his sunny room—
gin, port, and decanters of vin rouge and blanc. A
choice selection of fruits and cheeses was also on
hand. Before departing, the butler advised him that
the protocol for the evening involved donning the
garments in the wardrobe.

On his own, Franklin swung open the wardrobe
doors and laughed at the contents: the coarse brown
habit of a monk, a hemp sash, and a pair of leather
sandals. He heard carriage wheels on the gravel.
From his window he saw another visitor arrive and in
the distance, two more carriages were coming down
the drive.

That evening, any self-consciousness Franklin
might have possessed over his garb was cleansed
when he saw that every one of the forty gentlemen
assembling in Dashwood's great hall was similarly
attired. A servant promptly thrust a flute of champagne into his hand and he was warmly greeted by
men he had previously met in the corridors of power
at Whitehall. And in short order he was introduced
to other "friars" he didn't know, including John
Montagu, the fourth Earl of Sandwich, a haughty
and imperious man, the only one who doused Franklin with condescension.

"Philadelphia, you say," the tall man said down his
narrow nose. "I rather imagine they would have to
drag you back to a place such as that kicking and
screaming."

"Hardly," Franklin replied. "I believe Your Lordship would find it most satisfactory in all respects
though you would be hard-pressed to find a congregation of monks drinking champagne on Market
Street. Perhaps I could visit Your Lordship at Parliament to inform you about the recent activities in our
fair colony."

Franklin received a dismissive, "Perhaps."

Then, to the sound of an unseen gong, Dashwood
emerged from behind a curtain. He was decked out
in a bishop's robe with a red mitre perched upon his
large head.

"Welcome, Brothers! Welcome! It's been too long
since our last congregation, has it not? As always, I
offer a special welcome to our twelve superior monks,
who have already met this afternoon to discuss the
Order's business."

Franklin looked around and realized that a dozen
men wore red sashes around their habits instead of
hemp. One of them was Sandwich.

Dashwood continued, "We have decided to install
a new inferior monk tonight to add to our distin-
guished order. I give you Brother Benjamin Franklin,
our esteemed guest from Philadelphia."

Franklin bowed humbly and said to the portly man
beside him, "I have no idea what I've gotten into."

The man replied, with a leer, "You will not be dis-
appointed, Brother."

"Come, Brothers!" Dashwood shouted. "Our evening begins!"

With that, he led the group outside and through
a grove decorated with classical statues in indecent
poses. Franklin stopped in front of Hermes, the god
of lust, who was holding a red-tipped phallus as a
staff. He peered over his glasses and chortled at the

inscription on the base: *peni tente non penitenti*—a stiff penis is better than repentance.

Beyond the grove, Franklin could see in the fading evening light the facade of a mock Gothic church constructed of flint with chalk mortar. Above the main arch was carved the motto of the Order, *FAY CE QUE VOUDRAS*, do what you wish, which Franklin took as confirmation that an interesting time awaited.

The facade was in fact the entranceway to a series of natural caves and tunnels, which Dashwood had elaborately embellished over the years. The labyrinthine chalk walls were shaped into archways. Grand halls were chiseled out. A channel of natural still water was widened and dubbed the River Styx.

Their way was illuminated by candles, but Franklin could have scarcely gotten lost as all he had to do was follow the friar directly in front of him. Upon entry into an enormous chamber blazing with sooty torches and adorned with whimsical and weird faces carved into the chalk, Franklin saw a long banqueting table groaning under an abundance of roasted meats, pies, and sundry delicacies. Looking up, he was astonished to see a large, painted fresco, which aped classical themes but was surely the most pornographic group of images he had ever seen.

Dashwood took the place of honor, surrounded on each side by his superior monks. Then the inferiors were bade to take their seats.

"Bring in the nuns!" Dashwood declared.

Franklin had been fixed on a splendid, steaming leg of lamb, but he was persuaded to turn away from it at the sight of some three dozen young women flooding the chamber with their presence. All were dressed in the black habits of nuns, but their hair

flowed freely, and their habits had long slits allowing creamy thighs to flash into view. The nuns proceeded to pour wine and whisper provocative things
into monks' ears, generally involving their need to
be punished for their wickedness. Franklin reckoned
these were local girls pressed into service but one of
his table mates told him that many were imported
from London for the occasion.

After the most debauched meal of which Franklin
had ever partaken, the group moved through another
series of passageways into a large chamber, this one
much more dimly lit. It was apparent that this room
was set up as an abbey of sorts, complete with pews
and an altar.

Lord Sandwich, referring to Dashwood as the
abbot, called him to begin the mass and among general sniggering and catcalls, Dashwood drunkenly
offered an ersatz version of a Latin mass, replete
with profanities and double entendres. The assembled monks, who by now were dividing their attentions between Dashwood and canoodling nuns, grew
louder and louder in their responses and began to
openly call for the Devil to appear. And when the
congregation was in a high lather of fevered excite-
ment, Dashwood reached for and pulled a hidden
string, connected by a pulley to the top of a large
chest next to Sandwich's chair.

Out sprang a gibbering and shrieking baboon,
which burst from its confinement, scampered over
Sandwich's head, and ran amok among the howling
monks, who either broke into hysterics as Franklin
did or alternatively cowered in fear at the perceived
actual arrival of Satan.

The sight of this black creature appearing out of the
gloomy red atmosphere of the chamber, seemingly
conjured by their exhortations, unnerved Sandwich

so greatly that he promptly let loose a full bladder of urine and ran from the hall, shouting in alarm. It took a number of his peers to fetch him back and one of the nuns was dispatched to procure a mop to erase the evidence of his cowardice.

When order was eventually restored, Dashwood declared the black mass concluded, and upon reiterating their motto, *"Fay ce que voudras!"* the night took its inevitable turn. Franklin, for his part, was delightfully accosted by a comely nun with raven hair and clear skin who asked him if he would care to accompany her to a couch in one of the side chambers.

"Do you desire a lesson in the catechisms?" Franklin asked woozily.

"Wot's that?" the girl asked.

"If not, we can discuss current theories of electricity."

Again, a blank look.

"Never mind," Franklin said, as the girl pulled him to his feet. "I am a most patient teacher, and I am certain we can find a subject that interests you."

Although I departed England for Philadelphia in 1762, I was called back to Service and returned to England only two Years later. The political Situation in the Colonies had deteriorated. It was clear the odious Stamp Act was about to be passed by Parliament, and cognizant of the Foment this would cause throughout our American Colonies, I was dispatched once again to urge the Crown that it should make Efforts to deal differently with its American Cousins, to treat us with greater Felicity as a full Member of the British Empire, entitled to Representation in Parliament if we are to be asked to pay to the Crown Taxes upon our Goods.

Upon my return, I happily reestablished Residency with Mrs. Stevenson at my old Haunt on Craven Street. Though I had intended the Journey to be numbered in Months, the steadily worsening Climate between the Colonies and England turned a brief Trip into one lasting a Decade! I, of course, renewed my Friendships and made new Associations among Politicians, the Gentry, and Scientists both in England and indeed France. I must admit I also continued to serve rather faithfully as a Friar of St. Francis of Wycombe, for to do Otherwise would have severed not only important political Ties but have measurably diminished my Joie de Vivre.

And so, in 1775, the New Year just upon Us when I was grieving from my just received Family News, I was called on by Dashwood, who had by then inherited the Title from his Father and was now Baron Le Despencer.

Franklin was shocked at Le Despencer's appearance. He had not seen him for the better part of a year, and the man had gone downhill. Once hale and hearty with a perpetual spring to his step and an air of mischief in his eye he was pale and drawn, his inverted lower lip, once impish, now dry and forlorn.

Yet when Franklin voiced concern about his well-being, the baron brushed it off and told him he had come calling because of concern about his American friend's health.

"Tragic news about your wife's passing, old man. What a blow," he said, slumping into an armchair.

Franklin sighed heavily. "Her death was not a shock, Baron. She suffered a stroke some years back, and her health had declined. I could divine that from her letters well enough. My greatest sadness is that I was not at her side during these long years in England."

"You are a fine public servant, a credit to your compatriots, though I fear we shall be at arms soon enough. Is it, do you think, inevitable?"

"I fear it is. I have spent many years of my life endeavoring to find compromises and solutions, but I'm afraid the intransigence of the king and his Parliament has brought us to the brink."

"I hear," the baron said sadly, "that you will be departing these shores soon."

Franklin nodded. "I have some last maneuvers I would see through, but yes, I believe I will have to sail these old bones back across the sea to be with my people during the approaching storm."

"Then come with me to West Wycombe one last time for what may be the final meeting of the Friars. I've had my own small storms, I'm afraid, and I will be closing down our fraternal order."

Franklin knew well of Le Despencer's woes. Many were a direct result of that wretched baboon. Lord Sandwich had not taken his humiliation that night well, and the baron had found he was not the best of men to anger. In the intervening years, Le Despencer's political career had collapsed at the hands of Sandwich's marionette maneuverings, and neither had his business interests fared well. The expense of being England's leading lush was no longer tenable.

"I'm a bit old for the doings in your caves," Franklin said.

"By God, man, you're only two years my senior, so don't play at decrepitude. You must come! I will be bereft if you do not." He looked truly despondent.

Franklin reluctantly agreed to the baron's pathetic request, then purposely turned the conversation to the last-ditch efforts afoot to avert a great war.

Though Franklin had been in the West Wycombe caves many times, he couldn't remember a more desultory occasion. The twenty or so monks in attendance tried their best to appear merry, but none seemed up to the occasion. Even Le Despencer in his banqueting speech sounded more like a eulogizer than anything else. It was the end of an era, the monks were aging, and war was coming.

Yet the nuns buzzing about seemed out of touch with the mood of the place. Like the professionals they were, they stayed in character, showing a good bit of leg and saying all the right naughty things to spice up the evening. Franklin, in particular, given his fresh bereavement, was in no mood for frivolity, and, indeed, he felt silly wearing his monk's habit. But one girl persisted in her attentions to the sixty-eight-year-old statesman and succeeded in rallying his spirits.

She was a black-haired beauty with buttercream skin, certainly not yet twenty. During supper, she kept his wineglass full and insisted on licking his fingers clean, one by one when he was done. Then she pulled him off to one of the private rooms and sat upon his lap.

"You're a pretty lass," Franklin told her. "Have you been to these before?"

"Aye," the girl said with a thick northern accent, playing with his long, thinning hair.

"And what is your name?"

"Sister Abigail."

"Your real name."

"Abigail."

"I see," Franklin said. "You are not employing a nom de plume."

"A what?"

Franklin chuckled. "You're using your real name."

"Aye."

She put her hand under his habit, but he blocked its upward progress and removed it.

"You're a very sweet girl, and I will put good coin in your donation cup, but I would rather talk than play."

"Why?" the girl asked.

He slid her off his knee and had her sit beside him.

"Because I am old, and I am sad."

"Why are you sad?"

"Because I have recently received a letter from America informing me that my good wife has passed."

"Was she sick?"

"Indeed she was."

"It was her time," the girl said emphatically. "Everyone has their time. You shouldn't be sad. 'Tis God's will."

Franklin seemed happy to have been given entrée to a conversation topic.

"I'm not so sure I fully adhere to the Calvinist principles that everything under the sun is subject to God's predetermination. Surely there are some elements under the direct control of man."

"That is not so," the girl insisted. When she drew up her knees for comfort, her saucy nun's robe parted to reveal all.

Franklin rearranged her gown, mumbling, "I am apt to lose the direction of my thoughts. There, that's better. Abigail, you seem very sure of yourself on this point of theology. Why is that? Is that the way you were raised?"

"I'm sure because I know."

"To my mind, one can know something, truly know it, only via the powers of direct observation. Faith requires more of a leap because we cannot directly observe the provenance of God. The only things in life I feel I sincerely know are the things I have seen and studied."

"I know about you," Abigail said. "You're an inventor, ain't you?"

"I am indeed."

"You invented lightning."

At that Franklin nearly laughed himself off the settee. "Hardly, my dear! God takes credit for that. I merely chronicled the properties of lightning and invented the lightning rod to tame its wrath. How do you know of me?"

"I heard the baron talking."

"Where?"

"In his house."

"Do you live there?"

She nodded, but as she did, a tear dribbled down her cheek.

"Are you in the baron's employ?" Franklin asked. She nodded.

"But surely that is a good thing, is it not, rather than being on the streets like so many waifs?"

"I want t' go home."

"Then tell the baron, and he will surely let you go."

"He will not. I'm inventured."

Franklin smiled at that. "I believe you mean indentured. How did you wind up in indentured servitude?"

"I ran away from home. I shouldn't have, but I done it. A traveling man found me on the road and took me with him, made me do things with him and other men. He took me t' London, where he sold my indenture t' the baron. Now I'm indentured t' His Lordship. I'd need fifteen pounds to buy my freedom. And then I'd have t' find my way home."

Franklin shook his head. "What a tale of woe child! And fifteen pounds! A criminal sum given the circumstances and altogether a criminal enterprise. I shall speak to the baron and see what can be done."

She flung her arms around his neck, and pleaded, "Please take me home, kind sir. I'll do anything. Anything!"

He extricated himself, and said, "All I can do is speak to the man. I fear I have too much on my plate at the present to attend to your problems, worthy as they may be. A war is coming. My country is teeming with Abigails and I must try to save as many souls as I can."

"If they are doomed, they are doomed," she said petulantly.

"As you said," Franklin intoned. "Now run along. I would like to spend a while in solitude and contemplation like a proper monk."

She screwed her face into a stubborn pose. "Take me back to Yorkshire, and I'll show you the most amazing things. Things you could never imagine."

"What kind of things?"

"Proof there's a God in the sky. Proof he sets the fate of men."

Franklin raised his eyebrows. "Tell me what this proof is."

"No! If I tell you, you won't believe me. You must pay my indenture and take me home in a carriage under your protection."

"To Yorkshire? I simply cannot do that! I have pressing engagements, my dear. I must return soon to Philadelphia."

She went silent for a while, then said, "Then take me to a place called the Isle of Wight. Have you heard of it?"

"Indeed I have."

"Is it far?"

"Not very. A day from London. What is on the Isle of Wight?"

"There's proof there too. I'm sure of it."

It was late afternoon, and the sun over the Dales was providing little in the way of light or warmth. Flocks of sheep began huddling, and Harris hawks sailed the thermals searching for the last meal of the day. In the approaching dusk, the MI5 team rolled up to the Lightburn Farm.

Rob Melrose climbed out of the car, and said to Annie, "God, can you imagine living in a place like this. Might as well be in the Middle Ages."

She looked up at the steep, wild fells, and said, "I think it's quite beautiful."

"Right," Melrose said, "I don't expect any problems, but better be safe than sorry. Mitchell, come in with us so we can efficiently do a search if they consent. David, stay with the car."

The driver made a move for his shoulder pistol, but Melrose said, "Don't show any weapons, please. We're not going to war."

Annie knocked at the door, her two colleagues behind her. She waited half a minute, then knocked again. This time the door opened a few inches and Cacia peered out.

"Oh, hi," Annie said. "Remember me? Miss Locke

from the Security Services? Sorry to bother you again, but we'd like to come in and ask you a couple more questions?"

"About what?" was the frosty response.

"Well, actually, it's about the gentleman I was with earlier, Mr. Piper. You haven't seen him, have you?"

"Lost another one?" Cacia asked sharply.

"Yes, well, it seems so. It would really be very helpful if we could come in and chat about it."

Cacia nodded. "Just give me a few seconds."

The door closed, and Annie turned to Melrose with a shrug. "I think she's going to cooperate."

"Thought you said she was friendly," Melrose said.

"At least she didn't bless us out," Annie said.

Kenney and his team scrambled to get eyes on the front door of Lightburn Farm from a concealed vantage point across the road. When the MI5 vehicle entered the farmhouse lane, Kenney had Harper pull off the road and led his men on a dash by foot, toting their gear. They crossed the River Eden at a footbridge and headed uplands to the foothills of Great Boar Fell which was towering over them. About a quarter mile from Lightburn Farm they found a good stand of bushes.

Through binoculars, Kenney watched the front door open again and the three agents enter the house.

"What now?" Harper asked his boss.

Kenney said, "Hopefully, they'll leave with Piper. If so, we'll tail them back to the hotel or wherever and grab the son of a bitch quietly, then lean on him hard to find out if he knows anything about the postcards."

"And if they leave without him?"

Kenney breathed on his cupped hands to warm them. "Then we keep on trucking."

Cacia let them in. The hearth had a good fire going. Annie scanned the kitchen to the left and the sitting room to the right, both empty.

"We haven't seen your Mr. Piper again," Cacia said, eyeing her visitors nervously.

"That's odd," Annie said. Then she lied. "He said he was coming back here to ask you more questions.

"Well, he didn't."

Melrose came forward, thrusting out his chin. "Look here, Mrs. Lightburn, this is a serious matter for the authorities and I've come all the way from London to sort it out. We would like to search the premises to satisfy ourselves that Mr. Piper is not here."

"I told ya he wasn't," Cacia said truculently. "Why's that not enough for ya?"

"I'm not suggesting that you aren't being truthful, ma'am, but if I had a pound for every lie I've been told in my line of work, I'd be a wealthy man. I can't write in my report to my superior that I simply accepted the representations of a member of the public. I must insist that you allow us to have a look about."

Cacia's cheeks reddened. "And I say no t' you! You'll have t' leave."

Annie piped up, "Rob, let me talk to her alone, okay?"

Melrose stiffened and ignored her. "Look, we can do this the easy way or the hard way. Either you voluntarily consent to a search of your property, or we will be back here shortly with a judicial order and the local police. If you resist then, you'll be jailed."

Daniel Lightburn bounded down the stairs into their midst brandishing a shotgun, and shouting in rage, "You come here ont' my land and start makin' demands? You're threatening t' put us in jail? I don't think so, mister."

Mitchell reached into his jacket for his pistol and moved to shield Annie and Melrose. He'd done body-guard work for the Crown Protection Services and was probably operating on pure instinct.

For a split second the room was quiet until Annie saw the hatred and resolve in Daniel's face and screamed, "Nae!"

The shotgun was loaded with #8 birdshot. The scatter-blast tore through Mitchell's chest, piercing his heart and lungs. His body absorbed most but not all of the lethality. Melrose was hit with a half dozen pellets in his left cheek and eye and collapsed to the floor, writhing in agony. Mitchell teetered upright a few moments like a logged tree succumbing to grav-ity and fell down onto him, stone dead.

Annie caught a couple of pellets in her right leg, but she ignored the lancinating pain and dropped to her knees to tend to the wounded men. "Get an ambu-lance!" she shouted. "Right now!"

Two strapping young men, Haven's brothers, rushed down the stairs to help their father.

Daniel repumped the shotgun and kept it leveled at Melrose and Mitchell. "No ambulances! Boys, take their guns. Cacia, do something for that man t' shut him up and stop th' blood. Take 'em all downstairs."

Haven was on the stairs, crying at the sight of car-nage. Behind her, her two little cousins appeared wide-eyed. Their mother, Gail, ordered them back to their rooms then joined Annie and Cacia on the stone floor to tend to Melrose's bloody face.

Outside, the agent who'd stayed with the car reacted to the sound of the shotgun and began opening the driver-side door.

Before his foot touched the ground another blast fractured the air and peppered the car door. Blood began to ooze from his leg and flank. At the sight of Kheelan lining up another shot he threw the car into reverse and flew back down the lane.

More shots were fired, blowing out the windscreen, but the frantic driver reached the road and slammed the car into drive. Grimacing in pain he headed at speed toward Kirkby Stephen, voice-dialing Emergency Services.

From their post across the road, Kenney and his team watched in quiet fascination as the scene unfolded. The blast from inside the house was audible, and Kenney immediately identified it with a matter-of-fact, "Shots fired."

When the driver of the idling car was attacked, Lopez asked him, "What's our move, chief?"

"This isn't our shooting match, gentlemen. We're paid spectators. But I'll tell you one thing—I'm as pleased as a tick on a fat dog. This means that Piper's in there. These sons of bitches are doing the heavy lifting for us."

There was chaos inside. Haven's brothers peeled back a rug in the mudroom and yanked open a trapdoor. A steep staircase plunged into the ground. Daniel was barking orders to take the dead man to the barn; blindfold Annie with duct tape; wrap and tape a towel round Melrose's head.

Kheelan rushed in, breathing very hard, yelling that the driver had gotten away.

"Jesus, what are we t' do?" Cacia cried.

"Don't know," Daniel said. "I fuckin' well don't know. Boys, get 'em down th' stairs now! Cacia, tend their wounds down there. And make that man shut up even if you have t' finish 'im off. One dead, two dead, what's th' difference? Kheelan, fetch the other shotguns and give 'em to th' lads. We've got a war on our hands."

Blindfolded and in shock, Melrose and Annie were marched down the secret stairs. Cacia went first. At the bottom landing, she pushed open a large, heavy door that led directly into the Library at the opposite end from the dormitory and writers' room.

Annie could see none of it, not the books from 2027, not the endless stacks. She kept talking to Melrose, telling him he'd be okay, telling him to hang in there. But his only response were sharp breaths and groans.

Though he was loath to stop reading, Will laid down Franklin's journal the moment he heard the muffled retort.

Benjamin Franklin at Vectis! What did he find there?

But he had to stop. It's a gunshot, he thought. The cavalry's here.

He tucked the book under the mattress and woke Phillip.

"Get the cobwebs cleared, kiddo," he told the boy. "I think a rescue party's topside."

The second muffled shot confirmed his opinion.

They sat, chained to their bunks and anxiously waited. Finally, there were voices coming, not from the direction of the storeroom but from the anteroom connecting the writers' room and the Library.

The door opened, and Cacia came in. Will could tell instantly that something was very wrong and that rescue wasn't in the cards.

Melrose was brought in first, half-carried by Kheelan, his head wrapped in a bloody towel. Annie was next, limping and guided by one of Haven's brothers.

Will tried to stand, forgetting for a moment he was chained to the bunk. "Christ!" he said.

Phillip was shocked at the sight of the wounded captives, and said, "Dad?"

"It's all right, Phillip."

Annie turned her blindfolded face toward the direction of Will's voice. "Will? Is that you?"

"It's me. You're hurt." Blood was trickling down her leg. "Cacia, unlock me so I can help."

Kheelan said no, but Cacia did as he asked, whispering plaintively in his ear, "Don't try anything. There's one dead already."

Will rose and peeled the tape from Annie's face and hair as gently as he could. She looked around, frightened, and saw the rows of empty cots. "What is this place?"

"Later," Will said. Without asking permission, he raised her skirt up to look at her wounds. "Buckshot. Cacia, get me some clean bandages and some rubbing alcohol. And some matches and a tweezers."

"I'm okay," Annie said. "He needs the help."

"Who is he?" Will asked.

"My boss."

"Who got killed?"

"His name's Mitchell," she said, anguished. "An agent."

With Kheelan's scowling help, they got Melrose onto a cot. He immediately curled himself into a ball, his moaning growing louder.

"Does anyone know we're here?" Will asked Annie.

"Shut up!" Kheelan demanded.

Cacia intervened, "Kheelan, go back upstairs. You've got more important things t' do. Andrew, go back with 'im and fetch alcohol, bandages—all the things Will's asked for."

"Chain 'em all up first, Cacia," Kheelan insisted.

"They're not going anywhere. The doors are locked, and I'm watching," Cacia said.

"Not good enough," Kheelan huffed. "Andrew, take th' gun and shoot anyone if they try anything. I'll fetch th' supplies."

The young man nodded gravely and took the gun from his uncle but when Kheelan left, Cacia told him, as only a mother can, to keep it pointed at the ground.

Annie finally answered Will's question, loud enough for everyone to hear. "One of our agents escaped. The farm will be swarming with police within the hour."

Will and Annie were kneeling over Melrose, but it was Cacia who peeled back the towel. Melrose effected a defensive posture and raised his arms to fight her, garbled out some words, but then grew quiet as if his energy had been spent. His eye was swollen shut and was oozing with blood, and his cheek resembled bloody, fresh meat.

"He needs a hospital, Cacia," Will said. "We can't treat this. A pellet could have gone into his brain."

"No!" she said. "No hospitals. We've got t' deal with this 'ere."

Will was thinking fast. "Look, Cacia, you've got a little time before the police arrive. Carry him up, lay him beside the road. They'll find him and take care of him. You've got plenty of hostages here. One more won't make a difference."

She seemed to instantly take to the idea. "Andrew.

Go get Daniel or Kheelan to come down and 'elp. We're going t' do as Will suggests."

The young man screwed up his face. "But Uncle Kheelan said . . ."

"I don't care what he said! You'll mind your mother!"

Andrew stood his ground and half raised the shotgun.

"Will, will you promise you won't try anything while Andrew's gone."

Will said an emphatic yes, and Andrew reluctantly retreated.

The blood began flowing more aggressively through Melrose's torn eyelid and Cacia stood up. There were clean towels in the storeroom, and she went to get some.

Will saw that Annie was experiencing paroxysms of traumatic shivering. He got the blanket off his bed, wrapped it around her, and hugged her for added warmth.

"I'm sorry I ditched you," he said. "I had to do it to find Phillip."

"Hello, Phillip," she said weakly.

"Hey," the boy answered, frowning.

"What do they do down here?" she asked Will.

"I'll explain later. Let's concentrate on getting ourselves out of this mess."

She finally let loose and cried, apologizing between sobs, that a trained agent shouldn't be acting like this.

"It's okay," Will said, planting a kiss on her hair. "You're a human being first, an agent second."

"Dad, I'm right here," Phillip said in exasperation.

Will smiled. The boy was protecting the honor of his mother. He liked that. "Don't worry, kiddo," he said, waving his ring finger. "The wedding band's still on and your mom's number one."

Cacia ran back through the dormitory with some white towels and applied one to Melrose's eye.

"Cacia," Will said gently, "this is over. I'm really sorry it's come to this. I know this has been your life's work, and I know how important it is, but it's out of your hands now. You've got to let us go. You've got to surrender. For Haven, for you, for your whole family. If you don't, this will end badly."

Her lip trembled. "What about th' Library?" She gestured in the direction of the writers' room. "What about them?"

"I don't honestly know," Will said. "I'll do what I can, but like I said, it's not in your hands anymore."

"I know," Cacia said, with an abject sadness that gave Will a pang. "I've always known."

"How?" he asked.

"I can see things," she said softly. "Glimpses of th' future, not like them, mind you, but I *can* see things."

Will looked at her red hair and it clicked. He remembered what he'd discovered years ago in Cantwell Hall in England. That Nostradamus had a redheaded mother, a Gassonet, from a line that originated at Vectis. One of the rare female births from the union of a young woman and a savant. A red-haired girl born with powers of clairvoyance.

He smiled at her, and she smiled back.

"Yes," she said, "I'm born from them."

"Haven too? Can she see things too?"

"Aye. She's got something of th' gift, I suppose. That's why she summoned your Phillip. She knew it was going t' be th' right thing t' do."

"How does it end, Cacia?"

"I can't say for certain, but I still can't let ya go. Daniel won't agree and I'm his wife. The decision is Daniel's."

Kheelan and Andrew came back down, and Kheelan pulled Cacia to the far side of the dormitory. The two of them exchanged sharp words but when they came back Kheelan and Andrew pulled Melrose to his feet and hauled him toward the storeroom.

Cacia went to Will. "They're going t' do what you said—leave him by th' road. I've got t' chain ya and this lady. I promised 'im I would. I'll bring th' first-aid gear, and we'll tend t' 'er wounds. Just cooperate, will ya?"

"We can take her!" Annie cried. "She's not armed!"

"I can't risk Phillip's getting hurt," he replied. "Let her chain you."

When Cacia was gone, Annie asked from her cot, "She talked about a library? What did she mean?"

"These people are librarians," Will said. And then, in the quiet of their isolation room he proceeded to tell her what was on the other side of the door.

An hour later, Will was the only one awake. Phillip had dozed off again, and Annie, with the benefit of several shots of whiskey to help her through the pellet extractions, had passed out. Will strained to hear some signs from aboveground that the police had arrived, but he could hear nothing.

With a slice of time on his hands and his curiosity unabated, he reached under his mattress for the Franklin journal and began to read again.

Nothing I had ever experienced could have prepared me for the Sights I encountered that fateful Night. By the Light of Abigail's Lantern, a strange Universe was illuminated. I felt as if I had found Aladdin's Cave though the Riches within were far greater than a Hoard of Gold, Silver, and Jewels. For an old Printer such as Myself, a Man who had made his Fortune producing Manuscripts, it was the ultimate Joy finding the greatest Treasure known to Man within the Covers of finely bound Books.

With both feet on hard ground, Benjamin Franklin found himself surrounded by thick leather books and the sweet, musty aroma of the animal skins that had gone into creating them. Abigail was beside him, holding her lantern high.

"See, I told you," she said proudly. "I told you so."

"You told me I would find some proof that God exists, child, and all I see is a great subterranean library."

"It's nae an ordinary library, Mr. Franklin. Pick a book. Look inside."

He reached randomly for one at eye level and wriggled it off its shelf. On the tooled binding was a date: 1324. He opened it and the spine cracked as if it was the first time the pages had been parted. Realizing he lacked his reading glasses, he handed Abigail the book and fumbled for his spectacle case. Once the wire rims were in place, he reclaimed the book and scanned the page.

"It appears to be a registry of sorts. Names and dates. Curious sort of registry though. All manner of foreign names, not the mix of souls I'd imagine in these parts in the fourteenth century. Why would Chinese, Arabs, and Portuguese be on the Isle of Wight of all places?"

"Look at th' dates, Mr. Franklin," the girl urged.

"Ah, *natus* and *mors*, *mors* and *natus*, over and over. These are birth dates and death dates. I still don't see the larger purpose, nor do I understand the nature of the population recorded."

"I'll show you then," Abigail said. "Come with me."

Franklin slid the book back into its place and by the light of her lantern, she led him past case after case of identical leather books and at the center of the vast underground chamber they discovered a central corridor running like an arrow down the long axis. They made a left turn, but the girl saw that the dates on the book spines were going the wrong way, so she reversed direction, pulling the bewildered old man by the sleeve.

"Where are we going?" Franklin asked.

"To 1774."

"How, may I ask are there books dated 1774 when we are presently in 1774? Clearly this chamber has been sealed for some significant time."

All she said was, "You'll see."

"This place is foxing me," he said. Her lantern illuminated only twenty feet or so ahead of her. If there was an end to the corridor, he could not see it, and his weariness and bewilderment made his legs heavy and caused his feet to shuffle against the stones.

The dates were running ever closer to the present. Franklin was tempted time and again to take a book down and examine it but Abigail was moving ahead smartly and he wasn't keen on being left behind. But suddenly, while noting the date 1581 on the spines nearest to him he shouted at Abigail to halt. In the periphery of his vision, he saw something on the ground.

"Come here!"

Before she arrived, he held his lantern high and headed down the narrow row. There was a heap of cloth on the ground, a mass of brown-and-black material. He drew closer, then gasped sharply at the realization the mass was a clothed skeleton lying on its back.

The skull had adherent patches of leathery flesh and dark hair. A flat black cap lay beside it. Franklin knelt with the curiosity of a coroner and pointed out to the petrified girl that the back of the skull had been caved in, and that the stones underneath it were rust-stained with ancient blood. The skeleton's clothing was black—a padded, high-collared doublet, knee breeches, hose hanging loose on long bones, leather boots. The body lay on top of a long, black cloak, fur-trimmed at the collar.

"I'd say from the manner of his attire this gentleman drew his breath during the reign of Queen Elizabeth."

"When was that?" the girl asked.

"Look at the dates of the nearest books," Franklin said. "I'll venture he was interested in his present day much the same as we seem drawn to our present day. And he got his head staved in for his trouble. Do you still think we should gaze on books dated 1774?" he asked.

"We must if you're t' understand this place," Abigail persisted.

"Very well, we'll leave this gent to his repose. I fear him not. It's live ones who give me pause."

They carried on down the central corridor past books dated from the seventeenth century and into the eighteenth century. The closer they got to 1774, the greater Franklin's sense of apprehension. What was this place? What was it this girl intended to show him?

Finally, Franklin saw the first of the books with a 1774 date, but Abigail was still going deeper into the chamber.

"But here!" he called out. "Here is 1774!"

"We're almost there," she replied.

He followed her lead. At the first glimpse of a volume with a 1775 date, she backtracked, then plunged into the racks of books.

"Raise your lantern for me," she said.

She grabbed a book down, looked at a page, put it back, then moved a few feet and grabbed another.

"What are you looking for?" he asked impatiently.

"Tell me the date your wife passed on."

Franklin nearly dropped his lantern. "Why in heavens do you wish to know this?"

"Please. Just tell me."

"The nineteenth of December."

"What was her given name at birth?"

"What kind of question is that?"

"Just tell me!"

"Her name was Deborah Read."

"Spell it out for me."

"R-E-A-D. Really, child, this is ridiculous!"

After a few minutes of searching through book-cases her countenance changed from anxious to triumphant.

"Here, Mr. Franklin. Look at this!"

The page was crowded with names, but all of them seemed to disappear when he saw the name of Deborah Read written in a tight, quill-dipped scrawl.

Next to her name was written: *MORS 19 December 1774.*

Franklin's head was in a spin. He felt his knees weakening and he had to prop himself against one of the heavy bookcases.

"Do you understand now?" the girl asked.

He struggled to speak. "How is this possible?"

"The hands of them that wrote these books were guided by God. That's how."

"I simply cannot believe it. This is impossible."

"I'll show you more then," she said. "What date were you born?"

"Seventeenth of January, 1706."

"Let's find *you* then."

They reversed direction and ten minutes later Franklin was staring at his own name.

Benjamin Franklin Natus 17 January 1706

There was no place to sit, so he simply sat down upon the stone floor and beckoned Abigail to join him there.

"You must tell me everything. I have so many questions I scarce know where to begin. How did you know this library was here?"

"The knowledge of th' Library of Vectis has passed down within my family. I was certain it was so, but I was scared I wouldn't be able t' find it."

His face was reddening, and questions tumbled out in rapid fire. "Why does your family know of this place? What do you know about the men who wrote these books? How much of the future is foretold? Why . . ."

She cut him short. "Please, Mr. Franklin, rest yourself, or you'll be ill. I will tell you everything I know."

When Abigail was done imparting the oral history she had been raised upon, Franklin appeared exhausted. He had taken his ubiquitous notebook and drafting pencil from his pocket and jotted down some notes while she spoke. By the time he put the pencil down, he had written words like Vectis Abbey, monks, Order of the Names, writers, ginger hair, Clarissa Lightburn, Pinn.

He looked up wearily. "I have spent my life exploring that natural world which God has created. I have always had the utmost admiration for the work of our Creator, but now I see with utmost clarity that He firmly holds the reins to the fundamental elements of our destiny. It is truly awe-inspiring."

Abigail nodded in agreement.

"And you are telling me, dear girl, that this library enterprise continues unabated at your homestead in Yorkshire?" Franklin asked.

"Aye," she said. "That's why I left."

"Explain yourself."

"It was my time to bear one of 'em."

Franklin suddenly looked avuncular. "Ah, I see. But yet you wish to return."

"I shouldn't have run away," Abigail said. "I've seen a lot worse and done a lot worse in my time in th' baron's employ, down in th' caves like."

"I do understand." He stood and hobbled a few steps on his gouty foot. "Abigail, my time is short in England, but I will take you to Yorkshire. I will hire the finest carriage and the swiftest team of horses. The scientist in me cannot resist seeing these creatures in the flesh. But there is something we must do here first."

She looked very happy. "What?"

"How far into the future does this library go?"

"Ours begins in the year 2027, so I reckon up to then."

"My God!" Franklin exclaimed. "So enormously distant. It's quite overwhelming. My horizon of interest is far more modest. I only need to peer into the near future."

With that he began to write upon a fresh page of his notebook, then tore it out.

"Listen, Abigail, there are important doings in America. My fellows are fixing for a war with England. Soon they'll have their second Continental Congress in Philadelphia, and I hope to be there cheek by jowl. They'll be looking to me for counsel. Do we keep talking, or do we start fighting? Can we win, or will we certainly lose? I've a notion to help increase my wisdom considerably. On this paper is a list of the greatest statesmen in America. Though the task vexes me no end, knowing their dates of death will tell me much."

He showed her what he had written on the page:

John Adams
Thomas Jefferson
George Washington

Alexander Hamilton
John Jay
James Madison

Then he told her to take it.

"Let's work as fast as we can. We'll start at the present and wend our way into the future. We'll divide the labor. I will look for the dates of demise of these gentlemen for 1775 and the subsequent odd years. You'll do the same for 1776 and the even years. You see? If you find one of the names call me over immediately."

She needed more explaining, but once she understood the concept, they parted ways, and both of them began to pull down books.

Hours passed. In the darkness of the chamber, Franklin had no way of knowing that the night had long slipped away. Immersed in his task, he lost track of all his senses save the visual as he scanned an endless sea of souls for the names of interest.

One by one they appeared to him and Abigail until Franklin called the girl over and declared an end to the exercise, only one name undiscovered.

"Our job is well enough done," Franklin said. "All but Madison. You have found three, I have found two, and I have my answer."

"I found one more," she said, looking at the floor.

"You found Madison after all?" he asked.

"Nae. I found you."

Franklin sighed heavily. "I do not wish to know." There was a long, awkward silence until he added, "Is it soon?"

"It is not soon."

"Well, that's good, as I have much to do before my eternal sleep. So here's what we have: Washington— 14 December, 1799, Hamilton—12 July, 1804,

Adams and Jefferson—both incredibly on the same day—4 July, 1826, Jay—17 May, 1829. Madison, God bless his soul, outlives them all if we haven't missed him. Do you know what this means, Abigail?"

She shook her head.

"If there's a war coming, these men, our finest leaders, our generals, will not perish in the conflict; nor will they hang from a British yardarm. They will live fine, long lives. It means, Abigail, that if there is a fight with the English, then we will win! So I will tell this to my fellows in arms: let there be war!"

When Annie began to stir, Will hastily shoved the journal under the mattress. He hardly had time to process what he had read. Years earlier, he'd been astonished to find that the Library had influenced the likes of John Calvin and Nostradamus and even William Shakespeare. Now he'd learned that it had played a role in the American Revolutionary War! The revelation made him giddy but Annie's dry-throated voice brought him back to the moment.

"What time is it?" she asked, reaching with her free arm for the water bottle by her cot.

"Nearly seven. How's your leg?"

"Sore. Do you think Melrose got picked up?"

"Hope so, but I don't think his eye's going to be saved."

"I shouldn't say something so horrid, but I rather think a patch will suit him."

Phillip sniggered.

"You're up too," Will said. "How're you doing?"

"I need to take a leak," the boy said sullenly.

"You can use the pee bottle," Will suggested.

"I'm not going to use it with her here!" Phillip protested.

"Do you think the police have arrived yet?" Annie asked.

He shrugged. "There'd better be more than Community Patrol Officer Wilson. He wasn't even armed, was he?"

"We are capable of mounting the appropriate response to hostage situations, Will," Annie said defensively. "You have a dim view of our capabilities in this country."

"Well, let's just hope they can take down a few farmers with shotguns."

Phillip decided to shout at the top of his lungs, "I need to pee!"

Seconds later, Cacia came through the anteroom door with her son, Andrew.

"That's how you get things done around here," Phillip said.

Cacia organized bathroom breaks for all of them, and when everyone was rechained to their bunks, Andrew left her alone with them.

Cacia sat down wearily on one of the empty beds.

"So what's going on up there?" Will asked.

"We have quite a bit of company, I'd say," Cacia replied with a breathy sigh. "All th' police lights have turned th' sky blue. It's quite lovely in a way."

"You must surrender," Annie said, sounding tough and obviously drawing on some kind of hostage training she'd done earlier in her career.

"Must I?" Cacia said. She turned her back on Annie, and said to Will, "I wish none of this'd happened."

"Meant to be," Will said. "That's the funny thing about fate, but I don't need to tell you that."

She nodded gravely.

"Has a negotiator contacted you?" Will asked.

"By phone. A pleasant-sounding man—I took the

first call. He asked if you and Phillip were here, but Daniel wouldn't let me say."

"They're going to want something from you. A gesture to start things off right. Why don't you send Phillip out?"

"Daniel won't have it. He's stuck in. He's a stubborn man. I've always liked that in 'im."

"Then give them Annie."

"Also nae."

"What then?" Will asked. "How does Daniel think this'll end?"

"He doesn't know, does he?"

"But you do."

A single tear left her eye for her cheek. "Come and walk with me, Will," she said.

He held up his wrist, and she unlocked the cuff. In the anteroom, she asked if he wanted to stroll the Library.

"Could we sit with the writers without disturbing them?" he asked.

She said that would be all right. "Very little distracts 'em from their task."

They entered the writers' room, and the savants hardly looked up. Haven was there reading a schoolbook. Cacia told her she could go upstairs but warned her to stay away from the windows and keep her curtains closed.

"Are the police still there?" the girl asked.

Her mother nodded.

"Can I sit with Phillip?"

"If you're good," Cacia said. "Please don't take off his chain. It's for his own protection."

"Is that other woman still there?"

"Her name's Annie," Will said. "She's a good enough egg. She's scared too."

Will and Cacia sat at the front of the room watching the writers in silence. Will felt like one of two classroom teachers proctoring an examination as their students scribbled onto copybooks.

The seven writers had a look of utter concentration on their pale faces. Heads down, they moved their pens across the page without a sound. Will imagined that in centuries past the noise of the quills against parchment would have been cacophonous, but the only thing breaking the quiet was the occasional rustle of a page being turned. If they had to search their minds for what they would write next, it was not apparent. There was no turning of heads to the ceiling for inspiration, no sighs or utterances. They were efficient, well-oiled machines.

Will noticed that the oldest writer, a grizzled man with a wispy reddish beard, was drooling onto his blue shirt without seeming to take any note of it. Cacia rose to tend to him. There was a towel hanging from a peg at his station, and Cacia used it to wipe his face and shirt carefully and tenderly. A drop of saliva had found its way to his page, and Cacia blotted it.

Returning to Will's side, she said, "His name's Angus. I reckon he's eighty or thereabouts. There's something wrong with 'im, but it's beyond our ken t' fix it."

"I don't suppose the local doctor makes house calls," Will said.

"Not to this house he doesn't," she said, seemingly happy to have something to laugh at. "We've gotten quite good with home remedies. When they get a cough or fever, we put them in th' room you're in t' keep the others away from it. On th' whole, they're a healthy lot."

Will scanned the green-eyed faces. "Can I ask you something?"

"Aye."

"About your sons."

"Andrew and Douglas?"

"No, these sons."

She rose again and stood behind the youngest and put her hands on his shoulders. He briefly stopped writing at the touch but started again without looking up. "This is Robert. He's seventeen, but he looks younger, doesn't he?" Then she moved to Matthew. "And Matthew here is twenty-one. I was only nineteen when I had him. The rest are from my mother's time, may she rest in peace."

"How do your other children feel about them?"

She kissed Matthew's ginger hair and rejoined Will. "They accept it. It's what they know. And the girls know that when it's their time, they'll do th' right thing."

"But it's not going to happen now, Cacia. You know that. For better or worse, everything you've known is coming to an end. The police aren't going away."

Her whispered response was so faint he almost missed it. "I know, I know. What will become of 'em? I can see many things, Will, but when it comes t' them, I see nowt."

"I'll do everything in my power to help them and help you."

"They'll be put in a cage somewhere. People will come and look at 'em like they were in a zoo. I can't bear th' thought."

"Then we've got to do something. We need to control the situation while we still can."

"There's nothing t' do," she said in despair.

"Yes there is," Will said. "Let me help you."

Kenney and his men huddled in the bushes in the evening cold and watched through night-vision scopes as the police action unfolded below them. The narrow B road was clogged with police cars, ambulances, and a large command van from the Cumbrian Constabulary. A SWAT team had established positions, but Kenney derided their tactics. "Jesus, would you look at that! They've only got two shooters on the high ground behind the farm. The thing's as watertight as a submarine with a screen door."

Harper opened an MRE pouch and asked his boss whether he wanted to eat.

"What is it?" Kenney asked.

"Shit stew," Harper replied.

"Yeah, I'll definitely have one, but lemme call in first." He put his earpiece into place, spoke a command into his NetPen, and when connected he said, "This is Kenney. Give me Admiral Sage, Priority Alpha." He waited a few moments, and Sage was on the line.

"What's your status?" Sage asked him.

"Well, sir, we've probably got every policeman and their cousin within a hundred miles of here. We're monitoring their comm, and it sounds like they're not making much progress with the folks holed up inside the farmhouse. There's a bunch of MI5 guys clucking around reporting back to London every five seconds, but they're letting the police take the lead."

"Do we have any confirmation that Piper is inside?"

"None. But he's there. I'm sure of it. His son too. And Locke, the MI5 gal, is a definite. They picked up her boss, who was shot-up, by the side of the road along with the body of another agent."

"And you still don't know what the hell is going on in there?" Sage asked with obvious irritation.

"No, sir."

"No chatter about librarians?"

"That's a negative. Anything to tell me about the Chinese situation, Admiral?"

"Continued saber rattling. The diplomatic channels are full of chatter. Lots of smoke getting blown up lots of asses at the UN."

"Roger that," Kenney said. "Any changes to our mission package?"

"No, just keep out of the way and out of sight and continue visual and electronic surveillance. Report back in two hours or sooner if there are developments. Out."

"What did he say?" Lopez asked.

"Told us to keep quiet as mice and keep eyes on the target."

Harper handed Kenney a pouch of food. "Why do they say that? Quiet as a mouse?" he asked. "A mouse can make a hell of a racket if it's got a hard-on about something."

"Should be quiet as a bug, maybe," Lopez said.

Kenney chewed on his stew. "You have no idea how ignorant you are, Lopez. Bugs are among the noisiest creatures on the planet. Did you know that a tiny, little river bug called the water boatman makes a mating sound that's almost a hundred decibels? That's like sitting ten feet away from a goddamn freight train as it's barreling past. Know how they do it?"

He did not.

"The little bug's got a penis about as thick as a human hair—about like yours, Harper—and it rubs that sucker against some ridges on its abdomen kind of like a spoon against a washboard. And that's how it raises hell."

"How do you know that kind of shit, chief?" Lopez asked.

Kenney stuck his spoon into the stew, and said, "I don't know, Lopez, I just do."

You must be very proud of your father," Annie told Phillip.

The two of them had lain there side by side in awkward silence until she'd broken the ice.

"Yeah, I guess so," he said.

"I've wondered what it must be like, you know, being the child of a famous parent. My father's a chartered accountant."

"I never thought about it much."

"Didn't you? I saw that you won an essay contest with him as the subject."

He seemed embarrassed. "It was after his heart attack. I don't know why I wrote it."

"Well, don't worry, you don't have to explain it to me. But maybe you can tell me why you're here in Yorkshire. How did that come about?"

Before he could answer, Haven came into the room and sat on Phillip's bed, scowling at Annie.

Phillip nudged her, and said, "She just asked me why I came here."

"Did you tell 'er?" Haven asked.

"Not yet."

"He came 'cause I asked him t' come."

"Had you known each other?" Annie asked.

"No, I read 'is essay at school."

"Ah, that essay again," Annie said. "So why did you contact him?"

"You don't have to tell her," Phillip told her, shooting Annie a dirty look.

"Why is it I feel like the gooseberry at this party?" Annie said. "If you unlock my cuff, I'll happily wander off and leave the two of you on your own."

"Very funny," Haven said. "I'll tell ya. I thought Phillip could help let th' world know th' Horizon was nonsense. A girl in me school hung herself from worry. I thought I had t' do something about it."

"Well, I think that's very admirable, young lady. When this is over and done with, I'll make sure the authorities become aware of the good you've done."

Haven began to cry.

"I'm sorry I upset you," Annie said, "I . . ."

"Why don't you just shut up?" Phillip said sharply. "I wish you weren't here."

"We're in agreement on that score," Annie said. "Listen, Phillip, I'm not sure why you've got such a bad impression of me but . . ."

He interrupted her again, "It's because of the way you look at my father. It's like there's something going on. Is there?"

Annie smiled. "Your father is a perfect gentleman. Nothing transpired between us. I give you my word."

"That's good to know," Phillip said, "because my mom would kick your butt if you messed around with him."

Come into th' Library with me," Cacia said.

Will followed her through the anteroom. As soon as she closed the door to the Library behind her, she dissolved into tears.

"I didn't want them t' see me crying. They've never seen it before, and I don't know how they'd react."

"It doesn't seem to me they have much of a reaction to anything," Will said.

She staunched her sobs as best she could. "Oh but they do. You've got t' really know 'em like I do. It can be as little as a twitch at th' corner of their mouths or a particularly deep breath. They 'ave feelings."

Will sensed an opening, and he went for it. "You have feelings too."

She reached for him and pulled him against her body. He held her while she poured her heart out.

"It's been such a lonely life, Will. And a hard 'un. Constant toil. Secrecy. Isolation. I love Daniel, I swear it, but we're not close anymore, not intimate. He won't say, but I think he went funny about my having their children. He knows it's our lives, but it still affects a man, doesn't it?"

"I guess it would."

"I didn't want this life for me daughters. But we're Lightburns, and this is what we do. It's our obligation."

"I understand," he said. "I really do."

"It would be lovely, wouldn't it, if we could chuck away all th' fuss going on around us and all the obligations and lie down for a while, just th' two of us." She sighed, releasing him from her grasp. "But it would be over soon enough, then where'd we be?"

"Back here. Dealing with the biggest problem you've ever had."

"What can I do?"

"I need Phillip's NetPen. Do you still have it?"

"I put it on my windowsill for safekeepin'. Haven said th' sunlight charges it. I thought, just in case."

"That's good. Bring it to me as soon as you can."

"What would you do?"

"Knowledge is power, Cacia. It's the only weapon we've got. If the world doesn't know about your Library, then when the authorities take this place—and they will—they'll seize the books and suppress the hell out of it. They'll probably keep people in the dark about the Horizon, and they'll start up another Area 51 kind of place to exploit the data for military and political purposes. They might even kill us or lock us up to make sure no one ever knows."

"My God," she whispered.

"I was in the same situation years ago and the only way I saved myself was to leak the information about Area 51. We've got to do the same here."

"Who would ya tell?"

"Not my wife. She'd be obliged to keep the secret from the FBI. I can't compromise her. There's someone else. I think I can trust him. He'll be perfect. Please, Cacia, bring the NetPen to me now."

"I'd be betrayin' our family, our legacy. Generations of Lightburns. Wouldn't I?"

"No. You'd be saving your family and protecting its legacy. I know how this works. I know how it's going to end unless we work together. You know what I'm telling you is true."

With a nod of her fiery hair and a look of resolve, she left him there, free to wander on his own. The Library was so vast it was almost disorienting. Like staring into opposing mirrors, it seemed to go on infinitely. He had a momentary urge to head to the far end of it and browse the near future, but he stopped himself from doing that. He truly didn't want to know when he would die. Or Phillip. Or Nancy. Or his daughter, Laura. Or Nick. He never wanted to know. And he didn't want other people to know either.

Instead, he plucked out a book at random from the distant future. The page was for 21 May, 2440. The names he saw were a rainbow of diversity, dozens of languages and ethnicities.

The world is going to be all right, he thought.

Cacia came back, breathless, with Phillip's NetPen.

"I'm trusting you t' protect us," she said.

He took it from her and kissed her forehead. "I won't let you down."

And though he fumbled at the NetPen's unfamiliar

buttons, he managed to get off a flash photo of a long row of books.

Cacia chained Will back to his bunk and with a heavy glance, left him alone with Phillip and Annie.

"Look what I've got," Will said, pulling the NetPen from his pocket.

"She gave it to you?" Annie asked incredulously.

"She did."

"We've got to contact my headquarters, let them know the situation," she said.

"No, we're going to play this another way," Will said firmly. "Phillip, I need to send an encrypted message."

"You want to tunnel?" Phillip asked.

"Yeah, tunnel. Can you do it for me?"

"Sure."

"And I want to send the photo I just took."

"Give it to me. Do you want to type or dictate?"

"Type."

"Let me set up the screen for you, and you can start. Who're you sending it to?"

"Uncle Greg."

Will struggled, running his big fingers on the small virtual keyboard, but he managed to get it all down. He handed it back to Phillip, and said, "Send it."

There was a loud noise as the door to their room banged against the wooden partition.

Daniel came in, his eyes blazing with anger. Andrew was behind him, aping his father.

Daniel spotted the NetPen in Phillip's hand and snatched it away roughly.

"Andrew saw what his mother did, and he told me as soon as I came back from spyin' on those fuckers from th' barn." Daniel threw it on the floor and stomped on it twice with his boot, flattening the tube and sending small pieces of metal and plastic flying.

"Now tell me th' truth, lad, or I'll thrash you th' way I thrashed me wife."

Will couldn't stop himself. "Manly thing to do, Daniel. Beating your own wife. How'd you like to take a man on?"

"Go fuck yourself," Daniel said. "I asked you, boyo, did ya call anyone?"

Phillip looked at him squarely, and said, "No."

"Are ya lyin' t' me?"

"I swear. I was going to, but I didn't get the chance."

"All right then, we've got enough trouble out there without having t' worry 'bout you lot."

And with a final stamp of his boot, Daniel took his son and left.

Will wished he could put his arm around his son, but he couldn't, and besides, the kid would have been embarrassed by the gesture. "Did you send it?" he asked.

"Of course I did," the boy said proudly.

"You're an excellent liar," Annie said, approvingly. "There's a career for you in the intelligence services."

"I wasn't lying. He asked if I made a call," Phillip said. "He needs to ask better questions."

Greg Davis finished a late lunch and sent his assistant, Maggie, packing for the day. It was sleeting outside, so a bike ride was out of the question and there was little appeal to a walk. He stretched out on the sofa, fiddled with his curly hair, and took the TV off mute. CNN was running a story about the Chinese government's retaliation against the postcard affair by expelling a number of American diplomats in Beijing they accused of being CIA operatives. The US government was strenuously denying the accusations and was said to be weighing an appropriate response. When he'd finished with his sofa time he'd post a link to the story on *China Today*.

Though he'd gone bald on the top and his remaining hair was now salt and peppery, his appearance hadn't changed much from his days as a young newspaper reporter. People who hadn't seen him in twenty years instantly recognized him. Their friends called him and Laura, who had also kept the hippie throwback look of her twenties, the eternal couple.

The nerve center for Greg's media company was the second bedroom in his Greenpoint apartment in Brooklyn. For a two-employee company, Today

Media put out a lot of product. Greg's webzines blanketed the large immigrant communities in America with sites tailored to their interests. There were ones for Mexican-Americans, Cuban-Americans, Indian-Americans, Pakistani-Americans, Brazilian-Americans, Japanese-Americans but the one that was getting the most attention these days was *China Today*.

His concept was to aggregate news from home and abroad of relevance to the target audience, get knowledgeable freelancers to write original content, and sell ads aimed at the ethnic group. But for the past few years, his viewer numbers were too small to command good ad rates, and he eked out a paltry profit.

To his discomfort, his lifestyle was largely supported by his wife's book earnings. Laura had written nine novels, all of them reliable sellers. Her first book, *The Wrecking Ball,* loosely based on the breakup of her parents' marriage, had even been made into a film, owing to broad interest in Will Piper following his public disclosures. And though she had perpetually tried to establish her own identity apart from being Will Piper's daughter, she had been persuaded by her publisher to exploit her namesake once again with her latest book, *The Horizon.* Given the anxiety of the times, it wasn't surprising that the book had become her first bona fide best seller.

Yet far from bringing marital happiness, her success had merely stoked the long-simmering and unspoken rivalry that existed between her and Greg. Within days of her publisher's throwing her a party for hitting the *New York Times* fiction list, their arguments had become particularly nasty.

Then, out of the blue, Greg's fortunes turned in an unexpected way. Residents of New York's Chinatown began receiving postcards, and his Chinese Web site caught fire. Capitalizing on his role as the *Washington Post* reporter during the 2010 Area 51 exposé, *China Today* became the go-to site for breaking news and analysis for the Chinese-American community and for a lot of general readers as well. The ad dollars began to roll in and his fractured ego went on the mend. Laura noticed the difference and told him it was nice not living with a jerk. And when her father had his heart attack, Greg had been a proper supportive husband and son-in-law. Laura informed her kitchen cabinet of girlfriends that it was looking like their marriage was going to survive after all.

Laura came home, peeled off her rain-soaked coat, and sat down to take in the TV news.

"How was your workout?" Greg asked.

"Okay, I guess."

"You sound tired."

"I slept all right. It's the worrying."

"No news on your dad?"

"Nothing."

"Nick called," Greg said. Their son, off at prep school, was the same age as Phillip. Nancy and Laura famously had been pregnant together, and Will had come close to having to choose between attending the birth of his first son or first grandson.

"Everything okay?" Laura asked.

"He's fine. He just wanted to know if we'd heard anything about the guys." Then he added, "When was the last time you talked to Nancy?"

"Yesterday morning. I told you about that, didn't I?"

He nodded as if remembering. "How'd you say she sounded?"

"Stressed. She's worried out of her mind, but she can't get the Director to let her fly to England."

"Because of China?" he asked, waving at the TV.

"You know, it's China! The whole thing sucks for everyone but you."

"What's that supposed to mean?" he asked angrily.

"I'm sorry," she said. "I didn't mean anything by it. I'm a mess."

"Yeah."

She rose. "I'm going to take a shower."

He couldn't seem to let it pass and called after her, "Just because I'm finally making some money doesn't make me a villain, you know."

"Whatever." She sighed, closing the bedroom door.

Greg's NetPen chimed at the arrival of a new e-mail. He seemed inclined to ignore it, but after a while he snatched it off the coffee table and commanded it to read the message.

The husky female voice he'd chosen for the function purred, "Sender: Phillip Piper. Subject: For Your Eyes Only and Laura's Latin Eyes. Message: Encrypted. Sorry, read-mode unavailable."

Greg practically ran to his office and opened the e-mail on his work tablet. The body of the message was a jumble of machine code symbols with a header that read: tunnel protocol 1812.

"What the hell?" he mumbled.

He hit the command button on his NetPen and summoned the work number for his company's IT consultant.

"Hey, Nelson, it's Greg."

A calm voice came over the mobile, "What's up man?"

"I got an encrypted e-mail with something called tunnel protocol 1812. How do I open it?"

"It's an open-protocol encryption tool but it's heavy-duty. There've been some moves to ban it because bad guys use it for bad-guy shit, but it's still out there. You need a key to open it."

"What key? I don't have any key?"

"Then you're out of luck, man."

Greg raised his voice. "Nelson, this is a goddamn emergency. Life-and-death shit, okay? I need your help."

"I hear you, man. Why don't you forward it to me, and I'll take a look."

"No can do. We shouldn't even be talking on the phone. Come over to my place."

"In Brooklyn?"

"Jesus, Nelson, you're in Manhattan. What's the big deal?"

"It's like a different zip code, man."

"Take a cab. I need you here now."

Nelson Federman arrived an hour later bearing an irked expression on his young, chubby face. Greg had told Laura he was coming over to help him sort out a Net-site problem and she didn't seem to think twice about his presence. Although the stress had pretty much blocked her ability to write, she kept going through the motions and was hunched over her ancient laptop.

"Hey, Laura," Nelson said. "Got to love the old-school keyboard."

"I can't dictate," she said. "I'm too old to change the way I write."

"I liked your last book. When's the next one coming out?"

Greg interrupted the chitchat. "Come on, Nelson. Time's money," and beckoned him into the office and shut the door.

Nelson looked at the e-mail and rubbed his wispy goatee. "Look, the way these things work is there's usually a prearranged key that both sender and receiver already know. This guy Phillip? He didn't send you something in advance?"

"No, nothing."

"There's nothing I can do, man. This protocol is a 620-bit-key elliptic-curve algorithm. It may or may not be breakable. There's been some chatter in the hacker universe that some spook agencies can break something this big, but you'd need some kind of next-gen monster computer to do it." He looked at the work screen again, and said, "What do you make of the subject line?"

Greg read it out loud. "For Your Eyes Only and Laura's Latin Eyes. I don't know what he means by Laura's Latin Eyes."

"Well," Nelson said triumphantly, "there's your answer, dude. I'll bet that's the key."

"What? Laura's Latin Eyes?"

"If you're going to the trouble to tunnel, you're probably not putting the key out there. But this guy Phillip might be steering you to the right answer. Here, give me control of your machine."

Greg commanded a user change, and Nelson took over the voice commands, maneuvering to a hacker encryption site. He cut and pasted the e-mail message into the encryption engine and entered LaurasLatin-Eyes as the key.

Decryption Failure.

He tried some variants without success.

"Okay, man, what's cool about Laura's eyes?"

Greg thought for a few moments, and suddenly his face got animated. "They're different colors! One's blue and one's brown! Her father's always kidding her about it."

"Okay, then. Let's try that."

He spent a while trying every word combination of one is blue and one is brown he could muster.

Every time: *Decryption Failure.*

Nelson furrowed his brow, and said, "Hey, I know, maybe we need to be using the Latin words for blue and brown."

Ten minutes later, they'd looked up the words and exhausted all the permutations of *puteulanus* and *frons* with no luck, and Nelson started getting antsy, looking overly obviously at his watch.

Finally, Greg got out of his chair and opened the door, calling into the living room, "Laura. That thing with your eyes. Does it have a name?"

"Who wants to know?"

"Nelson is like obsessed with them."

"Hey!" Nelson said, defensively. "Leave me out of this."

She shouted through the door. "Glad you like them, Nelson. It's a congenital condition called *Heterochromia iridum.*"

Greg slammed the door and declared, "Latin!"

With Greg's help Nelson spelled out the term onto the log-in line, and said, "Enter."

Decryption Successful.

There was a lag of a couple of seconds, and the gibberish message turned into words and at the end was a photo.

Greg quickly stepped in front of the screen, blocking Nelson's view. "You're the best, Nelson. Double your bill and send it to me."

"Can't I read it, man?"

"You could. But then I'd have to kill you."

"I'm tripling my bill because you're such an A-hole, Greg."

When he was gone, Greg sat down and read the e-mail, stuffed to the gills with anticipation.

Greg:

Phillip and I need your help. Do not tell anyone, including Laura and especially don't tell Nancy for reasons I'll explain later. We are being held hostage at a farm in Pinn, Cumbria, England. Latitude = 54.4142, Longitude = −2.3323. You've got to get on a flight tonight and get to Pinn by tomorrow afternoon. Lightburn Farm is notated on the UK Ordnance Survey maps. About a hundred yards east of the farmhouse and about thirty yards off the north side of the B6259 is a small stone outbuilding with an open front. Be inside that building at 5 P.M. GMT. I will come for you. Someone on the inside is helping us. It may not be easy getting there undetected because the police have the farm surrounded, but you're a cagey old journalist, so I've got faith. Look at the picture, Greg, and you'll understand why you're the only one I can trust. There's a second Library. There is no Horizon.

Will

Blinking in disbelief, Greg looked at the image of a row of old bookcases containing a sea of leatherbound books. The ones nearest the camera were clearly marked: 2440.

Officer Brent Wilson was relieved from his post manning a roadblock on the B6259 long enough to get a mug of hot tea from the incident van. While he sat on a folding chair in the night chill enjoying the break he heard his name being called.

His Assistant Chief Constable was on the steps of
the incident van summoning him in. Still clutching
his mug he was led to the rear of the vehicle, duck-
ing his head to avoid cracking his skull against the
doorframes. The Chief Constable of the Cumbrian
Authority, John Raab, had arrived from Penrith and
was seated behind a desk.

"Officer Wilson," Raab said. "Have a seat and
carry on with your tea. There's a lazy wind blowing
out there."

"Aye, there is, sir," Wilson replied. "It's brutal."

"I'm told you met Annie Locke and Will Piper
when they first arrived in Kirkby Stephen."

"I did, aye."

"Tell me about them. Everything you can remember. I want to get a sense of how they might react
under threatening conditions. I asked the MI5 chaps
about her, and they acted like they'd be divulging national secrets."

"They were both very nice, very friendly I'd say. I
met them at th' station house and helped 'em print
up some flyers with th' boy's picture so they could
canvas th' town."

"What about Piper? What were your impressions?"

"Well, he's a big fellow. Not a youngster, but I
reckon he can handle himself. Far and away I thought
that this was a man worried sick about 'is son."

"And Miss Locke?"

"A go-getter, I suppose. Young and fit. Determined,
I'd say, the type who you'd bet on t' succeed in the Security Services."

"Pretty too."

"I'd agree with that."

"Piper's apparently got a reputation as a ladies'
man. Any sign of a personal connection between
them?"

"Sorry, sir?"

"It might affect their judgment and decision making under dangerous conditions."

Officer Wilson still seemed flummoxed by the question. "I think they'd just met that morning, sir."

"Very well, finish your tea and resume your post."

When Wilson was gone, the Assistant Chief Constable asked Raab, "We haven't attempted contact in about two hours. Would you like us to try again?"

"Yes, why not? Use the bullhorn this time. Keep hectoring them every five to ten minutes but vary the interval for maximal annoyance like the old Chinese water torture, eh? If we're not going to sleep tonight, neither should they."

"A farm like this, they could have enough provisions for a month. How long are we going to wait them out?"

"It's early days, Paul. We're hardly talking about the Siege of Orleans. We've got them well surrounded. They're not going anywhere. They haven't made any demands at this point. MI5 are bringing in some night-vision equipment and some listening gear. The American embassy is keen to know whether Piper and his son are indeed inside as we presume they are. We're going to keep our heads about us and take things step by step. And by the book."

Vice Chairman Yi had just finished giving a speech to the graduating class at the PLA Academy of Military Science in a western suburb of Beijing when his NetPen alerted him to an incoming encrypted request for a VidLink.

He asked for a private room and the Academy's Director ushered him into his office and left him there alone.

Yi unfurled the NetPen's screen and accepted the request. General Bo's face filled the screen. Yi could tell immediately from the man's wide eyes that the ordinarily unflappable general had something important to say.

Yi listened to the report and signed off with a simple, "Thank you, General. I understand."

He closed his eyes in gratitude and felt them fill with tears. When he'd wiped them dry with his handkerchief he summoned his personal secretary on a VidLink and told her, "Tell General Secretary Wen's people that I will be at his office in ten minutes. Tell them that I am coming to deliver the last straw."

Kenney stamped his feet against the frosty ground in a vain attempt to keep them warm. From time to time he'd part the bushes and take in the scene below through his night scope. He wasn't expecting significant activity that night, but you never knew. It was a waiting game, something his unit was exceptionally good at, but he would have preferred to be doing his waiting in shorts and T-shirt weather.

He became aware of his NetPen vibrating in his pocket. To maintain quiet, he put it on text mode and unfurled the screen. It was a priority message from Klepser, his head of electronic surveillance at Groom Lake. He sat down upon his rolled-up sleeping bag to read it.

An encrypted message had been sent from Phillip Piper to Greg Davis with a cryptic message line. The send location was Lightburn Farm.

Kenney knew damn well who Greg Davis was. Any historian of the humiliating debacle suffered by the watchers and Malcolm Frazier in 2010 knew that Davis was Piper's conduit. The leaker. And now Piper was probably using his son's mobile device to contact Davis again.

What the hell was going on?

Kenney scrambled up the hill forty yards to another clump of trees where he could talk softly without detection. He signaled to Lopez and Harper that everything was okay and called up Klepser on a VidLink.

"What's the level of encryption on that e-mail you just shot over?" Kenney asked.

"Six hundred twenty bits."

"Shit. The key's probably in the loopy subject line, don't you think?"

"Probably, but it won't be easy to figure it out since it's likely personalized."

"Like I said, shit."

"I think I can break it, chief."

"Yeah?"

"We've got a new algorithm I've been playing with. If you give me the authority to kick off everyone else using our systems I think I might have enough in-house computing power to crack it."

"You have my authority. If you can do it, I swear to God I'm going to fill your swimming pool with beer."

"I've got something else, chief. On a hunch, I put a tap on Davis's autopays. Fifteen minutes ago he bought a ticket from JFK to Glasgow, leaving 19:00 EST today."

"Son, once that pool of yours is full I'm also going to drop a squad of cheerleaders into it."

Nancy knocked sharply on the door and waited. She was about to knock again when she heard someone stirring inside. Laura opened the door and froze.

In a panicky voice, she said, "Oh my God, Nancy, what's wrong?"

"Nothing! I was in New York, and I thought I'd stop by."

"Dad's okay? And Phillip?"

Nancy came in and unwound her wet scarf. "I'm sorry I scared you. I should have called first. There's no change. They still don't know if they're at that farm. The MI5 people are keeping me in the loop pretty well but it's hard not being there."

In the kitchen, Laura put the kettle on. It was already hot from her last brew and it went straight to a boil. Nancy noticed that Laura's eyes were red.

"Are you going?" Laura asked.

"It's crunch time," Nancy said. "They want me to go to Beijing tomorrow with a DOJ delegation. Off the record, China's threatening to break off diplomatic contact and this is supposed to be a last-ditch effort to convince them our government has nothing to do with the postcards."

"But none of their diplomats in Washington actually died, did they?"

"It was a hoax but they still think it was a provocation from our side. But, Laura, I can't be going off to China with Phillip and Will in trouble. I just can't do it."

"So you're going to England instead?"

She put her thumb and forefinger an inch apart. "I'm this close. It'll end my career but that's the way it may have to go down."

She selected her herbal tea and while Laura poured, Nancy asked, "Is Greg here?"

"You missed him by about a half an hour."

"When's he coming back?"

"I don't think it's going to be for a few days."

Laura explained he'd finished a meeting with his IT consultant then rushed to the bedroom to pack a bag. He'd told her something came up, a big story that was going to help his business and that he'd have to go out of town for a while. He wouldn't tell her what was happening or where he was going but told her he'd call and tell her what was going on as soon as he could.

"Is that unusual for him?" Nancy asked.

"Completely." Laura started crying and Nancy realized her eyes must have been red for a while.

"So talk to me, honey."

"We've had problems. I thought things were getting better but maybe I misread the situation. I think he's having an affair."

"Do you have any evidence?"

"Not really."

Nancy shook her head and said, "When a wife suspects her husband's cheating she usually sneaks a few peeks at his e-mails and messages. Have you done that?"

"I'd never. I mean, did you ever do that to Dad?"

Nancy laughed. "I probably would have if your father ever used his phone or computer for more than paperweights. Do you know Greg's e-mail password?"

"No!" Laura said, horrified at the suggestion, but then seemed to warm to the idea, "But I don't think he ever logs off."

"Look, honey, if you want to take a look, I'll go along for moral support."

"You think I should?" Laura asked.

"The truth shall set you free. At least that's the saying."

Greg's office screen woke from sleep mode with Laura's command since she was an authorized user. She steered the device to Greg's e-mail account and as she'd thought, his account hadn't been logged off.

Nancy spotted it immediately: an e-mail from Phillip! She sputtered, "My God," and had Laura open it.

Nancy read the message line, and said, "It's encrypted." She looked at her watch. "It was sent two hours ago. It's from Phillip, but Will's got to be involved. I don't know what Laura's Latin eyes means but it doesn't sound like something that would come out of his mouth. It sounds like Will."

"I know what it means!" Laura said. "When Greg was working with his IT guy, they asked me what my eye condition was called—you know, the way my eyes are different colors. It's a Latin term: *Heterochromia iridum*."

"That's got to be the decryption key," Nancy said. "Will's still the smartest guy in the room. Laura, give me voice control of the computer."

Nancy quickly summoned up a tunneling program, transferred the coded message, and entered *Heterochromia iridum* as the key.

And there it was.

Nancy began to visibly tremble as she read the message. She fought to keep herself composed but her internal struggle between wife and mother and law-enforcement officer was showing.

"A second Library," she said, her voice wavering. "Someone wanted Phillip to know about it. Now Will wants Greg to know about it. It's history repeating itself. Listen, Laura. I know this is hard but for the sake of all of them you've got to keep this to yourself, okay?"

Laura was rummaging through a drawer. Behind some copy paper she pulled out a pack of cigarettes and a lighter. "Emergency stash," she said, lighting up. Her hand was shaking as she lit up. "I won't say anything to anybody. What are you going to do?"

Nancy was already in action. She had her assistant on the phone asking her to find out what flight Greg Davis was booked on. While she waited, she rehearsed what she was going to say to her boss. Since Will didn't want her to know about this it meant he didn't want the FBI to know. He had his reasons and she was going to follow his lead. When it came to other women, she didn't trust him as far as she could throw him. When it came to a case she trusted him with her life. And their son's.

The answer came. Greg was on BA Flight 231 to Glasgow, departing at 7 P.M. Nancy had the assistant book her a ticket on the same flight. Then she asked Laura for privacy so she could call her boss.

Director Parish sounded angry before the conversation even got going.

"Where the hell are you, Nancy?"

"I'm in New York City."

"Why?"

"Following up on a lead."

"Anything promising?"

"It's too early to tell. I'm going to need a few days to see how it pans out."

"Well, you don't have a few days. I want you at Andrews Air Force Base tomorrow morning on the State Department flight to Beijing."

She held her breath, then blurted out, "I'm sorry, sir, I can't be there."

There was an uncomfortable pause on the line. "I don't think I heard you properly. This is a direct order, Nancy."

"I'm aware of that. If you feel you need to relieve me of duty for this, I'll drop off my badge and weapon at the New York office. But I've got to run this lead down and I'm going to do it with or without a badge."

She couldn't tell whether the sound she heard was a sigh or a hiss of steam coming out of Parish's ears. "Jesus, Nancy, I hope to hell you know what you're doing. I'd hate to lose you. This is your first and last hall pass for insubordination."

Nancy spotted Greg at the British Airways departures pod buying a candy bar. She watched him for a while, trying to get a feel for his state of mind. She thought he was on the twitchy side but he was never a mellow guy. She'd always tried to be objective about him. It would have been easy enough to go along with Will's assessment, that he was opportunistic, that he had a chip on his shoulder for not living up to the promise of his early career, that he wasn't good enough for his daughter—but she preferred to see Greg through her own lens. In her book, he was a nice enough guy, a little on the ineffectual side, but she wouldn't wish the burden of being Will Piper's son-in-law on any man.

She had her own shopping to do having arrived with nothing but her handbag. She'd left her pistol with her driver so even her purse was light as a feather. She started by buying a roller bag at a luggage shop and proceeded to jump from store to store, filling it up with clothes and toiletries. When she was outfitted, she rolled the bag over to where Greg was seated and acted out a small scene.

"Greg? What are you doing here?"

His look of shock struck her as a rough blend of surprise and guilt.

"Nancy! Wow! I'm going to Scotland on business. What about you?"

She let the mask fall away. She said soberly, "I'm going to bring Will and Phillip home, Greg."

"Has anything changed?" he asked excitedly. "When I talked to Laura just a while ago, there was no news."

"That was before I knew for sure they were in that farmhouse in Pinn. Now I do."

"How'd you find out?"

She sat down beside him. "By reading your e-mail."

He deflated like a day-old soufflé. "I'm sorry, Nancy. You saw what Will wrote. He told me not to tell you. What was I supposed to do?"

She touched his sleeve. "You did what you thought you had to do. I don't blame you for it. But now I know, and I'm going with you. Can you believe it? A second Library?"

He nodded sharply. "It's incredible. It changes everything." He looked at her hard. "Does the FBI know too?"

She shook her head emphatically. "I'm a private

citizen for the next few days. Maybe longer. My boss is furious at me."

"Why?"

"For bailing on the China case."

"Still no leads?"

"None that I can talk about."

He nodded, then fidgeted in his seat and seemed on the brink of asking a question. Finally, he said, "How'd you get here so fast? I got the e-mail this afternoon. And how'd you decipher it?"

"I was at your apartment."

He was taken aback. "Why?"

"I was in New York. I thought I'd see Laura, give her some support. We got to talking, and one thing led to another. It was pretty apparent her eye condition was the cipher key."

"She looked at my e-mails?" he said with a certain resentment.

"It was my doing, Greg. She thought you were having an affair."

"Me? I'd be the last person."

"It's not my place but I think you guys may need to do some work on your marriage."

His face seemed to say, yeah, it's not your place. Instead, he said, "So what's the plan?"

"We follow Will's instructions to the letter," she said. "Hopefully he's worked out the endgame. If not, we're going to have to improvise, aren't we?"

As Nancy and Greg were negotiating their way to the rental-car lot at Glasgow Airport, Kenney was unzipping his sleeping bag, his breath producing pleasant puffs of vapor.

He asked Harper, who'd had the last four-hour watch, "Any developments?"

"Nothing. The police haven't made any moves. It's been quiet."

"They got tired of their bullshit bullhorn just in time for me to get some shut-eye. How good was that? What's for breakfast?"

"Energy bars or shit stew."

"I'll go with the bars."

Kenney's NetPen vibrated. As he read the screen message, a smile creased his face.

He looked like he wanted to shout it out, but he kept the decibels down. "Hallelujah! Klepser broke the encryption." He touched the screen to open the attachment and read it, and as he did, his jaw went slack. "Wake up Lopez," he said to Harper. "This is going to be a day we're going to remember for the rest of our lives."

In Nevada, Admiral Sage hadn't been asleep very long when his phone rang. His wife grumbled and pulled the covers over her head as he fumbled around the nightstand.

"Yeah?"

"Admiral, it's Kenney. I've got something."

"What is it?"

"We decrypted a message from Piper to his son-in-law, Greg Davis, the reporter who was involved . . ."

"I know who he is," the admiral growled.

"You need to hear the message verbatim."

As Kenney read it, the admiral shifted his posture from lying to sitting to standing beside the bed.

"Jesus fucking Christ," he said, when Kenney was done.

"Yes, sir. Jesus fucking Christ."

"Stand by while I call the Pentagon. And Kenney?"

"Yes, sir?"

"We may not be out of a job after all."

Neither Greg nor Nancy talked much during their two-and-a-half-hour ride from Glasgow to Pinn. For the most part Greg drove, relying on the nav system while Nancy stared at the misty landscape. Although there was no snow, save for the tops of the fells, the morning frost was still clinging to the verges and the meadows, and small melting icicles were dripping from the downspouts and gutters of village roofs.

They arrived in Kirkby Stephen at lunchtime, and with time to kill, they stopped at a café for sandwiches. There, they read the local newspaper splashed with stories on the front page about a mysterious police action in Pinn. At other tables it was clear that this was all that people were talking about but it was equally clear that no one knew the underlying facts. Nancy asked their waitress what she thought and got the two favorite theories: there was either a drugs factory at the farmhouse or some kind of armed religious cult. The girl added, "Fowks at Mallerstang are weird, ya know."

They waited until three to make the final drive to Lightburn Farm, and at three thirty, with only four kilometers to go to their destination, they hit a wall of traffic on the B road to Pinn. Nancy got out of the stopped car and asked one of the people milling beside their own halted vehicle.

"What's the matter?" she asked.

"There's a roadblock ahead," the motorist answered. "Some kind of police business." Some cars were executing three-point turns and reversing. "That's what I'm going t' do," the man said, climbing back into his car.

She poked her head into the open car window and told Greg, "We don't have all the time in the world. Let's pull off the road and hike the rest of the way."

Officer Wilson awoke with a start in the backseat of his patrol car. One of his fellow community patrol officers, a crusty older officer named Perkins, tossed a foil-wrapped bacon sandwich into his lap from the front.

"They passed these out but I let you have your kip," he said. "Sweet dreams?"

Wilson tried to stretch his legs without success. "Not likely. Can they do this?"

"Do what, marra?"

"Keep us on duty round th' clock without proper breaks."

"Don't bother ringin' your union steward. Since they've declared a police emergency they own your bollocks. Unless you choose t' return t' civilian life."

"I might just do that," Wilson said, unwrapping the sandwich. "I've got enough saved t' make it till th' Horizon without working."

Perkins snorted. "Your luck, the Horizon'll come and go, the world'll be dancing and singing, and you'll have t' blow your brains out 'cause you're bankrupt."

The sandwich was gone, wolfed down in a few

bites. Wilson looked at his watch. "Half two, and th' light's already startin' t' go. Let's take our posts."

"Thought you were packin' it in?"

"My missus would kill me if I spent the next year sittin' at home," Wilson said. Something caught his attention on the fells. "See that?"

"What?"

"There's some walkers over yon headin' toward th' farm."

"Christ's sake," Perkins said, opening his door. The cold air rushed in. "Tapped fools don't realize they're likely t' be shot. Come on."

The two officers strode up the fells waving their arms to get the attention of the walkers.

Nancy and Greg saw the policemen in the distance and swore. The hike had taken longer than Nancy thought it would. They'd taken a tack away from the easy visibility of the road which meant having to go partway up the fells. Their leather-soled shoes gripped the slippery slope poorly and there were stone walls to traverse.

"What do we do?" Greg asked. The stone outbuilding Will had described was within view.

"We've got to talk our way around them," she said.

They gingerly made their way down the fells toward the policemen. Nancy whispered to Greg to let her do the talking.

"Hello, Officers, is there a problem?"

"What do th' two of ya think you're doing?" Perkins asked.

"We're having a walk," she said.

"Is that right?" Wilson asked. "Didn't ya see th' roadblock up there?"

"We thought that was just for cars."

Perkins was looking at their street shoes. "If you lot are fells walkers then I'm the king of England."

Nancy smiled at them as coquettishly as she could. "Look, Officers, the truth is we're journalists. We're just trying to get close enough to observe what's going on and get a good story out. Could you give us a break?"

"Look, missy," Perkins said. "There's a police action in progress. If we had a few miles of incident tape we would've marked out a perimeter. So, we won't arrest ya for perverting the course of justice if you turn around and go back t' your vehicle wherever you've left it."

Nancy and Greg exchanged glances. They had no options. With desperate glances at the outbuilding ahead, they turned around and walked away.

Deep in a bunker at RAF Fylingdales, the joint UK and US Ballistic Weapons Warning System on the North York Moors, a British RAF radar tech and his US Air Force counterpart were manning their work screens during the evening shift.

At 16:33, a faint green circle appeared six kilometers north of Whitby, heading east to west from the direction of the North Sea. It was on screen for under two seconds then disappeared. None of the autoalarms triggered.

"Did you see that?" the British tech said.

"I think it's a glitch," the American answered.

The British tech didn't seem satisfied. "I'm playing it back."

He went into playback mode on another screen and slowed the image down. The ultrafaint signal from Fylingdale's phased-array radar system, if not an anomaly, was moving at 320 kilometers per hour close to the deck.

"I think it's birds," the American said.

"Pretty fast flippin' birds," the Brit answered. "It could be a stealth signal." He reached for a red handset.

"You're not telling me you're going to scramble jets over that piece of crap shadow!" the American exclaimed.

"That's exactly what I'm saying. I live here, mate. You don't."

Low clouds filled the Mallerstang Valley and filtered out much of the last afternoon light. The towering Wild Boar Fell rose to the east of Lightburn Farm and High Seat was to its west. The geography seemed to guard the farm from the coming night. Down on the valley floor, high-intensity floodlights powered by humming generators lit the terrain as if it were a film set.

The police on foot patrol were the first to hear it, a high-pitched whine that rapidly flared in volume. Something seemed to be approaching from the northeast. Officers Wilson and Perkins in position on the north side of the farm strained to see what they heard. The whine stabilized as if something that had been moving was now stationary.

Although he was half a mile away on the opposite side of the valley, Kenney was perhaps the first to identify the source of the noise.

He trained his night-vision scope on the western slope of the High Seat fell and saw a hovering helicopter and men making a rope egress.

"What the hell is going on?" he mumbled.

"What is it, chief?" Lopez asked.

"Someone's dropped in a special ops team."

"Is it us?" Harper said.

"Of course it's not us! I think we'd know about it, don't you?"

"Do you think the Brits know what's going on in there?" Harper asked.

"No way," Kenney said. "We're listening to all their comm. We haven't heard jack shit about a Library. Still, it's got to be the Brits. I mean, who the hell else could it be?"

"Can you make out any insignia on the chopper?" Lopez asked.

Kenney grunted a no and called Groom Lake.

A dozen special ops troops outfitted with short-barrel automatic rifles and night-vision headgear hit the slope of the fell and began racing downhill, sure-footed despite the slick grass.

Officer Wilson thought he saw the distant form of a man through the mist and radioed to the incident van. The Assistant Chief Constable picked up, and Wilson said, " 'Scuse me, Guv, do we have any of our blokes coming down High Seat?"

"Course we don't. What's making that bloody noise? Can you see anything?"

"I think . . ." Wilson dropped the radio and it dangled by his side. He instinctively felt his chest, and the last thing he saw before falling backward was his hands, wet and red.

Perkins managed to transmit a frantic, "Officer down! Officer down!" before he took a .50-caliber sniper round to his head and dropped stone-dead beside his partner.

Inside the incident van, Chief Constable Raab responded by shouting questions over the radio.

"All units, is the fire coming from the house or the barn?"

A series of responses flooded in jamming the airwaves and making it hard for Raab to process the info.

"Nothing from the house!"

"Not the barn!"

"It's coming from High Seat."

"Taking fire! Man down!"

"I see them! They look military!"

"There's a helicopter up on the fell!"

Raab turned to the Assistant Chief Constable, who had the look of a man who was going to be ill. "We're sitting ducks," Raab said. "We either turn tail or engage the hostiles."

A large-caliber round passed through the van well over their heads but they hit the floor nonetheless.

"What shall we do?" the Assistant Chief Constable croaked.

Raab said coolly, "Why don't you give the order to return fire while I call the MOD to see if I can find out what the hell is going on here."

Admiral Sage became unhinged and began screaming into his phone. It was immediately apparent to Kenney that he had no knowledge of the unfolding operation.

"It's got to be the British Army trying to take control of the facility," Sage yelled, "but I don't know how the hell they found out about it unless there's a leak at the Pentagon. The SecDef is meeting with the Joint Chiefs right now to formulate our own plan to present to the President."

Kenney interrupted him. "Admiral, I've seen four cops go down by sniper fire in the past minute. You think they'd be taking out their own guys?"

"If it's not them, who is it?"

"I don't know, sir."

"Jesus Christ, Kenney! Don't tell me you don't

know," he shouted. "Find out! I've got to break into the SecDef's meeting. Call me back."

Daniel Lightburn knelt on the floor of his bedroom and parted the curtains of a rear-facing window. His son Andrew crawled across the rug until he was next to him, "Are they comin'?"

Daniel motioned for him to keep his head down, and said, "Someone's comin' but it's nae th' police. I just saw a copper get his head blowed off."

"What should we do?"

"Are the women underground?"

"Yeah."

"You and me are gonna defend th' house. If they come in, we blast 'em. Kheelan and Douglas are still in th' barn, reet?"

Andrew nodded.

"Good. The bastards are coming down the fells, so th' barn's a good place t' take 'em on. You scared, son?"

"Wee bit."

"Don't be. If it's our time, it's our time. Simple as pie."

Nancy and Greg were just north of Lightburn Farm when the shooting began. Nancy pulled Greg down onto the cold grass and watched in amazement as tracer rounds came in showers off the fells. She saw the two officers who'd turned them back go down from long-range fire. By habit, she started to reach for her weapon which wasn't there.

She couldn't understand why it was taking so long for the police to return fire but the order must have been given because all of a sudden the officers started defending themselves with semiautomatic pistol and rifle fire.

"Someone knows about the Library, Greg, and they're trying to get to it."

He seemed too scared to lift his head. She heard a muffled, "Who?"

"I hope to hell it's not us."

"You mean Area 51?" he said.

She ignored the question. "We've got to get Phillip and Will out of there."

Will had spent all day chained to his bunk beside Phillip and Annie. Haven and Cacia had come down to deliver meals and Kheelan and Daniel had both paid surly visits to check their bonds. In the morning, while waiting for his turn in the lavatory, Will had seen one of the writers, the oldest one. The old man had looked through him as if he didn't exist.

During the morning, he had tried to keep things light for Phillip, making jokes and small talk with him and Annie, but the boy seemed to grow more choleric every time he and Annie exchanged a laugh or a smile.

In the afternoon, Will pulled in his horns and stayed quiet. While Phillip and Annie napped, he stared at his watch and counted down the hours until 5 P.M.

"Did you hear that?" Will asked, looking at the ceiling.

Though muffled, he recognized the prolonged and irregular staccato of automatic weapons—a firefight.

"It's started," Annie said, sitting up. "They're coming to rescue us."

"You think?" Will said. "I don't hear shotgun fire coming from the house."

"What then?"

"Beats me, but I don't like it. It's almost five. I hope Cacia's okay or we're kind of screwed."

Phillip tried not to look scared but Will could tell he was.

"Don't worry, kiddo," Will said. "We're going to get out of this fine and we're going to have some great stories for Mom."

The police dived for cover as rounds crashed into car doors and tree trunks. The unarmed Community Patrol Officers could only cower and try to survive while the SWAT members engaged an unseen foe, blindly firing bursts up to the fell.

Inside the incident van, the Assistant Chief Constable shouted at the driver to move the vehicle up the road out of the line of fire but as the driver took his place at the wheel a round shattered the glass and his head.

Two MI5 men scrambled into the van and hugged the floor as they made their way to the Chief Constable who was on the carpet with his mobile at his ear.

"I'm getting shunted from office to office at the MOD. Nobody seems to know anything," Raab bellowed.

"I'm awaiting a callback from our HQ," the MI5 officer said. "They don't know anything either."

"I've requested emergency backup from all the SWAT units within a fifty-mile radius but it's going to take a while."

Another large-caliber bullet tore through the last piece of glass in the van.

The MI5 man crawled closer to Raab's ear. "If we don't get out of here we're all dead."

The loudest noise any of them had ever heard sent everyone at the farm onto their bellies, hands to ears. It was the sound of a million screams.

Three RAF F–35C Lightning IIs roared overhead a mere two hundred yards off the ground. They had approached at Mach 1.2 from the Stainmore Gap and plunged south directly over the twin fells of Nine Standards Rigg and High Seat.

In the sliver of a second of airtime spent over the farm, the lead plane had taken a hundred infrared and thermal ultrahigh-speed photos of the ground activity, and as the planes banked for a second pass, the images were already on command screens at their base at RAF Boulmer, Northumberland and at the Ministry of Defense in London.

Group Captain Mike Rogers at RAF Boulmer was on hands-free with the MOD in Whitehall. The Chief of the Defense Staff, General Sir Robert Sandage, stood over his imaging techs shoulder to shoulder with the Minister of Defense, George Cotting.

"I see perhaps a dozen hostiles on 337," Rogers said, referring to the ID number of one wide-angle thermal image.

"I agree, yes," Sandage replied. "They were dropped there somehow. Have you got anything on that?"

"Hang on, sir," Rogers said. "We received a block of images in a burst." At Whitehall, the line went quiet for a few seconds until Rogers came back on excitedly, "Look at Image 732!"

A tech in Whitehall called up the photo. It showed a helicopter hovering off the slope of High Seat fell.

"Whose is it?" Minister Cotting asked.

"We won't see any markings from an overhead view," Sandage said. "Run it through our database, would you, Major," he calmly asked the tech.

The technician swiped his trackpad and called up an image-recognition program, which took seconds to find a match with one-hundred-percent probability. He projected it on the screen: the chopper was a stealth Mi–23/180.

Minister Cotting was the first to react verbally. "My God! Get me the Prime Minister."

The black-clad ground troops moved methodically down the fell toward the farmhouse, untouched by the random SWAT team fire and seemingly unperturbed by the RAF flyover. Two men who were ahead of the pack veered off toward the barn. They crept up to it and found the main door unlocked. One of them rolled it open just enough to enter and the other followed, his hand on the lead's shoulder.

"Shoot!" Kheelan shouted at his nephew Douglas from behind a bale of hay.

Shotgun blasts shredded the intruders and peppered the barn door with holes.

Kheelan pumped another shell into the chamber and cautiously approached the bloody men.

"I never shot no one before," his young nephew said, shivering.

"Watch th' side door," Kheelan said, ignoring the lad's feelings.

He pushed his boot under one of the prone bodies. With a grunt he flipped it over and shined his torch on it.

He blinked a few times at what he saw, but all he managed to say was, "Fuckin' hell!"

* * *

The Defense Minister stepped back to the command console, decidedly paler in complexion.

"What did the P.M. say?" General Sandage asked.

"He told us to engage." From the bewildered expression on Cotting's face, it was evident he hardly believed what was coming out of his own mouth. "How long will it take to get the SAS in there?"

"Too long," Sandage said. "The 22 SAS Regiment is at Credenhill in Hereford. I'm all for sending them, but we can get 1 Lancs there faster. They're in Yorkshire. In the meanwhile, I suggest we let the Lightnings have a go."

Right after the Lightnings made a second pass over the farm, the squadron leader received an order on his headset from RAF Boulmer.

"This is Group Captain Rogers. I am ordering you to immediately engage and destroy the hostiles."

The squadron leader banked left and with a catch in his voice asked Rogers to repeat the order.

When the order was confirmed, the pilot advised his wingmen to arm their weapons systems and assume attack mode.

Kenney was watching the aerial display through his scope and called out to his men, "They're coming around again."

There were a series of *booms* from 40mm cannon fire immediately followed by a huge thunderclap and bright explosion midway up the fell as the helicopter burst into flames and pitched into the hillside.

"This is unbelievable," Kenney called out. "We've got a goddamn war going on!"

* * *

The Lightnings pursued the ground troops with machine-gun fire and each time a shower of tracers slammed into the ground the crouching police let out a collective cheer.

Nancy was too engrossed in the aerial display to feel the cold and wet from the ground seeping through her clothes. Greg started to rise to his feet to get a better look but she pushed him back down.

"Just pray they think we're the good guys," she shouted to Greg. "Otherwise, we're going to get lit up."

With every pass of the Lightnings, the invaders made an effort to train small-arms fire against them but the jets streaked by far too quickly. The air-to-ground assault froze the troops in their positions about a hundred yards from the farmhouse and there the battle stood for twenty minutes or more when a new sound was heard over Mallerstang, the persistent thump of rotor blades.

Five AW159 Wildcat Lynx helicopters emblazoned with Union Jacks swooped out of the gloam and landed on the road beside the police positions.

A full company of 1 Lancs of the First Battalion, the Duke of Lancaster's Regiment, flooded the field of battle. The British Army regulars stormed the perimeter of the farm, effecting a pincer movement to the north and south. They methodically encircled the remaining special ops troops and fifteen minutes later, the last of the black-clad intruders was dead.

During the firefight stray rounds whistled over Nancy's and Greg's heads but a minute after the last shots were fired, she rose to her knees to assess the situation.

It was clear to her that the British forces had succeeded in the operation—against whom was the question. In the chaos of the battle's aftermath, as men were shouting for medics and the police were using bullhorns to warn the soldiers away from the farm buildings, Nancy decided to make her move. It was almost 6 P.M. but she still had her own mission to accomplish.

"Come on, Greg, let's go. I think we can make it."

She literally pulled him off the ground by his sleeve and tugged him through the dark field. Everyone was focused on the battleground and no one seemed to notice two civilians making a dash to an unassuming stone building a good distance from the farmhouse.

With fifty yards to go, Nancy tripped on something and went down hard. Greg helped her up, but looking back, she saw what had wrong-footed her, a piece of smoldering wreckage from the destroyed helicopter.

There was some kind of writing on it. In the dark, she couldn't be sure but she asked Greg, a proud polyglot, if he could make it out. He stooped over it, scared to touch the charred piece of metal.

"Can you read it?" she asked.

"It's Chinese!" he said. Then, with a voice bubbling with fear, he told her, "It says People's Liberation Army."

Kenney was scanning the battlefield with his night scope, sweeping from one hot spot to another, giving a running commentary to Lopez and Harper while simultaneously listening to intercepted traffic on the police and SWAT team's radio transmissions.

"Man alive, the army's just beaten the tar out of the guys in the helicopter. It's the power of numbers, boys. The Spartans may have been kick-ass fighters, but eventually the three hundred got reduced to zero by the Persians."

He paused to listen to a relay between a SWAT commander and Incident Control.

"You're not going to believe this," Harper told his men. "They've just IDed two of the corpses. They're PLA!"

"Palestinians?" Harper asked.

"No, you dumb shit! Not PLO. They're Chinese!"

"What do the Chinese want here?" Lopez asked.

"It ain't the Moo Shi Pork. It's the damned Library. Looks like they know it's here and looks like they're trying to get ahold of it. I've got to call Groom Lake."

Just then, something to the north of the farmhouse caught his attention. Two solitary figures were

making their way to a small stone building on the
periphery of the farm. He zoomed in. No uniforms.
Civilians.

"Hey, Harper, see if Davis has his mobile turned on."

Harper started tapping on his tablet.

"Yeah, it's on."

"Put it on a map."

Harper followed the order and handed the device
to Kenney.

The blinking yellow dot was approaching Lightburn Farm.

"Hello, Greg," Kenney said, looking through his
scope. "Nice to meet you, you son of a bitch. Now
who's your little friend?"

The wait was agonizing.

Even though the sounds were dampened, there was
no mistaking that all hell was breaking loose above
their heads. At each burst of gunfire Will gritted his
teeth and pulled at his handcuff. What he hated most
was his inability to shield Phillip. A father's job was
to protect his son and he hadn't done that, had he?
And even in the best of times, what kind of father
had he been? The kind who spends his time living on
his boat while his family fends for itself in another
state. He was mad at himself but this wasn't the time
for self-analysis.

Instead, he was brimming with questions.

Where was Cacia?

Was the house under attack?

Had she been killed or wounded?

It was six o'clock. If Greg had made it to Pinn had
he been able to navigate the mayhem and get to the
meeting point?

The door to their detention room creaked open.

She was there, tears in her eyes.

Will said, "Cacia."

"It's horrible." She could hardly stand.

Annie and Phillip seemed stricken by her agonized look.

"So many dead," she said. "Why?"

"Who's dead?" Will asked. "Tell me what's happening."

"Some men came off th' fell firing at t' police and killing 'em. The police fired back. Then airplanes came and fired ont' th' fells. Then British Army men came by helicopter and killed all th' men up on the fell. Kheelan and Douglas killed two of 'em in the barn. So much killin'! Why?"

"Undo my cuff," Will said softly.

When she did so, he rose and held her tightly, letting her cry into his shoulder. Annie chose to look at the floor.

"Who were the men on the fells?" he asked.

"I don't know, I don't know."

"All right, Cacia, here's what we need to do. The fellow I told you about, the one who can help us—I don't know if he was able to make it here, but we've got to see. Unchain Phillip and Annie and let's go there."

She stepped back and wiped her face with her palms. "Daniel and Kheelan are in a lather. There's no telling what they'll do. If they come down 'ere and find everyone missin', I don't know what'll happen." She pointed at Phillip and Annie. "It's safer for th' two of you to stay put. I'll take you to the stairs, Will. We'll see if your man's here, but so 'elp me, if this was a trick t' let th' police in . . ." She took a pistol from a deep pocket in her sweater. It was old and small, a relic of the Second World War.

"It's not a trick."

She put the pistol back. "Okay then, let's go."

Will winked at Phillip for reassurance and followed her out. They climbed the stairs slowly, straining to hear if there was any sign of the police or the army on the other side of the trapdoor. It was quiet. At the top of the stairs, Will gripped the latch, turned it, and pushed against the hatch.

It lifted a few inches.

It was dark but he saw a pair of tasseled loafers a few feet away. Greg's usual style.

Will threw open the hatch, letting it fall fully open on its hinges and climbed to the third from last step, high enough for his torso to be above floor level.

It *was* Greg, blinking at him in the dark.

"Is he there?" Cacia called out a few steps behind.

Will ignored her. "Greg, my man! You made it!"

Before Greg could answer, Will saw someone standing behind him. He tensed. Then he saw her.

Nancy stepped into the clear and ran to him, dropping to her knees and kissing him.

"Who the hell's there?" Cacia called out angrily. "Tell me! I'm going t' shoot!"

Caught between a woman with a gun and a wife who'd been far from his mind, Will was momentarily lost for words.

"It's okay, Cacia. It's Greg and my wife."

"Let me through," Cacia said.

He climbed into the hangar and let Cacia come up behind him.

Nancy looked like she wanted to pounce on Cacia's weapon but Will talked her down.

"Nancy, take it easy," he said. "Let's go see Phillip, all right? We need to have a good talk about things." Then he addressed Greg. "Jesus, Greg, I told you not to tell Nancy. I mean I'm happy to see you Nancy, but

I didn't want any complications. This is complicated enough."

"The FBI doesn't know, Will," she said. "I'm here on my own. And Greg didn't tell me. I found out."

Will was bewildered. He turned to Cacia, staring at her shaking gun hand. "It's not exactly what I promised you but it doesn't change anything. Nancy can help. She'll help us make our case." He looked out into the black night. "Let's go back down the stairs quick and get to work before someone see us. Someone launched an assault. Someone's already trying to take the Library away from you."

"Who?" Cacia asked. "Who was it? The British government?"

"No," Nancy said. "The British Army fought them off. It was the Chinese."

"The Chinese?" Will said, stringing together a bunch of epithets. "How the hell did *they* get involved?"

"I don't know," Nancy said, "but I'm sure a lot of people are scrambling like crazy for the answer."

Will turned to Cacia and begged her to put the gun away. She shook her head sadly and started down the stairs, saying, "Come on then, but there'll be hell t' pay when Daniel finds out. Last one down's got t' close th' hatch."

As they descended underground and entered the storeroom, Will took Nancy's hand and squeezed it hard.

"Is Phillip okay?" she whispered.

"He's fine," he said. "If I were alone, I'd have risked busting out of here. But with him . . ."

"Thank God you didn't," she said. "What is this place?"

"There's so much to tell you. Let's just start with Phillip."

Greg was already taking pictures of the stocked shelves of the storeroom with his NetPen. Cacia saw the flashes and was about to protest when Will said, "He needs to take photos, Cacia. It's part of the plan, remember?"

She kept quiet and proceeded to the far end of the room.

"Who is she?" Nancy whispered.

"The mother of the girl who persuaded Phillip to come here."

"She seems to do everything you say," Nancy said.

Will chose his words carefully. "I've gotten her to understand our interests are aligned."

Nancy smiled at that. "I'm sure you have."

They entered the dormitory.

Greg seemed to understand the purpose of the cots because he immediately began to shoot pictures of them.

"Good," Will said. "Get a wide shot of them."

Nancy understood too. "Christ, Will, you're not saying this is an active operation, are you?"

"It is. Completely active."

"Where are they?" Greg asked.

"Close by. You'll see them soon."

There was a glow coming from the top of the partitioned room. Nancy seemed to sense her son was there because she ran ahead of Will and despite Cacia's protests, flung open the door.

Before he got there, Will heard, "Mom!" then he heard Nancy crying with relief and anger at the sight of her son, dirty and chained to a bed.

Will, Greg, and Cacia joined them in the small room.

"Undo his handcuff!" Nancy demanded. She was sitting beside the boy, hugging him. For his part, Phillip seemed embarrassed but happy to see her.

"Was that the FBI doing all the shooting up there?" Phillip asked.

"No, sweetheart," she said. "I'm here as a civilian."

Phillip saw Greg behind his parents. "Uncle Greg?"

"Hey, Phillip," Greg said. "I'm glad you're okay."

Nancy repeated her demand that Phillip be unchained and Will gently made the same plea. "We're beyond that now, Cacia. Undo his cuff."

As Cacia knelt to unlock the handcuff another voice said, "What about me?"

Annie had been virtually invisible during the reunion but Nancy saw her in the corner bunk and asked, "Who the hell are you?"

"Annie Locke, with the Security Services. I'm very pleased to meet you, Assistant Director. I've heard a lot about you."

Nancy looked at her, then Cacia and smirked at both attractive women. "You've had a lot of help, haven't you, Will?"

Will nodded sheepishly. "Annie, if Cacia frees you up, will you promise not to run off or make trouble?"

Annie pointed to her leg wounds. "I don't think I'll be sprinting away. I promise."

Cacia sighed and unlocked her too.

"Thank you, Cacia," Will said. "Now we've got to get Greg into the Library for pictures. You feeling like a journalist again, Greg?" Will asked.

"I've always been a journalist," Greg said.

"Sorry. Didn't come out right," Will said. "But this is going to be a helluva story, and it's going to be yours to tell. And let me promise you something. When it's time to write a book about this, it's going to be you writing it, not me."

Greg looked at the ground avoiding eye contact and nodded.

Just then, they all heard a young man calling out, "Ma? You down here?" and Andrew came into the room. He was brandishing a shotgun. He looked around with a look of high confusion and alarm, turned tail, and ran away with Cacia calling after him to come back.

Mr. President, I have Prime Minister Hastings on the line."

Midnight was approaching in Washington. President Dumont was in the White House Situation Room, casually dressed, surrounded by his National Security team. He thanked the operator and when he heard the click of her signing off, threw the call onto the speaker, and said, "Martin, we've been monitoring the attack in Yorkshire and your response. What can you tell me?"

The Prime Minister was clearly stressed, his voice a quarter of an octave higher than usual. "I was going to call you in a few minutes, John. Just sorting through all this with my Defense staff. But I can say unequivocally that all the intruders were killed. One of their commandos was given the opportunity of surrendering but he shot himself."

"My folks are telling me it was the Forty-second GA out of Guangzhou," the President said. "It's their best special ops unit, like your SAS and our Seals. Apparently they call themselves the Sharp Sword of Southern China."

"Well, we have absolutely no idea why China would take this historic and unprecedented step, an act of war aimed at a bloody farm in Cumbria, for God's sake! I've got the Chinese ambassador waiting for me downstairs, and he'd better have an explanation! The area is remote and the immediate environs were cordoned off due to an ongoing police action involving hostages but the media are starting to get wind of it and we don't think we can keep a ring around it for very long. The British public will demand a harsh response."

The President shook his head at his staff and rolled his eyes. "Martin, you're not going to be declaring war on China, for Christ's sake. We've got to pursue this through diplomatic channels."

"It's well and good for you to say that, Mr. President," the Prime Minister said, getting formal, "but if the shoe were on the other foot, imagine how the American public would react. Let me repeat, this was an act of war!" One of Hastings's advisors must have urged him to tone it down because he immediately followed up with, "Look, John. The first thing we need to do is find out what in God's name their intent was. Then we can calibrate our response."

The President rocked back on his padded swivel chair. "Well, Martin. We might be able to help you with that. We know exactly what the Chinese want with that farm of yours."

Daniel and Kheelan barreled into the small room with fire in their eyes, waving their weapons and shouting.

Will raised his hands, and said, "Easy, Daniel. Everything's all right. This is my son-in-law, Greg, and my wife, Nancy. They're here to help you. Believe me."

"Don't you tell me t' go easy, mister!" Daniel bellowed. "We've got a war going on outside and we've got people coming into my home like it was a public way. Are you behind this, Cacia?"

She nodded, but replied steadily, "You've got t'

listen t' Will, Daniel. We can't survive this on our own. Not now."

"You women'll be the death of me!" he shouted. "You and Haven've brought ruin upon us."

"It was meant t' happen," she said firmly. "You know that better than anyone. The names of all th' men who died out there this evening—all of them are written in one of th' books."

When Daniel's face softened with sadness, Kheelan took up the cudgel.

"Let's not forget that we're holding th' good cards, Danny," he said. "We've got hostages, and now we've got two more. They're not gonna fuck with us while we've got hostages."

Will jumped in. "Hostages are meaningless. You're meaningless. The stakes are too high. We're all just flies who're going to be swatted away. I hate saying this in front of my family but unless we take control of this situation we're either going to be dead—which isn't something we can change—or we're going to be locked away in some damn hole so we can't tell the world what's been happening here."

"If hostages were meaningless, the police would've knocked our doors down already," Kheelan spat.

Will shook his head. "The game's changed, friend. Where've you been the last hour? Who do you think attacked the farm?"

"Haven't a clue," Kheelan said. "But they were foreigners. I personally sent a couple of them to hell."

"Yeah, they were foreigners, all right," Will said. "They were Chinese."

"You're joking," Daniel said. "That's daft."

"My husband's telling you the truth," Nancy said. "They were Chinese special forces."

Kheelan let the weight of his shotgun point the

barrel toward the floor. "I saw their faces. They *were* Chinese."

"I don't know how they knew you have a Library," Will said, "but they do. And my guess is they don't want the British or the Americans to have it. They want it. If they'd gotten in here we all would've been killed or wounded. And the same thing's going to happen if the Americans come or the British. We're expendable."

"And my lads?" Cacia asked. "What about them?"

Will could tell she was talking about the writers, not her sons.

"They'll want them," he said. "If only to study them like lab rats. You've got books going out hundreds of years. I'm not sure they'll much care about continued production."

Cacia's lower lip trembled. "Daniel and Kheelan, listen t' me good. Will Piper's a good man. I trust him t' do the right thing by us. Let 'im tell you 'is plan."

Kheelan began swearing again but Daniel cut him off. "Let the man talk, Kheelan."

Will laid it all out. He told them how with Greg's help back in 2010, he'd defeated the US government's attempt to destroy him by publicly revealing the existence of the Vectis Library.

"We neutralized them by bringing it out into the light of day. We defanged them, made them harmless. We've got to do the same thing with your Library. Let Greg take photos of the Library and the writers. Give him a tour and let him write the story of his life and put it out tonight on one of his NetZines. It'll spread like wildfire. The whole world will know about it within the hour."

"Then what?" Daniel asked.

"Then we talk to the police, the army, whoever they put out there to negotiate with us," Will said.

"We give them your demands: You get a seat at the table deciding where the Library's going to go because it can't stay here anymore. If you want to look after the writers in the future, you're going to have to demand it, Cacia. You're going to want immunity from prosecution."

Annie couldn't keep silent. She pointed at Kheelan. "I'm sorry, but this man killed one of our agents in cold blood and seriously wounded another."

"Kheelan will have to answer for that," Will said. "There's no getting around it, Daniel."

Daniel grunted and avoided looking at his brother. "All right. I've heard your proposal. We're going t' go off and discuss this as a family, like we always do. We'll be back with our decision, but until then, we can't have ya with the run of th' place. You and you," he said pointing at Greg and Nancy. "Empty out your pockets. Cacia, fetch more handcuffs and get everyone locked down again."

His wife started to object, but he pleaded with her, "For th' love of God, woman, would you please just mind me this one time?"

Nancy went first, presenting her passport, FBI credentials, a government-issue NetPen. Then Kheelan patted her down under Will's icy stare.

Greg was next. He seemed uneasy and fumbled through his pockets for his gear, slowly producing a NetPen, a wallet, a notepad, and some pens. "That's it," he declared.

Kheelan frisked him and was about to step away when he exclaimed, "What's this?" He thrust his hand into Greg's right pants pocket and came out with an olive green cylinder, two inches shorter than his NetPen.

"I forgot about that," Greg said. "It's my other NetPen, the one I use for work."

"Is it now?" Daniel asked.

Nancy interrupted the sudden silence. "I don't think so, Greg. I think we've got a problem."

Will was taken aback. "Nancy, what are you saying?"

"Let me take a look at that," she said to Kheelan. "I've got a feeling I know what it is and I don't think any of us are going to like it."

Daniel made Kheelan hand it to her.

She inspected it, and said, "I've seen these in training videos. They're personalized by fingerprint and heavily encrypted. Greg, I want you to push on the button with your thumb."

He hesitated, but Daniel pointed his gun and forced him to do it.

The polymer screen unfurled and brightly lit up. A man's face appeared on the screen, wearing a military cap.

He called out Greg's name and began speaking rapidly in Chinese.

Greg collapsed onto his haunches like an exhausted fugitive who'd been hounded and finally cornered.

Will's mouth started to open, forming the first of a litany of questions, while Kheelan grabbed the mobile device from Nancy's hand, threw it down, and angrily smashed it with the butt of his shotgun. He did the same to Nancy's NetPen and dispersed the electronic bits with his boot.

"There's nothing to discuss now, is there, Daniel?" Kheelan said. "We're not going t' make ourselves known t' offcomers. We're not negotiating with th' police. We're going t' defend our land and our lives. Come on, let's lock these bastards up and get back t' our places lest we get overrun without putting up a good fight."

Two more cots were dragged into the isolation room to accommodate Nancy and Greg. Reshackled, the prisoners were left on their own.

Greg was uncommunicative, sullen, avoiding everyone's glances. Nancy spoke about him in the third person as if he wasn't there.

"The postcards came from *him*, Will."

Will and Phillip both asked, "Why?" simultaneously.

"He's going to have to tell us," Nancy said, "but we've got CCTV images of him making deposits in the right post office boxes in Manhattan on the right days. He's one of the few people in the world outside of the Area 51 crowd who've had the database pass through his hands. Every federal department, including your favorite guys, Will, the watchers, have been scrubbed for leaks. It's not coming from inside. It's him. He's been a suspect for a couple of days. I kept it to myself, went to his apartment, followed him to the airport. I didn't want to believe it."

"He's got opportunity—maybe," Will said. "What about motive?"

Nancy stared at him, "Well, Greg?"

They all stared, waiting for him to give an account of himself but he stayed mute, glancing at them furtively then looking away, until Will finally said, "Here's the deal, Greg. You need to come clean with us. We're your family. We haven't always been on the same page and if I've been to blame, I apologize, but I'm scared as hell about Phillip and we've got to maximize his chances of getting out of this. So I'm appealing to you. What's your role in this? What do the Chinese want?"

Greg began talking in a monotone, keeping his eyes on the floor. He wasn't explicit about motivations but Will could easily enough fill in the blanks on that: chronic disappointments, a career overshadowed by his wife's, financial woes, unfulfilled aspirations. He'd been approached by a man who worked in the Chinese delegation at the United Nations. The guy was friendly, interested in his Web site for Chinese-Americans. He said the Chinese government was keen on positive cultural exchanges and wanted to help improve his circulation and outreach, help with articles about China. He offered money, envelopes of cash, modest amounts at first, saying that discretion was important. That's how it started. He got friendly with the man—lunches, dinners, clubbing. Will imagined Greg would have been susceptible to expensive food and wine, maybe some escorts thrown into the mix. Finally, the big ask came. The US database from Area 51. Had he managed to retain a copy? If so, the Chinese government might pay him handsomely.

Then Greg made the shocking admission. On the day in 2009 that Will e-mailed him the Area 51 database, Greg had stopped into a Georgetown Apple store and logged onto his *Washington Post* e-mail account. When no one was looking, he transferred the file onto a thumb drive. Simple as that. Later, when the Justice Department clamped down on the *Post*'s copy and confiscated all electronic files on the newspaper's servers, they found no evidence of a download from inside the company.

Why had he done it? He swore he never looked up dates of death, but Will didn't believe him. The Godlike temptation would have been too great. Greg's explanation was vague. It was like stealing the *Mona Lisa*. You could never tell anyone you had it. It would be yours alone to admire. But the feeling of power—

Greg insisted he didn't give his Chinese friend the database. That, he asserted, would have been treasonous. The man cajoled him, lavished him with a Rolex, the one still on his wrist (which he'd told Laura was a knockoff), danced around the subject until they hit on a compromise. Greg would do their bidding for them. He'd look up names—for a price, a good price, but toward what end, he wanted to know? After all, the database was almost spent. The Horizon was approaching.

The Chinese request was unusual. They wanted him

to find Chinese-Americans or Chinese nationals—it didn't matter—people with upcoming dates of death.

They wanted him to send postcards, mimicking the style of the Doomsday killer, calculated to garner the maximum media attention. They never told him why, but he thought it was obvious. The Chinese government wanted to create the artifice that the US government was behind a provocation. They wanted the political leverage to flex their muscles around the world as the aggrieved party.

The price was agreed upon and he began to mail the cards. It wasn't a great crime, was it? After all, these were people who were going to die anyway. He wasn't *killing* them.

His last act was to mail a set of fake cards to the Chinese embassy staff in Washington. None of the targets were in the US database anyway. He did as he was instructed. It was to be his final act for them. Again, as far as he was concerned, no harm, no foul. The Ambassador and his people were never in any danger.

His final payment was received. Thankfully, he was done. He wasn't cut out for a clandestine life, for all the stress. He'd made some good money, enough to make the final push to the Horizon pleasant as hell. He and Laura would travel, buy nice things, have a blast. It was over.

But Will's e-mail opened up a new world of possibilities and he couldn't ignore them.

The Horizon was just a date! The world carried on. More money—a lot more money—would be handy. This was information that might command millions.

He immediately contacted his embassy handler on the secure NetPen they'd given him. He was correct about their interest.

Before he went to the airport, his contact had met him at a Brooklyn coffee shop and exchanged a case containing $2 million for a copy of Will's e-mail message. The money was now sitting in the back of his office closet under a few boxes of sneakers. What the Chinese did with Will's e-mail, he didn't know.

"It's pretty obvious what they did with it, Greg," Will said. "They sent in troops to take the farm. First, they'll plant their flag. Second, they'll start talking about getting control of the material."

Greg fell silent again, talked out. He mumbled something about being very tired and faced the wall, curling himself into a fetal position.

"Everyone's going to want it," Nancy said.

Annie chimed in defensively, "The UK government will never relinquish its rightful claim. It's simply unthinkable."

Nancy replied tartly, "We'll see about that."

Will looked at both women and shook his head. "This is going to get ugly," he said. "Extremely ugly."

Prime Minister Hastings received the Chinese Ambassador in the Terracotta Room at 10 Downing Street. Given the circumstances, the two men did not exchange handshakes. Ambassador Chou spoke impeccable English so translators were not required. He had come with a single aide.

"Her Majesty's Government requires an urgent and thorough explanation for your government's illegal and outrageous military intrusion onto our sovereign territory," Hastings demanded before Chou had time to fully plant himself into his seat.

Chou cleared his throat, and, by his pinched expression, it was apparent he was not relishing the meeting. "I am sincerely sorry that such an action was considered necessary by my government. The leadership felt there was no alternative."

"No alternative to the hostile invasion of the United Kingdom?" Hastings bellowed.

"You see," Chou continued, his voice tension-pitched, "as the most populous country in the world, with 1.5 billion people, we cannot be at a disadvantage with respect to all available planning resources. You must be aware what is present in Yorkshire."

"I am. Of course," the Prime Minister said.

"For eighty years, the United States has had the rather distinct advantage of possessing the Library of Vectis," the ambassador said. "They leveraged this resource to their exclusive advantage. They did not share any of the data with you prior to 2010, am I correct?"

The Prime Minister exchanged an uncomfortable glance with his Foreign Secretary. "Since then, we've had selective access," Hastings said.

"Well, Prime Minister, how is it that the United States, which had no sovereign right to the Library, was allowed to control this critical asset?"

"It was a decision made by Winston Churchill a very long time ago. He undoubtedly thought it was the right thing to do at the moment. That doesn't mean it would be the right thing to do today. And listen here, Ambassador Chou, how can any of this come close to justifying your country's de facto act of war?"

Chou winced at the word. " 'War' is an unfortunate and premature terminology, Prime Minister. Our intrusion onto British territory was our way of asserting our undeniable claim which we doubted would be taken seriously without such an act. These books contain the names and dates of births and deaths. Not only for British citizens. Not only for

American citizens. But for all the peoples in the world. China has the most people and must therefore control the resource. We will be happy to discuss ways in which the United Kingdom can have, as you put it, selective access, for your own social and political needs."

Hastings was volcanic. "You invade my country, then tell us we can have sloppy seconds? Are you out of your minds? Do you . . ."

An aide entered the formal room with a note, which when passed to the Prime Minister interrupted him in midsentence.

Hastings read the note quickly and struggled to maintain his composure. "Mr. Ambassador, I've just been informed that your North Sea Fleet led by the carrier *Wen Jiabao* and a number of Type 094 nuclear submarines is off the Faroe Islands proceeding at speed toward the North Sea and presumably the eastern coast of Britain. This meeting is over. You will remove yourself along with your entire ambassadorial staff and return to your country. A formal letter will be forthcoming, but you may assume that as of now our two countries no longer enjoy diplomatic contact."

The Prime Minister made a flurry of calls. A meeting of his national security group was scheduled for the COBR in an hour's time. The Defense Minister was ordered to increase Britain's threat level to Critical and inform all Heads of Service to configure their forces accordingly. An emergency Parliament debate was called for the next morning. The king was summoned out of a charity event and briefed. The Press Association was contacted and urged to hold off on reporting on news emanating from Yorkshire until the morning. The P.M.'s spokesman began drafting standby statements and an address to the nation.

Then Hastings rang Washington.

"Mr. President, I've had the most extraordinary meeting with Ambassador Chou. The Chinese are making no bones about it. They want this new Library and they seem prepared to seize it by force if necessary. Their North Sea Fleet is off the Faroes proceeding at full speed toward our coast."

President Dumont was in the Situation Room. Surrounded by his staff, he quickly replied, "Yeah, we're tracking them. The Chinese position is certainly not acceptable, is it, Martin?"

"It is not. For your information, we have gone to Threat Level Critical and I will have Parliament debate a declaration of war unless the Chinese stand down and offer an apology and some form of compensation. If we do find it necessary to make a war declaration, we will be assuming the full cooperation and support of the United States and NATO."

The line went completely silent. Hastings pointed to his mute button, alerting his own staff of his assumption that the President had put them on mute.

When the line came to life again a few seconds later, Dumont said, "Let's not be hasty with any declarations, Martin. Once the toothpaste's out of the tube, it's going to be a bitch putting it back inside. Our belief in Washington is that the Chinese feel reasonably comfortable pushing Britain around. They might not feel nearly as bullish going at it with the United States."

Hastings furrowed his brow, and said, "That's precisely why it's imperative for you and our NATO allies to make the strongest possible statements of support directly to the Chinese government and to do so tonight."

The President replied fluidly, "Here's the thing, Martin. Our view is that you're vulnerable as hell up there in Yorkshire. The Chinese are going to figure you're going to have trouble defending a remote site against the kind of attack their North Sea Fleet can muster. They're also going to figure that NATO might not be up to the fight. I mean, are we really going to escalate this thing to World War III over a bunch of books?"

"NATO has a moral and a legal duty to support us!" Hastings exploded. "Are you honestly telling me that your intentions are otherwise?"

"No, no, I'm not saying that at all. I'm just passing on our concerns, which, I might add, are shared by the Germans and the French. We just think that the most prudent way to deal with this crisis is to get these damn books out of there as quickly as possible. If we do that, what are the Chinese going to attack? An empty room?"

The Prime Minister calmed down a notch. "We have had a preliminary discussion on our end of moving the Library to a more secure location. There are a number of deep bunkers associated with military installations that may be suitable."

The line went mute again and stayed that way for an awkward interval. "Sorry about that," the President said, "To be frank, it's our view that the best place for the Library is in Groom Lake, Nevada. I mean, think about it. We've already got a state-of-the-art, bomb-proof, earthquake-proof underground facility and all the supercomputers and analysts to properly handle the material. We were going to mothball it, but we can easily modify it to take the new merchandise. It would cost you tens of billions of dollars to build something that already exists at Area 51, and if you went down that road, it would take you years to be in a position to exploit the intel. We'd be more than happy for you to station a team of analysts at Groom Lake so you can query the database from time to time and reap the benefits along with the United States. What do you say, Martin? We've got our troops at Mildenhall on alert. Just give the word and we'll have all necessary transport and manpower up there in Yorkshire in no time. We'll knock down any local resistance at the farm for you, deal with the hostage situation up there, clean out the books by daybreak, and have them on the way to Nevada. The Chinese will be rip-shit but we don't think they're going to do anything about it. They'll storm and thunder but they won't be taking on the United States on our home court."

Hastings's aides were making furious hand gestures to go onto mute so they could advise him how to respond. He ignored them, and said icily, "Mr. President, your offer is very kind, but the answer is no. The Library was created on British soil and will stay on British soil. Winston Churchill made a dreadful mistake in 1947 by giving away a national treasure. I shall not make the same one."

A cold front blew across the Dales and cleared the sky of mist. The crescent moon became visible, sharply defined against the blackness of the night. The air was fresh and crystalline.

The scene playing out below Kenney's position was controlled and orderly. Army units were deploying themselves around Lightburn Farm, vastly supplementing and reinforcing the police presence. Ambulances had come and gone. From the incessant foot traffic going in and out of the incident van, Kenney assumed a fierce discussion had taken place over jurisdiction but when the police fell behind army units in a second-line stance, it was pretty clear the army had dominated.

Kenney grabbed his vibrating communicator. Admiral Sage had been calling regularly for updates but this time the conversation began differently.

"The situation's gone critical here," Sage said. "I've got a mission for you."

"Yes, sir," Kenney said, sensing that saying anything else would not be well received.

"The Pentagon and the White House want you and your men to be the thin end of the wedge. I know there are only three of you but your unit's the best in our arsenal. That's what I told them."

"Thank you, sir," Kenney replied warily.

"The United States has made a determination that the new Library belongs here in Groom Lake and obviously, I'm highly supportive of this. I'm sure you are too."

Kenney lobbed in his agreement.

"The Brits don't seem really keen on this idea, so here's the plan. If, over the next few hours, diplomatic efforts to resolve the matter break down, you will covertly insert your team inside the farm at 0200 and take control of the assets. Once you have achieved your objective, US Army and Air Force elements based at RAF Mildenhall will arrive to suppress any local opposition by force if necessary and transport the Library to Groom Lake."

"What about the hostages, sir?"

"We have carte blanche, Captain. I've had personal assurances there will be no questions asked. You won't have to write any after-action reports. Once the mission is initiated, the hostages and any nationals inside the farm need to be neutralized. This operation needs to be leak-proof. Understood?"

"Completely understood, sir. My men and I will prepare a plan and await a go order."

When he signed off, one thought beat all others to the top of his list.

Will Piper's going down, and I'm the one who's going to do it.

The landline at Lightburn Farm rang incessantly but Daniel refused to answer it. The family was keeping low, away from the drawn curtains. The authorities hadn't cut the electricity but Daniel and Kheelan warned the women and children to expect it. Upstairs, Cacia and her sister, Gail, tried to get the two young girls to bed with a pretended show of normality. Haven participated in the ruse by reading them their favorite bedtime story.

Douglas prowled the underground rooms in case anyone came at them from the storeroom side and while he was down there, he looked in on the hostages and the writers who were engaged in their labors oblivious to the drama.

Kheelan had snuck back to the barn to keep watch on the rear of the property and Daniel manned the house with Andrew, who was biting at his lip and obsessively rubbing the metal parts of his shotgun with an oiled rag.

When the phone began ringing again after the briefest interval of quiet, Cacia called down the stairs for Daniel to pick up and talk to them so the girls could fall asleep.

Daniel swore at her, then crept on his belly, muttering that it wouldn't surprise him if a sniper was going to open fire in the vicinity of the phone. "What d' you want now?" Daniel asked into the handset.

"With whom am I speaking?" The voice was starchy and cool.

"This is Daniel Lightburn. Who the hell is this?"

"My name is Colonel Barry Woolford, British Army. I'm in charge of this operation, Mr. Lightburn. I wonder if I might have a chat with you in person."

"Nae chance, marra."

"I see. In that case, let's have the chat now, over the phone. How would that be?"

"Suit yourself," Daniel said. "But I've got nowt t' say t' you 'cepting that you should leave me and my family be and get off me land. Understand?"

"Yes, I hear you loud and clear, but I'm afraid it isn't so simple. You see, we know exactly what you have, Lightburn, and more to the point, the Chinese know what you have, and they appear to want it very badly. We dealt with their small attempt to get to you but unfortunately, they are massing quite a sub-stantial invasion force and I rather doubt their next attempt will be as easily repelled. I'm concerned for the safety of you and your loved ones, not to mention the hostages you have."

"They're my concerns, not yours," Daniel snapped.

"Yes, once again, I've got to disagree. Let me get to the point. Our proposal is to come in peacefully, take control of the hostages, and assess the logistics. You and your loved ones will be taken to safety and given full immunity even with respect to the shoot-ing that occurred earlier. Isn't that splendid news? But we need for this to occur soon or I'm afraid the generous offer will be withdrawn."

"And what will ya do if I tell you t' stuff your gen-erous offer?" Daniel asked mockingly.

"Then we'll come in quite heavily, and, if you resist, I can assume there will be catastrophic casualties on your side. But we don't want that to happen, do we?"

"Fuck off."

"I see," the colonel said, evenly. "Tell you what, you discuss it among your people and I'll ring you back in a short while. I do hope we can come to a satisfactory agreement, Mr. Lightburn. This is a critical time for you, your country, and the entire world. There will be a resolution one way or another. The stakes couldn't be higher."

Will's mind was racing, working on scenarios and contingencies but he kept getting interrupted by all the little dramas playing out within their cramped confines.

Whether out of anger or fear or mortification, Greg had regressed to the point where he was refusing to converse with the rest of them. He kept his face glued to the wall although he periodically shouted to their unseen captors that he had to go to the bathroom.

Cacia had chained Nancy to the cot between Phillip and Will, perhaps in a sympathetic effort to keep the family unit together. Nancy, for her part, doted on Phillip, but the boy was in no mood to be mothered in front of an audience.

Nancy wasn't exactly giving Will the cold shoulder; she did ask with appropriate concern how he was doing and whether his heart was behaving. But she kept glaring ferociously at Annie and at one point whispered to Will, "She's very pretty."

Will replied that he hadn't noticed.

But she persisted, "Why do you think MI5 assigned her to you? You don't think they know their customer?"

"Jesus, Nancy," he whispered. "I was here to find Phillip, not fool around."

"Cacia's attractive too," she whispered back. "She's also giving you the look."

Will was exasperated. "Don't you think we've got bigger fish to fry?"

Cacia and Haven came in with trays of food and drink. This time, the women weren't left on their own. Douglas looked on moodily, apparently tasked with watching over his mother and sister.

Greg loudly demanded the bathroom again. Douglas grumbled, and took him off at gunpoint.

Cacia saw an opening and stood over Will's bed.

"Daniel's had a call with an army man who says we've got t' give up and turn th' Library over t' them. He says if we don't, they're going t' come in shooting and that if we all get killed or wounded, it'll be on his head not theirs."

Nancy spoke up before Will could. "I've got to get in touch with the FBI. They don't even know I'm in here. The US needs to intervene with the British. There's got to be a way to resolve this without bloodshed. Are there any other mobile phones you can bring down here, Mrs. Lightburn?"

"Kheelan smashed all of yours. We've only got the wired one upstairs."

Will shook his head wearily. "I'm sorry, Nancy, but that's not going to work. It doesn't matter if it's the Americans or the Brits or both of them cooperating. They're going to want the same thing—to control the Library and silence us, one way or another."

"What about the Chinese?" Nancy asked.

"Who knows," Will said. "Maybe they'll be given access to the Library as part of a grand bargain. But they'll all want the public kept in the dark so governments and militaries can play God with the dates.

You saw their reaction when we shined a light on Area 51. For Christ's sake, they probably won't even let the world know the Horizon's a false date."

"What's your plan then?" Nancy asked.

Will looked at her, then looked at Cacia. "I say we join forces with the Lightburns. I say we fight the bastards together. The only thing that's going to stop them is effective opposition. That's the only way to bring them to the negotiating table. We've got to make them understand they're only getting the Library if the world is informed about it, we and the Lightburns get safe passage and Cacia gets to decide what happens to the writers."

While he said this, Cacia was nodding in agreement.

"For the love of God, Cacia," Will implored, "can you get Daniel and Kheelan to let us help them defend your farm?"

She said she'd try and flew out, leaving Haven behind and telling Douglas she'd be back soon.

Haven stood stiffly among them, seemingly uncomfortable among new faces.

Phillip gave her a little wave with his free hand, and said, "Mom, this is my friend, Haven."

Nancy's stern expression melted into a smile. "Hi, Haven," she said. "All this stuff must be pretty upsetting."

"I'm okay," Haven said softly. "I'm worried about the little girls though, me cousins. The gunfire's making 'em cry."

"Oh my," Nancy said. "We've got to make all this craziness stop, don't we?"

Haven nodded.

"You asked Phillip to come to England, I hear."

"I did. And he did. I'm sorry I got him int' all this mess though."

Phillip interjected, "I'm not sorry. I mean it is messed up, but I'm glad I got to meet you."

Douglas marched Greg back in and rechained him. Nancy asked the young man if she could also go to the bathroom and Will piped up that he'd like to go too. Douglas warned against trying anything, unlocked both of them and ushered them away. When they left, Haven seized the opportunity to sit beside Phillip on his cot.

In the anteroom, Will wrapped his hand around Nancy's and gave it a little squeeze.

"I wish you weren't here, but I'm glad you are," he said. "Does that make sense?"

"Kind of," she said, squeezing back. "In a Will Piper sort of way."

"Remember the promise I made to you in the hospital?"

"Which one? About the cheeseburgers or the women?"

He laughed. "The women. I've been good. I wanted you to know."

"I'll choose to believe you."

Just then, the door to the writers' room opened and one of them came out on his way to the lavatory.

"Hang on," Douglas said to them. "Let 'im go first."

Nancy was thunderstruck at the sight of the ginger-haired young man. The writer gave her the most fleeting of looks before shuffling past and reaching for the doorknob.

When the lavatory door closed behind him, Nancy said to Will, "That's one of them, yes?"

"In the flesh."

"I kind of pictured them wearing monk's robes."

"At least they've got sandals."

"Do they talk?"

"Not that I've seen."

Will said, "Douglas, will you let my wife take a peek into their room?"

The young man raised his gun slightly and said, "Ten seconds. No more."

With that, he opened the door to the writers' room a crack, allowed her to peer in, then closed it.

"My God," she said. "It's unbelievable."

The young writer exited the bathroom and shuffled away.

Douglas said to her, "Go on, your turn. I shouldn't expect he's put th' seat down."

Ten minutes after all of them were recuffed, Cacia came back down, but she wasn't alone. Daniel and Kheelan were behind her. They ordered Douglas upstairs to take up Daniel's abandoned position.

Daniel glared at Will and looked like he was going to shout at him, but instead he asked with a forced calm, "Okay then, mister, tell me your proposal."

Will laid out his plan. He'd hastily pieced it together, and as it spilled out, he was pleased it sounded rational.

"So do you have any fertilizer?" Will asked.

"We do," Daniel said. "This is a working farm. How do you think we support the writers and all?"

"And do you have any gas, any petrol?"

"Aye. In the barn. For the tractor."

"And you've got shotgun shells obviously."

"Plenty."

"And jerry cans. I know you've got them."

"Aye."

"And a bag of sugar and a roll of cotton string?"

"I have that," Cacia said.

Will smiled. "Then we've got the fixings."

"Tell me why I should trust you?" Daniel said.

"Because it looks like fate's put us on the same side. We're both fighting to save our families."

Annie was having nothing of it. "Well, I'm certainly not on your side. You've killed and wounded MI5 agents and you intend to kill and maim members of the police and military. I'll play no role in that."

Will gently said, "Annie, if I were in your shoes I'd agree with you one hundred percent. But here's the thing. If they get control of the Library, they may or may not let you go back to your normal life. They might consider you a liability, and liabilities sometimes disappear."

"Nevertheless, I will not help you," she said defiantly.

"There'll be a way to use her," Nancy said. "Keep her locked up until we're ready. And Greg too. He's no longer one of us."

Daniel breathed a heavy sigh and told Cacia to unchain Will, Nancy, and Phillip, and leave Annie and Greg shackled.

"Come on," Will said, standing up and stretching. "Let's go cooking."

The scene in the Lightburn kitchen had an air of domesticity. After Kheelan's defiant outburst against releasing them, he settled down and grudgingly shuttled back and forth to the barn fetching ingredients. Will stirred the chemicals in Cacia's largest saucepans while Nancy emptied shotgun shells into a mixing bowl, all the while talking about her experience of a lifetime, walking through the vast Library chamber on the way to the farmhouse stairs. Under Will's tutelage, Phillip and Haven dipped string into a slurry of sugar water and black powder to make detonation cord. Cacia hovered, providing utensils as needed, and her sister-in-law, Gail, poked her head in from time to time when she wasn't upstairs with her sleeping girls. Daniel, his sons, and Kheelan kept up the watch through peepholes torn through the curtains.

"How did you say you know how to do this?" Nancy asked.

Will chuckled and put the ladle down. "I used to be in law enforcement. Remember? You think all I know how to do is catch fish."

"I'm in law enforcement too, and I don't know how to make a bomb."

"You got promoted into management too fast."

The telephone rang incessantly during their production run but they ignored it. When they were finished, there was enough liquid for four jerry cans. Will carefully placed lengths of homemade detonation cord into the mouths of each can and secured them with wads of Cacia's cut-up tea towels.

"Will they work?" Cacia asked.

Will pointed to Phillip and Haven. "If the kids made a good detcord, they should."

"If your recipe was good, then it's good," Phillip said.

"Then it should make a pretty great fireball," Will answered. "Let's just hope we don't hurt anyone."

They went back underground, carrying two jerry cans with them and walked back through the Library to the isolation room.

"What's that?" Annie said, pointing at the cans.

"What's it look like?" Nancy replied.

"I think you've all gone mad," Annie said. "Completely bonkers. One minute you're hostages, the next you're terrorists."

Will took the handcuff key from Cacia and freed Annie. "It's time for you to go, Annie. I'm sure the place is crawling with MI5. Go and find your people and tell them they'll be making a huge mistake if they storm the farm. Tell them we've got a dozen bombs and we'll use them. Go get your leg properly tended to."

"Come with me," Cacia said, gesturing in the direction of the Library. "You're going out this way, through the house."

Will bent over Greg and undid his cuff. "You're going too, Greg."

Greg blinked a few times and stood up.

"I'm scared," he said.

"I'm sure you are," Will said.

"What'll happen to me?"

"I honestly don't know. The feds don't know your role yet but I expect it'll come out soon enough, won't it, Nancy."

She nodded. "I'll have to turn you in when I get the chance," Nancy said sadly.

"Maybe the Chinese will take you in," Will said.

Greg teared up. "I'm sorry."

"I'm sure you are," Will said.

"Will you tell Laura that I love her?"

"You'll be able to do it yourself," Will answered.

"You think?"

"Look, Greg, you're BTH. I looked you up years ago, when I had the database."

"I'll bet you looked up Greg Davis, right?"

Will nodded.

"You know I was adopted, Will. You should have searched on Tanner, my birth name."

Will remembered the day in 2009. He'd only had a few frantic minutes before the police arrived to look up the dates for some of the people who were important to him. He felt sick to his stomach. For his daughter's sake, he patted Greg on the back and sent him off with Cacia.

Vice Chairman Yi was seated in the Foreign Intelligence Command Center at the Ministry of State Security beside General Bo. A concave wall at the front of the room displayed a variety of real-time satellite and thermal images of Pinn.

"See there?" a senior analyst told the men, springing to his feet and pointing to a moving dot on one of the images. "He's on the move."

"What would you like us to do?" General Bo asked Yi.

Yi understood that the question was deferential, but he was annoyed the general felt a need to ask. The answer was obvious. "We have discussed the scenario, General, and there is no reason to alter our plan."

Annie waved a white tea towel furiously over her head as she limped out the front door of the farmhouse, then ran the best she could toward the road and a squad of soldiers. Greg came too, head down, holding his own towel limply.

Overhead, a black-and-gray bird of prey the size of an osprey silently swooped from the black sky.

But it wasn't a bird.

The Chinese microdrone homed onto the signal emanating from Greg's Rolex.

A missile the size of a fat fountain pen let loose and streaked into his chest, exploding on impact.

The percussion was loud enough that Will heard it underground.

He wasn't sure, but he had a pretty good idea what it was.

Will left one of the bombs at the base of the stairs leading up to the hangar and the other at the stairs going from the Library up to the house. He and Nancy went back upstairs to the farmhouse with Cacia and left Phillip and Haven underground for their safety.

In the lounge, the telephone was ringing again, but this time Will picked it up.

"How're you doing?" he said defiantly.

Colonel Woolford replied with a challenging tone, "With whom am I speaking?"

"My name's Will Piper."

"I see. Mr. Piper, this is Colonel Barry Woolford, British Army. I've been informed by Miss Locke that you've gone off the deep end."

"I wouldn't describe it that way, Colonel."

"Well, maybe that's a bit of a disparagement. Perhaps I should call it the Stockholm Syndrome, identifying with one's captors."

"I'd call it a straight-up survival instinct. You see, I know how this is going to be played out. You come in, or the Americans come in, or the Chinese come in—it doesn't matter who—and your interest is going

to be the Library. The Lightburns, my family, everyone else down here are going to be liabilities. You're
going to want this completely watertight and leak-
proof."

"I'm a military man, Mr. Piper. I have a narrow
remit. But I'm sure that once you and your family are
safe, you'll be able to state your concerns to the appropriate civilian authorities."

"Colonel, I'm not going to argue about something I
know to be factual. I'm here to tell you that everything
that Annie Locke told you is true. We're making our
stand here. If you come in uninvited, you'll be met
with lethal force. Now that may not scare a tough
guy like I'm sure you are, but here's something that
might scare you. If you come in shooting, you will
not get the Library, you'll get ashes. As the responsible field officer, your ass will be as burned as the
books. Do you understand me?"

After a pause, the colonel replied that he understood
perfectly and asked what it was that Will wanted.

"Send in a BBC crew broadcasting live. We'll be
watching on television to make sure it's not bogus.
Once the BBC transmits a complete tour of the place,
then we'll walk out of here. And another thing, have
the journalists bring in a pardon letter for the Lightburns signed by the Home Secretary."

"Anything else?" Woolford asked with an exasperated officiousness.

"Yeah, tell me if Greg Davis is dead."

"He is."

"How did he die?"

"To be perfectly honest, I'm not at all sure. It's
under investigation."

Just before he hung up Will said, "I'd look to the
east, Colonel. Call me back when you've got an
answer."

* * *

I should sit with 'em," Haven said. "Do you want t' come?"

Phillip followed her into the writers' room. All of the ginger-haired men looked up at her. Though they never smiled, it seemed as if their faces softened in her presence.

She and Phillip sat at the front of the room, watching them do their work.

"What year are they working on?" Phillip asked her.

"They're up to 2611."

"It's hard to imagine so far into the future," he said. "It'd be cool to see if there're any strange names like aliens from another planet. Do you ever look?"

"Nae."

"Why not?"

"It's not me place t' look."

"Can I?"

"I don't think ya should," she said. "They're acting funny today."

Phillip didn't know their baseline behavior, but he saw what she meant. None of them were writing fluidly. They'd start and stop, their pens floating hesitantly over their pages. And when they weren't writing, they fidgeted in their chairs as if trying to find a comfortable position. Angus, the oldest scribe was hardly writing at all. Instead, he was blankly staring at his page and drooling more than usual, rendering his page soggy and unusable.

"Maybe they're spooked by all the noise outside," Phillip said, "and all the new people."

Haven got up and took a fresh towel. She went to Angus and wiped his face and blotted the drool from his shirt and the page. "Let me give ya a new one," she told him, heading toward the end of the table, where a ream of paper was at the ready.

Matthew, the twenty-one-year-old writer with reddish stubble on his chin suddenly rose from his chair, grunting loudly. He was thin, as they all were, and not very strong, but with an unexpected quickness he grabbed Haven around the waist and threw her to the ground.

"Hey!" Phillip shouted.

Haven struggled and protested under Matthew's weight. The young man tried to push up her dress. He was wild-eyed now, pushing his hardness against her while the other writers continued their business as if nothing were transpiring.

Phillip ran over and straddled Matthew trying to lift him off the wriggling girl. He was too heavy to shift, so Phillip got his attention by punching him in the right ear, the left ear, the right again.

Matthew yelped in pain and rolled off, covering his ears from further blows.

"Please, Phillip, don't hurt 'im!" Haven cried.

"I'll kill him!" Phillip yelled, balling his fist up again.

"No! He's out of sorts. He must've thought it was 'is time."

She got up, smoothed out her dress, and knelt beside the cowering writer. "It's okay, Matthew. It's okay," she said soothingly. "No one's going t' hurt ya. No one's mad at ya. Phillip, help me get him t' 'is chair."

Reluctantly, Phillip obliged. Matthew sat mutely for a while, then picked up his pen, wrote a single entry, then stopped. A drop of blood from a cut on his temple had fallen onto his page and he looked at it, transfixed.

Haven ran for a towel and held it against his small gash.

"Did this ever happen to you before?" Phillip asked suddenly.

"Nae."

"But it's supposed to happen sometime, isn't it?"

"It's our way, Phillip," she said in little more than a whisper. "I don't have t' like it. My mother and aunt didn't have t' like it."

Phillip only said, "Oh, man . . ."

She took Phillip's hand with a breathy sigh.

He held it tightly, and said, "It's not going to happen now, Haven. You heard my dad. Your life's going to change."

"Aye, it's going to change all right," she said, pushing her red hair from her eyes to wipe at her tears.

Okay, next chess move," Will said, handing the lounge phone to Nancy. "Make your call."

"I'm sure the Brits will be listening in," she said.

"It doesn't matter. Play to the audience."

She called Director Parish's office line at the FBI. It was almost 8 P.M. in Washington, but she figured he'd still be there, and he was.

He asked where she was, and when she told him, he went off like a Roman candle, spouting about insubordination again.

"You've got to get beyond that," Nancy told him. "I'm here, and we've got a very serious situation brewing."

"Is this a secure line?" he asked.

"It is not."

"Then I need to be careful. Suffice it to say, Nancy, we've got a good idea what's going on in Pinn and there's a high degree of interest in the assets. However, there appear to be other interested parties."

"The British Army's already informed us they're

preparing to enter by force. It's pretty clear the Chinese are closing in too."

Parish puffed out a blast of held breath. "How do you know about that?"

"It's a long story, but I know who the postcard sender is. He's dead. He was connected to the Chinese."

"Jesus."

"We need your help," she said. "This is a life-and-death situation here. We need you to persuade the British to agree to our demands." She told him about the live camera crew, the clemency letter for the Lightburns. Otherwise, no one was going to get the Library intact.

Parish listened, then answered her, sounding as tense as she'd ever heard. "There's a problem with this, Nancy, and I don't mind saying this over a non-secure line because I think everyone knows the score. The US government and the British government are no longer on the same team on this matter. They're going to do what they need to do, and we're going to do what we need to do. And, God help us, the Chinese apparently feel the same way. This is not going to end with all of us around the campfire singing 'Kumbaya.'"

At 1:00 A.M. Kenney got the call he was waiting for. "It's a go from the White House," Admiral Sage told him. "At 0200, you are to covertly enter the compound and secure the target. Once you have succeeded, you will be joined by one or more JSOC Seal teams, who will drop in and take control of the assets. They will be supported by the Third Ranger Battalion who are about to deploy from RAF Mildenhall. The Brits have suspended our takeoff and landing rights at all our shared RAF facilities, but we're in a fuck-'em mode. The Rangers are going to keep the Brits busy long enough for us to get a fleet of heavy-lift choppers in and get the books crated and out the door. You will start with 2027 and get as many decades and centuries of material as humanly possible before we vacate. Is that understood?"

"Yes, sir," Kenney said, his heart thumping. "What about the Chinese?"

"Looks like they're coming too," the admiral said excitedly. "Their fleet's close to striking distance. You let the Rangers and the Air Force worry about them. Also, the Brits aren't about to let the Chinese march in without a good fight. Stay focused on your objective and do not fail."

During a brief period of quiet, Cacia put the kettle on and made tea. She called Daniel from the lounge and handed him his favorite mug before serving up Nancy and Will. The four of them sat on the kitchen floor for fear of sniper fire though Nancy told them nowhere inside was really safe from a large-caliber rifle coupled with a thermal scope.

"That's comfortin'," Cacia said, taking a sip.

"Sorry," Nancy said. "I'm a full-disclosure gal."

"Can I ask you how long th' two of you've been married?" she asked.

"Sixteen years," Will said. "Sixteen good years. How about you two?"

"Twenty-five," Daniel said. "Time marches on, don't it?"

Nancy nodded in agreement, and said, "We've lived every year of our marriage assuming that 2027 might be the end. You guys are probably the only family in the world who knew that wasn't so."

"Maybe you were better off not knowin'," Cacia said.

"Why?" Will asked.

"Well, look at th' two of ya," Cacia said. "I've seen the way ya sneak glances at each other. You look like you're very much in love, like newlyweds. Maybe th' thought of th' Horizon's kept things fresh."

Daniel asked his wife, "Then how do you explain our marital bliss?"

"Oh, please!" Cacia said, giving him a little kick. "You're a bit old t' be becoming a comedian, aren't ya?"

The phone rang.

Will frog-walked to the lounge and picked it up. The colonel was on the line.

"Woolford here. Is this Piper?"

"I hope you're calling to tell me the BBC crew is on the way."

"Alas, no."

"Wrong move," Will said.

"Look, I think it's best not to beat about the bush," the colonel said. "Your proposal was discussed at the highest levels. It did not fly. In fact, it was batted down quite vigorously. The Lightburns are criminals and must come to justice. And the books are a national resource, and as such they must be protected from certain foreign powers which threaten to usurp them. I'm afraid I'm going to have to give *you* an ultimatum. Come out within the hour—hands on head, one by one—or we're coming in. Do you clearly understand, Mr. Piper?"

"Here's what I understand," Will shouted. "I understand that you're going to go down in history as one particularly sorry and ignorant asshole." Then he slammed down the phone, crept back into the kitchen, sat cross-legged on the floor, and resumed his tea drinking.

"That went well," Nancy said, stroking his leg.

"Is 'e always like that?" Cacia asked, laughing a bit.

"Believe it or not, he's mellowed with age."

In the COBR at Whitehall, Prime Minister Hastings was informed that President Dumont was on the line. He accepted the call and put it on speaker.

Gone were the "Johns" and the informalities. "Mr. Prime Minister," the President said, "historians will not treat us well unless we make a last-ditch effort to resolve our differences with compromise."

"And what is your definition of compromise, Mr. President?"

"It's a three-point plan. We take control of the Library, we help you stare down the Chinese and send the North Sea Fleet packing back to Tianjin, and we let you permanently station a team of analysts at Groom Lake to query the database once it's up and running."

Hastings looked around his conference table at the shaking heads of his ministers and Defense staff.

"This 'compromise,' Mr. President, sounds remarkably identical to your initial demand. Now here's my idea of compromise. We will control this British Library in a British facility to be constructed on British soil, you will fulfill your NATO obligations and help us chase the Chinese away, and we will let you station a team of analysts in Britain to query the database when, as you say, it's up and running."

President Dumont replied swiftly. "Not going to work, Mr. Prime Minister. We feel strongly about this. Our legal people have reviewed the letter agreement Churchill and Truman signed back in 1947, and they're satisfied that the term 'Library' encompasses the material you've got in Pinn. So, it's the property of the United States of America, and we intend to claim our property."

Hastings rose in his chair out of anger and with a sense of the importance of the moment. "Let me warn you, Mr. President, that movement of men and materials from any of your installations on our RAF bases will be considered a hostile act and will be dealt with accordingly. We are, as you are well aware, a nuclear power, and an invasion of our sovereignty by China, by you, by any nation whatsoever, is a de facto act of war."

Saddle up."

Kenney chambered a round into his assault rifle, and Lopez and Harper followed suit. They shoved their nonessential gear under some frosted undergrowth and crept down the hill.

Kenney led them toward the road, steering wide of the concentration of police and military massed in front of the farm. Their target was a group of three apparently unarmed or lightly armed policemen on the northernmost boundary of the property who'd been marginalized by the heavy presence of SWAT officers and army troops. He'd been watching them through his scope and liked what he saw. They'd make easy pickings.

They moved on their targets smoothly and quietly the way big cats descend on their prey until close enough to pounce.

The policemen were milling across the road on the verge trying to keep warm by stamping their feet. The watchers made their final rush across the road with pumalike speed. Each had one target and they descended on their assigned man with tactical knives. Killing wasn't so hard, but putting a man down without a sound escaping from his throat was an art. Kenney held his man while he died so that his blood spilled onto the ground, not his police uniform. He quickly checked to see how Lopez and Harper were getting on. All three of them were in a tight synchrony of mayhem.

After dragging the bodies behind a hedge, they stripped them of their outerwear and emerged from the bushes looking very much like community patrol officers, their rifles concealed under their anoraks.

"Okay, let's get this party started," Kenney said.

They began walking along the road toward the farmhouse. A squad of 1 Lancs was planted on the edge of the road in a defensive position, with half of them trained on the farm and the other half protecting their flank. Kenney and his men marched right past them, keeping silent as one of the soldiers made a wisecrack about them getting their heads blown off. Once clear of the squad, Kenney headed into the field, zeroing in on the small stone hangar.

It was 1:55 A.M.

A task unit from Seal Team 6, some forty men, were already in position on High Seat. They came in the same way the Chinese had but so low their helicopters didn't produce a single radar echo. They were using the burned-out hulk of the PLA chopper for cover.

Through his scope, their commanding lieutenant had eyes on Kenney as he led his men toward the outbuilding.

His targeting officer said, "They should've tasked us for entry."

The lieutenant replied, "You don't know about the Groom Lake guys, do you? They're as good as we are. Some say better."

* * *

In the COBR, the Minister of Defense looked up from his screen, and blurted out, "I've just been informed that dozens of helicopters and fixed-wing aircraft have violated our no-fly rule at Mildenhall and deployed. They are heading northwest."

"Toward Cumbria?" the Prime Minister asked.

"It would seem so," the Minister answered. "Hang on, I've got another alert coming in." He put his headset back on to hear the message from the monitoring station at RAF Fylingdales, then peeled it off to announce, "When it rains it pours. It seems the Chinese have launched an array of air assets from the carrier *Wen Jiabao*. We are under attack on two fronts, Prime Minister."

Hastings sat down hard and searched the faces of his people. "May I have the committee's recommendations?" he asked through his constricted larynx.

The Defense Minister said as evenly as he could, "I believe it is the consensus around this table, Prime Minister, that we cannot fight and win a two-front war with these kinds of adversaries. If we deploy nuclear-armed cruise missiles, we will be hit back in kind, and the destruction of civilian life would be unacceptable. Our two options are to stand down and let the Americans and the Chinese fight it out on British soil, or deploy 1 Lancs to seize the Library before the others lay claim to it. At least with that option, we'd be in the driver's seat."

Hastings thumped the table with his fist and winced at the pain he'd caused himself. "All right, do it! Send in our lads."

Nancy and I could use some guns," Will told Daniel.

"Don't know 'bout that," Daniel grumbled.

"If they come in firing, I want to be able to protect my son the best I can."

Cacia touched her husband's hand. "Let 'im, Daniel. We can trust 'im now, don't ya think?"

Daniel sighed and agreed. He, his sons, and Kheelan each had over-under shotguns, and Cacia had her old revolver which she gladly relinquished, holding it out, grip first.

"Who's the better shot?" Daniel asked.

Both Will and Nancy replied, "I am."

"All right," Will said, laughing. "Give it to her. I punch harder than she does."

Daniel crept over to a rear window, parted the curtains slightly, and turned his torch on and off twice. Immediately, the same signal came back from a barn window.

"Kheelan and Douglas are fine," Daniel said. He called upstairs for Andrew. The young man came down with his shotgun in one hand and his tea mug in the other. "Finish your tea, then go with 'em downstairs. I don't think they know about th' other way in, but ya never know. I'll stay in th' house with th' girls. We're stretched thin, but we'll do th' best we can. You okay, lad?"

Andrew had the Lightburn dark and flashing looks and the confidence of an oldest son. "If they come, I'm ready," he said.

"Good. I'm counting on ya," his father said.

Andrew led the way downstairs and through the Library, seemingly proud of his father's approbation. Will, Nancy, and Cacia followed.

They found Phillip and Haven sitting in the isolation room on Phillip's cot. The boy had his arm around her shoulder, and, to Will's surprise, he didn't remove it when they entered.

He's cocky, Will thought, just like me at his age.

Cacia looked at Haven with a mother's concern. "Are you all right?"

She and Phillip had agreed not to talk about the incident in the writers' room.

"I'm fine," she said. "We're just talking."

Nancy had never seen Phillip holding a girl. She was the only one who seemed embarrassed to be intruding. Will sensed it, and said, "Let's check on the storeroom."

The group left the kids behind and went into the dormitory. The homemade detonation cord snaked several meters from the middle of the dormitory, under the storeroom door, and into the neck of the jerry can. It wasn't much thicker than an untreated piece of string, so to inspect it, Will and Andrew had to walk its length.

"Think it'll work?" Andrew asked.

"I hope we don't have to find out," Will said.

Kenney surveyed the interior of the dark hangar through his night-vision goggles. There wasn't much there, some farm tools, a couple of hay bales.

He shed the police outer clothes, and his men did the same. "Check the floor for a hatch," he ordered.

Lopez found it immediately and with a nod from Kenney, he pulled it open by its iron ring, revealing a dark run of wooden stairs.

Kenney peered down the stairwell and checked his watch—0200.

"Curtain's up," he announced.

They clicked their safeties from safe to fire and, with Lopez and Harper leading the way, started down the stairs.

At the bottom, they found themselves in a tiny chamber chiseled out of the bedrock just large enough for the three of them. An old oak door confronted them. It was locked. Harper inspected it and concluded it might be too sturdy for a shoulder.

"Pick it or blow it?" Harper asked.

Kenney looked at his watch impatiently, and said, "Blow it."

Will heard the percussive pop and recognized it for what it was—a small charge of plastic explosive taking out the door lock.

"They're coming!" he shouted to Andrew. "Light the detcord!"

Kenney followed his men into a large storage room. He saw metal shelving stocked with dry goods and water cans. At the far end of the room was another door, open a crack, and Harper and Lopez approached it cautiously.

A second after Kenney told them to proceed, he noticed a five-gallon metal can on the floor near the opened door.

As Lopez pushed open the door, Kenney shouted, "Wait!"

At the threshold of the dormitory Harper and Lopez were momentarily blinded by the ceiling lights and had to switch off their night goggles. The first thing they saw when vision was reestablished was Andrew crouching on the ground with a butane lighter in his hand.

Lopez let off a burst from his rifle and caught the young man center mass, shredding his vital organs.

But the detcord was already lit. It hissed and smoked

as the gunpowder slurry burned and streaked, but two meters short of the door, it fizzled out.

Will dived behind one of the bed frames, heard the shout of a woman's voice, and saw Nancy hurdling cots until she was beside him, Cacia's old pistol in her hand.

Another burst of fire splattered the limestone wall above their heads.

"The can!" Will shouted. "Shoot the can!"

Harper moved up beside Lopez. He identified the threat, had Nancy in his sight, and moved his finger to the trigger.

Nancy didn't have a perfect line on the jerry can, so she squeezed her trigger five times, bracketing its approximate position.

One bullet hit home.

The fertilizer bomb flashed, then exploded, unleashing an inferno of white-hot energy within the confined space of the storage room.

What felled Harper and Lopez was almost medieval. The storage room door slammed shut, then disintegrated in the blink of an eye. Wooden splinters ranging in size from an eyelash to a forearm impaled them, head to toe, and dropped the both of them in the percussive wave.

Will draped himself over Nancy as best he could, but both of them were showered by debris and singed by a hot, fast cloud of vapors.

Kenney had been on the other side of the bomb from his men. He'd heard Nancy's shots rattling the metal shelving in the storeroom, and the moment before one of her slugs hit the jerry can, he'd managed to mutter, "Goddamn it to hell," and been blown back through the storage room into the stairwell by a column of fiery gases.

* * *

Colonel Woolford had just received the order from the Ministry of Defense to launch an assault on the farmhouse when he saw a fireball spouting from a small stone building at the northern edge of the farm.

He had no idea who had set off the explosion but he considered it timely. His hastily assembled attack plan had him utilizing snipers to remove identified threats in and around the farmhouse. There were no lines of sight into the house itself since curtains effectively obscured the targets. The barn was another matter. Two hostiles with weapons had been spotted through the windows by a forward sniper/spotter team.

Woolford radioed an order for the snipers to engage.

The Politburo Standing Committee was meeting in emergency session deep in a subbasement level of the August 1 Building of the Central Military Commission. Ordinarily, there were nine members, but General Secretary Wen was conspicuous in his absence.

"Wen Yun is ill," Vice Chairman Yi, told the men, with the slightest hint of a smile. "I can assure you he fully supports my recommendations, but the combination of stress and advancing age have proven to be too much for him. His doctors have placed him under sedation."

There was a murmur around the table, until one by one, the seven other supreme leaders of China told Yi they also supported him.

Yi nodded gravely, and said, "This is an historic moment, Comrades. Once we have this Library, we will solidify our position as the only true power in the world. We will not have to make excuses for our inaction. We will not have to hide our intentions behind slogans and platitudes. This is our moment. All we must do now is seize it. With your agreement, I will issue the order to the PLA."

They held their right hands up in unison and Yi was not embarrassed to let them see his tears.

Atop High Seat, the commander of the Seal task unit also saw the explosion blowing off the roof of the small stone building the watchers had entered.

"Something's gone wrong," he told his targeting officer. "What's the ETA of the Rangers?"

"About six minutes. Want me to raise base and ask if they've gotten a go sign from the Groom Lake entry team?"

"Negative," the commander said. "We've got to assume that team's been compromised. It's time to improvise. We're going in ourselves."

As the Seal unit began their rapid descent of High Seat, the commander wheeled around to look at the night sky from the east. The thumping he heard was choppers, all right, but they weren't friendlies. With a jolt, he recognized the insignia on the lead copter as it began raking his position with machine gun fire: the red star of the People's Liberation Army.

Daniel threw caution to the wind and parted his curtain a good way to try to see what was happening. In rapid sequence, he heard the fertilizer bomb, then the crack of rifle fire, then the staccato of machine guns on High Seat. Explosions and tracer fire up on the hill cast enough illumination for him to recognize that the sky was thick with helicopters.

He failed to see Kheelan being felled by a sniper round to his forehead, but with horror he did see his son Douglas running like a frightened animal from the barn to the house. And he let out an anguished cry when the young man crumpled into a heap a few paces from the back door when a 1 Lancs sniper ended his life too.

Once Will saw that Nancy wasn't seriously hurt, he shouted for her to go back to Phillip. He sprang from their hiding place, ran to Harper and Lopez, and picked up one of their rifles. Then he pushed their breathing but bloody bodies with his shoe, ready to put rounds into them. But it wasn't necessary.

Who were they?

He found a wallet, thin with minimal contents. But the cash told the story: dollars.

Then he saw the driver's license. Nevada.

The watchers are here.

He ran toward the storage room, prepared to engage survivors, but there was only an empty, blackened chamber reeking of diesel fuel. Then he turned tail, picked up the second rifle, and found Nancy huddled with Cacia and the kids in the isolation room, all of them sobbing in shock and horror.

They heard Daniel's shouting coming from the direction of the Library. When he came barreling in with Gail and the two young girls, they were all crying.

"It's hell out there," he cried. "They killed Douglas, for Christ's sake. I haven't seen Kheelan." He looked around frantically, and asked, "Where's Andrew?"

Cacia could only point toward the dormitory and wail.

Daniel collapsed to his knees. "Oh, Jesus . . ."

Will dropped beside him and looked at him squarely. "Who's coming? From what direction?"

Daniel delivered a monotone response, his emotion replaced with dull shock. "The British for sure on the ground. All sides. Up on the fell, there's helicopters, firing at someone, not us. They've got red stars on 'em."

Will stood. "The Brits, the Chinese, the Americans. They're all fighting each other for the pot of gold."

The dormitory door opened. Will took a longing look at his family and stepped out of the isolation room, rifle at his shoulder, finger curled on the trigger.

He immediately lowered the barrel.

The writers were entering in single file.

With their blank expressions, they filed past, paying him the scantest attention. Will called back into the isolation room, "It's just the writers!"

Cacia came out, touching each one on the shoulder as they shuffled by heading for their cots. "It's their bedtime," she said through heavy tears. "This is what they do."

The dormitory was full of acrid smoke. Puddles of blood surrounded the bodies of the two moaning watchers, but the writers hardly seemed to notice. Two of them, the older ones, coughed a few times to clear their throats, but none were deterred from kicking off their sandals and slipping under their bedding. Soon, seven ginger-haired heads protruded from beneath blankets.

All of the survivors stood behind Will, watching the writers' bedtime routine.

Outside, dulled by the thick limestone, the deadly sounds of a furious battle raged on.

"There's only one thing we can do," Will said.

Nancy seemed to know what he was going to say and nodded at him.

He spoke his mind, laid out his intentions. The Li-

brary was a precious thing, but men were going to
take it from them and use it for their own ends.

"I don't know what its purpose is," he said. "Maybe
it exists as a testament to something we can't understand, but I don't think it should be exploited by
governments. You've been good Librarians. You've
protected it your whole lives. I know it'll be hard, but
let me do this."

Cacia and Daniel reached for each other's hands
and Cacia pulled Haven to her side. The girl had
been hunched over in grief, hardly able to stand.

Daniel finally said, "Aye. There's no other way."

"Stay here," Will said. "I'll be back in a couple of
minutes."

He slung the rifle over his shoulder, moved to Andrew's body, and when he found his pocketknife, he
headed toward the Library.

As he ran through the stacks he was aware he was
running through the centuries. A single thought
pounded through his mind.

The world's going on, goddamn it. We're going to
survive. I don't know what it's going to look like, but
it's going to survive.

A jerry can was sitting at the far end of the chamber in the stairwell leading to the house. Will picked
it up, careful not to dislodge the detcord. He carried
it back inside the Library, planting it on the floor
among the nearest decades, the books he knew would
be of greatest interest to the approaching troops.

He quickly inspected the detcord. He didn't want it
to fail like the last one, so he used Andrew's knife to
cut it shorter. He lit it with the young man's lighter
and ran like hell back through the central corridor.

He counted it out. He thought he'd have twenty
maybe twenty-five seconds, but he was off.

At the count of eighteen, with the exit door just ahead of him, the bomb ignited.

The shock wave lifted him off his feet and carried him through the door, which he'd mercifully left open.

When he regained consciousness, Nancy was kneeling over him on the anteroom floor, and the Library was a roaring inferno.

"Can you move?" she shouted.

"I think so." He hurt all over and his ears were whining like sirens.

"Come on!" she said, dragging him to his feet. "We've got to get out."

He stumbled along but had the presence of mind to duck into the isolation room to retrieve Ben Franklin's journal from beneath his mattress. It didn't fit in his pants pocket, so he undid his top button and shoved it down his shirt.

"What are you doing?" Nancy yelled. "Come on!"

In the dormitory, everyone was limply standing among the writers' beds and the casualties on the floor. Haven was doing her best to comfort and shield her little cousins. Cacia and Gail placed a blanket over Andrew's body, and holding hands with Daniel, they said a parting prayer.

"Make a white flag out of a sheet," Will yelled.

"Is it gone?" Cacia cried, gesturing toward the Library.

"It's gone," Will said. "Hurry. And get the writers mobilized to get out of here."

At the sound of the explosion, the writers had awoken. All of them had sat bolt upright, thrown off their bedclothes, and had begun fishing with their toes for their sandals. Now they were on their feet, their faces showing the first flickers of real emotion

Will had seen from them. It seemed like an agitated confusion, a psychic pain.

Gail ripped a white sheet, and Cacia grabbed the writer Angus by the shoulder, pointing him toward the storage-room exit.

But the other writers started walking in the other direction, toward the Library.

"No, this way!" Cacia shouted after them, but they kept on going. Even Angus, as old and frail as he was, managed to whip himself away from her grasp and follow his brethren.

Cacia ran to the dormitory threshold, already hot from the advancing fire, and tried to block their advance. But Matthew, who was young and strong, pushed past her, his face twitching in discomfort.

"Matthew, no! Daniel, Haven, help me!" Cacia screamed, but it was already too late. Three writers were in the anteroom, heading straight for the inferno.

Will felt the heat rising, and shouted at Daniel, "Tell her we've got to leave!"

Daniel held Haven back and yelled at Cacia, "It's what they want! We've got t' let them have their way!"

Three more of them shoved past Cacia and finally, there was only old Angus left behind. As he approached Cacia, his face seemed to soften at the sight of her abject grief. He stopped for a moment and met her gaze, then slowly followed the others into the conflagration.

"Good-bye, Father," she sobbed, falling to her knees.

Will shouted at Daniel to take up the rear and make sure everyone was leaving. He took Gail's white flag and gave it to Nancy, then led the way forward, his rifle in offensive position. Phillip took Haven's hand,

and she, in turn, took the hand of one of her cousins. Daniel picked up Cacia and half carried her. The ragged conga line moved toward the storage room.

Will made sure the room was clear before signaling Nancy to bring the rest of them forward. The stairwell was charred, but the stairs seemed solid enough. There was a flashlight on his assault rifle's rail and Will twisted it on to light the stairs. They were clear too.

At the top of the stairs, the hatch door was in the open position. Will pushed himself through like a Jack-in-the-box in case there were shooters. The small room was sooty but empty. He waited until all of them were aboveground and crammed into the small space before shouting out the bay, "We're coming out! We're unarmed. Do not shoot!"

A few seconds later, there was a reply, a British voice. "Who are you?"

"Will Piper. I'm coming out with my family and the Lightburns. We are not armed!"

"Proceed with your hands raised. One at a time!"

Will put his rifle down and took the flag from Nancy. "I hope these guys play fair," he said, touching her face.

"I'm right behind you," she said.

He showed the flag first, then showed himself, his free hand touching the sky. A squad of 1 Lancs was closing on the hangar. The farmhouse lit the sky, fire spurting from every window. On the fells, a battle was in full engagement. He caught a glimpse of a US fighter jet swooping low, blasting a helicopter with a missile.

A captain ran to him, rifle trained at his chest.

"There are seven more behind me," Will shouted. "Mostly women and children. All unarmed."

"Keep your hands up!" he was ordered.

"Captain, you get Colonel Woolford on the radio. Tell him the Library's been destroyed. Tell him to let the Americans and the Chinese know that. Tell him there's no point to any of this fighting anymore."

The squad encircled the civilians while the captain urgently relayed the message to his colonel.

Breathing hard, Will saw people trying to comfort each other. Phillip held on to a shivering Haven. Gail clutched her daughters to her side. Daniel supported Cacia's rubbery legs. He shouted at everyone to stay low. There was still a battle raging. He turned to Nancy, dropped his flag, and enveloped her in a bear hug, the kind she liked to get from him, the kind that made her feel safe.

Then an ugly shout pierced the night.

"This is for Malcolm Frazier you son of a bitch!"

Will let go of Nancy, pivoted toward the voice, and took a step to shield her from whatever was coming.

Out of the darkness, Kenney staggered forward, his face blast-ravaged and blackened. He had a combat knife in his hand and was on top of Will before he could react.

Will saw the glint of the knife, felt a pressure in his gut, and heard the crack of a rifle.

Kenney dropped hard, grunting and swearing.

The soldier who fired moved forward, about to squeeze off another round, but Will called him off, surprised that he was still standing and still able to talk.

Nancy was frantically ripping Will's buttons apart to get at the wound, but there was none. Franklin's journal fell out of his shirt, gouged from cover to cover.

A medic was called in and Will knelt beside Kenney.

"I can't feel my goddamned legs," Kenney moaned.

"Hang on," Will told him, "you're going to be okay."

Kenney seethed at him. "I know I am, you cock-sucking son of a bitch. I'm BTH."

Will stood up, and replied, "Well, mister, it looks like you're going to be BTH in a wheelchair. Enjoy the rest of your life. I hope it's a long one."

Their London hotel was comfortable and quiet, a good way station to sort through their obligations before they could fly home. It was a small, secluded place off the paparazzi circuit, and they had checked in under assumed names: Mr. and Mrs. Franklin and son. Franklin was, unsurprisingly, the first name that had popped into Will's head.

Interviews with the Cumbrian police, MI5, and the Ministry of Defense were behind them. The awful conversation with Laura and Nick about Greg was behind them. In the morning, they were going to attend a debrief at the US embassy with FBI officials and Justice Department lawyers. That meeting had been delayed until Britain and the US had restored some of their frayed diplomatic relations.

Phillip had his own room, Nancy and Will a nice suite. MI5 had arranged the accommodations, and Will hadn't paid attention to who was covering the tab. He figured he'd find out at checkout time. For the moment, he was luxuriating in a hot bath to soothe his bruised body, and when he was done soaking, he joined Nancy under the cool sheets and yielding mattress.

"How're you doing?" she asked.

"Sore. But trending toward happy."

She circled him with her arms. "Do you think Phillip's all right?"

"He's been through a lot for a guy his age. I hope so," Will said.

"He had a connection to Haven, don't you think?"

Will nodded. "I expect he's going to stay in touch with her. The heart's a heat-seeking missile."

She kissed him. "Your heart held up pretty well."

"It did everything a heart's supposed to do, I guess."

She withdrew one arm and lay on her back, looking at the fancy plaster ceiling. "No Horizon. It's like a weight's lifted off my chest. I feel I can breathe. I can live."

"What about the rest of the world?" he asked. "Don't they have the right to breathe and live too?"

"Don't you think the British or American government will put out a statement?" she asked. "I mean, they have to explain what happened at Pinn."

"Do they?" Will asked. "When was the last time the government did the right thing on this? If you ask me, we're the ones who are going to have to go public. We know the drill. We've done it before."

"The feds aren't going to like it."

He laughed. "Tough shit."

"I won't be able to stay at my job."

He ran his hand over her breasts. "Then you'll have to live on the boat with me."

"In your dreams."

She was sleepy and turned off her bedside light. Will had other ideas. The Franklin journal beckoned. He hadn't had the chance to finish it, and, anyway, it held a special place in his heart. It had saved his life.

The leather book was hard to open because Ken-

ney's knife had deformed and crimped every page.
He carefully pulled the pages apart until he found the
place where he'd stopped.

> *Armed with the powerful and strange
> Knowledge I now possessed, I felt the great-
> est of Urges to return to America to assist
> my Comrades during their Hour of Need
> and deliver unto Them the Assurance that
> should We fight the Crown, We would win.
> Yet I was equally compelled to delay my
> Journey until I had the unique Opportunity
> to accompany Abigail to Yorkshire to see for
> Myself the Perpetrators of these Marvels in
> Action. As a Scientist and a Natural Philoso-
> pher, I could not do Otherwise.*

After departing the Isle of Wight, Franklin traveled
with Abigail by coach from Lymington to London.
During that brief journey, he was engrossed in the
deepest of thought. Although it set the household
tongues clucking, he bade Mrs. Stevenson to accommodate Abigail in one of the servant's rooms while
he hastily arranged for the hire of the best carriage
and driver in London for the journey to Yorkshire.
In fine weather, the carriage man thought he could
make it to Mallerstang in four or five days, but this
was January, so Franklin was advised it might take
twice as long. A price was negotiated and the depar-
ture date was sealed.

Before they disembarked, Franklin penned a letter
to be taken by courier to Portsmouth to be put onto
the next packet ship to Philadelphia and from there
delivered to Virginia. It was addressed to the one
man in the colonies whom Franklin considered to be
the inevitable commanding general of colonial forces

should there be war, the planter and soldier, George Washington. In the letter, he told Washington that the mood in London was dark and that political and economic compromises were not likely to be forthcoming from the king. That said, he urged the Virginian to be of stout heart and prepare himself for the arduous path that lay ahead. As soon as he was able to conclude his affairs he, himself, would sail to Philadelphia and join the cause. And then he concluded, enigmatically but forcefully, "Ask Me not how I know this, but I know it with the full Force of God-given Certitude. If We Continentals should endeavor to throw off the Shackles of the Crown by Force, then We shall win. Again, my dear Washington, this is not merely the Belief of an old Optimist. I ask you to spread the Word among our Brethren in all the Colonies. It is a Fact. We shall win."

The journey to Pinn took even longer than the carriage man's most conservative estimate because they encountered not one but two wintry storms near Birmingham and Manchester.

When they finally arrived in Mallerstang, the Dales were blanketed in snow, and the midday sun on the fells was dazzling and blinding. Franklin endured the hardships of the adventure with stoicism and good humor, but he was a coughing, worn-out man, shivering under his travel blanket when they reached Pinn. Abigail had only been a partly suitable travel companion. Although she had been able to flatter him and make him laugh over the silliest of things, she had not been able to engage his mind in a substantial way. Every time she had glazed over at his pronouncements about science and nature, he had told her that if he were a magician, he'd have changed her into a member of the Royal Society to have a proper conversation. In the evenings, they had spent their nights in inns along the postal road to Scotland, and Franklin had immersed himself in writing inside his new blue leather journal about the circumstances that brought him to Vectis and now Pinn.

On their day of arrival, Abigail leaned out the carriage window and cried a river of tears at the sight of Lightburn Farm. And when her mother and father emerged from the farmhouse door to investigate the whinnies of strange horses, she sprang from the coach and threw herself into their arms. But Josiah Lightburn's pleasure at seeing the unexpected return of his daughter changed to fury at the sight of Dr. Franklin gingerly climbing down onto frozen ground on his gouty leg.

"Who's he then?" Josiah fumed.

"He's Benjamin Franklin," Abigail said. "He's a very famous man from America who's also th' kindest man I ever met. I was a stupid girl t' run away, but I never would have been able t' mend my ways without 'is help."

"Where were ya?" her mother Mary asked.

"London mostly."

"You came all the way from there?" Mary asked in shock.

Franklin strode forward, extending his hand. "We did indeed. A difficult journey, but we are here, safe in body and felicitous in spirit. I am happy to deliver unto your care your wayward daughter, who assures me she will not stray again."

"How can we ever repay you, kind sir?" Mary asked.

"I wish only a few days' lodgings to renew myself before returning to London. And lodgings for my driver and feed for his horses."

"You kinna stay here!" Josiah huffed.

"Father," Abigail said, "he knows about us. I took him t' Vectis. We found the reet place."

"You told an outcomer?" he raged.

"It was the only way I could persuade him t' pay off me indenture and take me home," she sobbed.

"All right, come inside," Josiah said gruffly. "Your man can stay in th' barn."

By the blazing hearth, with four generations of Lightburns clamoring to be with Abigail, Franklin sat in the best chair, warmed his cold feet, and drank a mug of strong ale.

"I promise you," he told Josiah, "on my oath as a gentleman, that I will never divulge the nature of what I have seen in Vectis or what I will see at Pinn. I have to know for myself, that is all. Your secret will be safe with me. I seek no profit from it."

"He's brought our Abigail back," Mary said, handing Franklin a bowl of stewed meat. "I can see by his eyes he's a good man we can trust."

"I'll think on it," Josiah said.

The following morning, Franklin awoke remarkably refreshed. Two children had been displaced from the bed to make room for him, and he was grateful for the comfort. He trundled down the stairs to the hearth, where Abigail had already assumed a burden of chores.

"I made some gruel for you," she said proudly. Then she leaned over and whispered in his ear. "Father said aye. I'm allowed t' take you below th' ground."

He wasn't about to postpone the venture to the secret chambers for the sake of gruel, so he waved off the meal and followed her eagerly down a clandestine stairway at the back of the house. As he slipped below the level of the floor, he caught sight of Josiah looking like he was about to spit.

And when he had descended as far as he could go, he felt the chill of the underground realm and caught a whiff of leather.

"Through here," Abigail said, pushing open a familiar door. She held up her torch. "It's just like Vectis."

Indeed it was.

He wandered through the Library of Pinn as he had done at Vectis, with a sense of wonder and rapture, feeling the spiritual power of the experience imbue his every fiber.

"It is enormous," he mumbled.

"Those Lightburns who came before us cut the stone with pickaxes," she said proudly.

"How far does it extend?" Franklin asked, holding his own torch ahead of him.

"I'll show ya."

They kept walking away from the direction of the house until the bookcase shelves became empty. He looked at the dates of the books most recently produced, and said, "So the volumes span 2027 to 2231. And by the looks of it there's plenty of room for more in the future."

"Aye," she said, "we carry on."

They walked the remaining empty space of the vast cavern until they came to a door.

"Through there?" Franklin asked.

"Through here," she agreed.

He felt the anticipation prickle the hairs on his neck.

The next chamber was smaller and brightly lit with dozens of fat candles.

And there they were!

A dozen ginger-haired men and boys sitting at tables all dressed in simple farmers' tunics, completely consumed by their labors to the point that they largely ignored the intrusion.

Franklin stood before them, watching them dip quills into ink-pots and scratch names and dates upon parchments.

He began to weep softly, and whispered as not to

disturb them. "From God's hand to their hands. My faith has always been firm, but it is now like a fortress. I am blessed to be in the presence of the divine."

Abigail walked among them, showing the tenderness of a wayward sister returning home. She touched shoulders and heads, and when she did, the pale faces and green eyes registered glimmers of contact.

Then one young writer shifted his chair back slightly and began to rise, but she firmly pushed his shoulders down, and said, "Nae, Isaac. Nae!"

Franklin understood immediately.

"I see!" he whispered. "That's how they are renewed! Is that why you ran away, Abigail?"

She nodded sadly. "But I don't mind now. I'll do me duty. The things I done whilst in the baron's service were a lot worse."

He spent a good hour underground, observing the writers, wandering the stacks, plucking books from shelves for perusal, and when he was done, he retired to his bedroom, opened his writing case, and resumed penning his journal.

At supper that night, Franklin was given a favored seat at the family table opposite Josiah. He thanked them profusely for allowing him the honor of seeing their noble venture and reiterated his vow that he would not divulge what he had seen and heard at Pinn.

Josiah looked at him skeptically, finished chewing his piece of mutton, and reached under his chair.

To Franklin's astonishment he had his blue journal in his hand.

Josiah's voice rose in anger. "We found this among your things when you was in th' privy. We can read and write, ya know. We can see you've written about Pinn, and you've written about Vectis. I say you're lyin'."

"Heavens no, my good man!" Franklin cried. "I keep a journal for my own uses only. As I age, my memory dims." He removed his bifocal spectacles and pointed at his face. "The only eyes that will ever see these pages are my own."

Josiah handed the journal to one of his brooding sons, and said, "Our work here's sacred. We're the keepers of these books. We can't have outcomers interfering. We made an exception with you because of th' kindness you showed t' our Abigail, and if you're th' gentleman you appear t' be, you'll honor your vow of silence. But you're not taking this journal. It stays 'ere."

"Very well." Franklin sighed. "It's probably for the best. I will leave in the morning, glad in heart that I have seen what I have seen. And while you, good sir, continue your enterprise in this beautiful valley, I will return to my country, where I will continue my enterprise to liberate my countrymen from their shackles."

So I conclude My Journal on this second Day of February, 1775. The Things I have seen at Vectis and at Pinn will stay with Me in the profoundest of Ways for the rest of My Life. I have witnessed the Span of Humanity to come. The Future of Man appears both bright and dark. The Brightness comes from the knowledge that Mankind will endure, not for years and decades, but for Centuries and perhaps Millennia. Yet the Darkness troubles me no End. At Vectis, I saw Years where the Word Mors appeared so many Times it made Me Numb: 1863; 1864; 1915; 1916; 1917; 1942; 1943; 1944; 1945. I can only assume that great and horrific Wars will consume Humanity. But nothing shook the Foundations of my Soul like the Observation I made at Pinn concerning the year 2027. Commencing on the sixteenth Day of the Month of October, Book after Book, Shelf after Shelf, Row after Row, a great Tide of Woe. By my Calculations, the unfathomable Number of One Billion Souls will perish during that single Month, which is far in the Future yet near enough to turn my Heart to Stone. What terrible Powers of Destruction will Men create to wreak this kind of Devastation? My only Consolation is that the books continue after this Annus Horibilis. *Births continue. Life continues, and Mankind seemingly finds a Way to endure. What a strange Adventure it is to be Human!*

Will put the journal down and wiped away his stinging tears.

Nancy was asleep by his side.

He nudged her awake as gently as he could.

And he told her. He *had* to tell her.

Into the night, they held each other and talked.

October 16, 2027. The Chinese. The Americans. The British. The seeds for what was coming must have been sown over those few days in the Yorkshire Dales.

"I think I'll leave Washington," she told him. "Phillip and I will come to Florida. We've got a year and a half before this happens. Let's spend it together in the sun. You can teach me how to fish."

He kissed her and tried to make her laugh. "It's going to be bad, really bad, but at least it's not the end of the world."

"You still want to go public with what's going to happen?" she asked.

He shook his head. "Let me sleep on it."

They made love, talked some more, and made love again. And when the first light of dawn made their curtains glow, they finally fell asleep.

You'll be in here," the matron said.

Prisoner #965876 stood in front of the cell and waited for the matron to unlock the door. New Hall Prison in West Yorkshire was built in the 1930s of red brick to resemble a fortress. It was overcrowded and noisy. Cells meant for one woman held two, and those meant for two held three.

The new prisoner held her bed linens, blanket and towels to her chest and stepped inside. The door slid closed behind her.

"Bloody 'ell," the other prisoner said. She was heavyset, with thick calves and ankles showing beneath a flimsy yellow prison dress. "I've had this to myself for just one bloody day, and they've filled it with fresh meat already." She pointed to the top bunk. "That's yours. My name's Sheila. I'm from Manchester. What are you in for?"

"Accessory to murder and defeating the course of justice."

"Oh yeah? Suppose you didn't do none of it, right?"

"I pled guilty."

Sheila thought that was hysterically funny. "You

needed a better lawyer! How much time'd they give you?"

"Two years."

"That's nothing. I got fifteen. They say I set my boyfriend on fire. I'm not daft like you. I pled not guilty, but they didn't buy none of it, did they? Whoever done it, he deserved it, the wanker. What's your name then?"

"Cacia."

Sheila stared her up and down. "Here, didn't I see you on the telly?"

"Can't say," Cacia said.

"Yeah, I did! You're from Mallerstang. You had that Library."

Cacia responded with an almost imperceptible nod and asked if she could stand on the lower bunk to make the upper. Sheila seemed to like the deference, and helped her with the sheets.

"What happened to your family then?"

Cacia answered with dry eyes. "I lost both of me sons. My husband's in prison waiting trial. He's charged with murder, and I expect he'll be sent away for a long, long time. I pled guilty t' get me time over with so I can get back t' me daughter. She's with me sister-in-law and her girls. They're put up on an estate in Kendal. I lost others too."

"How come you ain't crying when you're telling me all this?"

"I've had me fill o' tears."

The woman nodded. "Want some tea then?"

While Sheila waited for the kettle to boil, she launched into a pedestrian explanation that all the provisions on the shelf were hers and hers alone. Until Cacia received her first care package from the outside, she'd let her have some items on credit—with interest, of course. One biscuit would be repaid with two, one tea bag with three . . .

Cacia sat on her bunk, gazing through the barred window. A sliver of blue sky was visible above the prison ramparts. She thoroughly tuned out her cell-mate's recitation of repayment rules.

"Here, haven't you been listening to me? Do you or don't you want a fig biscuit?" Sheila waved one in the air.

Suddenly, Cacia jumped off the bunk and made for the stainless-steel toilet. She fell to her knees in front of it and began retching violently.

"Bloody 'ell! What's the matter with you, anyway?" Sheila shouted. "You'd better not be contagious."

Cacia looked up, wiped her mouth with the back of her hand and smiled.

"Don't worry, I'm not contagious," she said, caressing her belly. "It's only a touch o' morning sickness."